From the introduction to PragMagic . . .

When we first started working on this book, we were distressed to have two themes instead of one. One of these, *pragmatism,* involved logic and discipline. The other, *magic,* fairly exploded with a sense of risk, surprise, intuitiveness, mystery, and delight.

Then a serendipitous slip of the tongue gave us the word *pragmagic,* and we realized that *pragmatism* and *magic* are two sides of the same coin. When we put both ideas to use in our lives, they aren't so very different at all. In fact, we may learn that many things we always thought to be perfectly mundane are magical, indeed.

This book is about pragmatic magic—useful magic—magic that works in everyday life because it is grounded in practical information.

PRAGMAGIC offers specific techniques for understanding the processes of brain, body, and mind—techniques based on research for creating a rich and rewarding life.

Marilyn Ferguson's
book of
PRAGMAGIC

*Pragmatic Magic for Everyday Living—
Ten Years of Scientific Breakthroughs,
Exciting Ideas, and Personal Experiments
That Can Profoundly ChangeYour Life*

adapted and updated by Wim Coleman and Pat Perrin

illustrations by Kristin Ferguson

POCKET BOOKS
New York   London   Toronto   Sydney   Tokyo   Singapore

Paul and Sarah Edwards are the authors of the book *Working From Home: Everything You Need To Know To Live and Work Under the Same Roof,* 1987, Jeremy P. Tarcher, Inc. Through their weekly Los Angeles radio show "Here's To Your Success," which they co-host, the Working From Home Forum on CompuServe Information Service and speeches, they provide information and expertise for people to make it on their own. They consider the ability to visualize goals as a key ingredient in proceeding toward success. Sarah is a licensed clinical social worker.

An *Original* Publication of POCKET BOOKS

 POCKET BOOKS, a division of Simon & Schuster Inc.
1230 Avenue of the Americas, New York, NY 10020

ISBN: 0-671-66824-2

First Pocket Books trade paperback printing October 1990

10 9 8 7 6 5 4 3 2 1

POCKET and colophon are registered trademarks of Simon & Schuster Inc.

Design by Pat Perrin

Printed in the U.S.A.

In a sense, *PragMagic* has been written collectively over the years by the editors of *Brain/Mind Bulletin* and *Leading Edge Bulletin*. Noel McInnis and Connie Zweig deserve particular note for their extensive reporting, and Mike Ferguson for his ongoing editorial help.

Other *Brain/Mind* writers and editors have reported on a wealth of information, which now adds up to more than two million words. Their words will be found in these pages, and their names are listed below. This book is dedicated to them, with thanks.

Ray Gottlieb
Research Director

Harris Brotman	Meg Bundick
Scott Busby	Eric Ferguson
Clyde Ford	Noel McInnis
Brian Van der Horst	Connie Zweig

ACKNOWLEDGMENTS

It is a cliché to begin acknowledgments with the words "it is impossible to list the people who contributed to this book." In the case of *PragMagic*, it is quite true.

Our thanks are due to the literally hundreds of thinkers and researchers whose words, theories, ideas, and information appear in these pages. Their generosity is of a special order, and this is really their book. We are particularly grateful to those who have offered us fresh insights and information for *PragMagic*.

We are deeply grateful to our Pocket Books editor, Claire Zion, for her clarity, imagination, and persistence, without which *PragMagic* could never have happened. Particularly warm thanks are due to our research assistant, Sylvia Delgado, whose perseverance and clearheadedness during the course of the mammoth job of updating, letter-writing, and obtaining permissions was nothing short of heroic; she has been of great moral and practical support. Thanks also to Jim Uhls, Greg Wright, and Mike Weber for their valuable input; to the entire staff of *Brain/Mind Bulletin* for contributing in a number of ways; and, of course, to Marilyn Ferguson and Ray Gottlieb for entrusting us with our part of this extraordinary project.

Layout and typesetting for *PragMagic* was produced on Macintosh computers using Aldus PageMaker software.

—Pat Perrin and Wim Coleman

Grateful acknowledgment is made for permission to use the following materials:

page 13—EXERCISE: TRICKS FOR VISUALIZING printed by permission of Paul and Sarah Edwards.

page 15—"A 'Body Response' Script" from "A Bio-informational Theory of Emotional Imagery" by Peter J. Lang, *Psychophysiology*, 1979, *16*, 495–512. © 1979, The Society for Phychophysiological Research. Reprinted by permission of the author and the publisher.

pages 18–19—EXERCISE: DIFFERENT PERSPECTIVES printed by permission of Stuart Heller.

page 28—EXERCISE: MEETING YOURSELF printed by permission of Arnold Horwitz, Ph.D.

page 29—INVENTORY: INNER COMFORT printed by permission of Arnold Horwitz, Ph.D.

page 34—INVENTORY: INS AND OUTS printed by permission of William Gray, M.D.

page 42—EXERCISE: FOCUSING excerpted from *Focusing* (Bantam, 1981) and *Let Your Body Interpret Your Dreams* (Chiron, 1986) by Eugene Gendlin. Reprinted by permission of the author.

page 49—"Argonne National Laboratory Anti-Jet-Lag Diet," Argonne National Laboratory, Argonne, Illinois. Reprinted by permission.

page 53—EXERCISE: EXPLORING YOUR INNER COMFORT excerpted from *Hypnosis Questions and Answers* by Ernest Rossi (W. W. Norton, 1986). Reprinted by permission of the author.

page 55—EXERCISE: MONITORING HEMISPHERE DOMINANCE from "Altered States of Consciousness in Everyday Life: The Ultradian Rhythms" by Ernest Rossi, in *Handbook of Altered States of Consciousness* (Eds. B. Wolman and M. Ullman, Van Nostrand, 1986). Reprinted by permission.

page 58—Excerpt from *Second Wind* by William Russell (Random House, 1979). © William Russell 1979. Reprinted by permission of the author.

page 61—INVENTORY: WAKEFULNESS, The Stanford Sleepiness Scale by E. Hoddes, V. Zarcone, H. Smythe, R. Phillips, and W. C. Dement from *Psychophysiology* (10). Reprinted by permission of W. C. Dement.

page 62—INVENTORY: HEALTHY SLEEP, Eleven Rules for Better Sleep Hygiene excerpted from *The Sleep Disorders* by Peter Hauri, from a 1982 edition of *Current Concepts* series published by The Upjohn Company. Reprinted by permission of The Upjohn Company and Peter Hauri.

pages 63–64—"Remembering Dreams" excerpt and computer drawing from the newsletter *Brainstorms* (1987) by Howard Rheingold. Reprinted by permission of Howard Rheingold, designer of "Dreamworks," dream work software for the Macintosh.

page 67—EXERCISE: LUCID DREAMING, Steps for Lucid Dreaming (MILD) by Stephen LaBerge from *Lucid Dreaming* by Stephen LaBerge (J. P. Tarcher, 1985). Reprinted by permission of the author.

pages 68–71— "Thinking Styles" from the *Gregorc Style Delineator* by Anthony F. Gregorc (1985), Gregorc Associates, Inc., Columbia, Connecticut. Reprinted by permission of the author.

page 74–75—EXERCISE: CREATING A MANDALA from "Putting it All Together: A Mandala" and two examples of mandalas, exercise and illustrations from *The Creative Journal: The Art of Finding Yourself* by Lucia Cappacchione (Ohio University Press, 1979). Reprinted with the permission of the Ohio University Press, Athens.

pages 81–83—"Differences Between Males and Females" and EXERCISE: CATCHING YOUR BIASES, include excerpts from "Psychobiological Factors in the Development of Cognitive Gender Differences: An Effector Theory," by Karl Pribram and Diane McGuiness (1978). Reprinted by permission of Karl Pribram.

page 94—"The Hidden Observer," by permission of Ernest R. Hilgard, Professor of Psychology, Stanford University, Stanford, California 94305-2130.

page 100—INVENTORY: THE WORLD OF PROJECTIONS excerpted from *Projections: Our World of Imaginary Relationships* by James Halpern and Ilsa Halpern (Seaview/Putnam, 1983). © 1983 by James Halpern and Ilsa Halpern. Reprinted by permission of The Putnam Publishing Group.

page 130—INVENTORY: TWO LEARNING MODES, "Traditional and Accelerated Learning" reprinted by permission of the *A.L. Network News,* published by the Center for Accelerated Learning, Lake Geneva, Wisconsin 53147.

page 133—INVENTORY: TURNING UP THE LIGHTS excerpted from *Using Your Brain—for a Change* by Richard Bandler (Real People Press, © 1985). Reprinted by permission of Real People Press.

page 146—INVENTORY: HELPFUL ILLUSIONS printed by permission of Jonathon Brown.

page 150—INVENTORY: THE TRUSTING HEART adapted from *The Trusting Heart: Great News About Type A Behavior* by Redford Williams, M.D. (Times Books, © 1989). Reprinted by permission of Times Books, a Division of Random House, Inc.

page 159—INVENTORY: MANAGING RISKS excerpted from *Electric and Magnetic Fields from 60 Hertz Electric Power: What do we know about possible health risks?* by Granger Morgan and others, the Department of Engineering and Public Policy, Carnegie Mellon University, © 1989. Reprinted by permission of the author.

page 172—EXERCISE: FIRST STEPS IN LISTENING printed by permission of Alexandria Pierce, Ph.D.

page 173—EXERCISE: BEING MOVED BY SOUND printed by permission of Alexandria Pierce, Ph.D.

page 174—EXERCISE: ORGANIC MUSIC excerpted from *Self-Transformation Through Music* by Joanne Crandall (Theosophical Publishing, 1986). Reprinted by permission of the author.

page 180—"A New Creativity" summarizes a portion of *Coming to Our Senses* by Morris Berman (Simon & Schuster, 1989). © 1988 by Morris Berman. Reprinted by permission of Simon & Schuster, Inc.

page 180—INVENTORY: TOOLS OF IMAGINATION from "Four Creative Thinking Abilities and Restructuring Activities" in *The Creatively Gifted Child: Suggestions for Parents and Teachers* by J. Khatena (Vantage Press, 1978, pp. 24–26). © 1978 by J. Khatena. Reprinted by permission.

pages 182–184—INVENTORY: SATORI SKILLS excerpted from *The Search for Satori and Creativity* by E. Paul Torrance (Creative Education Foundation, 1979). Reprinted by permission of The Creative Foundation in association with Bearly Limited, Buffalo, New York, © 1979.

pages 188–189—EXERCISE: ENCOURAGING CREATIVITY IN CHILDREN from "Four Creative Thinking Abilities and Restructuring Activities" in *The Creatively Gifted Child: Suggestions for Parents and Teachers* by J. Khatena (Vantage Press, 1978, pp. 57–59). © 1978 by J. Khatena. Reprinted by permission.

page 231—INVENTORY: TRANSFORMATIONAL WORLDVIEW by Jack Drach from the 1982 *AHP Perspective* (originally *AHP Newsletter*). Reprinted by permission of the author.

page 236—INVENTORY: NEGOTIATING WITH HOMEOSTASIS printed by permission of George Leonard.

pages 243–244—INVENTORY: MORNINGNESS–EVENINGNESS from "A Self-assessment Questionnaire to Determine Morningness–Eveningness in Human Circadian Rhythms" by J.A. Horne and O. Ostberg, *International Journal of Chronobiology, 1976, 4, 97–100*). © Gordon and Breach Science Publishers, Ltd. Reprinted by permission.

pages 245–247—*EXERCISE*: OPEN FOCUS®—General Training © by Les Fehmi, Ph.D., Director of Princeton and Manhattan Behavior Medicine and Biofeedback Clinics. Open Focus® is a registered trademark of Biofeedback Computers, Inc. General Training was copyrighted © 1984 by Biofeedback Computers, Inc. Reprinted by permission.

pages 247–250 —EXERCISE: LEFT BRAIN/RIGHT BRAIN from *The Possible Human: A Course in Extending Your Physical, Mental and Creative Abilities* by Jean Houston (J. P. Tarcher, 1982). Reprinted by permission of the author.

pages 250–253 —EXERCISE: FREE FLIGHTS TO NOWHERE: LET YOUR PSYCHE DO THE WALKING from "How to Have a Mystical Experience" by Keith Harary, Ph.D., which first appeared in *Omni* magazine (December, 1988). Reprinted by permission.

CONTENTS

FOREWORD:

When I first discovered the fascinating frontiers of brain/mind research in the early 1970s, I felt compelled as a writer and a reporter to sift through the literature for the most exciting yet practical science. How did the findings relate to everyday life, liberty, and the pursuit of happiness.

This compulsion to understand the implications of cutting-edge research led me to the writing of a book, *The Brain Revolution* (Taplinger, 1973), and the founding of a periodical, *Brain/Mind Bulletin,* in 1975. The research also played a part in another book, *The Aquarian Conspiracy: Personal and Social Transformation in Our Time* (J. P. Tarcher, 1980, 1987).

PragMagic represents yet another telling of the ever-breaking story. In creating this guidebook from the *Bulletin* and related sources, Pat Perrin and Wim Coleman looked for material that related to the reader's most practical needs and higher ideals. They brought to the task their own lively curiosity, imagination, humor, gumption, and a lifelong fascination with how people evolve.

I first met Patricia Perrin in 1986 at a conference in the Midwest. A former high school teacher, she was completing her doctoral dissertation in art education at the University of Georgia. She was weaving together strands from new physics and sociology to show how these developments were almost uncannily paralleled in the world of art and literature.

Some months later a coworker introduced me to Wim Coleman, a gifted playwright with a keen interest in psychology. Wim had just moved to Los Angeles from Des Moines, Iowa. And not long after that Pat and Wim came via their separate ways to work at the *Brain/Mind* offices in L.A. They began remarking, casually enough, on their respect and liking for each other. So we should not have been surprised (as we were) when they announced one September day that they had married.

This new partnership seemed to stimulate boundless creative energy. Soon they had launched a wry, fanciful newsletter, the *jamais vu papers,* and assorted other projects. It seemed natural that they should team up to create a book inspired by the thousands of experiments in *Brain/Mind Bulletin.*

Naturally enough, *PragMagic* recruited the talents of Kristin Ferguson, who first began illustrating *Bulletin* stories in 1982 at the tender age of fifteen. (Incidentally, Kristin's artistic labors were interrupted during the course of the book for another kind of labor: the birth of her daughter, Katherine Grace Harrington.)

As research and good sense demonstrate, we human creatures flourish when we are encouraged, when we are challenged, and when we collaborate. This collaborative guidebook invites you to experiment, and in experimenting to discover new facets of yourself.

—Marilyn Ferguson
Los Angeles, April 1990

INTRODUCTION:

The history of *PragMagic* goes back to 1973, many years before it was even conceived. That year, Marilyn Ferguson published *The Brain Revolution: The Frontiers of Mind Research*. Very quickly, she discovered that she had become an unofficial clearinghouse, receiving a flood of scientific papers, requests for information, and offers to compare notes. This led her to found a newsletter, *Brain/Mind Bulletin*, in 1975. *Brain/Mind* itself quickly became a clearing-house for consciousness research from all over the world.

Since then, *Brain/Mind* has reported on breakthrough studies, papers, and conferences. It has kept abreast of current theories in brain science, psychology, learning, creativity, health, and states of consciousness. Over the years, it has featured interviews with scores of well-known people, offering new information, commentary, and personal advice on difficult situations.

Marilyn Ferguson's 1980 book, *The Aquarian Conspiracy,* further explored the implications of groundbreaking scientific studies in the areas of brain and consciousness research. That year, she established a second publication, *Leading Edge Bulletin,* to cover broad cultural shifts reflected in business, education, the arts, consumer groups, and political trends. In 1985, *Leading Edge* was merged with *Brain/Mind*.

With its distinguished history, the *Brain/Mind Bulletin* is an exceptional source of valid and reliable theories and techniques. But the reporting has had to be done piecemeal, as research and discoveries unfolded over a long period of time. Although each issue often speculated on connections between news items, space is limited in a newsletter, and a larger context was not always visible.

By 1987 it was clear that something needed to be done with all the reporting that had accumulated over the years. A new book was needed—an update, a synthesis to deal with the practical, personal implications of this staggering wealth of information.

PragMagic sifts, sorts, and updates information once published in the *Bulletin* and points out ways you can test it in your life. We've gone back to some of the researchers quoted in *Brain/Mind* for their most recent observations. This process led to new information and insights, presented here for the readers of *PragMagic*. The result is a "self-help" book of a different order—a practical guide to self-improvement. Limited neither to a particular set of theories nor the perspective of a single therapist, *PragMagic* draws on the theories, methods, and research data of hundreds of practitioners and scientists from many theoretical backgrounds. It will also serve as a companion piece to Marilyn Ferguson's forthcoming *The New Common Sense: Secrets of the Visionary Life* (New Stream Books).

Pragmatism and Magic

When we first started conceptualizing this book, we knew it would be full of hard-nosed, down-to-earth information. It was going to be a *pragmatic* book. It was also going to hint at the wonderful possibilities for human potential and transformation, and explore today's ever-expanding ideas about reality. It was going to be a book of *magic*.

We were, frankly, distressed to have two themes instead of one—and contradictory themes at that. One of them, *pragmatism,* involved logic and discipline. The other, *magic,* fairly exploded with a sense of risk, surprise, intuitiveness, mystery, and delight—effortless and flowing, not forced and methodical.

Then a serendipitous slip of the tongue gave us the word *pragmagic,* and we realized that *pragmatism* and *magic* are two sides of the same coin. When we put both ideas to use in our lives, they aren't so different at all. In fact, we may learn that many things we always thought to be pure fantasy are really very practical—and many things we always thought to be perfectly mundane are magical, indeed.

This book is about useful magic—magic that works in everyday life because it is grounded in practical information.

PragMagic offers specific techniques for understanding the processes of brain, body, and mind, and for bringing about meaningful changes in your personal life—techniques based on research in psychology and brain science, many of them studied by professionals in therapeutic fields. And it includes reviews of helpful books and other resources.

There are many ways to use this book. You can try out the exercises and therapies as personal experiments. Or they can be foundations on which to build other personal experiments. Here are useful tools, stimulating theories, and resources for creating a rich and rewarding life.

Using PragMagic

In this book, you'll find many different kinds of information on many different ideas. Sidebars adjacent to the main text expand on topics and contribute related material:

RESEARCH findings, taken from the pages of the *Brain/Mind Bulletin* or from new contacts, provide intriguing data and tell you how researchers arrived at their conclusions.

RESOURCES are books and other materials that have been reviewed in the past by *Brain/Mind,* with a few more recent additions.

COMMENTARIES from interviews and texts give individual perspectives on the ideas under discussion.

Quotations that seem to be appropriate and enlightening are also scattered among the sidebars of *PragMagic*.

Throughout *PragMagic* boxed INVENTORIES and EXERCISES invite you to try out some of the ideas for yourself. An Appendix includes longer or more complex activities.

Many of the exercises and experiential materials were provided by particular researchers or were based on specific studies. In these cases, the name of the person who authored them is clearly indicated.

Some were drawn from *Brain/Mind Bulletin* and *Leading Edge Bulletin,* or from the "Power of Knowing" seminars conducted by Marilyn Ferguson and Ray Gottlieb on a national tour in 1983 and 1984. We have developed other such materials based on our own experience or inspired by research ideas.

Sources

Brain/Mind Bulletin and *PragMagic* have gathered information from hundreds of scientific journals, magazines, and books. For the benefit of those who would like to follow up on specific research, journal names are followed by either the volume number or month and year of publication. Where the volume number is listed, we have also included the year the material was covered by *Brain/Mind* or *Leading Edge.* Book titles are followed by publisher and date. More specific documentation, including page numbers from periodicals and addresses of publishers, can be obtained by writing to *Brain/Mind Bulletin.* See the information page at the end of this book.

We have made every effort to update locations and titles of the many researchers who are listed here.

Techniques alone don't necessarily bring about change and may just result in the individual becoming a technician. . . . As long as we allow external forces—society, a teacher—to prescribe for us, to suggest our style of living, we're in a trap. We're totally dependent. . . . Now we're making people dependent on the holistic healer!

—Healing expert Jack Schwarz, in *Brain/Mind Bulletin* (1978)

Designing Your Own Curriculum

PragMagic is an eclectic collection of ideas and information, put together by people who believe that the only *true* education is *self*-education. *PragMagic* is not, in itself, a curriculum—but a tool for building your own curriculum.

The word *curriculum* comes from the Latin word *curricule,* having to do with "driving" or "chariots." A curriculum, then, is a vehicle for learning. Lots of self-help curricula come off the assembly line just like cars: one standard-issue "chariot" is supposed to be right for everyone. Exercises and activities are designed to be carried out systematically, step-by-step.

In *PragMagic*, we offer tools, materials, and information to custom-build your very own chariot, your own vehicle of learning.

Certainly, *PragMagic* can be read chronologically from beginning to end. Or you can select sections that interest you. Or, like many reference books, it can be opened at random for items that catch your eye.

In any case, pick and choose. See what seizes your interest. Try an exercise or an activity that looks interesting and find out where it leads. Does it offer intriguing insights? If it doesn't, look elsewhere. If it does, you may want to study the research surrounding it. Exercises and activities of your own are likely to come to mind. Also, scan the text and sidebars for related books. *PragMagic* is an ample source of reading lists. And check the index for related information to be found in other parts of the book.

A lot of us grew up in a solution-oriented culture. We got the idea that there was one right answer to every problem, and that a temporary solution was really not a solution. Problems were supposed to be things you could fix once and for all.

But now our sciences tell us that the whole universe is in a process of change, that our very bodies are made up of energy fields in motion. Psychologists now think of the personality itself as a developmental process. Philosophers think of belief systems as journeys rather than final resting places.

And so, in the pages of *PragMagic,* you will read more about the unfolding of a journey than the reaching of a destination. As all of our journeys continue far beyond the confines of this or any book, each reader will decide what to try out and discover what helps and what doesn't.

You can think of your journey as a dance—one that changes tempo and pattern but that has no ending. This way, you may find practicing pragmagic is a conscious way to enter into a process of growth: putting the elements of the dance into a comfortable balance; making joyful use of the wonder inherent in your everyday life.

—Pat Perrin and Wim Coleman

1.
DISCOVERING MAGIC:
Where to Begin?

The practice of pragmagic is a kind of alchemy. The ancient alchemical quest was, of course, the transmutation of matter, the making of gold out of "baser" elements. But the alchemists were not motivated by greed. Quite to the contrary. This quest was symbolic, a metaphor for a deeper quest—the transmutation of the self into a new, golden kind of human.

Where do we begin our contemporary alchemical quest? How do we discover magic in everyday life and learn to use it? Magic starts with a state of mind, a way of thinking. Before the practical tools and techniques can be of use, we each have to discover the internal sources of our own stories.

What is the story of your life? This question has to do with much more than just the total of things that have happened to you. What kind of character are you in the drama of your own life? How do you relate to the other characters? What kind of "script" are you acting out? What is the story of the culture within which you live? What do you expect to happen next? These questions are basic to the practice of pragmagic, and they will be addressed in various ways throughout this book.

This section builds a foundation for contemporary alchemy by investigating:

• how making stories may be fundamental to human thinking
• ways of discovering and shaping the stories by which we live
• the power of metaphor
• self-fulfilling prophecies
• using visualization and body-response techniques for insight and change

- thinking like a scientist
- trying out experimental beliefs

As you read this section, you will encounter research findings that support the idea that our brains and minds are magical raw materials for transformation. To practice pragmagic means to work ordinary wonders with ourselves and others.

The Power of Story

We all have certain ideas about how the world works: data, beliefs, experiences, and traditions. These are the "stories" on which we base our lives. Never mind, for now, deciding whether they are true or false. We have to pay attention to the fact that they are there. The most crucial thing about the stories we tell ourselves every day is how they shape our thinking.

"Making stories may, indeed, be fundamental to human thinking," said psychologist Renee Fuller at an annual meeting of the American Psychological Association. "The ability to comprehend a story—that is, to grasp meaning within a given context—may be more basic to human intelligence than anything measured by IQ tests.

"The need to make our life coherent, to make a story out of it, is probably so basic that we are unaware of its importance." From her experience with students, Fuller inferred that our basic concept of intelligence may be in error because it emphasizes the knowledge of data out of context: "Story cohesion, as the basic form of intellectual cohesion, is earlier in development and cognition than we had thought possible on the basis of IQ tests."

Fuller is president of Ball-Stick-Bird Publications, Inc., in Stony Brook, New York.

Although IQ tests have been credited with successfully predicting school performance, this success or failure has not always correlated with adult excellence. For example, Charles Darwin, Albert Einstein, George Patton, and Winston Churchill performed poorly in school.

Fuller suggested that these geniuses may have had difficulty because they were called on to perform tasks out of context—tasks similar to those on IQ tests. "Although they differ one from the other, [these thinkers] have in common an ability to make sense out of the world—to make a story out of what is going on. Darwin did this with his theory of evolution. . . . Einstein's laws of physics and relativity tried to tell us a story of the universe. Churchill made the history of the Second World War his story."

Story comprehension appears surprisingly early in child development, Fuller noted. "By the time a child is two, he begins to follow a story. Is his budding capacity to understand a story the development of intellectual cohesion? Is this new imposition of structure the reason for his sudden spurt in vocabulary?" Fuller said that before a child can understand and create stories, his vocabulary consists of four or five isolated words. "Then almost overnight his vocabulary explodes and he starts to make sentences. . . ."

Many people have no dream,
no clear image of the future.
Some have a dream, even a clear
image of the future but they are not
in love with it—they may feel that
it is not really them.
How might one search for her/his
identity and discover a dream and
fall in love with it? In my opinion,
this search for identity is one of the
most important things that a
person ever does. . . .
Sometimes a story—even a
fantasy—can capture the essence
of a problem such as this and
distill the truth more powerfully
than our most sophisticated
researchers and most complex
and ingenious computers.

—Paul Torrance
from "The Importance of
Falling in Love with 'Something'" in
The Creative Child and Adult Quarterly
(VIII, 1983)

EXERCISE: TWO STORIES

As a quick experiment, test the responses of your body to two quite different stories.

• First, just sit or stand quietly, close your eyes, and think intensely for a few minutes about some negative aspect of your life. For example, "I just can't get this work done (pass this class, stand this person, catch on to this game, etc.); there is just no way that I'm going to do this. . . ."

You get the idea, we're sure. As you concentrate on these messages, notice how your body feels. Is it tired or energized? Notice what emotions you feel.

• Now, try the same experiment with a positive statement that you can believe rather easily, such as: "This really comes naturally to me, I'm glad I got into this job (class, relationship, game, etc.) and want to do this again. . . ."

Can you feel changes in your body? Do your emotions change? Do you feel heavier or lighter?

INVENTORY: SELF-DESCRIPTION

Only when we are aware of the stories we live by can we begin to reinforce the ones we like and change the ones that might be doing us harm. The first step is to begin to notice what you are saying to yourself or to others. Messages such as "this is hard to do" or "I always have trouble with . . ." or better, "I can do that" are all clues to the kinds of the stories we tell ourselves.

When we start listening, it's often a surprise to discover just what our own stories are. For at least a full day, pay close attention to the messages that run through your mind, as well as to the things that you say aloud. If you can't catch them easily, then spend several days listening carefully to yourself.

Check the ones that apply, and/or add your own.

Comments I made to myself about how I look or how I feel about myself:
- ❏ I'm too fat/skinny
- ❏ My clothes are wrong
- ❏ My hair looks good
- ❏ I look younger than I am

_____

_____

Comments I made about how other people feel about me:
- ❏ They think I'm dumb
- ❏ They won't notice me
- ❏ They know I'm smart
- ❏ They think I'm cute

_____

_____

Comments I made about things that are difficult or impossible for me:
- ❏ This is so hard for me
- ❏ I'm too tired to do this

_____

_____

Comments I made about things that I can do well:
- ❏ I do know how
- ❏ This is my real talent

_____

_____

Other comments that I heard myself say internally or aloud that give me clues to the stories by which I live:

_____

_____

_____

_____

_____

INVENTORY, continued

The comments we make to ourselves add up to the stories we live by, and they often become self-fulfilling prophecies. Consider the comments you have listed. If they were made by someone else, or were about someone else, what kind of life story would that person have? For example, is this a story about a person who is helpless or who is able to take charge of things? Is this a story about a person who feels attractive? A person who works well with others?

Is this a story about a person who is headed for success? For trouble? Is this a story about a person who has excellent relationships? Is lonely?

Considering the comments I have made about myself, this is the negative story I tell myself:

_____

_____

I would like to change these parts of my negative story:

_____

_____

Considering the comments I have made about myself, this is the positive story I tell about myself:

_____

_____

I am particularly happy with these parts of my positive story:

_____

_____

_____

Considering the comments I have made about others, or about events that have happened, this is my story of the nature of the world in which I live:

_____

_____

_____

_____

Paying attention to your story is the first step in changing what you don't like in your life, and enhancing what you do like.

Form the habit of paying attention to the stories that run through your head every day. When you know which ones you want to change, look for the exercises in *PragMagic* that will help you do just that.

Remember, there is more of your story yet to come.

RESOURCE

From early childhood, when we learn Aesop's fables or the fairy tales of the Brothers Grimm, we are presented with many of life's essential lessons in the stories we read and hear.

In *The Call of Stories* (Houghton Mifflin, 1989), Harvard professor and psychiatrist Robert Coles reflects on the role stories have played in his own life. From childhood days listening to his parents read Dickens to each other, to discussing the lessons of Tolstoy's works with depressed and ill patients in later years, Coles has found the power of stories to be a wonderful way of linking human experiences.

Particularly known for his work with young people, Coles has, over time, seen stories help people overcome the fear of death, evoke empathy, and restore optimism. He also discovered that if psychiatric patients are offered the chance to present their own lives in story form, they are better able to find the roots of their problems.

"How to encompass in our minds the complexity of some lived moments in a life?" he muses. "How to embody in language the mix of heightened awareness and felt experience that reading a story can end up offering the reader? . . . A novel can . . . insinuate itself into a remembering, daydreaming, wondering life; can prompt laughter or tears; can inspire moments of amused reflection with respect to one's nature, accomplishments, flaws."

Living Our Own Stories

Intimately connected to our thinking processes as well as to our behaviors, stories are powerful influences. In fact, we are all living out the stories of our own lives. In the long run, each story will be complete with a beginning, middle, and end—it will become history. The extent to which we are able to shape our own whole-life story varies somewhat with our circumstances and our self-awareness.

However, that whole-life story is shaped by smaller stories we tell ourselves on a daily basis. Mini-stories show up in the comments we make about ourselves: "This is hard for me to do" or "I always have trouble with . . ." or even "I'm so tired." At the time we say them, such statements may seem absolutely true, but it's important to recognize that *our minds and our bodies are affected by them whether they are true or not.*

For example, a University of Michigan study indicated that pessimism may actually be hazardous to your health. When Christopher Peterson and colleagues did a 35-year follow-up of Harvard graduates, they found that those with negative interpretations of events were consistently sicker than their peers. (See report on page 141.)

Our commentaries about ourselves, about events, about others, constantly run through our minds. They are clues to how we are shaping our lives. Not only our physical and mental responses—but our expectations in life—are based on the stories we tell ourselves daily. We live according to what we believe is possible.

Are you, every day, telling yourself a story about a person who is blocked, exhausted, helpless to make changes? Or are you telling yourself a story that says you are capable, growing, learning, improving, and enjoying your life? When you start paying close attention to these comments, these clues to the story you're feeding into your own system, you might be surprised at what you find.

The stories in our minds spring from our personal beliefs as much as from our actual circumstances. Sometimes they have been taught to us by our parents or other authorities in our culture. They may be shaped by images from television, from advertising, from novels, or from schoolbooks. They are affected by all of those messages about what we are, what we should be, and what life is like.

Too often we fail to notice that some of our stories can be changed. This does not mean denying that certain problems exist in our lives. In fact, the first step is to give those problems our attention. When we do recognize our own power of story, we are ready to begin making revisions.

Metaphors

Most of us have learned about the power of metaphor and story by reading poetry and fiction. Good authors know it well. When we use metaphors—saying that one thing *is* something else—what we are saying is literally untrue, but it tells us something very true, indeed. Metaphors are especially powerful stories.

Jerome Bruner writes in *Actual Minds, Possible Worlds,* that metaphor, like story, fuels the problem-solving mind. "The history of science is full of [metaphors]. They are crutches to help us get up the abstract mountain. Once up, we throw them away, even hide them, in favor of a formal, logically consistent theory that (with luck) can be stated in mathematical or near-mathematical terms."

Knowing, feeling, and action cannot be separated, Bruner maintains. We *perfink*—perceive, feel, and think all at once. To separate the three is "like studying the planes of a crystal separately, losing sight of the crystal that gives them being."

Metaphors and Reading

Renee Fuller was one of the developers of an innovative reading method called Ball-Stick-Bird, which teaches students to use metaphor to describe the letters of the alphabet.

Ball-Stick-Bird simplifies the mechanics of reading by showing how each letter of the alphabet can be made with one or more of three basic forms—a circle (the ball), a line (stick), and an angle (bird). The combinations of images can be remembered as mini-stories. Word-building begins with the presentation of the second letter. By the time the student knows four letters he is reading stories.

The Ball-Stick-Bird method was designed to teach reading to learning-disabled children of superior abstract intelligence. By chance it was tried with several retarded individuals. They, too, learned to read, even though their IQ scores were so low that reading had been believed to be impossible for them. Repeated experiments since 1975

RESOURCES

Story is a way of knowing, not just an entertainment. In *Actual Minds, Possible Worlds* (Harvard University Press, 1986), Jerome Bruner, one of the fathers of the cognitive revolution in psychology, implies that stories may be more compelling than information.

In his book Bruner goes deeply and swiftly into the terra incognita of the story-telling mind. Story, he points out, implies intention. And human beings naturally assume intention, even when none is meant.

Russell A. Jones begins and ends *Self-Fulfilling Prophecies* (L. Erlbaum, 1977) with a statement by W. W. Wagar: "The ultimate function of prophecy is not to tell the future but to make it."

He has synthesized an impressive body of data from the annals of psychology and sociology as evidence of the role of expectation. This intelligent, scholarly volume makes an airtight case for the critical nature of our expectations for ourselves and others.

Jones concludes that our very acts of interpretation—our attempts to anticipate the future based on experience—help shape the future.

*the transformative power
of metaphors . . .*

*When we say
"Johnny runs fast,"
what have we said that
anyone except Johnny's
mother is apt to recall?
When we say that
"Johnny runs like a deer,"
we have provided a
memorable totemic image
to which our notion of
Johnny's speed might be
conveniently stapled.
Should we say, however, that
"Johnny is a deer,"
we have eternalized Johnny,
fitting him out forever with
antlers and hooves
from the unyielding deep
forest of primal
unconsciousness.*

—Tom Robbins
in *the jamais vu papers,* 1987

have shown that individuals with Stanford-Binet IQ scores as low as 20 can learn to read and comprehend stories.

Apparently, the heavy reliance on context—on providing a background of metaphor and story—is the secret of the success of this method. The retarded individuals who mastered reading with Ball-Stick-Bird had been unable even to learn the alphabet by other reading methods.

EXERCISE: MAKING METAPHORS

This activity is adapted from a classroom exercise. It can be done by one person alone. However, two or more participants will generate far more striking results.

Take 50 small note cards and write a word on each. A very small number of these can be adjectives or abstract nouns, but the vast majority need to be *concrete nouns*, naming a very specific person, place, or thing. Use no verbs or adverbs. Take some time collecting these words, a few days if you like. The idea is to collect words that are as interesting as possible to you.

Once the words have been collected, shuffle them together. Then randomly pull out pairs of the cards until you've found two words that can be combined into a metaphor. Try connecting them with the words "is a." Two seemingly contradictory criteria are required to create a metaphor: that the connection between the words be *literally untrue,* and yet that they share some common attribute, a *metaphorical link*.

For example, a statement such as "the *house* is a *mansion"* hardly qualifies; a house has a lot in common with a mansion, but the statement is literally *true,* and hence, no metaphor. "The *ukulele* is a *rock"* is literally untrue, but it is also nonsense; it is pretty hard to find any metaphorical link between these words. A case might be made for "the *telescope* is a *ladder";* the statement is not literally true, but telescopes, like ladders, help us to get from one place to another.

This exercise is not intended as a creative writing tool, but as an examination of the *effect* of metaphor. If you spend enough time at this activity, you are likely to find at least one combination of words that does more than just "qualify," that also elicits delight and surprise. Generating freshness, lending new vitality to old concepts, are principal purposes of metaphor—both in literature and in our lives.

A related exercise on page 10 and 11 is designed to help you make use of your skill in creating metaphors.

One retarded subject, Hal, demonstrated the importance of context to cognition. His central cortical blindness made it difficult for him to perceive the "bits" of information required for reading. Often he could not correctly identify two letters side by side, yet with Ball-Stick-Bird he learned to read fluently.

Expectations

Our expectations for the future are stories that we tell ourselves every day. They can become self-fulfilling prophecies, creating just what we expect. According to University of Georgia educational psychologist E. Paul Torrance, scientists have accumulated evidence that our image of the future determines our motivations. What we make an effort to learn and what we achieve is based on what we think is possible for ourselves. "In fact," Torrance wrote in *The Creative Child and Adult Quarterly* (VIII, 1983), "a person's image of the future may be a better predictor of future attainment than his past performances."

It is absolutely essential that we find that clear image of the future, Torrance says. Developing our story of our future is, indeed, a search for our own identity. If we do not have it, we will not work to become the person in our dream.

To learn how to tell a better story of our lives, of course it helps to have all the information we can about our own nature, our potential, our relationships, and our world. But first of all, we must pay attention to those stories we are already living by, and practice ways of changing the ones we don't like.

Visualization

To improve the stories you tell yourself, it is important to notice more than the words in your mind. You must also pay attention to the mental pictures there. Visualization is a powerful tool for gaining insight and for change. Exercises in visualization are recommended by many therapists and healers for work on specific physical and emotional problems. Some of them will appear throughout *PragMagic*.

(Continued on page 12)

RESEARCH

Our Expectations Affect Others as Well as Ourselves

Edward Jones, a Princeton University psychologist, has pointed out that the problem of self-fulfilling prophecy runs deeper than we imagine. It isn't just that we misread others, Jones reported in *Science* (234). We actively inspire them to behave in ways that can confirm our expectations. Experiments have also shown that perceivers underestimate their role in causing the other's behavior. *Brain/Mind Bulletin* reported on this work in 1987.

This "created social reality" is a serious issue that affects everything from stock prices to the arms race, not to mention everyday interactions. Jones reviewed studies in which people attributed conservative or liberal views to other experimental subjects even though they themselves pushed the buttons that caused the others to read statements prepared with one slant or another.

In another experiment, men were assigned to make "get-acquainted" telephone conversations. They were significantly friendlier when they thought they were talking to attractive women rather than plain ones. The women, who had randomly been assigned, were poised and confident in response to the callers who had been led to believe they were attractive. They tended to be uncomfortable and terse with the others.

In another study, aggressive boys interpreted ambiguous acts as hostile rather than accidental. Jones cited this as an example of how self-fulfilling prophecy might, in fact, escalate even in close relationships.

Cultural face-saving requires that we act as though we believe each other's self-presentation and the surface flow of conversation. This is one reason why erroneous "prophecies" are difficult to correct.

EXERCISE: BONE OF CONTENTION

In our last exercise, we practiced making metaphors. But metaphors are just a game with words unless we use them for their transformational value. How can you find metaphors for your own life, metaphors that empower you to change? Try the following technique for harnessing metaphors directly to your life:

Each of us is always *contending* with something—difficulties at work or in a relationship, money problems, etc. What is *your* present "bone of contention"? Write it down:

_____

_____

_____

_____

_____

_____

_____

Think of an animal *that you are like* in your contention. *Are you like* a migrating bird, a hungry wolf, a nut-gathering squirrel?

_____

If you are familiar with mythology, think of a mythical figure *that you are like* in your contention. Odysseus, fighting the cyclops? Persephone, carried away into the underworld? Hercules, facing his twelve labors? Borrow your myth from any tradition or culture—and don't feel presumptuous. Self-comparisons are part of what mythical figures are for.

_____

If you are not familiar with mythology, it shouldn't be hard to think of some popular figure, fictional or a celebrity, with whom to *liken* yourself in your contention—a sports figure, perhaps, or a character in a novel or movie.

_____

Notice that, in the exercise so far, we have worked in the tame and unthreatening language of simile— saying that *"I am like* such and such." Now it is time to leap into the more adventurous language of metaphor, where one of these figures will, in a sense, *become you,* and vice versa.

EXERCISE, continued

Choose the figure that appeals most to you. Make up a story *in which you are* the figure of your choice, facing the contention that presently concerns you. In a sense, you are letting this figure step in for you, and aligning yourself with, say, the speed and agility of a bird, the cleverness of Odysseus, or the lightning reflexes of a popular tennis player.

Write a brief narrative in which your figure strives and triumphs over the problem or contention of your choice. Don't worry about being realistic, and don't be bothered by the incongruity of a squirrel's handling your finances, or of Persephone's doing your spring cleaning. Be fanciful. Metaphors aren't supposed to be literally possible, after all.

_____

_____

_____

_____

_____

_____

_____

_____

_____

_____

_____

_____

_____

_____

_____

_____

_____

_____

_____

_____

_____

_____

_____

It is likely that your metaphorical figure called upon some interesting resources in dealing with your contention. Is there anything you can learn from the actions of your figure? Can you do something similar and achieve the same results? This is an example of how metaphors—and the power of story—can be used to achieve creative breakthroughs in our lives.

Imagery Tied to Vision

According to psychologist Ronald Finke of Texas A&M University, imagery facilitates or enhances visual perception. He reported in *Scientific American* (March 1986) that mental imagery appears to engage the brain's visual system and is subject to the same "optical illusions."

Just as with normal vision, a small or distant mental image is harder to distinguish than if one imagines it larger or closer. For example, he said, try to imagine an ant on a newspaper several feet away and then on the tip of a toothpick directly in front of your eyes.

In his experiments, three-dimensional images mentally "rotated" also seemed to correspond to the actual view of those images rotated in physical reality.

In his other work at MIT, Finke designed tests unpredictable enough that the outcome could not be guessed from prior experience. Students who wore prism glasses and attempted to point to a target were able to do so when they were asked to imagine the position of their hands.

The actual forming of an image depends on one's knowledge of the physical world. Once the image is formed, however, it can function in some ways like the object itself, activating certain neural mechanisms.

"In this way mental images may serve to modify perception itself," said Finke.

Therapist Sarah Edwards and husband/coworker Paul Edwards of Santa Monica, California, consider the ability to visualize goals a key ingredient in proceeding toward success. In their book, *Working From Home: Everything You Need To Know To Live and Work Under the Same Roof* (J. P. Tarcher, 1987), on the Los Angeles radio show they cohost, and in their CompuServe Information Service forum, they provide information and expertise for people to make it on their own.

Everyone visualizes, say the Edwardses. But the process is subliminal in many people—from one-fourth to one-third of the population. In those people, images are

EXERCISE: A DOOR OF PERCEPTION

These simple exercises provide practice in visualizing. Your mental images may not take the form of normal everyday vision, but you can use this opportunity to observe how you are "seeing"—how you know what the scene looks like. Take as much time with these as is comfortable for you. Do them as often as you like, or make up other things to visualize.

First, sit in a comfortable chair. Your spine should be straight and feet flat on the floor. (Lying down is okay, too, if you're not likely to fall asleep.) Close your eyes. As you do these exercises you may actually move your head and eyes in whatever way would be natural if you had your eyes open.

Relax for a few moments, just concentrating on deep and even breathing. Notice when you breathe in and when you breathe out. Allow your mind to quiet down from its normal activity. Keep your eyes closed.

• Think about a door you often go through—the front door to your house or apartment, for example. "See" it in your mind. Is it flat or is there paneling? Is there glass in it? What color is it? What does the doorknob or handle look like? Are there any other details that you can see? Imagine that you reach out and open the door and walk through it. What is the first thing that you see on the other side of the door?

• Now imagine that you are sitting alone in a beautiful place that is very familiar to you—your favorite place, whether it is real or make-believe. As you are sitting in this beautiful place, use your internal vision to look at the ground or floor directly in front of you. What do you see there? Look to your right to see what is just beside you. Take note of everything there, and then look to see what is beside you on your left. Finally, turn your head and raise your eyes to look straight ahead—into the distance. Take note of everything that you see before you. Sit and enjoy this beautiful place for a while, taking note of everything you see there.

EXERCISE: TRICKS FOR VISUALIZING

Paul and Sarah Edwards told *Brain/Mind Bulletin* that they suggest these strategies for people who have trouble visualizing.

• *Bridging.* Each of us has a preferred sensory mode in which it is easiest for us to visualize. Some people can hear music in their minds, others strongly imagine tastes or smells. To bridge, vividly imagine a series of flavors (lemon, toothpaste, salt, onion) and then try to slip into a visual image of each object.

• *Turning off verbal "noise."* Look around you for a few minutes without categorizing, labeling, or naming what you see: colors, shapes, movements. If you slip into naming, just gently return to trying to see without naming.

"Poor visualizers turn images into words," Sarah Edwards said. This transformation happens so quickly that they cannot detect the visual image in the split second before they name it. "These people are like tour guides to their own images." They are helped to visualize by processes that turn off the verbal noise—exercises that take them "out of their heads and into their senses." Relaxation and yoga can help.

• *Visual recall with slide projector.* Cap the lens of a slide projector with your hand. Uncap the lens for a second so you can see the projected image, then cover it again. Try to recall what you saw without naming the object itself—how it looked.

• *Evoking visual images of something you strongly enjoy looking at.* Twice a day, for one minute, practice imagining this favorite object, person, place, situation.

• *Evoking early childhood memories.* Remember all you can, clustering recollections of particular times, places, people. Do this twice a day. After a week, review the memories of the previous week. You should find that the earlier the memories, the less dominant the verbal component.

• *Dream recall.* Draw your dreams rather than recounting them verbally. This helps you stay in a visual rather than verbal mode.

• *Picture inner dialogues.* When you recognize different aspects of your personality in conflict, try to visualize cartoon characters for them.

RESEARCH

Body-Response Training

Peter Lang reported in *Psychophysiology* (16) on his body-response training methods. *Brain/Mind Bulletin* reported on this work in 1980.

His experimental subjects were first given progressive relaxation training. They were then divided into two groups, each trained differently.

The "stimulus" group was instructed to pay attention to visual and other sensory details in the scenes they imagined. Reports of personal body awareness or participation in the imagined scene were discouraged by the trainer, discounted as unimportant.

The "response" group was coached to describe their imagined breathing, muscular activity, eye movements, and other sensations, as well as visual details of the scene. The trainer praised them for reporting physiological sensations, especially those coinciding with the script.

After three one-hour training sessions, each subject listened to ten scripts—"neutral," "action," or "fear." (See sample scripts in opposite sidebar.) Afterward the subjects were given 30 seconds and told to "visualize the scene as vividly as possible, just as you practiced during the training sessions."

Action scenes included flying a kite, isometric exercises, and riding a bicycle. Fear scenes involved being trapped in a sauna, confronting a snake in the water, or a spider on a pillow. In neutral scenes, subjects imagined sitting on a lawn chair or walking on the sidewalk of a quiet street.

The scripts presented to the "stimulus" group referred only to the content of the scene. Those for the "response" group included physiologically arousing phrases.

In four out of five physiological measurements, "response" subjects were more intensely aroused than the "stimulus" group. Furthermore, the sequences of these responses followed the script.

essentially out of the range of conscious awareness, so fleeting they are missed.

Paul Edwards emphasized that visualization means bringing into consciousness phenomena that are already occurring—and learning to pay attention to them. Usually those who have difficulty visualizing are thinking in another sense language, he said. Their thoughts might be more auditory, tactile, somatic (body sensations), kinesthetic (movement), or gustatory (taste).

They may also be expecting too much. "Images are less clear than actual perceptions," he said, and they occur on a continuum from fragments to vivid, full-color motion pictures in your mind.

Techniques that unblock all of the sensory modes are important therapeutic tools to the Edwardses. One client is an engineer who visualizes structural models and blueprints in detail but can't remember what he has heard. He has vivid visual images of conversations he has participated in but can't recall what was said.

They also noted that imagery can be helpful to those getting through depression, and emphasized the importance of visualization in decision-making: "It's valuable for people to be able to picture outcomes of how they'd like their lives to go." That, of course, mirrors Paul Torrance's concern with our images of the future—our inner stories that determine the direction of our lives.

Body-Response Imagery

Of course, as the Edwardses pointed out, there is more to visualization than just "seeing." You can improve visualization exercises by including physical reactions in your "script"—for example, breathing, heart rate, and reactions to heat and cold. Imagery is not something that just happens in the mind's eye; it integrates the responses of your entire body. And it seems that the power of imagination can make the difference when it comes to making therapy work.

Psychologist Peter Lang at the University of Florida, Gainesville, described some of his imagery studies for *PragMagic*. He noted that in clinical work and research, imaginal procedures are very common. Therapists often ask the patient to imagine some experience or situation that involves the focus of their anxiety. After sustained imagining, the patient often reports—and the therapist observes—a reduction of fear when there is an actual confrontation with the object. Imagery has served as a substitute for experience with the thing that is feared.

"An imaginal confrontation is modifying a confrontation in the real world," Lang said. "Why should that occur?"

When he started recording physiological responses during imaginings, "the dramatic thing we found was that those patients who showed an appropriate physiology of fear when they imagined frightening material were the patients who improved." And the patients whose psychological conditions did not improve were the patients who tended not to show that physiological response.

This happened even though "all the patients professed to be imagining the material very vividly. They were indeed all saying they were quite afraid. In point of fact, the imagery we looked at specifically for these tests were images that the patients said were so frightening that they could not continue." Nevertheless, he found that for many of these patients there were no physiological responses.

"It led us to consider—well, what's important here? Maybe the important thing is not what a person visualizes in the mind's eye, if the mind's eye exists, but rather the behavior that occurs"—the response of the body.

Lang reported in *Psychophysiology* on an elaborate series of experiments he and his colleagues carried out while he was at the University of Wisconsin (see sidebars). They were focusing on emotional imagery in response to verbal instructions—typical of the therapeutic situation.

College students were coached by "scripts" to imagine either a heightened visual response or heightened physical response to a specific situation. The results show a connection between mental images and the body's response to them. "The image is not a stimulus in the head, but an active response process," Lang said.

"Myths permeate all areas of modern life," say David Feinstein and Stanley Krippner, both professors of psychology, in defining the ideas behind *Personal Mythology* (J. P. Tarcher, 1988).

"Your personal mythology acts as a lens that colors your perceptions according to its own assumptions and values. It highlights certain possibilities and shadows others. Through it, you view the ever-changing panorama of your experiences in the world.

"Unlike such terms as scripts, attitudes or beliefs, myth is able to encompass the archetypal dimensions of the unconscious mind, which transcends early conditioning and cultural setting. A mythic outlook also reminds you that you are part of a larger picture than your immediate concerns."

Presenting techniques the authors have employed since the midseventies, the book describes a series of personal rituals to help people overcome the historic fears and biases that have become their "myth."

For example:

• A woman whose emotional "helper" role eventually leaves her with no time of her own

• A man raised in the Depression who ends up valuing money more than love

After recognizing the myth, subjects work to create a "countermyth"—a new, more balanced sense of personal destiny that reconciles old wounds and tendencies. Chronically timid people realize they have the capacity for assertion; money-lovers redirect their love.

"The task of weaving this renewed mythology into the fabric of your life can add fresh meaning and purpose to your journey," the authors say. "In addition, by coming to understand your own mythic process, you become more adept at understanding the mythology of your society and more able to skillfully participate in its evolution."

Personal Experiments and Experimental Beliefs

Theories and research results from many scientists and therapists are presented in *PragMagic*. But this information is only of intellectual interest until you check out its relevance to your life. If you feel skeptical about some theory or research presented in *PragMagic*, but you like the idea it suggests, then try it out as an experimental belief: for a day or two, act as though it were true.

Stuart Heller, a "movement psychologist" at John F. Kennedy University, discussed that idea for *PragMagic*. "Experimental believing is just another term for scientific method," he said. "It says, let us utilize the very method that allowed us to understand physical reality. It is an excellent method. To do any experiment, you have to have a hypothesis. The more you practice it, the more clear you get on what you do and don't believe."

Feeling Your Story

Trying out an experimental belief is not just an intellectual decision. You have to find out how the new belief *feels* in your whole body. When you take different perspectives on the world, you are not just affecting your thoughts. The story you are living affects you physically, too. In fact, according to Stuart Heller, the way you move expresses your beliefs quite clearly.

"Story is more than words," Heller explained. Changing our story means changing the *way* we think and the *way* we move. "The most primitive people in the most primitive traditions know that song is not separate from dance. And story is not a mental construct; it is actually a pattern of tensions, actually shapes the way you move."

So if you only change your story verbally—without integrating it completely into your behavior—you haven't actually changed your story.

A shift of belief demands a shift in movement, Heller says. For example, as he pointed out in a 1983 interview with *Brain/Mind Bulletin,* a person may have a heartfelt insight into a fear of self-assertion, yet not change because of a still-fearful posture. "Each new understanding requires a congruence of physical knowing." It is difficult, for example, to be courageous if you habitually stand in a cringing and timid position. Your feelings respond to the messages from your body as well as those from your brain.

"It is not enough to work on *either* the body *or* the mind," Heller continued. "Changing one's thinking typically makes no difference to the body. Likewise, releasing physical tensions doesn't affect underlying beliefs. But you can affect both by directly altering the movement pattern that connects them." If the postural personality does not change, he said, a new understanding is *only* a change of mind, not a transformation.

Identifying With Beliefs

Discomfort with letting go of beliefs, Heller said, comes from this fear of overall change. When faced with conflict or paradox, people tend to adopt *one* of the positions rather than enlarging their view to include both, even though they may be settling for a partial truth.

For example, when listening to the opposing sides of a family quarrel, we may miss subtle ways in which the positions are really similar. If we feel that we must decide which side is right—and which one is wrong—we may not be able to step back and discover other alternatives.

This either/or attitude translates into a particular body pattern, Heller said, such as always aggressive or always submissive poses. The body-set then further reinforces the polarized thinking. When we repress half of a complex truth or get caught in switching back and forth, our bodies reflect the lack of integration. The natural pulsation is blocked. Breathing is shallow. We lose present-time awareness.

"We resist new ideas because they would change our lives. When we begin to let go, our old identities scream for consistency. One 'I' becomes more sacred than the others, and we design ways to protect it. We'll do almost anything to hang on to who we think we are."

(Continued on page 20)

What if you were to discover that half the things you believed to be true were actually false— but you didn't know which half?

If beliefs change like the seasons, what is their appropriate role in our everyday lives? Movement psychologist Stuart Heller recommends that we try out "experimental beliefs" while remaining aware of their built-in limitations. Tentatively held beliefs can change easily, as the evidence changes.

Beliefs themselves are not the issue. They are useful illusions, enabling us to manage experience. . . . The problem is our relationship to them. To believe in something is to breathe life into it. If we know what we believe, we know what we empower. However, if we do not choose our beliefs—if, through our failure to question, they choose us, then we are unaware of the impact of our assumptions. . . . If, wide awake, we choose to believe in something, we can also choose to let it go when the time comes.

—Connie Zweig
Brain/Mind Bulletin, 1984

EXERCISE: DIFFERENT PERSPECTIVES

This is a slightly modified form of an exercise that Stuart Heller suggests as a way to begin noticing how it feels to look at the world in different ways. Although this may seem like a very simple beginning, it puts you in touch with your own *physical* responses to different perspectives. Give yourself time to feel the physical changes.

FOCUS ON THE BOXES ONE AT A TIME. COVER UP THOSE YOU ARE NOT USING.

STEP #1

Look at the vertical line

and let every muscle in your body change.

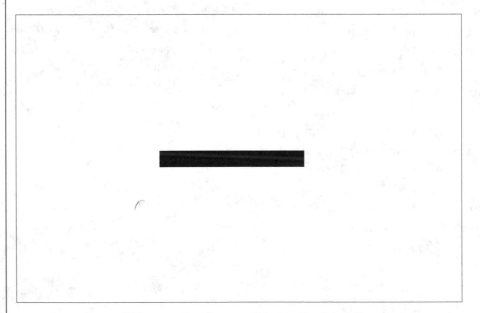

STEP #2

Look at the horizontal line

and let every muscle in your body change.

Did you notice that you did actually change?
Did you feel taller and thinner when you contemplated the vertical?
Did you feel shorter and wider when you contemplated the horizontal?

See how you feel contemplating them together.

STEP #3

Alternate between
the vertical and
the horizontal

*and let every muscle
in your body
change.*

STEP #4

Look at the vertical
and the horizontal
together

*and let every muscle
in your body
change.*

NEXT: Look around your immediate environment and notice the verticals and let every muscle in your body change.

NEXT: Look around your immediate environment and notice the horizontals and let every muscle in your body change.

It is easy to stop the changes.

And it becomes easier with practice to allow the changes.

RESOURCES

"We are all believers," Peter Lemesurier says in *Beyond All Belief* (Element Books, 1984). "Belief is the very tool with which we make sense of what, in our earliest years, necessarily seems to us a confused and chaotic reality. Yet possibly it is the child who sees the world more nearly as it is, and we adults who use belief as a filter to help us see the world as we want to see it."

Belief and knowledge exist in an uneasy rivalry, he suggests. "The more we find out, the more our cherished beliefs have to go overboard." If beliefs are useful tools, illusions that allow us to cut experience into manageable bits, there is a point at which they are too crude to advance our further understanding. They prevent our experiencing a deeper, more seamless reality.

Ruthlessly, Lemesurier dismantles certainty. Sensory experience, descriptions of the physical universe, political ideologies, religions, even the "open" or "new age" versions of reality—all are explored in terms of limiting beliefs. He plays avantgarde findings against each other to illustrate that *nothing* is absolute.

He carries his arguments to their logical conclusion: Consciousness alone is real. The reality that remains after belief is burned away is evolving consciousness itself, the summary mind that perceives.

We can tap this greater entity's awakening psyche, which Lemesurier calls "Earthchild," by keeping in touch with the newest scientific research and by observing and recording our dreams. We can learn to interpret the signals that the unconscious continually feeds into our waking experience.

Human awareness alone can further the destiny of this larger mind, he tells us. We must not limit it by prematurely crystallizing experience into belief.

If It Feels Right . . .

Striving for what "feels right" has its pitfalls, too. For *PragMagic*, Heller said that "using pleasure and pain as your measuring device is guaranteed to lead to failure. Pleasure/pain is not the proper feedback device. Addiction is based on comfort. We are addicts as long as we use that system."

We have all had to make painful decisions—ending tormenting relationships, for example—that feel very bad at the time but which are for the better in the end.

Steps in Changing Your Story

And changing a story isn't a single process that's over and done with. Heller outlined these steps from what he calls his "Course in Ordinary."

First step: "I got it." You feel as if something's changed. For example, maybe you've had a sudden insight into why you have really been afraid to look for a new job. So you feel as if you can go ahead, now that you understand the problem.

Next step: "I lost it." The change you thought you'd achieved seems to have vanished. What people don't realize is that it's *supposed* to vanish. You've been hit by too much information to incorporate it all at once. Don't despair. Just remember all the fragments you can.

Whatever you realized about your situation may seem less important now, but commit it to memory nevertheless. Continue to work with what you have discovered, even if the sense of achievement has faded.

Next: "I know it." You'll sense when you've put your initial insight back together again. When you can go through this period of doubt without giving up, the insight that you had can return and be fully integrated into your life.

Heller relates this to getting kicked out of the Garden: "So people feel this primordial, archetypal kind of guilt and shame for forgetting." But if they know that forgetting is to be expected, they can go ahead with the process.

It will help if you can also look at your current beliefs as experimental beliefs. They are, after all, ideas that you have developed to suit the way you want to live. But many of them are probably not immovable "facts." As scientists know well, what we think of as facts do change.

EXERCISE: CREATING A BETTER STORY

Try this exercise for practice in creating a new story for yourself. Choose a situation that represents a story you would like to live—something you might expect to happen, or a complete fantasy. Remember that this is not necessarily a method of bringing about that specific story, but it is a technique for improving the image, and therefore the expectations, in your own mind. Your ability to visualize a joyful story can be very effective in shaping your actual future.

You might decide to work on a story about a relationship, or something you would like to do, or just being somewhere alone, feeling good and enjoying yourself. In any case, it is important that you have yourself in the picture, acting out some part of the new story.

You will probably find it helpful to do this kind of exercise many times, with the same stories or with different stories.

Read this exercise over thoroughly so that you know what to do. Better yet, have someone read it to you or put it on tape. In that case, be sure to leave a few moments after each direction or question, so you have time for the experience.

During this kind of visualization, some people find it very helpful to actually turn their head, move their eyes, and even reach out with their hands as though actually looking at something, or touching something. Do whatever seems comfortable and effective for you. First relax your body and mind. Use your own favorite procedure for relaxing, or follow the simple instructions for relaxing we gave you on page 12.

• With your eyes closed, begin to "see" yourself in a situation that you feel would be an improved story for you. For the present, just set the scene without any action taking place.

Now, with your eyes still closed, "look" about you—right, left, up, down, behind you. Catalog in your mind the things around you. See just what the scene looks like. If something undesirable appears, just gently insist that you are going to have things exactly as you want them—this is your story, after all.

• Now, staying in the same scene, give your attention to your senses of smell and taste. Are there outdoor or indoor odors? Is the air fresh? Are there foods or beverages in your scene? If so, take a bite or sip of something you like. How does it taste? What other odors and tastes are there?

• Now, staying in the same scene, focus on your sense of hearing. Are other people making sounds around you? Is anyone talking? Singing? Can you hear birds or other sounds of nature? Any other sounds?

• Now, staying in the same scene, give your attention to your sense of touch and other physical sensations. Is it warm or cool? Is there a breeze or is the air still? What do the clothes you are wearing (if any) or surfaces you are touching feel like? What other things can you feel?

• Now, staying in the same scene, focus on your emotions and physical responses. How do you feel about the scene you have created? Are you pleased? Delighted? Is there anything that worries you? What other feelings do you have? How is your body responding to these feelings? Are you blushing or cool? Is your heart beating fast or is it calm? Is your breathing fast or slow? Are your hands warm or cool? What other responses does your body have to your feelings?

• Now continue with the same scene, and let any action occur that you wish. Talk with people who are there, and walk (or dance) through your scenario. Do whatever you want.

Whenever possible, be aware of all your senses and of your emotional and physical responses to your new story. Enjoy your new story and return to it, or create others, whenever you wish.

RESEARCH

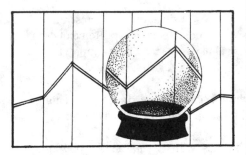

Present Attitudes Color Future Visions

Los Angeles psychologist Andrew Leeds used "hypnotic future progression" in a clinical study of precognition—knowledge of the future. In 1984, *Brain/Mind Bulletin* reported on Leeds's work from his unpublished doctoral dissertation.

The technique of hypnotic reorientation in time sheds light on the relationship between the quality of our inner lives and our expectations of the future. Leeds said: "Our initial findings don't support the idea of hypnotic progression as a window onto an objective future. But they may shed light on some of the reasons for fears of global catastrophe."

Subjects' visions of the future were catastrophic or utopian depending on the quality of previous peak experiences. Those who had undergone significant psychedelic, mystical, or near-death experiences reported more optimistic, utopian future worlds. Those with limited previous peak experiences tended to report global catastrophe.

Leeds hypnotized 25 volunteers independently, reorienting them 200 years in the future. He used the *remote* future to account for the possibility of guessing. "Imagine yourself in 1783, just after the Revolutionary War," he explained. "Try to project what America would be like 200 years in the future. You see the futility of trying to extrapolate from current trends."

Thinking Like a Scientist

Besides thinking like an alchemist and a storyteller, it's important to be able to think like a scientist. This doesn't mean that we undertake elaborate and rigorous laboratory research. But in order to carry out our own personal experiments and have confidence in the results, it will help to adopt the characteristics of the best scientific minds.

Scientists are not really so separate from the rest of us. In *On Becoming a Person* (Houghton Mifflin, 1972), Carl Rogers points out that science is not something external and impersonal, a body of knowledge "out there." He suggests that "science exists only in people." Recognizing a problem, investigating it, coming to a tentative conclusion, communicating results, and making use of findings are all activities that people carry out in their everyday lives.

A scientist, first of all, is curious. Like any of us, a scientist wants to know more about something and sets out to find out, directing a great deal of attention to the questions at hand. Readers of this book have already taken those first steps.

Rogers describes the creative phase of science as a time when a particular person pursuing certain aims and values becomes immersed in the experience. "He senses the field in which he is interested, he lives it. He does more than 'think' about it—he lets his organism take over and react to it, both on a knowing and an unknowing level."

Scientists not only want to know what all the facts are—but also what all the facts *mean*. At this point, you might gather all the available information and discoveries from your investigation and simply make a hypothesis. Developing a hunch, says Rogers, is the most important phase of science.

The next question is: "But does it check with reality?" Because we find it easy to "believe something which later experience shows is not so," we design a test for our idea. We can consult with others, use control groups, statistics, logic, any scientific tool that seems appropriate.

"Thus scientific methodology is seen for what it truly is—a way of preventing me from deceiving myself in regard to my creatively formed subjective hunches, which have developed out of the relationship between me and my material," Rogers says.

You might want to try out your theory as an experimental belief or devise a specific test for it. It is still a matter of your own personal judgment how to test your hunch and how much credibility to give to the results. Rogers writes, "If I have selected and used intelligently all the precautions against self-deception which I have been able to assimilate from others or to devise myself, then I will give my tentative belief to the findings which have emerged. I will regard them as a springboard for further investigation and further seeking."

Finally, we can check our ideas with others who have been interested in the same questions. We gain a certain amount of security if those others have made similar observations or have come to the same conclusions. We may also uncover other questions that will be exciting to investigate, as well as other ways to test the validity of the tentative conclusions we have reached.

> *Science,*
> *as well as therapy,*
> *as well as all other*
> *aspects of living,*
> *is rooted in and based upon*
> *the immediate, subjective*
> *experience of a person.*
> *It springs from the inner,*
> *total, organismic experiencing*
> *which is only partially and*
> *imperfectly communicable.*
> *It is one phase of*
> *subjective living.*
>
> —Carl Rogers
> *On Becoming a Person*
> (Houghton Mifflin, 1972)

NOTES:

2.
BEING MAGIC:
Your Story

How well do you know yourself? Could you describe yourself to someone else as vividly and effectively as you might describe a friend or acquaintance? Sometimes we are called upon to do so—when we're interviewing for a job, for example.

How do you feel in such situations? Most of us experience some degree of discomfort and self-consciousness. Why is this so? After all, we are our own raw material. We should be intimately familiar with ourselves, and able to proudly and accurately trumpet our strengths, as well as to acknowledge our weaknesses.

It's time to consider the role of self-analysis and self-understanding in our lives. Avoiding the issue altogether doesn't help anybody—not us and not those around us.

The practice of pragmagic is meant to enrich our lives and help us discover how deeply we can contribute to the lives of others. While it may mean some intense focus on ourselves, it also demands learning more about our relationships with others and our interactions with the world. It means learning to analyze and improve our own stories.

In this section you will find information about such issues as:

- problems caused by a lack of self-esteem
- how feelings organize our thinking
- how emotions we can't express affect our health
- cycles in our levels of energy and awareness
- the nature of consciousness
- how to make the best use of sleep
- the power of dreams
- the subtleties of human relationships
- ways of determining our own personality "types"

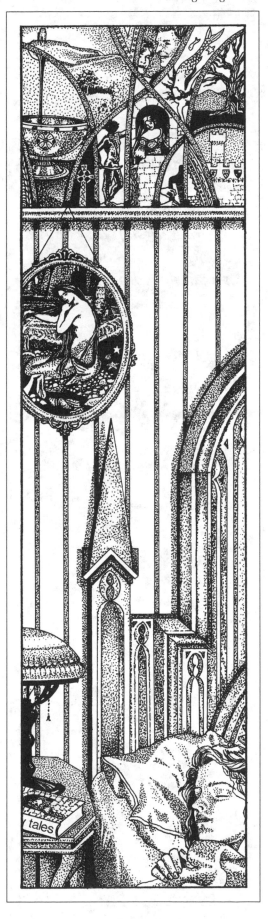

The research reported here suggests how we experience the world is more complicated than we may have realized. How we perceive other people may well be rooted in how we perceive ourselves. These concepts, in turn, can deeply affect what we expect from life. What we know and believe about ourselves are the materials from which we build our own stories.

There is not a more perplexing affair in life to me than to set about telling anyone who I am— for there is scarce anybody I cannot give a better account of than of myself; and I have often wished I could do it in a single word—and have an end of it.

—Laurence Sterne
A Sentimental Journey Through France and Italy
(Penguin, 1986)

Self-esteem

If the thought of focusing intensely on yourself makes you uncomfortable, it may be because rigorous self-examination is often suspect in our culture. Giving attention to yourself is said to be self-indulgent, narcissistic.

Like many of us, you may have been taught to be modest and self-effacing—perhaps even at the cost of your own self-esteem. However, self-esteem may be closely connected to the development of personal responsibility, maintenance of good health, and kindness to others. We do deserve our own attention.

Emotional Anemia

Emotional anemia is a deficiency in our ability to accept ourselves—or even to acknowledge affection, appreciation, and closeness from others.

Arnold Horwitz, a psychologist in private practice in Beverly Hills, California, told *Brain/Mind Bulletin* in 1982 that his clients commonly avoid positive recognition. They refuse to accept others' appreciation of their good points, competence, skills, and resources. "Usually it's not that these people lack appreciation," said Horwitz, "but that they have great difficulty acknowledging and accepting appreciation." He traced the tendency to childhood, when most clients were told that making positive statements about themselves was "bragging" or "showing off." They were taught to "be humble," to deny that compliments from others were true.

"Is that all there is?" was the attitude Horwitz encountered in his clients. They expressed a sense that they were missing something, but "what they are missing most is their own appreciation of themselves."

He helps these clients become aware of how they discount the giver of the gift of appreciation or change the

(Continued on page 30)

There is no value-judgment more important to man— no factor more decisive in his psychological development and motivation— than the estimate he passes on himself.

—Nathaniel Branden
from *A Nathaniel Branden Anthology*
(Houghton Mifflin, 1980)

INVENTORY: RECEIVING PRAISE

To check your own response to appreciation, try the following scenario: Imagine you are an office worker and have spent several days of hard work on a particular task. You passed it along to your supervisor this morning. It is afternoon now, and your supervisor has just called all your fellow employees together to praise your work. How do you feel? What do you do?

Now, think back to the last time you received such praise, a time that closely approximates the imaginary scenario above, whether in the workplace, at home, in a recreational setting, etc. Be very specific. What were your reactions?

Did you experience any bodily responses? For example:
- ❏ Did you blush?
- ❏ Did you break out in a smile?
- ❏ Did you feel yourself slump, as if trying to hide?
- ❏ Did you feel yourself straighten up?

What did you *do* upon receiving the praise?
- ❏ I simply thanked the person offering it.
- ❏ I denied that I deserved it.
- ❏ I hastily changed the subject.
- ❏ I froze and said nothing until the moment passed.

Which of the following most accurately reflects your *inner thoughts* at receiving this praise?
- ❏ "I deserve this praise, and it's nice to get it."
- ❏ "I don't trust this person's judgment; he/she isn't qualified to assess my work."
- ❏ "This person simply doesn't know the 'real me.'"
- ❏ "I wish people wouldn't embarrass me like this."

The capacity to accept praise is more valuable than we may have been led to believe; our own responses are well worth our attention.

EXERCISE: MEETING YOURSELF

This is a technique that Arnold Horwitz uses with his clients. The first thing he asks is the commitment to carry it out consistently. "It takes about three to four weeks to begin to change behavioral patterns," he explains.

Horwitz encourages clients to make eye-to-eye contact every morning with their image in the mirror. He also suggests that the client place a picture of him/herself as a three- to seven-year-old child in the mirror. This helps put them back in touch with the "child within." "This way," he says, "they see themselves as that little person, recognizing that the child is still inside themselves."

You proceed step by step:
• Spend 30 seconds in front of the mirror doing slow, deep breathing. This desensitizes the experience, allowing you to make eye contact while physiologically comfortable.
• Put your hand over your heart. This is somehow quieting and self-connecting.
• Speak self-affirmations very slowly, word by word, and with conviction—"Not like a laundry list," insists Horwitz. "Then the words are only going into a bag, and not into yourself."

Initially, this exercise can be very difficult. "Two to three minutes can seem like forever at first," says Horwitz.

His list includes such highly affirming statements as:
• I love you.
• I have strength.
• I'm a fine person.

Certain statements are particularly sensitive and demanding:
• I'm scared. It's okay for me to be scared and I will get through this.
• I have enough now to enjoy my life.
• I deserve to be loved.
• I have a right to change my parental rules about living my life.

Horwitz's clients strive to incorporate an entire list of 30 affirmations, but for their first mirror work they deal with only three to five, such as those listed here.

INVENTORY: INNER COMFORT

What questions should we consider regarding our own self-esteem? Horwitz suggests that we begin by asking which of these is true:

- ❏ I am usually comfortable with myself.
- ❏ I am usually *un*comfortable with myself.

If you find those statements too abstract, go on to these more tangible questions:

- What physiological responses come from just considering the *question* of whether I am comfortable with myself or not? (Do I relax or tighten up? Where do I tighten up? List specific physical *sensations.*)

_____

_____

_____

- What do I *say* about myself during the day? (Do I speak well of myself? Or do I put myself down? List specific *statements* you commonly make about yourself.)

_____

_____

_____

If you have determined that you are *un*comfortable with yourself, you may need to reconsider the standards you are setting for yourself. Disappointment and pain arise out of striving toward exalted standards, out of not being able to measure up to an ideal. List the following:

- What are my specific *standards* for success?

_____

_____

_____

- Who are the *models* I compare myself to? (Family members, peers, celebrity figures, etc.?)

_____

_____

_____

Horwitz points out that people who strive toward impossible ideals tend always to "raise the ante" whenever they find themselves approaching success, setting a new set of unattainable standards so that they never quite "make it." People need to focus on them*selves,* rather than upon misleading expectations.

These lists and checklists may help you to enhance your awareness of how you respond to praise. *Attention,* as always, is an all-important word—not only toward how we respond to the judgments and assessments of others, but toward how *we* feel about *ourselves.* It is always important to consider the question: "When I receive praise, do I accept it or deflect it?" But we also need to be able to praise *ourselves* objectively and sincerely, quite apart from accepting praise from others.

subject to avoid positive recognition. He also counsels them to actively ask for, give, and accept positive recognition. "People aren't mind readers. You have to tell them when you need something. And you inevitably increase the probability of getting more from life if you ask for more, whether it's hugs, attention, or involvement."

COMMENTARY

Attention to Self-esteem Is the Law in California

California lawmakers were among the first to turn their attention to what they believe may be a root cause of crime and anti-social behavior: low self-esteem. A special task force was created by law in a 1986 bill designed by Assemblyman John Vasconcellos. The 25-member group included psychologists, counselors, bureaucrats, educators, legislators, law enforcement officials, and homemakers.

The ongoing job of the "California Task Force to Promote Self-esteem and Personal and Social Responsibility" is to collate all available data on self-esteem and to discuss its significance and social implications. Robert Ball, executive director of the task force, emphasized that real self-esteem leads to responsible behavior.

Vasconcellos based his approach on the work of Carl Rogers, the late humanistic psychologist who believed that human beings, like all other organisms, have a natural tendency to fulfill their inherent possibilities.

In his 1977 book, *Carl Rogers on Personal Power* (Delacorte Press), Rogers wrote: "As the client is more acceptant of self, the possibility of being in command of self becomes greater and greater. . . . As the client becomes more self-aware, more self-acceptant, less defensive and more open, she finds at last some of the freedom to grow and change in the directions natural to the human organism. Life is now in her hands, to be lived as an individual."

EXERCISE: UNCOVERING OLD ASSUMPTIONS

This group exercise can be especially effective for finding the sources of problems with self-esteem.

Distribute small slips of paper to each person. If there are six or more people in your group, three slips apiece will be enough. Smaller groups may want to give six slips to each person.

Next, have participants write down negative traits attributed to them as children—one to a slip. Perhaps these were labels imposed by others; or perhaps they were ideas participants had about themselves. (Examples: fat, skinny, slow, bookish, clumsy, etc.)

Toss the slips on the floor and scramble them up. Then have each person draw a slip at random. Each person will read the slip he or she has picked to the rest of the group.

As each slip is read, take a moment to discuss it. There will usually be plenty of spontaneous commentary and comparison.

Discuss these questions:
• Have many of you shared the same traits, real or imagined?
• Does it surprise you that others have shared your experience?
• How have traits attributed to you in childhood shaped your adult life?

It is usually liberating to realize that you are not alone in having been labeled as a child. It is also beneficial to realize that you are no longer so constricted by some early belief.

And of course, not all childhood labels are negative. To remove the aura of negativity from this exercise, perform the same activity concerning one gift or strength attributed to each of you as children.

Self-esteem and Health

Experience as a therapist has led Horwitz to perceive emotional anemia—the inability to acknowledge or accept appreciation—as a possible cause of physical problems. He found that people who avoided positive recognition reported more obsessive-compulsive behavior, greater depression or anxiety, and more disordered thinking. He also cited studies indicating that individuals who lack strong social ties or intimate social relationships are more likely to suffer premature death from heart disease, cancer, or suicide than those who have significant social contacts.

As his clients learn to accept positive recognition, Horwitz said, they report relief from many symptoms, including headaches, faintness, loss of sexual appetite, poor memory, uncontrolled temper, self-blaming, lower-back pain, feelings of inferiority, hopelessness, and chronic nausea.

"From this perspective, the concept of illness needs to be broadened to include an awareness of how we interact with one another," he said.

In a more recent interview for *PragMagic,* Horwitz offered this metaphor for the inner malnourishment of emotional anemia: "Some people might go to a gourmet restaurant where the best food in the world is served, and they might put food on a fork or even in their mouth, but they won't swallow. If they go about things this way for long enough, they'll starve."

When we're starving, whether physically or emotionally, we are likely to do desperate things. And most of us, when desperate, have a tendency to look for *external* factors to resolve our desperation. Drug, food, and other abuses arise out of this "internal experience of emotional malnourishment. People are often unaware that they have a responsibility to take care of themselves emotionally."

Horowitz describes this external behavior as "smoke from the fire of internal conflict."

Attention to the Child Within

He also points out that we need to give some special attention to the child who we once were—because that child still lives within us. Horwitz wants some of his clients to understand that they are "abusing" this child. He explains that when you fail to nurture the child who still

RESOURCES

Honoring the Self by Nathaniel Branden (J. P. Tarcher, 1983). "Self-esteem," says Branden, "is the reputation we acquire with ourselves."

Unrewarded choices lead to low self-esteem, then to an expectation that life will be difficult—and so it is. Our sense of self is the original self-fulfilling prophecy.

Drawing on her work with gifted people, Swiss psychoanalyst Alice Miller writes in *Prisoners of Childhood* (Basic Books, 1981) of the ways in which well-meaning parents emotionally damage their children. The children—denied respect and understanding—in turn become parents who cannot empathize with their own children.

Unconscious of the patterns that set this early cycle in motion, both generations become "prisoners of childhood."

When a child adapts to its parents' needs due to fear of the loss of love, he can develop an "as if" personality, revealing only what is expected of him, Miller says. To achieve this, he kills a part of himself, developing the "art of not experiencing feelings."

A "well-behaved, reliable, convenient child" emerges, a child who in fact was never a child at all. The natural contact with emotions that is essential to self-esteem is lost.

Miller redefines narcissism as both a healthy self-love and a set of disorders leading, she believes, to depression and perfectionism. If parents learn to respect a child's feelings, she says, even when the feelings are misunderstood the child can get a sense of being the center of his own activity.

dwells within your present self, or when you say cruel things to that child, it is "a form of child abuse."

For example, most of us would disapprove if we heard a parent describing a child as "stupid, foolish, no good, hateful, or terrible," or telling a child, "I can't stand you." But people say these things to themselves and think it's perfectly normal—statements as destructive as "You're never going to make it" or "You're not a winner."

Good Self-esteem

But what constitutes good self-esteem? Horwitz describes it as "being at a point in your experience where you feel comfortable with you. . . .You can be honest about what you do, and what effect your behavior has on yourself and on others. This occurs when you have learned to accept yourself and confront your own behavior."

Partly due to the plethora of self-help books and radio psychologists, many people are able to "talk the talk, but may not have learned how to walk the walk," said Horwitz.

"I've heard a lot of people, either in my life or in my practice, who use words like 'responsibility.' Often, they had the right words but were not responsive to their own or to other people's needs. They were not paying attention to nurturing the child within. Even if they are not overtly or physically ill, they are not enjoying complete health either. They are experiencing emotional anemia."

In my opinion it is the spontaneous emotional life that carries the thread of humanity in our species. Thus, whether one is dealing with an emotionally driven zealot or with a de-emotionalized scientist who has lost the meaning of the work he has done, the result is the same— a disregard for humanity in terms of caring and feeling.

—William Gray
in *Brain/Mind Bulletin* (1982)

Feelings

Our feelings about people and events are sometimes considered strictly personal issues. Our inner emotional states are often thought to be best kept separate from our actions. We may be told that the intelligent way to make important decisions is to "keep your feelings out of it."

But now it seems that thinking may not be separate from feeling.

Researchers are discovering intimate links between feelings and knowledge and behavior. They are also developing theories that help us understand the problems that arise when we don't *experience* what we are feeling. These studies suggest that feelings are just too important to be ignored.

Feeling-Tones

According to a comprehensive theory developed by psychiatrist William Gray of Newton Center, Massachusetts, *all* thoughts and memories are coded by subtle "feeling-tones," and the brain actually uses feelings to structure information. Even when we are not conscious of subtle feelings, Gray believes they underlie everything we know. When we are cut off from our feelings, it becomes much more difficult to make mental connections. Abstract information is hard to remember because it is not connected with our emotional records.

Paul LaViolette, a systems theorist and staff researcher for the Starburst Foundation in Portland, Oregon, has further developed Gray's theoretical work. *Brain/Mind Bulletin* interviewed Gray and LaViolette in 1982.

LaViolette said that, although "many people believe consciousness is generated by particular physical effects at particular brain sites," the feeling-tone model suggests consciousness is located in the structure and relation between the feelings themselves. "That is, *consciousness is transcendent.* The brain may be conceived of as a kind of sophisticated weaving machine that allows feeling-tones to feel and affect themselves, and thereby to weave themselves into complex tapestries—our thoughts."

Gray believes that feelings may be the organizers of the mind and of the personality. Gray told *Brain/Mind Bulletin* that in infancy we experience a basic set of feelings such as contentment, rejection, anger, fear. Just as the primary colors red, yellow, and blue are blended into millions of hues, these "primary" emotions become changed through our life experience into many feeling-tones.

He thinks that human beings have achieved greater intelligence than other species because of the richer supply of emotional nuances available to them.

RESEARCH

Cognitive Complexity and Emotional Range

Research at the University of Massachusetts suggests a correlation between emotional and cognitive (information processing) complexity and strongly supports the Gray-LaViolette model. The late psychologist Shula Sommers described the studies in the *Journal of Personality and Social Psychology* (41). *Brain/Mind Bulletin* reported the work in 1982.

The study showed that the wider the range of one's emotional expressions, the more complex is one's intellectual expression.

Fifty-four psychology students were asked to make up stories for two ambiguous illustrations showing five human figures, then to retell the stories from the viewpoint of each story character.

Students were then assigned to write brief descriptions of their best friends. Finally they were asked to construct stories about three different situations: a boy's first day at school, a dispute between college roommates, an argument between spouses.

The complexity of the students' stories and descriptions correlated with both the number and variety of emotional terms they used.

RESEARCH

Parents' Emotional Support Predicts Kids' Well-being

Parental affection and encouragement of independence registered as the two clearest predictors of adult happiness and effective social functioning, Judith Richman and Joseph Flaherty of the University of Illinois Psychiatry Department reported in the *Journal of Nervous and Mental Disease* (175). In a study of 100 medical students, the young adults' views of the style in which they were reared correlated strongly with later mental health problems. *Brain/Mind Bulletin* reported the research in 1988.

Students who said their parents had supported them emotionally and had encouraged them to be independent showed high self-esteem and intellectual flexibility. Depression and personality problems were associated with the father's coldness or with overprotection by either parent.

Social relationships, surprisingly, did not protect the students against depressive moods. Rather, the students' moods seemed to color their social relationships. Moods also particularly affected the sense of being in control.

The effect of moods on other personality traits was less clear. The researchers said they were unsure whether characteristics such as low self-esteem, dependency, and rigidity cause depression or vice versa.

Imbalances

There are two basic emotional/cognitive imbalances that Gray considers "defective forms of mental function":

• *Being driven* by emotion "leads to such inhumanity as mob psychology."

• *Losing touch* with the emotional basis of one's thinking results in uncaring, "a pathologically sterilized form of thought."

The Gray-LaViolette model both transcends and resolves the age-old argument: Which is more important, heart or mind? According to their studies, feeling and knowing, the realms of heart and mind, cannot be separated.

INVENTORY: INS AND OUTS

In the drawing at the right:

The fence is to keep students in.

The fence is to keep people out.

Your response to this drawing, according to William Gray, is a clue to whether you have a tendency to feel locked in or locked out.

Did you think the fence is to keep students in? You may be particularly bothered whenever you feel locked in.

Did you think the fence is to keep people out? Perhaps you are more disturbed when you feel locked out.

Another indication: Would it bother you more to go to the library for a book you really needed and find yourself locked out, or to be reading late in the library and discover that you had been locked in? The imaginary scenario that is most disturbing can tell you which kind of real-life situations are troublesome for you.

Feeling Locked In or Locked Out

William Gray began developing his theory of linked emotional and cognitive structures as he researched creativity and learning in the 1960s and began publishing his ideas in the early 1970s. Practical application followed in his court work when he realized that criminals and adolescent repeat offenders could not say why they had committed crimes or antisocial acts. Their motives, he hypothesized, "came from parts of the brain that do not possess verbal language capacity."

Gray identified what he believes to be a basic cause of criminal activity: intense feelings of being either "locked out" of family or other groups—or "locked in." The two types of behavior are developed from different kinds of life experiences and produce different kinds of antisocial responses. In terms of criminal behavior, people who feel locked out commit break-and-enter offenses such as burglary and rape; locked-in people react with dissenting acts such as truancy, fire-setting, and prostitution.

Gray teaches his clients who feel locked out that socially acceptable strategies can be used to "break in," such as interrupting conversations, knocking on doors, and applying for jobs. Break-in alternatives are often no more elaborate than learning to approach parents or friends with the desire to talk about something.

Locked-in clients are harder to treat, Gray said, because most attempts to deal with their rebellious behavior increase their locked-in feelings. In one case, he gave a 12-year-old who kept running away from home a supply of dimes so that he could, instead, telephone a series of people he trusted.

Feelings in Everyday Life

Gray stressed that moderate locked-in and locked-out feelings are essential to the development of privacy and community. Neither breaking in nor breaking out is a specifically criminal activity, but simply a human trait that can be exercised in healthy, growth-producing ways.

We are genetically predisposed to react when we feel that we are being either locked in or locked out, Gray commented for *PragMagic*. A particular sensitivity to either state may be activated by our early experience.

Although Gray's work has focused on criminal behavior, most of us can remember times when we felt shut out

---

RESEARCH

Neuropeptides Link Emotions, Brain, and Body

"The same chemicals that control mood in the brain control the tissue integrity of the body," Candace Pert, then chief of brain biochemistry for the National Institute of Mental Health, told *Brain/Mind Bulletin* in 1986. Judging from the role of the peptides and their effects on mood, Pert suggested that "emotions are the key to health."

Neuropeptides are so basic that they exist even in single-celled life. There are 50 or 60 known neuropeptides, which are made directly from the DNA.

The neuropeptides link the nervous system, endocrine system, and immune system. They transmit, receive, and monitor the flow of information, and adapt accordingly.

The peptides are associated with a variety of moods and states—pleasure, pain, learning, appetite, sexuality, and anxiety. As regulators of mood, they may help to integrate behavior. They also alter consciousness.

The limbic brain, rich in neuropeptides, extends its tentacles into the brain stem and cortex more extensively than once believed. But the substances and their receptors are also strategically located throughout the body.

"The emotions are not just in the brain," Pert said. "They're in the body." Even certain hormones, such as insulin, have turned out to be part of the peptide system. One peptide, CCK, affects gut action. CCK forms a lining from the esophagus through the intestines. "This may explain why some people talk about 'gut feelings.'"

Passion Can Be Adolescent Inspiration or Undoing

"Passion can be the prod for great achievement or the cause of great downfall," said Rutgers psychologist Jeannette Haviland, who is studying the effect of mood on adolescent intelligence. *Brain/Mind Bulletin* reported her work in 1988.

A lack of emotional coping skills may prove to be a time bomb in the cognitive development of adolescents. "In a nutshell, if you have normal emotional development in childhood, the passion of adolescence can produce positive change. If the coping skills aren't there, emotional swings can produce disturbance and fragmentation."

The study of young people aged 12 to 15 was drawn from adolescents' diaries tracking daily mood shifts over a three-week period. "We found that reports of mood correlated with tests on coping," Haviland said. "In juveniles, passion itself creates the need to control."

The diaries are also analyzed for evidence of emotional blocking and intellectual change. As one example, she points out the diary entry of a student who had been raped. The student wrote: "Mommy and Daddy would have a fit if they knew, but *I didn't find it as traumatic as everybody seems to make it.* The fact is that this particular fellow had already had a few six-packs too many. *It had nothing to do with me.*"

Haviland predicted that the student would later show striking cognitive deterioration. "It's as if blocking off thought about rape will block other thinking."

of a group we wanted to be with, or felt trapped in a situation we wanted to escape. Each of us develops a tendency to be more distressed by one kind of situation than the other—a helpful thing to realize about our friends as well as about ourselves.

Learning to recognize the most troubling situation can be the first step in determining a solution, for example: breaking into conversations and career opportunities, or taking that badly needed vacation away from it all.

Alexithymia

Some people who have real difficulty in finding words to describe how they feel are not resisting or repressing their emotions but are simply not experiencing them. It is as though the feelings had never taken place. The condition is called alexithymia (meaning "without words for feelings"). It is not so much a disorder as a type of mental functioning that can be helpful in a crisis, but becomes a serious problem if the state is prolonged.

Alexithymia is often associated with severe trauma. Stuart Shipko, now a Los Angeles psychiatrist in private practice, and associates William Alvarez and Nicholas Noviello found the condition in 41% of 22 Vietnam combat veterans suffering from post-traumatic stress disorder.

Reporting their findings in *Psychotherapy and Psychosomatics* in 1983, they observed that the ability to avoid experiencing emotions can actually be helpful when conditions are so severe that appropriate emotions might make purposeful action impossible. They noted that "several of the alexithymic combat veterans could clearly identify the incident which resulted in a conscious decision to suppress their experience of emotion. These individuals felt that it was the only way to continue fighting."

However, the absence of emotion persisted for 10 to 15 years. The patients were aware of their lack of feeling even when faced with the death of a parent or the birth of a child. Even though the original blunting of feeling was voluntary, and the patients were aware of their emotional differences from other people, it proved difficult to reset their "emotional thermostats" for different conditions.

In a 1987 interview with *Brain/Mind Bulletin,* Shipko observed that, on a practical level, all people in society must sometimes stifle emotions in order to carry out a necessary task.

The ability to do so is present in all of us; it is innate, like the more familiar "fight-or-flight" response. But sometimes this natural mechanism becomes vastly over-developed. In some cases, the numbing results from a turbulent childhood. Sometimes it arises out of rigid family structures, or homes in which emotions are considered "unimportant."

Shipko described what he called the "John Wayne syndrome." The detached husband brings in his wife, who is hysterical because the husband refuses to interact with her on a feeling level. "I treat the husband," Shipko said.

Treating Alexithymia

Shipko addressed the issue of treating alexithymia for *PragMagic*. He said, "My clinical observation is that when you unfreeze your emotions, you can't really progress until you do deal with the things you've frozen out. They seem to stay alive as issues in the unconscious." But when emotions become unfrozen, "people who originally seemed like poor therapy candidates can become quite good ones, if you start with a discussion of *feelings*."

Shipko says it is possible to monitor alexithymia as a stress management technique. "The tricky thing about stress," he says, "is to identify it." Sometimes, when undergoing stress, you can feel the stress before you can actually pinpoint what or who is causing it. "But sometimes," he says, "when you're really under a lot of stress, you don't feel any annoyance. There's just the sort of vague emptiness and discomfort of alexithymia."

Paying attention to these reactions can be valuable. When you recognize an alexithymic reaction to stress, you can be quite sure that "I'm overworked and cannot really empathize with my spouse or people around me." You can be aware of your stress and take into account how it will affect your responses.

Natural and Unnatural Alexithymia

According to Shipko, there is such a thing as "natural" alexithymia. For example, life stages may take an alexithymic turn. "Our twenties are pretty much an alexithymic stage," he said, "where action is valued at the expense of emotion." Traditionally, this is when people

(Continued on page 40)

RESEARCH

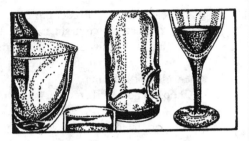

Alcoholics May Lack the Ability to Feel and Express Emotions

In two studies, Janusz Rybakowski and his colleagues in the Psychiatry Department of the Medical Academy, Bydgoszcz, Poland, tested patients at an alcoholism treatment center. They found that three out of four alcoholics may be alexithymic—essentially unaware of and unable to express their emotions. This rate is drastically higher than that for the general population.

Rybakowski reported the first study in *Drug and Alcohol Dependence* (21). *Brain/Mind Bulletin* discussed it and the more recent unpublished study in 1989.

The Polish researchers found that the following percentages met the psychological criteria for alexithymia:

	%
Study 1	78
Study 2	80
overall population	10

The authors speculated that the biological and psychological factors in alexithymia leave people vulnerable to alcoholism.

For example, alexithymics, like alcoholics, have been shown to have tendencies toward prolonged reactions to stress. It may be that alcohol enables alexithymics to relax as well as helping them express themselves with more emotion.

INVENTORY: FEELING YOUR FEELINGS

The capacity "not to feel our own feelings" is common to all of us, and it is likely that we have all experienced alexithymic states at one time or another. Since alexithymia literally means "without words for feelings," check yourself out with this little inventory of your "emotional vocabulary." To put it simply, how do you *know* that you are feeling a particular emotion? It's not a common question in our culture, but one well worth asking.

Choose a powerful emotion that you believe yourself to have some knowledge and experience of—*joy,* perhaps, or *hatred, love, disgust, pleasure, rage,* or *amusement.* Visualizing a recent situation in which you experienced such a powerful emotion will help you in describing it.

How do you know this emotion when you experience it? List your symptoms according to the following categories:

Physical symptoms (might include racing heart, sweaty palms, flushed face, etc.)

_____

_____

_____

_____

_____

Mental symptoms (might include confused thoughts, accelerated ideas, particular mental images, etc.)

_____

_____

_____

_____

_____

Other (basic self-knowledge, perhaps; a strong memory of past emotion; a firm knowledge of what "pushes your buttons")

_____

_____

_____

_____

_____

Were you able to list more under one category than under another? Perhaps the most important aspect of this inventory is not so much *what* symptoms you list as how *easy* it is to list them. If you needed another sheet, congratulate yourself on the state of your emotional vocabulary.

INVENTORY: CHECKING IN, CHECKING OUT

Here is a self-inventory for recognizing some of the more commonplace examples of alexithymia. It involves looking back on *several specific scenes* of stress in your life—whatever is freshest in your memory and recalling the scene in as much sensory detail as possible. Then ask yourself certain questions about these situations. Check the response *nearest* to what you experienced.

For example:

A moment of personal or interpersonal stress: a quarrel, a confrontation, a moment of grief, loss of a relationship, etc. Which of the following was true?
- ❏ I experienced little or no emotion during the situation, only a vague sense of discomfort and stress.
- ❏ I was intensely aware of my emotions throughout the situation.

A situation of occupational or competitive stress: an impending deadline, an interval of overwork, or professional conflict. Which of the following was true?
- ❏ I was only aware of taking care of the tasks at hand and a general sense of discomfort and stress; I was essentially unaware of my emotions.
- ❏ I was at least as aware of my feelings as of the tasks at hand.

Stress in a crisis situation: being a crime victim, involvement in an accident, etc. Which of the following was true?
- ❏ Most of my emotions were lost in the shock and confusion of the situation.
- ❏ I was overwhelmed by my feelings.

In one or more of the above situations, it is possible that you were essentially unaware of your feelings at the time and could not have described them as you were feeling them. If so, choose *one* such situation, and check which of the following statements was true about it:
- ❏ The situation demanded quick thinking and alert and ready action.
- ❏ I was really powerless to affect the situation. My role was a passive one.

Lastly, consider how your emotions were eventually handled in a situation in which you did not, initially, experience them:
- ❏ My emotions came to the surface immediately after the situation was resolved.
- ❏ My emotions came to the surface much, much later.
- ❏ My emotions never really came to the surface.

Monitoring your own alexithymic reactions can prove very valuable as a stress-management tactic. Being self-aware of degrees of alexithymia can clue you in to the kind and amount of stress you are under —and what you can reasonably expect from yourself under the circumstances.

RESEARCH

Psychosomatic Disorders and Alexithymia

A study by psychologists Marvin Acklin and Gene Alexander of The Queen's Medical Center in Honolulu supported the theory that people with psychosomatic disorders tend also to be alexithymic. They reported their findings in the *Journal of Nervous and Mental Disease* (176). *Brain/Mind Bulletin* reported their research in 1989.

In particular, they found a clear association between lack of emotional expression, deficits in fantasy, and low-back pain.

Acklin and Alexander studied subjects suffering from gastrointestinal disorders, dermatitis, low-back pain, and migraine. Based on the results of the Rorschach test, they found that psychosomatic patients were substantially more likely overall to qualify as alexithymic than a healthy control group.

However, there was a considerable disparity between the groups. While all had high rates of alexithymia in comparison to healthy controls, back-pain patients showed the highest rates.

are making their way in the world: finding a career, buying a house, settling into marriage, etc.

But to make your next set of decisions, you need an awareness of your emotions. Relationships begin to demand more attention. An alexithymic person can be quite helpless in marital power struggles. When things go wrong, "you can get a *vague* sense of uneasiness, but really not know why or where it's coming from."

At such a point, alexithymia is "kind of like the antithesis of transformation. You're stuck in a black hole of unawareness."

Alexithymia "predisposes one to physical disease," said Shipko, "as well as to psychological perception of disease. This is a state which definitely leads to greater physical as well as mental illness, and also is highly incapacitating on a psychosocial level."

William Rickles, a Los Angeles psychiatrist in private practice, told *Brain/Mind* in 1987 that alexithymics may appear supernormal since they try to be cheerful or stoic. But when a major crisis occurs, they cannot rebound. And they may become panicky and subject to uncontrollable outbursts. Their lack of psychological resources causes them to translate their loss into physical symptoms such as vomiting, racing heart, and pain.

The Lack of Words

In a more recent interview for *PragMagic,* Rickles emphasized the *verbal* aspect of alexithymia. It is, quite literally, an inability to put emotions into words.

By way of analogy, he speaks of the Eskimos, who "have thirty-two words for snow, as opposed to our four or five adjectives." Sometimes, people are likewise limited in their words for emotions. Alexithymia arises out of a person's lack of *nuance* in emotional expression—both inwardly and outwardly.

Paradoxically, alexithymics sometimes believe themselves to be extremely emotional, and even appear so to others. "When alexithymics do express emotions," he explains, "it is a gross kind of expression." Tantrums and rages are common. Such people suffer from a lack of "midrange emotions." They experience only the emotions at the extreme ends of the spectrum and few if any of the ones in between.

He relates alexithymia to the Freudian concept of *disavowal,* as opposed to *denial.* "Denial is a kind of crazy defense, in which you declare that something never happened. Disavowal is when you say, 'Sure, it happened, but it doesn't mean anything.'"

Rickles acknowledges that alexithymia can serve a constructive purpose, but "only in extreme situations."

Does alexithymia have a genetic aspect? Rickles points out that there is some indication that identical twins are more predisposed to share alexithymia than fraternal twins. Still, cultural and environmental influences obviously play a tremendous role.

Focusing—the Felt Shift

When psychotherapy works, what is happening?

Eugene Gendlin of the University of Chicago Department of Behavioral Sciences asked himself that question after realizing that some people who undertake therapy will not improve appreciably—and that those who will get better can be identified from the start.

Over the years he analyzed and refined the process by which "naturals" get better. This evolved into a technique he calls "focusing," which has attracted considerable attention for its effectiveness.

Focusing can be done with a therapist, with a friend, in a group, or alone. It can be very useful to begin working on important changes in your everyday life. In this technique, you start with a vague *bodily* feeling of current problems, then identify one to work on. Gendlin describes the problem as a kind of aura, a diffuse feeling of worry or discomfort. Your body carries this kind of vague, preverbal feeling for any individual in your life and for any particular problem.

A Sense of Relief

Gendlin uses the common nagging feeling that one has forgotten something as an example of such a vague bodily sense or "aura" of the problem and its release.

Aboard a plane, for instance, you might continue to stew, trying to think what you have left behind. A forgotten item may come to mind, but if there isn't a sense of release, you know that it isn't the one bothering you. *Suddenly you remember—and there's no doubt this time.*

In the focusing technique, instead of thinking or talking about a problem and keeping it at a distance, the individual allows a physically felt step toward resolution to emerge from within. The steps to recognition and solution

RESOURCES

In his book *The Language of the Heart* (Basic Books, 1985), psychologist James Lynch addresses the dilemma of alexithymia, likening it to the difficulty of identifying color blindness. He says that just as those who are color-blind have no idea what they have missed, alexithymic patients "cannot tell you what it feels like to be sad, angry, or in love—except in rational terms."

But perhaps the oddest irony of alexithymia is that people who have a *professional* need to understand emotions sometimes don't. He writes that Sigmund Freud, the founder of psychoanalysis, was probably a prime example of an acute alexithymic. "Brilliantly rational about human feelings, Freud himself may have had great difficulty feeling his own feelings or, for that matter, feeling those of his patients."

Inner Joy by Harold Bloomfield and Robert Kory (Wyden Books/Harper & Row, 1980) extends psychology beyond mere adjustment. The authors discuss the concept of anhedonia—the inability to experience pleasure. They examine the causes of joylessness and point out irrational beliefs that underlie our life-denying behaviors. The authors offer an array of strategies and experiments designed to break the walls of the prison of anhedonia.

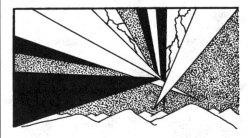

Focusing by Eugene Gendlin (Bantam, 1981) is the how-to book on the technique.

Cassette tapes: *Introduction to Experiential Focusing* and *Complete Beginning Training Program* are available from The Focusing Institute in Chicago.

RESEARCH

The Anatomy of Insight

Norman S. Don of the Kairos Foundation and the University of Illinois at Chicago has detected EEG patterns that coincide with sudden shifts in conscious experience—a phenomenon he calls "the facilitation response." *Brain/Mind Bulletin* reported on his work in 1977.

Every time the subjects experienced a sudden insight, an "Aha!"—what Eugene Gendlin calls a "felt shift"—an analysis of the EEG showed that the dominant alpha frequency and its subharmonics had peaked in power *just prior to* the shift in consciousness, or insight.

The subjects were engaged in the attentional, meditationlike procedure of "focusing." They verbalized into an audio recorder simultaneous with EEG measurement from the left occipital region (back of the head). Later the subjects scored their audiotapes for the moments of greatest consciousness change.

Without exception, Don said, those events were accompanied by the distinctive EEG pattern. The moments when the subjects said they felt the most stuck coincided with "a statistically significant collapse of the power in the dominant alpha frequency and its subharmonics."

One of Don's subjects reported a mystical "white-light" state of consciousness during the session, describing a flow of love and joy: "everything connected by . . . silver threads." There was a corresponding EEG change, but with more power in the subharmonic frequencies in the theta and delta parts of the EEG.

are *experienced* as being correct, rather than guessed at or rationalized.

The "feeling" of the problem and the felt shift are not clearly identifiable emotions in the usual sense (anger, fear, or sorrow) so much as they are a direct sensing of complex feelings. "Focusing doesn't move you from concept to concept," says Gendlin. "Rather, it's concept/experience/concept/experience, etc."

Sometimes, Gendlin says, the shift takes place without a verbal tag. "This kind of shift feels as if you forgot what you wanted to say. It comes back, you get a body shift—but you still don't say it. Usually this is something hard to conceptualize; a whole new constellation is changing. You have new concepts and you need a new way of talking. The old way wouldn't handle it.

"Wait a while. Stay with it. Usually, it's going against all your old concepts, the old way of cutting things. Meanwhile the experience is demanding something new and radical."

EXERCISE: FOCUSING

Just sit quietly and allow a vague bodily feeling of current problems to come into your mind, then:

• Pick one to work on. It can concern anything—something that went wrong yesterday in an encounter with a spouse, friend, or coworker, for instance. Think of it in general terms: "all-about-John," or "all-about-that-argument-with-John," rather than trying to pinpoint anything specific.

• Just hold that vague sense of the problem for a few seconds or half a minute. *A phrase or a single word will usually emerge.* (The time will vary. This technique comes quicker to some people than to others.)

If that phrase or word or image fits, the feeling will usually emerge. What physical quality does it have? Is it heavy? Tight? Jumpy? You'll experience a physical sense of fit. Now ask your body sense "what is it about this whole situation that generates this body quality?" If it answers, you'll experience a *felt shift*—a sense of release, a feeling of physical and psychological relief, a change that offers a fresh perspective, even though that was only one step.

—Adapted from *Focusing,* by Eugene Gendlin

Learning to Focus

Anyone can learn to pay attention to the preverbal process, Gendlin believes, and can draw it into clear expression. The implicit becomes explicit. Still, some people who are "out of touch with their feelings" may find they have trouble focusing. "They have to be willing to discover that emotions are in their body."

In the meditative state fostered by focusing, you address a question to your bodily sense of the problem. You ask what the problem is really about. To the surprise of some participants, a small step toward resolution emerges.

The person feels a physicial sense of release—and psychological relief, too, although the problem has only been changed and not resolved. Resolution usually requires further steps. People vary in how quickly they learn to focus.

Too Hot to Handle?

Occasionally, people come up against material they are afraid to handle. For example, perhaps you bring up some unhappy childhood experience you really don't want to remember.

Gendlin says that's perfectly okay. "You may not be ready for everything you touch upon. Some things are too hot to handle." He tells people, "If it's too scary, consider that you now know it's there. Make a door between you and the problem. You have your hand on the doorknob, and you can go back anytime, letting in as much as you can handle. You aren't avoiding it. You know where it is and you can work on it slowly."

Using Focusing

Gendlin observes that changes in our culture have made such techniques more approachable: "Now there's a lot of talk about being in touch with your feelings, so people are more willing to try."

He distinguishes focusing from meditation: "Focusing is an active process. It oscillates on the line between normal consciousness and meditation. Material comes from what seems like below, and you're there to respond to it—but below the thinking, jumping-around level.

"It's easier to respond from that line than from the depth of meditation or hypnosis, where you generally experience some discomfort in shifting back to normal consciousness. That's not so in focusing.

COMMENTARY

Biology of Mood, Behavior

For most people, a brisk ten-minute walk generates energy and a positive outlook comparable to the natural late-morning energy peak that many people experience, Robert Thayer of California State University, Long Beach, told *Brain/Mind Bulletin* in 1986.

We are often subject to a common error in our thought processes, Thayer said. We are pessimistic about future demands because of our current tiredness. Unthinkingly, we project a low-energy state into the future— we expect our exhaustion to continue.

If we were more sensitive to our internal signals, we might learn to schedule activities appropriate to our varying levels of energy. We might also be less discouraged by how we perceive our problems when we're tired, recognizing that within a few hours or days—or after a brisk walk— things will look different.

COMMENTARY

Cycles and the Workplace

Most of us do not need to be told that our working routines often go against the grain of our natural cycles. Carl Englund told *PragMagic,* "The problem is that we live in a workday world in which large numbers of people have to be organized to interact with the rest of the world. Companies establish work hours, whether it's a day or night shift, and everyone is supposed to comply."

Englund is particularly concerned about schedules that force particular times for eating, getting up, and going to sleep. "People should do shift work that they are well suited for," he says. For many, night shifts can be detrimental to health; such people will be miserable and exhausted all the time. But for others, nights may be "their best time for working, when they're alive and awake. They'd rather sleep during the day.

"This is where self-monitoring helps. If you're half-dead during most of the day, can't function, and just don't seem to be able to get up until nine or ten in the morning, you're probably a person who either has some severe desynchronization problems, or, personality-wise, you may be better suited to a later-day operation."

Englund says that "the best management style is one in which people are told, 'This is what the job is. Here's when we need to get it done. Work on it as you will to get it done by then.' That allows a person to set their own hours and their own work base in a very natural way."

There are obviously settings in which this kind of management won't work well—for example, on an assembly line. "But the consequence of not paying attention, at least to the people who are very radically different in chronopsychological or chronobiological variables and personal makeup, is that they end up making a lot of errors and having accidents."

"It's good to focus before meditating. A Zen master used the same expression I use: 'Before you meditate, see what you're carrying with you, put it in front of you.' Then you can go into meditation with a body that's free of that stuff. Otherwise, meditation amplifies it."

"Unlike most therapeutic approaches, focusing need not try to 'fix' anything in one step, so you're not under any pressure to achieve certain results. It does solve problems, so it's practical, but in its essence it creates changes in consciousness," says Linda Olsen Webber, a therapist with the Los Angeles Center for Healing Arts, and a former student of Gendlin's. She told *Brain/Mind Bulletin* in 1979 that she has used focusing for a whole range of psychotherapeutic approaches.

"I think the therapy of the future will be based on the experiencing process," she said. "It won't be so much a matter of the sectarian wars within different schools of psychology. Focusing mobilizes inner experience. It is the essence of what we know below the level of awareness."

Cycles

Most of us experience mood swings, and sometimes we are even aware of patterns in them. Our emotions cycle through highs and lows, often on a regular basis. There are also other cycles, driven by environmental factors and by our bodies' own mechanisms, that affect our lives. Among the most pronounced of these are our ultradian rhythms, lasting from 90 to 120 minutes, and circadian rhythms, which span the average day.

Research not only explains the sources of some of these cycles, it also reveals techniques for paying attention to them and learning to make use of them.

Chronopsychology

Evidence that human physical and mental processes vary greatly according to circadian (*circa* = around; *dian* = a day) and other temporal cycles sparked the emergence of a field of body/mind study: chronopsychology. The term refers to the effects of biological rhythms on physical, cognitive, and emotional behavior.

There is a tremendous range of such rhythms. Perhaps the briefest are 90-minute ultradian cycles (*ultra* = beyond; *dian* = a day; or in other words, "more often than daily"). On a much broader scale, we also experience annual cycles associated with seasonal changes.

The Best Time of Day

Research psychologist Carl Englund, a division head at the Naval Health Research Center in San Diego, has studied circadian or daily rhythms, which seem to correspond with the 24-hour light and dark cycles.

Englund began his circadian research in 1975, to define the purpose and scope of chronopsychology. He used a self-monitoring process in which a number of different exercises were used. Variations in psychomotor ability were tested by periodic finger counting and tapping activities. Changes in intellectual performance were tested by exercises in short-term memory, random num-

---

INVENTORY: AT THE RIGHT TIME

Englund found that circadian cycles create daily fluctuations in our moods and capacities. So, many events and activities have a "best" or most likely time of day. The following are some typical examples:

• Short-term memory is less effective in the afternoon, but at this same time long-term memory improves.

• Reading speed declines during the day, but comprehension increases.

• Intellectual performance is greatest in late afternoon and early evening.

• Maximum tolerance of pain occurs between late afternoon and early morning.

• Human birth is most common at four A.M., death at six A.M.

• Error-proneness among night-shift workers also is greatest about four A.M.

• The activity phase of most circadian rhythms peaks in early afternoon. Rest phases peak shortly after midnight.

COMMENTARY

Cycles and Education

"There's no question that our educational systems are way out of sync with our learning cycles," Carl Englund told *PragMagic*. "First, they start too early in the day. Second, schedule predominates over people as the driving factor. I believe certain academic things should not be taught in the morning, and others should not be taught in the afternoon. For example, students would be better off doing physical activities in the afternoon rather than in the morning."

Englund thinks schedules are a tremendous problem. "Some schools are starting at six-thirty and seven o'clock in the morning. Nobody's prepared for a lecture or for absorbing material at that time.

"The assumption is generally made that, as the number of hours in school increases, the amount of learning increases. That may be true, but you can carry it too far. School days are scheduled so that there isn't appropriate time for appropriate study or socializing. Students get 20-minute lunch periods, or can't go to the bathroom when they need to. And consequently, you're forced into a schedule where you need to cram junk food. By the time students get back from one of these 20-minute lunch periods, they fall asleep in class.

"There are a lot of things we could do to make the school learning schedule much more appropriate." To do so, Englund said, would mean "making human considerations more predominant than bureaucratic or schedule-type considerations."

RESEARCH

Light a Potent Factor
in Body Clocks, Calendars

Psychiatrists Peter Mueller and Robert Davies of Fair Oaks Hospital, Summit, N.J., reporting in *Archives of General Psychiatry* (43), said that winter depression has a counterpart: summer agitation. Summer symptoms—anxious, racing thoughts—can be precipitated or worsened by full-spectrum light. *Brain/Mind Bulletin* discussed this work in 1986.

Of 47 patients studied, they focused on 17 whose collective hospital admissions totaled 71. Fifty-one of the hospitalizations occurred between March and August.

Winter depressives are often treated with artificial light. Mueller and Davies reported success in treating the seasonal syndrome with colored glasses: red for fall/winter, polarized blue-green for spring/summer.

ber addition, and reading skills. Subjects were also tested for variations in mood and wakefulness, and for physiological changes in oral temperature and pulse.

Englund told a 1981 meeting of the American Psychological Association in Los Angeles that psychologists can no longer afford to ignore circadian cycles. "Without a time reference, biological and psychological events cannot be appropriately placed in perspective. Also, social or environmental changes during the day may have less impact on the individual than the normal fluctuations seen in circadian rhythms.

"The evidence concerning the effects of time-of-day upon the outcome of experiments has been so pervasive that some researchers have become suspicious of observations that fail to account for this factor," said Englund.

These rhythms, says Englund, are "nature's way of placing our bodies in harmony with the environment and the world we live in. It's the natural way to adjust to the major environmental variables that interact with us: the dark-light cycle, heat or temperature cycle, and seasonal

EXERCISE: SELF-OBSERVATION

Carl Englund suggests the following very simple self-monitoring technique to determine your own daily cycles. It requires no equipment other than a stopwatch:

Start the stopwatch. Then move your right thumb from the tip of one finger to the next, starting with your index finger, as quickly as you can, counting as you go. Go back and forth counting up to 25. You should arrive back at your index finger at the count of 25. Stop the stopwatch.

"This is a really good indication of how efficient your nervous system is at the moment," says Englund. "If you make a mistake, start all over again." The two crucial pieces of information to gather from such a psychomotor exercise are:
- How accurate were you?
- How fast were you?

Keep a record of your results, taking note of both your speed and accuracy. Compare results from successive days. A profile will emerge of your daily cycles—your alert, wakeful, and productive periods, and your less energetic, sleepy periods.

Englund notes that in order to gain the most useful data from this exercise, you need to do this every hour during your waking days for two weeks.

changes. Our bodies respond to these things, just as a thermostat responds to the temperature cycle in a room."

Getting Out of Sync

Our rhythms sometimes get out of sync, and the results can be severe. Any of a number of factors may cause this, including changes in lifestyle, diet, or schedule. People who make many transoceanic flights, and consequently experience frequent jet lag, suffer from considerable desynchronization—the disruption of their natural rhythms.

And there are even instances of mass desynchronization. "When we change to daylight savings time," Englund told *PragMagic,* "accident rates go up. There are more work-related accidents, more car accidents, and more things get broken around the house, until people re-sync into their cycle. A person is a whole hour off in time for several days. It takes quite a bit of time to adjust to that."

Englund points out that even our weekends may tend to put us in a state of desynchronization. "The Monday-morning blues stems from the fact that people have essentially *altered* their rhythmic nature. They've eaten differently, maybe more or at different times. They may have partied and consumed a lot of alcohol, which is directly related to sleep disturbances. So they may not have slept as well. By doing those kind of things, you alter your rhythmic nature. Then, of course, it takes time to re-sync. And it usually takes Monday to do that."

Overriding Cycles

We have all sorts of tricks and devices for overriding these cycles, including caffeine. Sometimes they may backfire. "A little bit of caffeine goes a long way," says Englund. "Most people use it excessively. And there are some gastrointestinal problems as well as cardiovascular problems associated with excessive caffeine. People should not use it unless they absolutely need to.

"It's useful on, say, those Monday mornings when you have to get up but don't want to. And what you really need to do is get up your speed. So you drink a warm cup of coffee with a little caffeine in it, and it advances the phase of your basic body rhythms. It gets them started faster so they reach their peak faster. You don't need very much of it. And the warmth of the liquid itself increases the body temperature. Temperature increases are associated with the alert phases of the cycle."

RESEARCH

Mood Disorders Tied to Body-Rhythm Disturbance

Disturbances of daily rhythms may underlie some symptoms of manic-depressive illness, according to researcher Daniel Kripke and coworkers at the Veterans Administration Hospital in San Diego. They reported their findings in *Biological Psychiatry* (13). *Brain/Mind Bulletin* reported their research in 1978.

Kripke and his colleagues evaluated seven manic-depressives over complete cycles of mood swing to ascertain the relationship between mood and various physiological changes such as blood pressure or body temperature. In five of the seven case studies, peaks of activity advanced to an earlier time each day.

When cycles become out of phase with each other, they may cause a "beat phenomenon." That is, some body systems are free-running and others are sychronized with the environment. The new phase relationships may disturb the brain chemistry.

When the body temperature peaked after midnight, depression seemed to occur. Mania correlated with a return to a temperature peak in late afternoon or evening.

Body Clocks and Bonding

Research at the University of Colorado suggests that circadian disruption may be an important component of reaction to loss and separation, according to Martin Reite and Psychiatry Department colleagues, reporting in *Chronobiologia* (9). This experiment was reported in *Brain/Mind Bulletin* in 1982.

When infant monkeys were separated from their mothers, they became depressed and their circadian rhythms became disorganized. The disruption of circadian rhythms in the infant monkeys did not run its full course until they were reunited with their mothers.

The accompanying depression was preceded by alteration in the timing and amplitude of body temperature and heart-rate rhythms. "Our findings support the notion of a strong association between affective behavior and the regulation of circadian systems."

This partially explains the apparent "placebo effect" of decaffeinated coffee, although there is still a small percent of caffeine present in such beverages. "People should treat it like any other drug," says Englund, "as of use on those occasions when you need that extra effort."

Regarding self-monitoring for cycles, Englund says that "in most cases, you don't have to take any actual measurements to get some objective data on yourself. You just exercise a little sensitivity to your own well-being. Be sensitive to when you are hungry, sensitive to sleepiness and when you need a rest period, sensitive to your best times for study, performance, or work.

"People should pay attention, not to what they're forced to in their sleep-wake cycles, but to what their real preferences are."

An inventory for determining whether you are a morning or evening person is included in the Appendix of *PragMagic*.

Jet Lag

Certainly one of the most infamous and commonplace disturbances of circadian rhythms is jet lag, the desynchronization of eating and sleeping schedules that accompanies major time-zone shifts. Charles Ehret, a biologist at the Argonne National Laboratory in Illinois, has made some discoveries about this bane of the traveler:

• Westbound travelers, who lengthen their days, adjust more rapidly than eastbound passengers, who don't feel tired at the new local bedtime.

• People over age 30 have more difficulty adjusting.

• Introverts and neurotic persons have greater adjustment difficulties than extroverts.

But due to Ehret's work, airborne passengers traveling across several time zones now have a way to minimize jet lag. He has developed a diet that helps the body adapt its circadian rhythms to changes in time zones. The Anti-Jet-Lag Diet (reproduced at right) is published on a wallet-sized folder.

The diet, which begins three days before the flight, involves alternate fasting and feasting. It also schedules the consumption of coffee or other sources of caffeine to help "reset" body rhythms. One's diet while airborne and immediately thereafter is also prescribed. Ehret offers a second tactic for those who do not wish to watch their diets before traveling: fasting on the day of departure.

ARGONNE NATIONAL LABORATORY
ANTI-JET-LAG DIET

The Argonne Anti-Jet-Lag Diet is helping travelers quickly adjust their bodies' internal clocks to new time zones. It is also being used to speed the adjustment of shiftworkers, such as power-plant operators, to periodically rotating clock hours. The diet was developed by Dr. Charles F. Ehret of Argonne's Division of Biological and Medical Research as an application of his fundamental studies of the daily biological rhythms of animals. Argonne National Laboratory is one of the U. S. Department of Energy's major centers of research in energy and the fundamental sciences.

How to avoid jet lag:

1. DETERMINE BREAKFAST TIME at destination on day of arrival.

2. FEAST•FAST•FEAST•FAST on home time. Start three days before departure day. On day one, FEAST; eat heartily with high-protein breakfast and lunch and a high-carbohydrate dinner. No coffee except between 3 and 5 P.M. On day two, FAST on light meals of salads, light soups, fruits, and juices. Again, no coffee except between 3 and 5 P.M. On day three, FEAST again. On day four, departure day, FAST; if you drink caffeinated beverages, take them in morning when traveling west, or between 6 and 11 P.M. when traveling east. Going west, you may fast only half a day.

3. BREAK FINAL FAST at destination breakfast time. No alcohol on plane. If flight is long enough, sleep until normal breakfast time at destination, but no later. Wake up and FEAST on high-protein breakfast. Stay awake, active. Continue day's meals according to meal times at destination.

FEAST on high-protein breakfasts and lunches to stimulate the body's active cycle. Suitable meals include steak, eggs, hamburgers, high-protein cereals, green beans.

FEAST on high-carbohydrate suppers to stimulate sleep. They include spaghetti and other pastas (but no meatballs), crepes (but no meat filling), potatoes, other starchy vegetables, and sweet desserts.

FAST days help deplete the liver's store of carbohydrates and prepare the body's clock for resetting. Suitable foods include fruit, light soups, broths, skimpy salads, unbuttered toast, half pieces of bread. Keep calories and carbohydrates to a minimum.

		COUNTDOWN			
		1 FEAST	2 FAST	3 FEAST	4 FAST	BREAK FINAL FAST
O N H O M E T I M E	B	🐄	🍊	🐄	🍊	Westbound: If you drink caffeinated beverages, take them morning before departure. Eastbound: Take them between 6 and 11 P.M. If flight is long enough, sleep until destination time. Wake up and FEAST, beginning with a high-protein breakfast. Lights on. Stay awake and active.
	L	🐄	🍎	🐄	🍎	
	S	🍝	🍲	🍝	🍲	

Coffee, tea, cola, other caffeinated beverages
allowed only between 3 and 5 P.M.

*Select any moment
and examine what is going on
in your mind. There are
visual images, perhaps of a
favorite face. A song, with
words and melody, refuses to
go away. There is a
particular mood, perhaps of
anticipation, perhaps of love,
perhaps of sorrow. There are
ideas, there are problems you
are trying to solve, there are
thoughts, and there are plans.
You are looking at your
waking consciousness.*

—*States of Consciousness*
(Teachers College Press,
Columbia University, 1981)
an instructional unit produced by the
Human Behavior Curriculum Project of
the American Psychological Association

Consciousness

Once it may have seemed that everyone knew what it meant to be conscious—or unconscious. Consciousness was taken as a given, and its variations or anomalies were seldom discussed. "Consciousness" is the word we use to indicate our awareness—of ourselves, of others, of everything around us. If something happens but we are not aware of it, we say we are not conscious of it. If we are aware of nothing at all, we are unconscious.

Around the turn of the century, Sigmund Freud described the subconscious, full of thoughts and feelings that we do not even know about consciously. Freud believed that this information was really only accessible with the help of a psychoanalyst.

Then came what has sometimes been called "the consciousness revolution" of the 1970s, generated by biofeedback research, meditation, an interest in "altered states of consciousness," and research in the specialized functions of the brain's hemispheres. Suddenly it seemed that there were more kinds or "states" of consciousness—and more ways of accessing them—than anyone had ever supposed.

Since then, scientific study has brought us exciting new information about consciousness, but has not really clarified the definition. Many scientists still feel as biofeedback researcher Elmer Green of the Menninger Foundation did at a 1980 conference sponsored by the Institute of Noetic Sciences: "It's too early to define consciousness," he said. "We're better off describing what it does."

Altered States of Consciousness

There are many techniques—focusing, some forms of meditation, hypnosis, and visualization, among others—designed to bring information and feelings from the subconscious into the conscious mind. States of mind that can be achieved through those methods and through the use of certain drugs are often referred to as "altered states," indicating something different from the state in which most of us spend our waking hours. However, it can no longer be supposed that exactly the same state of consciousness is "normal" for everyone, or that we all experience altered states in the same ways.

The nature of our consciousness at any particular time depends on the focus of our attention. The techniques of meditation and hypnosis are designed to focus our attention in ways that are different from our everyday manner. Gaining control over the way in which we pay attention is emphasized in many exercises throughout *PragMagic*.

Meditation

Meditation techniques are used in various ways in the West. Some groups follow specific ancient traditions, while others devise their own methods of changing consciousness and making use of the insights they gain.

Psychologist Jean Houston has written a number of books and gives frequent workshops that include both physically active and meditative exercises. We have included an exercise from one of her books, *The Possible Human* (J. P. Tarcher, 1982), in the Appendix to *PragMagic*. This exercise integrates visualizing with other sensory experiences and also focuses the participant's attention on three-dimensional space. Since it is a long exercise, you should arrange to have someone read it aloud to you, or have it put on tape so that you can use it as often as you wish. However, you might want to turn to page 247 now and take a quick look at Houston's method.

In her discussion of the exercise, Houston comments that things are happening to the participant on many levels. "Teachers who have used this exercise with their classes report that their students enjoy the experience and then are more relaxed and alert as they address the other areas of their schoolwork. They begin to regard their brains as allies rather than poorly programmed robots, and they are delighted to find that their brains have a sense of

Our normal waking consciousness, rational consciousness as we call it, is but one special type of consciousness, whilst all about it, parted from it by the filmiest of screens, there lie potential forms of consciousness entirely different. We may go through life without suspecting their existence; but apply the requisite stimulus, and at a touch they are there in all their completeness, definite types of mentality which probably somewhere have their field of application and adaptation. No account of the universe in its totality can be final which leaves these other forms of consciousness quite disregarded. . . . At any rate, they forbid a premature closing of our accounts with reality.

—William James
The Varieties of Religious Experience
(Harvard University Press, 1902, 1963)

RESOURCES

Consciousness & Tradition by Jacob Needleman (Crossroad, 1982) is a series of essays on religion, psychiatry, philosophy, culture, science, and medicine by a brilliant philosopher.

Beyond the Brain by psychiatrist Stanislav Grof (State University of New York Press, 1985) summarizes the rich paradigm that has emerged from the author's quarter century of psychotherapy and consciousness research.

The Possible Human: A Course in Extending Your Physical, Mental, and Creative Abilities by Jean Houston (J. P. Tarcher, 1982) is a master course in awakening all aspects of consciousness.

The Meditative Mind by Daniel Goleman (J. P. Tarcher, 1988) traces the roots of meditative attentional training in several cultures and includes instructions on how to meditate, as well as reports of research on the meditative state.

Goleman describes two different kinds of altered states of consciousness that are fundamental attentional strategies in meditation. "Concentration leads the meditator to become one-pointed and finally to merge his attention with its object. Mindfulness leads the meditator to witness the workings of his own mind, coming to perceive with detachment the finer segments of his stream of thought. The altered states produced by each approach are radically different."

It is this attentional retraining, Goleman says, which "gives meditation its unique cognitive effects, such as increasing the meditator's concentration and empathy." Attentional training is also the difference between meditation and mere relaxation.

whimsy and play. Some who have felt sluggish and sleepy experience renewed energy. One Texas rancher found his brain saying to *him,* 'Where have *you* been all my life?' Many experience an unexpected sense of reverence for their brain; the brain has truly become Thou, an active partner in the process of co-creation."

Houston says that when this kind and duration of attention is directed toward the brain "more blood goes to the brain, bringing nourishing oxygen." As you imagine the hand becoming warm and heavy and the forehead cool, theoretically congested blood in the head is relieved and more blood is directed toward the hand.

Houston notes that the same process is used in training people to relieve migraine headaches. "Some people experience a temporary feeling of constriction in the skull after doing this exercise. This is often followed by increased mental acuity and cognitive clarity."

The Everyday Trance

Most of us are unaware of the state that Los Angeles psychologist Ernest Rossi calls the "everyday trance." He explained his views in the anthology *Handbook of Altered States of Consciousness* (Eds. B. Wolman and M. Ullman, Van Nostrand, 1986).

Rossi was a longtime collaborator of the late Milton Erickson, a psychologist who was regarded as one of the world leaders in the field of medical hypnosis. Rossi points out that recent research confirms Erickson's idea that people enter a natural trance periodically throughout the day. Skilled hypnotists have long recognized these trances by behavioral clues.

Rossi himself has become a conscientious observer of these subtle clues, which include slight alterations in visible pulse movements, blushing, a slowing down of swallowing and eye blinking, and a change in breathing. The pupils dilate, the eyelids droop, and the body becomes less generally mobile.

One striking aspect about the everyday trance is that it is often masked by amnesia. "In fact," writes Rossi, "these are the moments when perfectly 'normal' people experience illusions and split-second hallucinations—which, however, are then quickly dismissed . . ."

The mind wanders, memories awaken spontaneously, and, Rossi explains, "we even experience spontaneous bursts of socially acceptable age regression: a business executive will burst into a boyhood whistle; a scholar will attempt to 'make a basket' with a wadded piece of paper. ... After 20 or 30 minutes we are surprised to discover how much time we have 'wasted,' and we dutifully snap ourselves back to an alert, work state."

Some people catch musing, fleeting glimpses of the "big picture." Others become so entranced that they neither see nor hear. Others may feel discomfort and suppress "personal truths that come unbidden during these naturally unguarded periods."

EXERCISE: EXPLORING YOUR INNER COMFORT

Psychologist Ernest Rossi offers the following advice to his patients:

"You can use a natural form of self-hypnosis by simply letting yourself really enjoy taking a break whenever you need to throughout the day. You simply close your eyes and tune into the parts of your body that are most comfortable. When you locate the comfort you can simply enjoy it and allow it to deepen and spread throughout your body all by itself. Comfort is more than just a word or a lazy state. Really going deeply into comfort means you have turned on your parasympathetic system—your natural relaxation response. This is the easiest way to maximize the healing benefits of the rest phase of your body's natural ultradian rhythms.

"As you explore your inner comfort you can *wonder* how your creative unconscious is going to deal with whatever symptom, problem or issue that you want it to deal with. Your unconscious is the inner regulator of all your biological and mental processes. If you have problems it is probably because some unfortunate programming from the past has interfered with the natural processes of regulation within your unconscious. By accepting and letting yourself enjoy the normal periods of ultradian rest as they occur throughout the day, you are allowing your body/mind's natural self-regulation to heal and resolve your problems.

"Your attitude toward your symptom and yourself is very important during this form of healing hypnosis. *Your symptom or problem is actually your friend!* Your symptom is a signal that a creative change is needed in your life. During your periods of comfort in ultradian self-hypnosis, you will often receive quiet insights about your life, what you really want, and how to get it. A new thoughtfulness, joy, greater awareness, and maturity can result from the regular practice of ultradian self-hypnosis."

—from *Hypnosis Questions and Answers*
Zilbergeld, B., Edelstein, M., and Araoz, D., eds.
(W. W. Norton, 1986)

COMMENTARY

Ultradian Cycles

The biological rhythms that govern sleep and dreaming also may facilitate hypnotherapy, Ernest Rossi said at a 1981 advanced training seminar sponsored by the Southern California Society of Clinical Hypnosis.

Rossi referred to the ultradian cycle, which alternates between 90 and 100 minutes of activity and 10 to 20 minutes of rest. At night the rest phase corresponds to rapid-eye-movement (REM) sleep, when most physical activity is minimal and conscious dreaming is most prominent.

The ultradian cycle affects waking behavior; it also probably accounts for the timing of midmorning and midafternoon "coffee breaks." During the cycle's rest phase, when the right brain hemisphere is dominant, speech and reflexes (such as eye-blinks) are slower.

Perceptive hypnotherapists, Rossi said, can use this natural state of "trance readiness."

Rossi began studying ultradian cycles after observing that the late psychologist Milton Erickson's hypnosis sessions lasted 90 to 120 minutes or longer, rather than the standard 50-minute "hour." Rossi's review of ultradian research suggested that Erickson's exemplary success at inducing hypnosis was less that of a "master manipulator" than that of a facilitator of his patients' most susceptible moments. Erickson's long sessions were certain to include the periodic rest cycle likely to be missed in a standard session.

Since right-brain dominance is associated with intuitive and introspective behavior, Rossi speculated that depression, anxiety, and other emotional disorders may represent failure to focus attention inward during ultradian rest phases.

RESEARCH

Breathing and Brain Hemispheres

Researcher Debra Werntz, together with colleagues in San Diego, reported in *Human Neurobiology* (6) that breathing out of only one nostril stimulates activity in the brain hemisphere on the opposite side. *Brain/ Mind Bulletin* discussed the studies in 1988.

Forced breathing through one nostril generated almost immediate EEG changes. Five out of five untrained subjects produced "relatively greater integrated amplitudes" in the opposing hemisphere, Werntz wrote. The switch was successful in 25 of 31 attempts by the same subjects.

Earlier experiments have shown that EEG activity can be triggered by air inflow through the nasal mucosa without lung involvement. Local anesthesia of the mucosal membrane counters the effects of the airflow on cortical activity.

Hemispheric Dominance

A simple breathing exercise makes it easy to affect our short-term brain hemisphere dominance at will. The exercise is an example of voluntary control of body/mind states and is a link between Eastern and Western concepts of medicine.

Human Neurobiology (6) reported the discovery of a direct relationship between brain activity and the nasal cycle—alternation of congestion and decongestion in the nasal passages. This work was discussed in a 1988 issue of *Brain/Mind Bulletin.*

When airflow is more free in one nostril, the opposite hemisphere is relatively more dominant. Forceful breathing through the more congested nostril awakens the less-dominant hemisphere.

EEG responses showed a consistent relationship between nasal airflow and cerebral dominance in all frequencies (alpha, theta, delta, and beta).

"The nose is an instrument that can be used for altering cortical activity," David Shannahoff-Khalsa, then of the Salk Institute for Biological Studies, told *Brain/Mind Bulletin.* (Khalsa's research is now directed through The Khalsa Foundation for Medical Science.) "The nose is far more than an olfactory device. Discovering this is like finding a new sense."

Shannahoff-Khalsa and three co-researchers, Floyd Bloom of the Salk Institute (currently at Scripps Clinic and Research Foundation), and Debra Werntz and Reginald Bickford of the University of California, San Diego, School of Medicine, demonstrated the first conclusive evidence of a link between this cycle and the nervous system. The cycle of alternating hemispheric dominance in human beings and marine mammals has been confirmed in other laboratories.

The Science of Breathing in Other Cultures

Chinese scientists showed great interest in the research, Shannahoff-Khalsa said, because it added a new dimension of understanding to their theories of yin (passive) and yang (active) bodymind states.

The discovery also means that Eastern medical concepts need no longer remain foreign to Western science, he said. "There is a true science of breathing, discovered by the yogis, which is the equivalent of a technology of the

EXERCISE: MONITORING HEMISPHERE DOMINANCE

Your nasal cycles can be a useful key to a better understanding of your current states of consciousness. Here are three ways of monitoring nasal dominance. These are based on information from Los Angeles psychologist Ernest Rossi's chapter in *Handbook of Altered States of Consciousness* (Eds. B. Wolman and M. Ullman, Van Nostrand, 1986) entitled "Altered States of Consciousness in Everyday Life: The Ultradian Rhythms."

The Mirror-Condensation Method: Hold a small pocket mirror under your nose. Quickly but gently (for two or three seconds), exhale onto the mirror. Small but visible patterns will form under each nostril. The larger of the two represents the less-congested nostril. Rossi describes this as "a very simple but reliable measurement method used by yoga breathing experts in studying their own nasal cycles."

The Sound of Exhalation: Use your thumb to close off one nostril, then exhale quickly and sharply through the other. Do the same on the other side. Do the two sides sound slightly different? *The side with the higher pitch* is the more congested of the two.

Tactile Sensations Method: This method may take a bit more practice than the others. Take a slow, steady, inhalation. Can you tell by *sensation* which side is more congested than the other? If not, try a short, sharp inhalation. If the two sides seem about the same, you may want to use the mirror-condensation method and compare the results. If the two sides are identical, Rossi says, this is "because the nasal cycle is in the midst of its shift from one side to the other."

By checking your nasal dominance repeatedly during a day, you can get some idea of how frequently your nostrils switch dominance. You may wish to ask yourself, what is your state of mind during each phase of your cycle?

You may want to jot down some observations during the course of the day. For example:
- Less congestion in the left nostril suggests greater right-brain activity; at these times, one is typically in a dreamier, more intuitive state of mind. Is this true for you?
- Less congestion in the right nostril suggests greater left-brain activity; at these times, one is typically more alert, more prone to practical, intellectual problem-solving. Is this true for you?

You can switch this dominance at will, and thus alter your state of consciousness. There are at least two simple ways to do this:
- Rossi points out that it can be done by shifting your body position, sitting or lying, from one side to another. Frequently, the nostril that is "down" will become more congested. If you've been intellectually active, and hence more "left-brained," simply lying meditatively on your back can switch you from a dominant right nostril to a dominant left one.
- As David Shannahoff-Khalsa has pointed out elsewhere, forceful breathing through the more congested nostril awakens the less-dominant hemisphere.

Body Sides Switch Dominance

The sides of the *body* switch regularly in concentrations of certain chemicals, according to David Shannahoff-Khalsa, Michael Ziegler, and Brian Kennedy, who conducted their research at the University of California, San Diego, School of Medicine. Their findings were reported in *Life Sciences* (38) and covered by *Brain/Mind Bulletin* in 1986.

Researchers sampled nervous-system transmitters by taking blood from both arms every seven and a half minutes for periods of three to six hours. They found that specific neurotransmitters were more elevated on one side or the other every one or three hours.

"This discovery offers a real window on the relationship of mind to metabolism," said Khalsa, mentioned on the previous pages. The investigation followed up on earlier studies at the University of California and Salk Institute showing left and right alternations in nasal breathing coincident with the alternating rhythms of cerebral hemispheric activity.

Khalsa sees the cycles as a key to voluntary alteration of metabolism, mood, and cognition. Identifying the crossover point is especially significant.

"My chief interest is to investigate and provide credibility for the concepts and techniques of yogic medicine. A yogi is an individual who has learned to consciously control this lateralized rhythm of mind and metabolism."

mind." The suspected correlation of nasal cycles and overall body function, if substantiated, could support ancient yogic teachings about *pranayama,* or the breath.

The implication of this ancient technology of the mind is that we are not helpless victims of a given emotional state. "If you want to alter an unwanted state," he said, "just breathe through the more congested nostril."

This is not a new insight, he observed. Millennia-old yogic traditions prescribe many techniques for inducing or altering mental and physiological states via precise, rhythmic breathing through a single nostril or in sequences involving both. The brain hemispheres may be thus integrated or selectively activated.

Open Focus®

"What makes man special is the capacity to become aware of strategies of awareness," Les Fehmi, a physiological psychologist at the New Jersey Princeton Biofeedback Clinic, says in his *Open Focus Handbook* (1982). (Open Focus® is a registered trademark of Biofeedback Computers, Inc.) Many people, such as the stockbroker described in the right sidebar, pay attention to the world only with a "tense kind of concentration." They do not know that there is any other way.

We can learn to choose a style of attention appropriate for a given situation, Fehmi told *Brain/Mind Bulletin* in 1983. This implies that we have to release our mind's grip on a particular bias—the way we are accustomed to experiencing our world. "Paying attention to attention can directly affect our bodies as well as our minds," Fehmi said. Attentional training is being used to alter a variety of complaints: pain, listlessness, low blood sugar, even the bleeding of hemophilia.

Styles of Attention

Research conducted by Fehmi and his colleagues at clinics in New York, New Jersey, and Pennsylvania has shown that people employ a variety of attentional styles in their daily lives. For example, people who habitually use a narrow, objective focus tend to become rigid and fixated. They are usually not aware of body sensations or emotions. Others may have a narrow focus that is intensely absorbed, as when we are lost in the sensation of a deep massage or enjoyment of a concert. Some individuals also get absorbed in feelings. Some are able to focus diffusely on an entire scene, performing a task (driving a car, playing a sport) while maintaining a sense of both the foreground action and peripheral activity.

Our usual ways of paying attention to the world may be products of environment, past history, or heredity. "Narrow focus" is a common but unproductive style. As we learn to drop narrow focus, Fehmi said, relaxation is a natural side effect.

"Optimal performance includes effortless attention that is specifically focused on a task and simultaneously open to surrounding experience," Fehmi said. Once we learn to use Open Focus, it generalizes to daily life. Like the juggler who effortlessly handles all the balls at once, we can maintain wide awareness and perform tasks at the same time.

Biofeedback Offers a Clue

Fehmi first discovered Open Focus by accident. Years ago he was struggling to gain control of his brainwave pattern as reflected by a biofeedback machine. One day, at a peak of frustration, he suddenly gave up. At that moment, the machine began to reflect the high-amplitude, in-phase pattern associated with a calm, coherent mental state. "After that, I learned to let go more and more. As I did, the experience became increasingly pleasant."

For *PragMagic,* Fehmi said that he had noticed more than 20 years ago that only certain things produced the increased alpha amplitude and synchrony that he sought. Questions about space—for example, "Can you imagine the space between your eyes?"—proved much more powerful than just asking clients to imagine a beautiful scene or to relax.

Fehmi wondered why that might be so. He finally came to understand that the real difference was in the way a person pays attention. In using Open Focus "you include all your senses simultaneously and you're more centered in the experience."

In our culture, most people are overly biased toward narrow-focus objective attention, he said. "When they can't stay that way all day, they think something's wrong with them." The ordinary person who has never thought about attention—the process itself—is surprised to learn that a different way of paying attention is "a solution to many, many problems."

COMMENTARY

"The game would be in a white heat of competition, and yet somehow I wouldn't feel competitive—which is a miracle in itself. I'd be putting out the maximum, straining, coughing up parts of my lungs as we ran, and yet I never felt the pain. The game would move so quickly that every fake, cut and pass would be surprising, yet nothing could surprise me. It was almost as if we were playing in slow motion.

"During those spells, I could almost sense how the next play would develop and where the next shot would be taken. Even before the other team brought the ball in bounds, I could feel it so keenly that I'd want to shout to my teammates, "It's coming there"—except that I knew that everything would change if I did.

"My premonitions would be consistently correct, and I always felt then that I not only knew all the Celtics by heart but also all the opposing players, and that they all knew me. There have been many times in my career when I felt moved or joyful, but these were the moments when I had chills pulsing up and down my spine.

"Sometimes the feeling would last all the way to the end of the game. On the five or ten occasions when the game ended at that special level, I literally did not care who had won. If we lost, I'd still be as free and high as a skyhawk."

— Bill Russell of the Boston Celtics
in *Second Wind*
(Random House, 1979)

Using Open Focus

However, when he trains world-class athletes and coaches, Fehmi finds that they readily accept Open Focus because they already know it. They just want to learn how to achieve it more easily. The state frequently reported by athletes—in which time seems to slow down and everything happens easily and perfectly—is an example of their use of the Open Focus state.

Fehmi's clients use tapes he provides to practice Open Focus exercises at home, and at his office they learn the technique in the presence of EEG biofeedback equipment. When the EEG changes, they get feedback that tells them when they're trying too hard. Fehmi says that he gets them to take it a whole lot easier. "They learn in a much more passive way than they're used to." Using the exercises in combination with biofeedback is more efficient, Fehmi says. With the exercises alone, "you're still moving ahead, but you're just not moving ahead as efficiently." In any case, however, "the longer you use the techniques the more intimate and subtle your awareness becomes and the more direct your experience of that awareness becomes."

An exercise designed to introduce you to Open Focus is included in the Appendix of *PragMagic*.

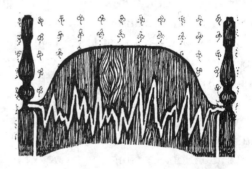

Sleep and Dreaming

Sleeping and wakefulness are not tidily distinct states, but rather interdependent ones. We can learn to pay attention to sleep cycles and to shape them to our advantage. And the world of dreams is another realm of experience, with similarities to both sleep and waking, that can give us valuable information.

Sleep

"The sleep-wake alternation in humans is an example of a circadian rhythm, which requires about 24 hours to complete," says Peter Hauri, professor of psychology and director of the Insomnia Program at the Mayo Clinic, in *The Sleep Disorders,* a 1982 publication of the Upjohn Company. Hauri reported that "when human beings are placed in an underground cave with artificial light, plenty of food, but no clock, they still maintain a circadian rhythm. However, under such constant conditions, the cycle rarely lasts exactly 24 hours." He said that humans typically settle into longer rhythms, between 24 and 28 hours. Sleep-wake cycles up to 50 hours long have been observed.

Not all people need the same amount of sleep. Hauri noted that some adults sleep three hours a night or less without problems while others sleep ten to twelve hours and feel deprived if they get less.

Some people—Thomas Edison was an example—apparently require only a few hours' sleep and perhaps occasional naps. Can the rest of us decrease our sleep time? Hauri said "the answer is a qualified 'yes.'" Some research has indicated the possibility, but "the long-range effects of curtailing sleep are unknown."

Sleep Diet

Researcher L. C. Johnson and coworkers at the Naval Health Research Center, San Diego, and the University of California–Irvine reported in *Psychophysiology* (14) that the key might be *gradual* sleep reduction, which may enable the body to adjust to the change. Subjects in the study—four couples aged 21 to 28—cut their total sleep time by half-hour increments every two weeks until they could not tolerate further reduction. The gradual sleep-reduction period covered six to eight months. The study was reported by *Brain/Mind Bulletin* in 1977.

Before the experiment, three of the couples had slept an average of 8 hours nightly and one couple slept 6.5 hours. They all reduced their average sleep time (see table on page 60). Their performance was not significantly impaired nor were there major psychological changes. After the study, when their total sleep time increased but eventually stabilized at a lower level than they had once been accustomed to, they all reported feeling well.

RESEARCH

Preventive Napping More Effective Than Catch-up Sleep

Well-placed naps may serve us better than prolonged sleep after an accumulated "sleep debt," David Dinges and his team of researchers at the Institute of Pennsylvania Hospital reported in *Sleep* (10). Those anticipating jet lag or all-night studying will benefit more by napping prior to sleep loss than by napping the next day. *Brain/Mind Bulletin* covered this research in 1988.

The researchers deprived 40 healthy young adults of all but one two-hour nap during 56 hours of sustained wakefulness. The timing of nap opportunities coincided with the daily peaks (12–2 P.M.) or troughs (4–6 P.M.) of alertness and occurred at hours 6, 18, 30, 42, or 56 for different groups. They measured reaction time (alertness), subjective feelings of sleepiness, and body temperature changes throughout the experiment.

Reaction-time performance was better for subjects who napped at either 6 or 18 hours after starting. The later the nap, the worse the scores. The superior reaction time of the early nappers held for more than 24 hours, through the second night. The later nappers' improvement was less "robust" and shorter lived. Whether the nap coincided with a peak or trough did not influence reaction time.

David Dinges and his team were surprised by several of the findings. The naps did not seem to affect mood or feelings of sleepiness. Nappers seemed unaware of their improved performance. Indeed, the benefits for reaction time of the 6th-hour nap were not evident until 12 hours later.

As expected, the subjects were not as sleepy before their 6th- and 18th-hour naps as they were before the later naps. The early naps were lighter, contained less slow-wave sleep, and were substantially shorter in length.

The benefits of the earlier, lighter naps were surprising because it is usually assumed that deeper sleep is more beneficial than lighter sleep.

Couple	Average hours sleep before study	Average hours sleep reduced to
A	8	5.5
B	8	5
C	8	4.5
D	6.5	5

Couples A, B, and C were still averaging a significant reduction in total sleep time a year after the experiment ended. Couple D, already operating on only 6.5 hours' sleep, reduced it to 5 during the study but returned to 6.5 during the follow-up period.

The researchers pointed out that they are not recommending a reduced sleep diet for everyone but suggested that "adequately motivated persons following a gradual sleep-reduction regimen" are likely to achieve a similar change.

Sleepiness

Most normal adults are seriously sleepy through much of the day, according to William Dement, director of the Sleep Disorders Clinic and Laboratory at Stanford University School of Medicine. Although this frequent sleepiness undermines their effectiveness, he said, most adults feel this is normal. In studying sleepiness and alertness as states of consciousness, he and his coworkers have discovered that "some people may not ever reach the maximum of their potential . . . simply because they never really wake up!"

The performance of a person who is sleepy may be impaired without their knowing it and without its being evident to others.

In addition to the Stanford Sleepiness Scale, which is subjective, Dement's team also used such measurements as pupil dilation, task performance, reaction time, and EEG.

The Stanford workers also found that the sleepiness-alertness cycle does not necessarily correlate with rest-activity cycles. Peak sleepiness may not occur at conventional sleeping hours, Dement said.

Hauri also reported that "sleep disorders are common; in 1979, about 50 million adults in the United States reported 'trouble with sleeping.' Each year, about 10 million Americans consult a physician about their sleep."

RESEARCH

One Night's Sleep Loss Can Hamper Creative Ability

One night's sleep loss can seriously impair a person's ability to think along new lines, according to J. A. Horne and co-workers at Loughborough University in England. They reported in *Sleep* (11) on their comparison of a group of subjects who went sleepless for 32 hours to a group who slept normally. *Brain/Mind Bulletin* reported their research in 1989.

Both groups, who had earlier scored equally on the same tests, took three tests of creative thinking and one involving convergent thinking—thinking along established lines. The creativity tests included:

• Abstract imagining, such as explaining how many things a cardboard box could be used for

• Finishing drawings

• Moving rows of beads and pegs to create a defined pattern

• Generating words beginning with the same letter

On all the creative thinking tests, the sleep-deprived subjects performed substantially worse when retested than the control group. They had poorer scores and required longer planning time before beginning certain tests. Though the control group improved on its initial scores through familiarity, those who had not slept actually scored lower.

As expected, no significant differences between groups were found on the test of convergent (noncreative) thinking.

INVENTORY: WAKEFULNESS

How awake are you? You can check youself on the Stanford scale of 1 to 7—alert to nearly asleep.

The Stanford Sleepiness Scale is a self-rating scale that has been found to be highly correlated with performance on tasks that are sensitive to sleep loss, such as memory and adding figures. Self-rating on the SSS at various times throughout the day may provide useful information on the effects of sleep loss as well as on the effects of medications.

The statements and their scale values are:

1. Feeling active and vital; alert; wide awake.
2. Functioning at a high level, but not at peak; able to concentrate.
3. Relaxed; awake, not at full alertness; responsive.
4. A little foggy; not at peak; let down.
5. Fogginess; beginning to lose interest in remaining awake; slowed down.
6. Sleepiness; prefer to be lying down; fighting sleep; woozy.
7. Almost in reverie; sleep onset soon; lost struggle to remain awake.

—E. Hoddes, V. Zarcone, H. Smythe, R. Phillips, and W. C. Dement, *Psychophysiology* (10)

RESEARCH

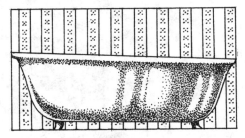

Warm Baths Deepen Sleep

A well-timed warm bath does indeed deepen your sleep, J. A. Horne and his associates at Loughborough University in Leicestershire, England, reported in *Sleep* (10). And, they said, the heat of an inflatable hair-drier hood may do the same thing. This discovery was cited in a 1988 issue of *Brain/Mind Bulletin*.

Healthy young adult subjects had a 2° C increase in body temperature after soaking 30 minutes in warm bubble baths at five P.M. and nine P.M. The early bath caused no changes in sleep, but the late bath resulted in significant rises in both stage four and slow-wave sleep.

Aspirin blocked the effects of the warming. The body heat rose regardless of whether the bather had taken aspirin or a placebo. (Aspirin lowers body temperatures only in case of fever, the researchers said.) "It's possible—this is pure speculation—that aspirin blocks biochemicals that are increased from brain-warming," Horne told *Brain/Mind Bulletin*.

There is no evidence that an increase in deep sleep will help insomnia, he said, "but sitting in a warm bath does promote sleep."

He suggested that those with mild or moderate insomnia may be helped by learning the "behavior and rules of good sleep hygiene"—listed on the following page.

Lingering in bed "to savor the last moments of sleep," for example, may lead to insomnia. Getting up before being totally "slept out" will reset your internal clock for a better match with daily activities.

Becoming upset about insomnia causes more stress and more trouble sleeping. Hauri recommends that "if, in the middle of the night, one cannot sleep (yet is comfortable and unconcerned), relaxing in bed seems best; sleep may return." However, if you become frustrated and upset, he suggests that "reading or engaging in a quiet hobby should occupy the mind."

RESEARCH

Active Days Aid Sleep

Why does an interesting but unstressful day seem to make us sleep unusually well, whereas an emotionally demanding day can leave us tired but wide awake?

J. A. Horne and coworkers discovered that slow-wave sleep increased after a "behaviorally active day." *Brain/Mind Bulletin* reported the research in 1986.

The subjects spent four-day periods in a sleep-research project. On one of the four days, they were unexpectedly taken on an outing. They were driven to another city, went to a shopping center with a museum, a scenic spot, a small amusement park/zoo, then went to a movie.

That night they fell asleep more quickly than on the other nights. They spent longer than usual periods in slow-wave sleep and awoke feeling refreshed.

INVENTORY: HEALTHY SLEEP

Eleven Rules for Better Sleep Hygiene:

1. Sleep as much as needed to feel refreshed and healthy during the following day, but not more. Curtailing the time in bed seems to solidify sleep; excessively long times in bed seem related to fragmented and shallow sleep.

2. A regular arousal time in the morning strengthens circadian cycling, and finally, leads to regular times of sleep onset.

3. A steady daily amount of exercise probably deepens sleep; occasional exercise does not necessarily improve sleep the following night.

4. Occasional loud noises (e.g., aircraft flyovers) disturb sleep even in people who are not awakened by noises and cannot remember them in the morning. Sound-attenuated bedrooms may help those who must sleep close to noise.

5. Although excessively warm rooms disturb sleep, there is no evidence that an excessively cold room solidifies sleep.

6. Hunger may disturb sleep; a light snack may help sleep.

7. An occasional sleeping pill may be of some benefit, but their chronic use is ineffective in most insomniacs.

8. Caffeine in the evening disturbs sleep, even in those who feel it does not.

9. Alcohol helps tense people fall asleep more easily, but the ensuing sleep is then fragmented.

10. People who feel angry and frustrated because they cannot sleep should not try harder and harder to fall asleep but should turn on the light and do something different.

11. The chronic use of tobacco disturbs sleep.

—from *The Sleep Disorders,* by Peter Hauri; an edition of *Current Concepts,* published by The Upjohn Company, 1982.

Dreaming

Periods of rapid-eye-movement (REM) sleep, in which closed eyes dart rapidly back and forth, are the times when most dreaming takes place. REM sleep has long been known to be highly active: heart rate, respiration, and brain-wave patterns resemble the waking state. REM sleep may be as different from non-REM (NREM) sleep as it is from being awake.

Peter Hauri notes that "the REM state is behaviorally similar to normal sleep (one lies in bed with eyes closed and diminished responsiveness to the environment), but it resembles wakefulness in other aspects (desynchronized EEG, arousal in many physiologic systems)."

To remember a dream, Hauri reminds us, "we must awaken directly from REM sleep and then consciously think about the dream." People who think that they seldom or never dream simply awaken less often from the REM state and "they are less interested in their internal life than are regular dreamers." He says that we should remember that we "have created the dream, are responsible for it, and should neither fear it nor laugh it off."

Remembering Dreams

"We all learn how to turn on televisions, ride elevators, and open pop-top cans, but nobody teaches us how to dream. I've always thought there was something anomalous about that," says Howard Rheingold in his newsletter, *Brainstorms* (1987).

Rheingold got interested in dreams after editing a manuscript on lucid dreaming by Stanford psychologist Stephen LaBerge. Deciding that "dreaming is a skill, like tying your shoelaces or driving a car," Rheingold set about to learn how to do it.

The secrets, he reports, include getting started and being persistent. After recording dreams when you wake up, he suggests transcribing and expanding your notes into a journal. "Try to think up a title or headline for each dream: 'Big Machines Chase Me!' or 'Jungian Minuet in Monte Carlo.'"

After he had accumulated a stack of journals, Rheingold realized that it would be easier to check back for relationships between dreams and useful insights if he systematized his record-keeping. He devoted a double-page spread to important dreams, giving them a title and

---

RESOURCES

Wide Awake at 3:00 A.M. by Richard Coleman (W. H. Freeman, 1986) is a researcher's guided tour through the wonders of insomnia, biological clocks, shiftwork, and jet lag. It has a bright writing style, with many interesting side trips, including the story of a man who has not slept since World War II.

Secrets of Sleep by Alexander Borbely (Basic Books, 1986) is a Swiss investigator's summary of sleep research for the lay reader. Practical and captivating.

The Sleep Disorders by Peter Hauri (1982) is one of a *Current Concepts* series published by The Upjohn Corporation. The booklet provides a clear and concise roundup of basic facts on sleep problems, with some material on dreams. A chapter on "Disorders of Excessive Somnolence" is by William Orr, Director of the Sleep Disorders Center at Presbyterian Hospital in Oklahoma City.

Dream Pretraining
Aids Therapy

In order to enhance dream recall in clients who had difficulty talking about personal matters, researchers awakened some subjects during REM sleep. Psychologist Rosalind Cartwright of Rush-Presbyterian-St. Luke's Medical Center in Chicago and her associates reported their research in *Archives of General Psychiatry* (57). It was cited in a 1980 issue of *Brain/Mind Bulletin*.

All of their subjects (ages 18 to 41) had voluntarily sought help at the counseling center for problems ranging from mild to severe. All had been judged in need of at least ten hours' psychotherapy but unlikely to remain in treatment.

For eight nights they were monitored in a sleep laboratory. Some were awakened during REM sleep, others during non-REM periods. The technician asked a set of standard questions in the morning: "What do you remember from last night?" "Do you see any ways in which these dreams relate to things happening in your life now?"

The subjects then were assigned to therapists who were unaware that an experiment was in progress and who did not specifically work with dreams. Based on the later evaluation of "blind" judges who listened to tapes of the sessions, the dream-trained subjects developed "therapy-appropriate behaviors" more quickly than the untrained. They were able to talk about personal matters and express emotions more easily.

A later pilot study explored the effectiveness of a daytime "dream modeling workshop." Each day, participants watched a ten-minute videotape showing individuals discussing their dreams with another person.

"The videotapes worked almost as well as the REM condition," Cartwright told *Brain/Mind Bulletin*. "After the first or second tape, subjects shifted their attention to dreams of their own that they wished to interpret."

a few lines of description, and leaving space for comments or interpretations.

On the right-hand page he made a sketch. "The object was not to attempt to visually depict the dream scene—I'm not exactly a professional artist, and who has the time to draw out all their dreams?—but to jog my 'right brain' thinking processes through the mechanism of image-creation."

Rheingold's dream journal, from *Brainstorms* (1987)

Sometimes he left the interpretation area blank. "I found that the process of browsing for blank interpretations sometimes jogged my pattern-recognition capabilities, and suddenly I would see the outlines of a dream message that had repeated itself in different forms."

Even Rheingold's shorthand memory-aids were overwhelmed by the sheer volume of messages. When his single notebook grew into a stack, it occurred to him that a computerized database could do the job. He designed *Dreamworks* to take over the details of record-keeping and cross-indexing.

Interpreting Dreams

The interpretation of dreams is a personal matter. You may find that a dream means something quite different to you than a superficially similar dream does to a friend.

It is important to get to know *your own* symbols, responses to archetypal images, and personal ways of making connections between dreams and everyday life. Some people find meaning simply by taking time to discover what a dream makes them think of. For some,

EXERCISE: DREAM CATCHING

The first step in any work with dreams is, of course, remembering them. The remarkable thing about dreams is how quickly they can disappear. Something you remember upon first awakening may be gone by the time you're on your feet. The memory of a dream you're sure you'll never forget may vanish by midday.

Most of us also have dreams we remember very well for long periods of time. But even those who often remember many dreams can call up more by recording them, and often begin spontaneous lucid dreaming—realizing that you're dreaming while still experiencing the dream.

Virtually everyone can improve his or her memory of dreams. The technique most often recommended is a simple one: write down everything you remember about your dream as soon as you wake up. Take these simple steps:

• Place a notebook and pen beside your bed, where you can reach it with the least effort.
• Before you go to sleep at night, tell yourself you're going to remember a dream and record it.
• When you wake up, start recalling your dream before you even open your eyes. Then, write *something* down immediately—one word, a fragment of a sentence, if that's all you can remember.
• If you can't remember what *happened* during the dream, try to get a word that expresses how you *felt,* emotionally (frightened, confused, happy) or physically (cold, hot, tired).

Some people teach themselves to wake up during the night and record their dreams.

If dream memory has been difficult for you, it may seem, at first, that you remember nothing at all. But try to get just one word that says something about what you were dreaming. Catching even one word will usually produce greater memory on following nights. Catching one dream will often lead to memories of earlier dreams from the same night. It may be like following a thread backward into the night from dream to dream.

RESOURCES

DreamWorks (Logical Design Works, San Jose, California) is Rheingold's computer software for the Macintosh. It includes a selection of built-in images that can be modified and mixed. New images can also be created.

The program will locate other recorded dreams that used the same images or key words, or that occurred on the same day of the week.

Working with Dreams by Montague Ullman and Nan Zimmerman (Delacorte Press, 1979) is a clearly written book.

Ullman, a psychiatrist, founded the famous dream laboratory at the Maimonides Medical Center in New York and is known for his extensive studies of dream telepathy. Zimmerman is a writer and teacher whose lifelong interest in dream journals led her to collaborate with Ullman not only on the book but in conducting study groups.

"If you want to learn how to appreciate and learn from your dreams," Ullman wrote in the foreword, "there are some straightforward ways of doing so. These ways require some courage and, sometimes, some friends, but they do not require any expert knowledge of dream theory, or dream research or of clinical technique...."

The book draws on well-known dream theorists (Jung, Freud, others), literature, history, anthropology, and contemporary sources. There are helpful guidelines to remembering, recording, and considering one's dreams and suggestions for how to set up a group for studying dreams.

Ullman and Zimmerman say that the dream groups nearly always generate evidence of telepathy, a subject they cover in one of the chapters.

dreams are loaded with puns and metaphors about real-life people and events.

Our dreams take place in the context of ourselves and it may be more important to discover how we feel about them than to pin down exactly what they mean.

In *The Inward Arc* (Shambhala, 1985) psychologist Frances Vaughan mentions an interesting technique based on Gestalt therapy. "One effective method for deciphering the messages the psyche offers to convey to consciousness through dreams is role-playing the various figures in

Dreams of Flying

About a third of the population has reported dreams in which they could fly.

Sigmund Freud interpreted flying dreams as symbolizing sexual intercourse. In contrast, Carl Jung felt they forecasted a potential for changing one's life in a profound way.

T. L. Brink, a California psychologist, reported in *Journal of Altered States of Consciousness* (5) his finding that people who have flying dreams feel more in control of their lives and able to shape their own destinies than those who said they had no such dreams. They score higher on several measures of creativity than those who don't report flying dreams. This discovery was reported in *Brain/Mind Bulletin* in 1979.

The best interpretations of his survey of more than 200 college students, Brink said, "would be that the experience of flying dreams is directly associated with an increase in self-confidence, sense of freedom, and creativeness."

After noting the observation of some contemporary psychotherapists that "flying dreams characterize clients who are beginning to rise above their circumstances and are beginning to take control of their lives," Brink proposed that such psychotherapeutic flying dreams might be induced in clients through training.

the dream. When one is willing to take the part of every figure in the dream, to own the projections and recognize each one as an aspect of the whole Self, the process of differentiation and reintegration begins. . . .This enables one to view the self and the world from different points of view, recognizing the relativity and plasticity of them all."

Lucid Dreaming

Lucid dreamers are people who report being aware that they are dreaming—a phenomenon that has triggered a renaissance of interest in sleep and dream research. A skilled lucid dreamer can turn a nightmare into a pleasurable experience.

Lucid dreaming may occur when a dreamer decides to "pinch myself and see if I'm dreaming," and discovers that he or she *is*. Some people become aware that they are dreaming when the situation gets too nightmarish, and learn how to wake themselves up. Others just spontaneously recognize that what they are experiencing is a dream.

After becoming lucid, it is possible to keep on dreaming. One lucid dreamer told *PragMagic* that, once when she realized she was dreaming and that the dream was not going to disappear, she crossed the street, went into a restaurant and into the women's room to look in the mirror to see what she looked like. Fascinated by her completely different appearance, she simply continued with the dream story.

Other lucid dreamers say they have enjoyed seeing how they can control or change the dream story. Some report that flying is their favorite dream sport.

Practical uses of lucid dreaming may include a greater lucidity during waking and greater access to the unconscious for solutions to problems.

Learning Lucid Dreaming

"Dreaming lucidly of doing something is more like actually doing it than like imagining it," Stephen LaBerge, a pioneering researcher, wrote in *Lucid Dreaming*. His lab at the Sleep Research Center at Stanford has made records of EEG and muscular activity during lucid dreaming and worked on designing a more reliable means to induce lucidity.

Among the informative materials LaBerge includes in his book are techniques for inducing lucid dreams developed by German researcher Paul Tholey, of the Johann Goethe University (Frankfurt am Main) psychology department. Tholey's methods were derived from more than a decade of research with over 200 subjects:

"According to Tholey, the most effective method for achieving lucidity is to develop 'a critical-reflective attitude' toward your state of consciousness, by asking yourself whether or not you are dreaming while you are awake. He stresses the importance of asking the critical question ('Am I dreaming or not?') as frequently as possible, at least five to ten times a day, and in every situation that seems dreamlike.

EXERCISE: LUCID DREAMING

In *Lucid Dreaming*, Stephen LaBerge describes a number of ways to learn lucid dreaming. One of them he calls MILD for Mnemonic Induction of Lucid Dreams.

"MILD is based on nothing more complex or esoteric than our ability to remember that there are actions we wish to perform in the future. Aside from writing ourselves memos (a device of little use here, for obvious reasons!), we do this by forming a mental connection between what we want to do and the future circumstances in which we intend to do it. Making this connection is greatly facilitated by the mnemonic device—the memory aid—of visualizing yourself doing what it is you intend to remember. It is also helpful to verbalize the intention: 'When such-and-such happens, I want to remember to do so-and-so.' For example: 'When I pass the bank, I want to remember to draw out some cash.'"

His specific steps for lucid dreaming are:

1. During the early morning when you awaken spontaneously from a dream, go over the dream several times until you have memorized it.

2. Then, while lying in bed and returning to sleep, say to yourself, "Next time I'm dreaming, I want to remember to recognize that I'm dreaming."

3. Visualize yourself as being back in the dream just rehearsed; only this time, see yourself realizing that you are, in fact, dreaming.

4. Repeat steps two and three until you feel your intention is clearly fixed or you fall asleep.

RESOURCES

Dreams & the Growth of Personality: Expanding Awareness in Psychotherapy by Ernest Rossi (Brunner/Mazel, 1985) is a second edition of Rossi's 1972 book. The volume focuses on the expansion of awareness through modern depth psychology, particularly through the understanding of dreams. Rossi illustrates the processes of psychological growth with the dreams and visions of a gifted young woman, who is called Davina. This new edition includes a review of current theories and work on dreaming, including lucid dreaming.

According to *Lucid Dreaming: The Power of Being Awake and Aware in Your Dreams* by Stephen LaBerge (J. P. Tarcher, 1985), the commonly held belief "it was only a dream" may be toppled by the latest findings on lucid-dream research.

At the Stanford University Sleep Research Center, LaBerge has found that lucid dreaming is a learnable skill that enriches life by enhancing creativity, physical coordination and problem-solving, he says. It can also provide a technique for spiritual development.

Coupled with the latest sleep-lab techniques, this skill opens a window on the unconscious, enabling a measurable approach to a once mysterious realm.

Lucidity Letter (The Lucidity Institute, Stanford, CA), edited by psychologist Jane Gackenbach, is a journal of research reports that are related to lucid dreaming.

The Enneagram by Helen Palmer (Harper & Row, 1989) is a comprehensive introduction to an ancient system of personality types.

Derived from Sufi lore, the system was first used in the West and given the name Enneagram by George Gurdjieff, who employed it with his students. However, he did not pass it on in any detail, and it was not until the 1970s that Chilean psychiatrist Oscar Ichazo introduced it to America.

The system identifies nine basic personality types, such as "The Performer," "The Boss," and "The Tragic Romantic." Each features its own central fixations and preoccupations.

Palmer, considered the country's leading practitioner, analyzes each type, then offers specific advice on ways to improve and pitfalls to avoid. Lucid and scholarly, the book also covers empirical research.

"The Enneagram is part of a teaching tradition that views personality preoccupations as teachers or indicators of latent abilities that unfold during the development of higher consciousness," Palmer says.

"The power of the system lies in the fact that ordinary patterns of personality, those very habits of heart and mind that we tend to dismiss as merely neurotic, are seen as potential access points into higher states of awareness."

"Asking the question at bedtime and while falling asleep is also favorable. Following this technique, most people will have their first lucid dream within a month, Tholey reports, and some will succeed on the very first night."

How do you deal with threatening characters? Tholey's subjects find that strong positive action is more effective than placating or attacking. Questioning dream characters, LaBerge suggested, may produce valuable information from the unconscious.

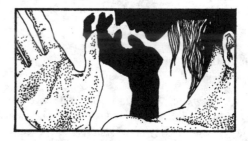

Defining Yourself

We respond to the world and to other people in highly individualized ways. Some of these seem to be "wired in," built into our physical systems. Others are developed at a cultural or a psychological level.

How can we tell which is which? What can we each learn about our own style of living? Are there others like us? Research brings us a collection of fascinating theories and a number of positive alternatives.

Among these descriptions of personality types you may recognize something about yourself—find a perspective enlightening or a tool useful. Several of the theories overlap; some offer quite separate viewpoints. But they all reflect our fascination with learning more about who we are.

Thinking Styles

Our thinking style may determine our whole orientation to life. According to Columbia, Connecticut, educator Tony Gregorc, each style or preferred learning pattern includes a particular view of reality, an ordering ability, a sense of time, and a creative mode.

Each of us has the capacity to use every thinking style, Gregorc told *Leading Edge Bulletin* in 1983. In each of us are some of the personality traits of all types. But Gregorc's research on students revealed that 90% of them had affinities to one particular style.

Gregorc divides thinking styles into two areas: perception and ordering. Four major modes emerge from different combinations of these abilities:

Concrete Sequential

People with this style (CS's) gather information primarily through direct sensory experience—"seeing is believing." The "real" world is the concrete world of the senses, which they seek to make orderly and predictable. They are adept at gathering, labeling, and controlling things.

Their thinking is methodical and deliberate—"a train of thought." They like to follow step-by-step directions and will easily defer to "experts." Their creativity, though not original, is expressed in manufacturing concrete products. And their sense of time is of a distinct past, present, and future.

As parents, dominant CS's tend to be disciplinarians, sticking to a regular routine. As friends, they are stable and dependable and expect the same of others. At work they can't tolerate distraction and expect their coworkers to be dedicated and task-oriented. They often strive for perfection, paying attention to detail and interpreting everything literally.

CS's tend to dress conventionally and keep their desks neat and orderly. They have highly developed senses and may name the perfume someone is wearing or the vintage of a wine they drink. They frequently attribute a subjective experience to something from the environment.

Abstract Sequential

These people live mostly in the abstract, nonphysical world of thought. Words and symbols—such as peace and justice—are real for them. An AS can easily become an eternal student.

Dominant AS's order life like a branching tree, with parts extending from a common base. Time is seen in terms of the present, the historical past, and a long-range future.

AS's can outline, compare, and categorize data better than others. They may be excellent synthesizers of infor-

---

RESEARCH

Intuitives and Intellectuals

A study reported in *The Journal of General Psychology* (99) by James Giannini of the department of psychiatry, Yale Medical School, suggests that individuals who favor an "intuitive" process in trying to interpret nonverbal cues are not particularly receptive to external reinforcement—and their performance may actually be worsened by it. Those favoring an "intellectual" or analytical approach, however, perform better when rewarded. *Brain/Mind Bulletin* reported on this study in 1978.

Experimental subjects watched videotapes of male students who were winning either pennies, quarters, or jackpots. The experimental subjects were supposed to guess, by facial expression, whether the people in the videotaped sequences won large or small amounts. The subjects gave their answers under two conditions—reinforced and nonreinforced. In the reinforced condition, they got a dime from a slot machine every time they were right.

After the experiments, the subjects described their procedures for judging. They were designated "intellectual" if they described a trial-and-error system, "intuitive" if they said "I just knew" or otherwise described feelings.

"Intuitives" responded almost instantly during each trial period. "Intellectuals" postponed their response until late in the period.

The "intellectuals" were significantly more accurate than the "intuitives" when their answers were reinforced, but when they were not, the "intuitives" scored significantly higher. Males and females were evenly distributed in the two categories.

"Intuitives" were not only less able to use external cues but their accuracy also declined with reinforcement. The researchers conjectured that the external reinforcement—the dime from the slot machine—may interfere with attention to internal cues.

RESEARCH

Vocal Clues—A Holonomic Key

The human voice may contain a complete personality profile of the speaker—including fundamental dynamics, deep purpose, stress, and learning styles—which can be identified by a trained listener.

Sandra Seagal, a psychologist living in Topanga Canyon, California, and working abroad as well as in the U.S.A., discovered her ability to discern three distinct sets of dynamics in everyone's voice. These "tones," she believes, reflect the relative functioning of mental, emotional, and physical expression and development. High voice frequencies seem to relate to mental functioning, medium-range frequencies to emotions, and low-range to sensory perception. "We listen to what is deep in people, to what is sounding in them," Seagal told *Leading Edge Bulletin*.

From 1979 to the present, she and her associates have seen approximately 30,000 people from over 25 cultures. The voice was, for her, a key that unlocked understanding of fundamental human dynamics, which cross age, gender, and culture.

Seagal's research has resulted in human development programs for a number of organizations and also teacher training programs directed toward understanding the personality dynamics of students and their styles of learning.

mation, eager to share new concepts with others and to impress people with what they know. But they reject as irrational anything that doesn't fit with their view of the world.

Dominant AS's may appear flighty because of their quick and active minds, typified by the "absentminded professor." They can arrive somewhere by car or foot unable to remember how they got there. They are not averse to change but are notorious for their "yes-buts." Because they need to weigh all the data, they may argue intelligently—and with polysyllabic words—and still end up unable to make a decision.

AS parents set high standards for their children, emphasizing proper manners and achievement in school. Although they may be loving, they are not demonstrative and may appear aloof.

AS employees defer to authority and dislike environmental distractions. Typically, they are unconcerned with clothes but will collect objects that symbolize knowledge.

Abstract Random

The "real" world for the dominant AR is the world of feelings and imagination. Some have uncanny intuition and the capacity to sense nuances of atmosphere and mood. Their world is ever-changing and fluid, and they know it through "gut response."

Dominant AR's seek personal meaning in experience. To them, events seem to flow in meaningful coincidences. They live to the fullest in the moment. And they believe a single person or event can make a significant difference. AR's can easily establish rapport with others, feeling both sympathy and empathy. They care more about the quality or refinement of experiences than about their quantity. They use their sensitivity to refine things through art and music.

AR's are typically idealists, approaching life through a passionate range of emotions. They communicate with sound, color, and gesture and use metaphoric language.

AR's find routine and orderliness boring and nonessential. Their offices and homes may look like jungles to others. As parents, they get immersed in their children's games and are often the youngsters' biggest supporters.

Concrete Random

The physical world is real for dominant CR's but is seen as a launching pad for more important things. Their ordering ability is random, intuitive, arising out of a stream of consciousness with no apparent beginning or end. For this reason they see the possibility of new, unpredicted events taking place.

CR's use instinct to register the concrete world as a starting point. Then they use intuition to see into and beyond objects, to gain insight and unlock the message encoded in all things. The message they seek is unity.

CR's may ignore theoretical considerations and make startling leaps in their efforts to discover underlying principles. These leaps are validated for CR's through intense probing, but the search often results in still newer, unexpected options. CR's focus on processes and their applications. They are typically more concerned with ideals than objects. The products of their creativity tend to be unique and the result of risk.

CR's often instigate change. As troubleshooters, they predict possibilities rather than events and convey them through metaphors, not models. They strive to understand the "why" rather than the "how" of things.

CR's do not like to be fenced in. They need a rich environment and ample personal space. Words do not convey true meaning for them, though they are colorful, informative conversationalists. They like people, have a natural curiosity, and keep four or five irons in the fire at all times. CR parents are not disciplinarians, often allowing their children much experimentation.

CR's often frustrate friends by anticipating the punch line of a story with their excellent, impulsive intuition.

Self-observation

Robert Thayer, a psychologist at California State University at Long Beach, teaches a course in Systematic Self-observation. One of the most crucial activities in this course is journal-keeping.

Journals can tell us a great deal about our everyday cycles and how they affect our moods. Thayer told *PragMagic* that the time of day influences whether we feel optimistic or pessimistic about our problems. An ongoing personal issue appears less pressing during the

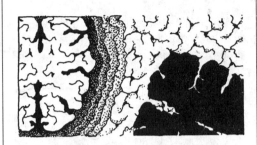

RESOURCES

Several valuable testing materials are available for self-assessment and self-analysis, on an institutional or personal level. Among these are:

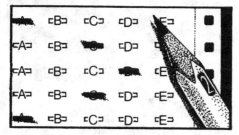

The Gregorc Style Delineator, designed by Anthony Gregorc (see related text). Simple multiple-choice questions, accompanied by detailed and sophisticated materials concerning scoring and interpretation, offer a superb analysis of one's personal style—Concrete Sequential, Abstract Sequential, Abstract Random, or Concrete Random.

WKOPAY ("What Kind of Person Are You?"), designed by E. Paul Torrance, and SAM ("Something About Myself") designed by Torrance and Joe Khatena of the Department of Educational Psychology of Mississippi State University, cover a wide variety of issues, including initiative, self-strength, individuality, self-confidence, awareness of others, disciplined imagination, and others.

late morning and early evening, worse in middle to late afternoon. Mild exercise seems to be an antidote for the low.

We tend to think of peaks and valleys in mood as a single cycle, but this is not so, according to Thayer. Our peaks and valleys really reflect how two other cycles combine—the first being our high and low energy levels, and the second being our degree of relaxation or "tense arousal."

The time-of-day differences were small but persistent in a group of college students ages 20 to 33 at California State University, Long Beach. Participants had been chosen because they had reported "bothersome" long-standing problems—being overweight, painfully separated from a spouse, caught between battling parents.

The moods are natural altered states that "can be overridden in any one situation," said Thayer, "but they're influential over time."

Thoughts can be unrealistically optimistic as well as pessimistic, he said. During high-energy phases you can overestimate your own resources.

Once you learn about your cycles, you can make educated self-observations. When you become depressed or anxious, you can ask yourself questions about recent diet, sleep, and exercise, and better understand your current moods.

Drawing as a Tool

Recording our self-observations need not be limited to writing. In his *Thinking Course for Juniors* (Direct Educational Services, Ltd., 1974) Edward DeBono says that drawing is a good thinking medium.

One reason, DeBono explains, is that drawing makes for commitment. "A drawing cannot be half one thing and half another. You have to draw something definite."

And in drawing, "things are not left hanging in the air as they might have been with language." There are no loose ends.

A most important advantage to drawing is that it is all visible at once. "This means that you can see the whole process and the interactions at one glance. You can see the gaps at once. If you want to change something, you do so at once and immediately see the consequences. You can also build things up gradually."

Drawings are easy to modify, DeBono points out. And organization is required. "With a verbal description, inconsistencies and even contradictions are not obvious at once—but with a drawing they are. Things have to be related. Loose and sloppy thinking is obvious to the child himself."

But drawing is not just for children. Try the mandala exercise on the following pages.

Being Magic 73

RESOURCE

In 1926 a young Englishwoman decided to start keeping a journal so that she might better understand those moments that brought her happiness. Seven years later she had completed an account of self-discovery that took her from a naive examination of delights into the reasons for her boredom, anxiety, sense of inadequacy, expanded and contracted consciousness, and monstrous fears of annihilation.

In *A Life of One's Own* (J. P. Tarcher, 1981), Joanna Field (a pseudonym of Marion Milner) shows us that a curious, observant individual, by trial and error, can come to insights about the mind's workings that parallel the findings of psychology and philosophy.

She uncovered subliminal, childish thought patterns she came to call "blind thinking." And she learned to achieve a kind of wide attention that brought her clarity, communication, a loss of self-consciousness, and even transcendence.

Her values changed. "When I was living blindly, I was pulled this way and that by all manner of different wants, but when I stopped to look at them their clamor died down, and I became aware of others that seemed to emerge from far deeper down in myself."

EXERCISE: CREATING A MANDALA

In *The Creative Journal: The Art of Finding Yourself* (Ohio University Press, 1979), artist and educator Lucia Capacchione focuses on drawing as a means of journal-keeping. In an exercise entitled "Putting It All Together: A Mandala," she explains how to create your own mandala—and what it can mean to you. If you haven't started your own journal, you can use the space above for your first attempt at this exercise:

Imagine yourself in the center of a blank journal page before you. Close your eyes and picture yourself located there, looking out at the world from your place in the center of the page. Then think about all the qualities you possess. Meditate upon them. Picture them in your mind's eye. After you have let these random thoughts and images pass through your mind, open your eyes.

First make a dot in the center of the page. Then draw a border around the page as a frame for your design. It can be any shape: circle, square, hexagon (six-sided figure), octagon (eight-sided).

EXERCISE, continued

Now, return to the center point and focus your attention there. Say:

This *is my center*.

Then draw an image or symbol in that central area which represents your unique inner core. Then let images, colors, shapes, and lines unfold outward, emanating from your center design. Let this evolve into a self-contained graphic expression of your many aspects integrated into wholeness.

Uses: The word *mandala* means circle in Sanskrit. The mandala, a design form which radiates out from a center, is ancient and universal, appearing in the art, architecture, and dance of cultures everywhere. It is the "magic circle" and often has a ritual, religious symbolism as in the rose window of medieval churches. Here, it is intended as a drawing meditation for centering and integrating the self. In times of confusion or stress it is a way to "collect your thoughts" or "gather your wits" or "pull yourself together."

In the process of creating a mandala you can reach into deep levels of your Self. This can be done repeatedly as a part of the ongoing process of integration. It is a tool for developing centeredness through outward expression in graphic art.

The mandalas below are examples of first attempts reproduced from *The Creative Journal*.

NOTES:

3.
CONNECTING MAGIC:

Ifs, Ands, or Buts?

So now we've spent some time practicing the process of self-definition. What next? Certainly, it makes good sense to bring our growing self-awareness into the world around us—to *connect* with our world.

Of course we're by no means through defining ourselves. We never are. As we examine the vast field of human multiplicity, our self-defining continues. Who are the "selves" who live inside each of us? And how many are there? How can we make the most of this community that dwells inside us? How can our various selves be good neighbors? And what kind of untapped talents do we hold? *Connecting* with this vast world of selves—both inward and outward—is essential to the practice of pragmagic.

When we start regarding each human being as a kind of society, the issue of human interaction takes on increased subtlety and sophistication. This section will deal with:

• getting to know our many "selves," and dealing with the multiplicity of those around us

• how we can better grasp some of the subtleties of human communication and interaction, beyond the merely verbal

• information on bonding, at every phase of our lives

• what we can learn from projections and archetypes

• how we can tap our best resources as workers

• how we can relate more effectively to those who work with us

I think every adult needs a relationship with a child, a real flesh-and-blood child, so that we can imagine what it will be like as that child's life unfolds into the future.

—Mary Catherine Bateson
in Bill Moyers, *A World of Ideas*
(Doubleday, 1989)

How we can take a holistic view of multiple selves and complex relationshps? Holism is the theory that the universe can be seen in terms of interacting wholes that are more than the mere sum of the individual parts. We need to give our attention to the *relationships* among our inner selves and between ourselves and others. And we have to include all of them.

Our motto might become: *Holism means never saying "but."* In a complex and diverse world, we should try to live increasingly *in*clusive lives. We must *connect* in as many ways as possible. Every time we say the word "but," we implicitly exclude something, make an exception, say that something doesn't belong. It is, of course, unreasonable and impossible to insist on forcibly dropping the word "but" from the language. Still, the practice of pragmagic means living with increasingly fewer "buts"—and a lot more "ifs" and "ands."

Human Interactions

Sooner or later, our efforts at self-study must lead to an examination of how we relate to other people, and how other people relate to each other. How do we communicate? How do we detect falsehoods? How do human beings condition one another's behavior? What is the basis of human attractiveness?

Insights into ourselves can be brought to bear on our understanding of those around us. An acceptance of human uniqueness is invaluable in relationships.

The Language of the Eyes

Eye contact is the primary regulator of communication, judging from a growing body of research. Patricia Webbink, a Maryland psychologist, summarized the state of research to date in her book, *The Power of the Eyes* (Springer Publishing Co., 1986).

Webbink notes that just as people are about to speak, they look away from each other. At the ends of phrases and sentences they look up briefly. When they finish speaking, they give the listener a more prolonged gaze. "At this point the other person will look away and begin to speak."

In groups, the person last looked at by the speaker is the likeliest to gain the floor.

Gaze patterns vary from one culture to another. In a typical interaction among the British or Americans, eye contact will occur 10% to 30% of the time, for periods of about one second.

The rate of gaze shifts and the duration of each gaze seem to be agreed upon by both partners in an interaction, as if they had come to a consensus about how long each would look at the other. There were reliable differences between *pairs* of people as well as in individuals.

In pairs, the listener usually looks at the speaker twice as much as the speaker looks at the listener. But in groups, people seek eye contact 70% of the time while speaking and a little less than half the time while listening.

Breakdowns in the flow of conversation, Webbink said, may be due to different patterns of eye contact. Those who have different cultural backgrounds and thus different gaze behavior will have trouble synchronizing in a conversation.

The "language of the eyes" also reveals the distribution of power in social relationships. Established leaders look less at subordinates, but the subordinate gazes at the leader to signal respect, seek approval, or monitor the leader's reactions.

Looking away signals submission or peaceful intention. Females use more such submissive gestures with their eyes than males. In spite of this, they also use more eye contact, regardless of whether they are conversing with men or women. People can change their visual behavior to reflect a new perception of their own dominance or submissiveness.

The power of visual behavior is probably primal, she said. "Light-sensitive cells of some kind are common to most life forms and eyes were a relatively early development in vertebrate life-forms."

INVENTORY: EYE CONTACT

Do you pay attention to your own eye-contact habits? Make mental notes during your next one-on-one conversation, and jot them down afterward. Ask yourself, specifically:

What do I do with my eyes during *the moment before* I address someone?
- ❑ I make eye contact with the person.
- ❑ I look away.

What do I do with my eyes during *the course of speaking* to someone?
- ❑ I maintain eye contact most of the time.
- ❑ I maintain eye contact little of the time.

What do I do with my eyes when I *finish* addressing someone?
- ❑ I make conclusive eye contact.
- ❑ I look away.

Patricia Webbink suggests that most of us divert our gaze when we begin to speak, look intermittently at each other during conversation, then make eye contact in conclusion. Is this true for you?

You might find it interesting to alter your eye contact habits consciously during a conversation. While speaking to someone, consciously *make less eye contact* than usual. Or consciously *make more eye contact* than usual. Once again, make mental notes, and jot them down afterward.

How did each of these changes affect the level of communication in the conversation?

_____

_____

_____

_____

How did the person you were speaking to react to the change of eye contact?

_____

_____

_____

_____

Did you feel any different in one situation vs. the other (awkward, aggressive, etc.)?

_____

_____

Human Differences

Years of research have demonstrated that males and females show clear, important perceptual differences from infancy on. In addition, females are more empathic and communicative, males more skilled at mechanical tasks.

But where do these differences come from? According to Diane McGuinness of the University of California at Santa Cruz and Karl Pribram of Stanford University, they can be traced back to early hormonal influences, which directly affect sensory perception. In a 1978 study of sex differences, "Psychobiological Factors in the Development of Cognitive Gender Differences: An Effector Theory," the researchers presented a remarkable new theory.

According to McGuinness and Pribram, these perceptual differences lead to biased behavior, resulting in anatomical differences in the growth of the nervous system, leading in turn to differences in behavior and brain development—differences that are ultimately reinforced by society itself.

Differences Between Males and Females

Their survey included hundreds of experiments covering many decades. The more reliable differences included:

• Males are superior in visual acuity, except in dim light, where women excel. Males are more sensitive to both brightness and smell. Visual phenomena, such as afterimages, differ in the sexes.

• Males react more to "noxious" extremes of temperature.

• Females have greater sensitivity in taste, "overwhelming" sensitivity in touch, especially in their fingers and hands. From childhood women show superior hearing. Around the level of 85 decibels, females perceive the volume of any sound as twice as loud as it is perceived by males.

• By age one, boys play more than girls with objects other than toys, devising novel uses for them. Females are superior in performing new motor skills. Three-year-old girls were more responsive than boys to new playmates.

• Infant girls are comforted more by speech and singing, boys by touch. Although mothers reinforce vocaliza-

---

RESEARCH

Despite Testing Results, Sex Biases Remain

Young boys and girls generally perform equally well on tests of reading and mathematics, but inaccurate sexual stereotyping remains common, researchers at the University of Michigan concluded. Harold Stevenson and coworkers at the University of Michigan Center for Human Growth and Development (Ann Arbor) studied thousands of kindergarten, first-grade, and fifth-grade students in Chicago, Taiwan, and Japan.

They found that the pattern exists in both Asia and America and indicates that gender differences in later life are at least partially the result of parental bias and myth. *Brain/Mind Bulletin* reported their research in 1989.

On tests in all three countries, kindergartners of both sexes had essentially equal scores for matching and identifying letters. They were also similar in their ability to count, to identify numbers, and in memory and verbal/spatial skills.

First- and fifth-graders, tested for reading comprehension, math problem-solving, and cognitive ability, also had virtually identical scores. Although gender differences did show in two tests, in neither case were differences considered significant.

Nevertheless, mothers rated boys and girls differently.

Mothers who said girls were better readers than boys:

Japanese	79%
Taiwanese	54%
American	35%

Less than 2% of the mothers surveyed took the opposite point of view. Mothers also consistently rated boys better in math, whether they rated their own children or children in general.

"If a parent expects a child to do better in one area than another," said Max Lummis, a researcher on the project, "eventually the child probably will. By the time a student takes high school achievement tests, the pattern has been reinforced."

EXERCISE: CATCHING YOUR BIASES

None of us is completely free from feelings of prejudice. But it does no good to run away from these assumptions and try to maintain that basic human differences do not exist. As Pribram and McGuinness point out, "problems arise not because stereotypes are inaccurate, but because value judgments are inevitably applied to them."

Consider any group of people for which you know yourself to harbor preconceptions and prejudgments, whether based on gender, ethnicism, religion, age, or any other category.

Examples might include: assuming that certain racial or nationalistic groups either have or lack exceptional responsibility or industriousness; expecting helpless emotionalism or rational clarity from either males or females; expecting intelligence or reliability from a particular age group, etc. Some of these preconceptions may be positive and some negative, but take some time to think about the ones you hold.

First, list these preconceptions and assumptions—positive or negative—as completely as you can:

_____

_____

_____

_____

_____

_____

_____

_____

_____

_____

Going back to the first list, place a mark by all the *negative* assumptions. Instead of trying to obliterate these assumptions, see how many of them can be placed in a *positive* light. To use an example of McGuinness and Pribram in their "plea for cultural reevaluation," the female disposition toward empathy and communicativeness is too often perceived as weakness and irrationality. Can any of your negative assumptions be turned inside out? List them:

_____

_____

_____

_____

_____

_____

_____

_____

_____

_____

tion more in male children, girls have greater clarity and quality of speech throughout childhood. Girls sing in tune better; there are six times as many male monotones as female. And although mothers interact physically more with infant sons than daughters, boys show greater childhood interest in objects than in people.

• At an early age, females are more sensitive to social context, based on situational cues, even where facial expression contradicts behavior. Their vicarious responses to other people's feelings are more accurate, but males are equally able to assess and categorize another's feelings.

• Males are superior in spatial-mechanical tasks and reaction time, but females excel at fine motor dexterity.

• Females are superior in most forms of verbal and visual memory, and they process verbal stimuli faster and more accurately.

So what is the answer to the age-old question of whether environment or heredity brings about these differences between men and women? McGuinness and Pribram concluded that they result from both. Innate physiological differences from infancy are deeply enhanced by our culture throughout life.

But their research on male-female differences produced a striking byproduct. They also unmasked a cultural tendency to find negative implications in human uniqueness. McGuinness and Pribram entered "a plea for cultural reevaluation." (See sidebar.) Why, they asked, can't we see these differences in a positive light? Uniqueness is all too often suspect in our culture.

The "Enemy"

Our impulse to attribute negative characteristics to anyone who is different from ourselves leads, of course, to the making of enemies. How do we come to hate another person? How does this process perpetuate itself?

Throughout history, enemies have had many faces. Today, the face of "the enemy" is no longer human, according to Sam Keen, author of *Faces of the Enemy* (see sidebar, page 84), who spoke at a 1983 San Francisco conference on the process of enemy-making. He traced the history of wartime propaganda to show "how hard we work to condition people to kill." The propaganda imagery revealed the efforts of different cultures to portray "the enemy" in several ways:

COMMENTARY

A Plea for Cultural Reevaluation

"Status derives from a system of values and in all cultures is particularly associated with male and female role stereotypes. Problems arise not because stereotypes are inaccurate, but because value judgments are inevitably applied to them. It was seen from . . . data that females are communicative, show a greater interest in people than males, and that they may also be more sensitive to contextual and emotional forms of communication.

"Sensitivity to persons is a quality which is profoundly important in maintaining a stable social system. Yet several authors imply that such female characteristics render them unable to carry out logical thought."

"All statements of this type carry the implicit assumption that to be assertive, independent and unfeeling is good, but to have characteristics of sensitivity and cooperativeness is bad. In spite of these assumptions, it seems, rather, that traits of aggression, competitiveness, coupled with a lack of empathy and sensitivity to others, are the very characteristics that lead to the downfall of civilized life."

"The authors put forward a plea for the reassessment of cultural *values,* with the suggestion than an emphasis on communicative and communal skills be introduced not only in our academic institutions but in our culture as a whole. The plea is concerned not so much with the argument that the talents of men and women be treated equally but that men and women are *different*. What needs to be made equal is the value placed upon these differences."

—Diane McGuinness and Karl Pribram
"Psychobiological Factors in the
Development of Cognitive Gender
Differences: An Effector Theory"
(a 1978 study)

RESOURCE

Sam Keen's *Faces of the Enemy: Reflections of the Hostile Imagination* (Harper & Row, 1986) is an extraordinary volume, richly illustrated with posters and cartoons, many in color. He illuminates material that could be merely depressing, and gracefully penetrates causes of human conflict.

The archetypes of the enemy include stranger, aggressor, God-hater, barbarian, beast, impersonal weapons machine, and worthy opponent.

Women, he says, have not been able to gain power because they have never entered fully into the paradigm of violence. If we can make the rearing of gentle people an ultimate concern, the art of fathering and mothering "might become the center of a new definition of heroism."

The Barbarous Jap
U.S., W.W. II

The Pentagon—Mindless Power
U.S.S.R.

Lady Macbeth—Britain
Washing away the blood guilt for the
bombing of civilians
Germany, W.W. II

• Seeing the enemy as an atheist means he is an enemy of God, Keen said, providing theological justification for killing. "All wars, in effect, are holy wars. The enemy plays a role by which evil is redeemed—and the winners prove they are on God's side."

• Seeing the enemy as a barbarian alien to cultural refinement justifies the idea that he is not fit for survival.

• Seeing the enemy as a loathsome beast contaminating the world implies that he is therefore deserving of sterilization.

• Seeing the enemy as death implies that we engage in war to avoid death, defeating the "final enemy" and gaining immortality.

Keen noted that "primitive" peoples typically place warfare in a different context—the battle between the forces of chaos and cosmos. "These people realize that something must die for something to be born. For this

---

EXERCISE: A COMMUNICATION STRATEGY

How do we maintain productive, nurturing bonds with our peers through common disagreement? The late Carl Rogers, in his book *On Becoming a Person*, asserts the importance of "seeing the other point of view" (see sidebar). He proposes a simple experiment to help in such situations:

When an argument arises, whether between a couple, with friends, or within a small group, stop the discussion and make this rule:

"Each person can speak up for himself only after he has first restated the ideas and feelings of the previous speaker accurately, and to that speaker's satisfaction."

This means that, before you get to present your own point of view, you must "really achieve the other speaker's frame of reference—to understand his thoughts and feelings so well that you could summarize them for him."

Although it sounds simple, Rogers says that "if you try it, you will discover it is one of the most difficult things you have ever tried to do." And understanding the other person's point of view may change your own position rather drastically. At the least, the emotional charge of the opinions will be dissipated and you will discover exactly what it is that you do disagree on.

First, practice this method with minor problems. Then you'll have an excellent technique ready when a big and emotionally charged disagreement comes up. You'll be able to suggest and demonstrate the experiment to others.

COMMENTARY

Carl Rogers on "Seeing the Other Point of View"

How is it that bonds of friendship and family so often turn into enmity? One of the most obvious hazards to our social and family bonds is common, everyday disagreement. The late Carl Rogers discusses this pitfall in his classic work *On Becoming a Person: A Therapist's View of Psychotherapy* (Houghton Mifflin, 1961). Rogers points out that when we hear someone give their opinion on something, our first response is to judge the opinion—and the person who holds it. For example, when someone says that they agree with a speaker or disagree with the platform of a political party, we immediately agree or disagree with that person, whether we express what we feel or not. The stronger our emotional response, the stronger our judgment.

This natural tendency to judge, evaluate, to approve or disapprove, Rogers calls "the major barrier to mutual interpersonal communication." When each person is making a judgment from their own frame of reference, there is "really nothing which could be called communication in any genuine sense."

Developing the ability to see the other point of view, Rogers says, "is the most effective agent we know for altering the basic personality structure of an individual, and improving his relationships and his communications with others."

Parent-Infant Bonding (C. V. Mosby, 1982) by Marshall H. Klaus and John H. Kenell is a comprehensive look at the relationship of the entire family to the birth of a new member. The authors, professors of pediatrics at Case Western Reserve University School of Medicine, report their own research and studies by others.

In a chapter on "Labor, Birth, and Bonding," Klaus and Kennell discuss some provocative data and conclusions:

• New scientific evidence concerning obstetric practices "may be obscured, suppressed, or not fully evaluated if it is not in tune with our society's system of beliefs."

• In contrast to hospital births, the woman who gives birth at home often appears to be in a remarkable state of ecstasy immediately after birth.

• Research supports the recognition of a "sensitive period" soon after birth, during which close contact between the mother and full-term infant improves the quality of their long-term bond.

• During the first hour after birth, the infant is in a quiet, alert state, "ideally equipped for the important first meeting with his parents."

• When given the opportunity to be alone with their newborns, fathers "spend almost exactly the same amount of time as mothers in holding, touching, and looking at them."

• "Well over 80% of mothers have postpartum blues, with crying sometime during hospitalization." The authors speculate that "the mother-infant separation, the assignment of most of the caretaking responsibility to 'experts,' the concerns about ability to care for the newborn at home, and the limiting of visitors are major factors."

• Some women experience the first feelings of love for their infant at later times: during or even after the first week.

• In spite of typical hospital separations, most parents manage to bond with their children. "The human is highly adaptable, and there are many fail-safe routes to attachment."

reason it's enough for them to shed only symbolic blood or to cease fighting after only one death."

In days of chivalry, too, the enemy took on another value—worthy opponent. "Chivalrous warriors, or members of military castes such as samurai and Kshatriya, saw the enemy as fellow professionals. They studied their tactics and thought of war as the highest game, an ordeal of manhood."

With the advent of nuclear weapons, however, the role of the enemy has changed drastically. "The enemy of this era no longer has a human face. It is the weapons systems that can destroy us all." The machine has replaced the warrior as the agent of the next war, Keen said. Martial virtues, no longer needed, are replaced by technological competence. And "we no longer see the target because it has become you and me—the entire civilian population."

Bonding

Bonding is a lifelong issue. It begins before birth. It continues into childhood and remains an issue even in adulthood. We're making new bonds all the time—bonds with friends, coworkers, new family members.

But what does bonding mean in terms of our growth and well-being? What constitutes a *healthy* bond? And how do the bonds we make early in life resonate through the rest of life?

An investigation of bonding leads us to examine the ties that hold human beings together in families, friendships, and other relationships. Violence, autism, child abuse, manipulation, hostile sexual behavior, and addictive behavior have been identified as the results of a lack of human bonding.

Affectional Bonding

What are the biological roots of human bonding? Are there brain or hormonal mechanisms involved in the development of affection or of antisocial behavior? Increasing scientific and social interest in these questions led to a 1980 conference called Developmental Biology of the Affectional Bond. The five-day seminar at Big Sur, California was cosponsored by the University of California–Berkeley health and medical sciences program, the life sciences division of Stanford Research Institute, the Esalen Institute, and several foundations.

Conference participants represented a variety of specialties: neuropsychology, sociology, medicine, education, clinical psychology, sexology, and philosophy. They focused on the brain processes that might be involved in familial, sexual, and social bonding. Peter Levine of the University of California–Berkeley, a conference organizer, said that a better understanding of biological mechanisms might offer society tools to help understand and deal with the roots of violence and the many social problems that may be traceable to the failure to bond.

Touch and Movement

Touch and movement contribute to brain growth, according to James Prescott of the National Institute of Child Health and Human Development. Depriving infant mammals of either touch or movement always results in antisocial behavior, he noted. He suggested that the brain system that regulates balance by sensing gravity (the vestibular-cerebellar pathway) also plays a major role in the development of normal social behavior. A lack of movement, depriving that system of stimulation, may be the critical factor in social withdrawal, he said.

Prescott showed films of withdrawn or hyperactive children who were spun around in an office swivel chair. This stimulation led to brief but pronounced changes in behavior. The children settled down momentarily, appeared delighted, and for the first time, allowed themselves to be touched.

RESOURCES

Facial Expressions of Infants

Brain/Mind Bulletin reported in 1982 on a University of Miami Medical School study indicating that newborn babies mimic happy, sad, or surprised faces and may be innately disposed to perceive facial expressions.

Researcher Tiffany Field and her colleagues reported in the study of 74 infants, averaging 36 hours old, that the babies could detect and imitate these expressions as modeled by an adult. Infants' brows, eyes, and mouth movements tended to conform to those of the model.

The infants' facial movements were recorded by observers who could not see the models' expressions. Split-screen video-taping of the infants' and models' expressions were used to check the observers' reliability.

Field noted that happy, sad, and surprised facial expressions have been observed in young infants of numerous cultures. "Because of their early appearance and apparent universality, these basic facial expressions may reflect innate processes," she concluded.

Child Abuse

The most clear sign of the failure of affectional bonding is child abuse, even though it can still be difficult to detect. "In the clinic, abusive parents usually wear the mask of normalcy," John Money, a medical psychologist at Johns Hopkins Hospital, told the Esalen conference.

Money was speaking specifically about children who fail to make growth hormones and who become dwarfs as a sequel to abuse and neglect at home. They have the syndrome of psychosocial or abuse dwarfism. Those who fail to grow physically and normally in a neglectful or abusive environment actually do resume normal growth—judging from hormonal changes—within days after being placed in a friendly setting.

He said that the abused dwarf is an involuntary martyr whose martyrdom becomes "a deeply imbedded trait in his personality, imperative to survival." For him abuse is an inevitable part of life.

INVENTORY: CHILD-ABUSE WARNING SIGNS

Brain/Mind Bulletin asked John Money, an authority on child abuse, for a checklist that might be useful to counselors, physicians, teachers, and others on the lookout for possible child abuse.

Money's warning signs:
• Abused children are often retarded in physical growth, speech, social skills, and schoolwork.
• They may seem socially isolated, living in their own world. They may fail to cry when hurt, yet appear sad and alone.
• The sleep of abused children is disturbed and irregular, their sleeping arrangements often inadequate. Food and water are restricted, eating and drinking irregular.
• Abused children are sometimes seen rocking, banging their heads, mutilating themselves, picking at themselves.
• Abused children and their mothers typically have not related to one another, even from the day of birth. The mother has rejected and felt rejected by the baby.
• The parents cover up for one another and rationalize their behavior ("Spare the rod and spoil the child"). Furthermore, the children themselves seldom disclose abuse. Investigators should check with neighbors, friends, and relatives.
• Where there are several children in the family, usually only one is the victim of neglect and abuse. The other children may join in the maltreatment and conspire to cover it up.

"It is pointless for an Eskimo to complain about ice, snow, and subzero weather. They constitute the only environment he knows. An abused child doesn't complain about the only environment he knows." Just as the kicked dog repeatedly returns for affection, Money said, "so abused children relentlessly try to meet their abusers' demands, as if trying finally to win love and appreciation."

Abusive parents are in need of help themselves, Money said. Threatening them with punishment makes it all the more difficult to detect and prevent their pathological behavior. Child abuse is often part of an overall pattern of aggressive sexuality, suggesting that sex therapies might help remedy the problem, he added.

Drug Abuse and the Failure to Bond

The failure to make appropriate social bonds—to get reward from interpersonal relationships—often leads to drug abuse. Dave Smith, the physician who founded the Haight-Ashbury Drug Abuse Clinic in San Francisco in 1967, said that the pleasure of the drug high becomes a kind of substitute relationship. "We hear from our clients all the time about their fears of intimacy and closeness. They say the drugs help them escape."

Either they use the drugs to block out their anxiety about closeness in a sexual situation or they substitute the drugs altogether for sex and other forms of social interaction. "The high failure rate of recovery from addiction," Smith said, "is due in part to the failure to help the addicts function socially and sexually without drugs." Rehabilitation should include therapy that focuses on the ability to relate to others, sexually and otherwise, he said.

It may be that rewarding human interaction causes the brain to release or synthesize specific chemicals, creating a kind of social "high." Jaak Panksepp of Ohio State University, Bowling Green, pointed out that the distress experienced in the loss of love—loneliness, loss of appetite, crying, despondency, psychic pain, irritability, insomnia—resembles the symptoms of narcotic withdrawal. Among the connections between narcotic addiction and social bonding:

• The highest incidence of narcotic addiction in the U.S. has usually been among the socially uprooted—first-generation immigrants and the "long-term dispossessed of the ghettos."

• In a British study, 85% of the addicts had a background of poor family relations.

COMMENTARY

Research Is "Me-search"

Do researchers experience a form of bonding with their work? "Research is me-search," psychiatrist Julian Silverman told participants in a 1980 Big Sur, California, conference on "Developmental Biology of the Affectional Bond." What a scientist chooses to observe is significant, he said.

"What are you doing in your research that tells you who you are? What do you have to learn about yourself in this investigation? What you're working on is really your problem—just as a teacher teaches what he most needs to learn."

Conference coordinator Peter Levine summed up the five days of research reports, ranging from clinical psychology to brain research: "The essence of the conference is the discovered commonalities underlying the researchers' wide divergence."

The scientists conceded that a central concern of their own lives—human bonding—was mirrored by their observations of the phenomenon in animals and humans.

Joe Kamiya of Langley-Porter Institute, San Francisco, urged the researchers to talk more openly about their own relationship to their work. He also said that successful biofeedback training appears to hinge upon the development of a bond between subject and trainer.

He said that 20 years of brain-wave biofeedback research led him to the hypothesis that the nature of the subject-experimenter relationship is "a major variable" in predicting whether or not an individual will succeed in the training. Those subjects with whom he felt a rapport learned more quickly and easily than those with whom there was no such relationship.

Helping Your Aging Parents by James Halpern (McGraw Hill, 1987) deals with family relationships, discussing how to gain sibling cooperation in caring for elderly parents, and also ways to enlist neighborhood or community help. It confronts certain emotional issues. For example, some of us are utterly unable to confront our parents at all, while others are wrapped up in angry relationships with parents, full of conflict but really no more communicative.

Family Therapy in Clinical Practice by Murray Bowen (Aronson, 1978) is a collection of papers on family systems therapy. The last chapter describes Bowen's own reentry into the life of his family, describing his use of letter writing and other techniques.

The Dance of Anger by Harriet Lerner (Harper & Row, 1985) combines family systems theory with a feminist approach.

Giving In to Get Your Way by Terry Dobson and Victor Miller (Delacorte Press, 1978). Despite the title, the advice in this remarkably readable, valuable book is not manipulative.

The authors' "Attack-tics" approach is based in part on the Japanese martial art, aikido. The individual under attack learns to divert the negative energy of others to positive ends. This psychological aikido is illustrated with hundreds of examples.

"Attack-tics" also incorporates the rehearsal and training aspects of theater. Dobson is an aikido teacher, and Miller developed "theater games" so that actors and directors could experiment with the dynamics of relationships.

The authors build a convincing and useful set of metaphors for understanding "the geometry of conflict." Their advice is couched in direct, contemporary language, yet it dovetails with ancient wisdom. "Centering" is the keystone to their system, as it is in aikido and theater.

• Addicts personify the opiates, referring to the drug as their friend, family, loved one.

• Many persons alleviate their suffering in the continuous seeking of company, much as addicts turn to their opiates.

Family Systems Therapy

James Halpern, a psychologist in private practice in Manhattan and a professor of psychology at the State University of New York, New Paltz, told *PragMagic* that he is convinced that you will have no trouble getting along with friends and associates "if you have an intimate relationship with your mother and your father and your siblings—that is, if you can speak with members of your immediate family about things that matter to you without defending yourself or attacking them, and if you can be *yourself* in those relationships."

EXERCISE: A LETTER HOME

Many of us have unresolved conflicts with our parents that we will never be able to sort out face-to-face. Perhaps our parents have died or are not available for one reason or another. Or perhaps the task of directly confronting our parents is simply too much for us to imagine. In such cases, as James Halpern points out, an alternate therapy is letter writing.

If your parents are alive and your letter is full of anger and bitterness, Halpern points out, there is certainly no need to send the letter. That's not going to help. The real purpose of this simple technique is to allow your emotions to surface. The act of writing your thoughts and feelings down, then reading them over and studying them, may be very helpful and instructive to you. The letter is for you.

Based on Halpern's technique, write a letter home. Whether your parents are still alive or not, write a long letter to either or both of them about everything that has bothered you or has made you happy in your relationship. Some of the things that come out may surprise you, but try not to hold anything back or hide any of your feelings from yourself.

A letter such as this can be especially helpful when you read it again a few days (or even months or years) later. Of course, it can be followed by others, and by letters to other family members.

While in his book *Projections* (Seaview/Putnam, 1983), Halpern addressed the problem of illusory relationships, in clinical practice he focuses more closely on actual family relationships. His particular approach is called family systems therapy.

Like other therapists who use this method, Halpern points out that "the blueprint for our relationships with our children, with our friends, our lovers, husbands, wives, or on the job, comes from the family of origin."

"So I send people back to their families," explains Halpern. Of course, there's a lot of prior planning involved. Before working out problems with family members, patients need to consider carefully potential snares and pitfalls, how this or that is likely to go wrong, and "how the interaction is likely to fall into the same rut" and how to avoid having that happen.

"If you can't talk to your mother or your father, or you're still furious with your father, that's going to come up in other relationships. If you work it out in the cauldron of the family, the rest is easy."

This process doesn't necessarily involve literal family confrontations. After all, it is sometimes impossible for patients actually to meet with family members and resolve difficult issues. In the case of many adult patients, parents may be dead. But the issues are essentially the same. The focus of therapy is to help clients find more satisfying relationships by resolving anger, roles, and expectations that arose from family relationships.

Halpern acknowledges the influence of Washington, D.C., therapist Murray Bowen, with whom he shares the conviction that "you don't have to get the whole family together in front of the therapist, but that the main work is still to have the person resolve the issues with the members of their family."

COMMENTARY

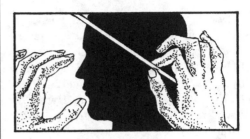

Conductor and Orchestra

"I liken the human mind to a symphony orchestra," says John Beahrs in *Unity and Multiplicity* (Brunner/Mazel, 1982, see sidebar on following page). He describes the healthy mind as a unity made up of many parts, "each with its own sense of selfhood, functioning together in a cooperative enterprise under the leadership of an executive, the conductor."

Many things can go wrong with an orchestra, he says: warfare between sections, exhaustion, a drunken conductor, others competing for leadership. Similar things might go wrong with the human mind.

The possibilities are endless, Beahrs says, but the treatment principles remain simple: do what allows each part to remain itself and still enhance the whole group—or Self. The conductor must be decisive, but respect the individual members.

RESOURCE

Drawing on his psychiatric experience in treating multiple personalities, therapist John Beahrs looks at multiplicity in the light of normal behavior, pathology, and hypnosis in *Unity and Multiplicity: Multilevel Consciousness of Self in Hypnosis, Psychiatric Disorder and Mental Health* (Brunner/Mazel, 1982).

He points out that, despite an increasing "burden of knowledge" in brain research and psychology, there are great gaps in our understanding of human behavior. Much psychological theory, Beahrs believes, is complicated by a failure to recognize the simple fact of multiplicity. When people seem to violate commonplace tenets of life, the likeliest reason is that the multiple selves are in conflict. Either two personalities are evenly matched, paralyzing action, or one may be sabotaging the efforts of another.

Beahrs, like many therapists who have worked with multiples, came to believe that a crowd of selves, even in normal people, is not a figure of speech but a reality.

In a very real way we may all be covert multiple personalities, Beahrs believes. Our obliviousness of these selves, not the multiplicity itself, is the problem. We defeat ourselves without knowing why.

Our component selves may have conflicting beliefs. The personality experiencing itself as "I" at the moment—the self in the driver's seat—can be unaware of information known to another subpersonality. That which we consider unconscious behavior may, in fact, be a conscious choice of one of the parts.

In Beahrs's theory of co-consciousness, the organizing self is not single in any absolute sense but is "a relatively unitary experience that lends us our sense of identity and direction."

Beahrs, who worked with hypnosis researcher Ernest Hilgard and the late Milton Erickson, has the hypnotherapist's perspective on the unconscious. Rather than a cauldron of fury crying for suppression, it is seen as "the source of all life and growth."

Multiplicity

Our relationships with others are vastly complicated by the fact that each of us is not really a singular and unified self. Each of us is many different people, coping daily with others who are just as varied and multiple as ourselves. As philosopher Daniel C. Dennett put it in *the jamais vu papers* (July 1988), "There are rather more biographies around than there are people."

The extraordinary phenomenon of multiple personality disorder may be only a dramatic—and tragic—overstatement of everyone's normal, waking condition. Each of us contains many different "selves" who take turns directing us through our lives. Living under the illusion that one is a unified, singular "self" may limit one's potential. How much better to become acquainted with our many selves and use the full energy of the team.

But there are other kinds of multiplicity. We may project illusory perceptions onto those around us, and consequently wind up living in imaginary relationships. It is crucial to be able to tell the real from the fancied in human interchanges—but often supremely difficult.

Harnessing the multiplicity of ourselves and those around us is a challenge indeed. We can start by identifying multiples inside ourselves and also by gaining a better understanding of our own projections onto the lives of others. A look at archetypes (mythic images some believe are common to all humans) can be helpful in grasping the vast multiplicity of human experience.

Multiple Personality Disorder

Multiple personality disorder is a *dissociative* condition—*dissociation* being defined in Funk and Wagnalls's *Standard College Dictionary* as "the process whereby a set of ideas, feelings, etc., loses most of its relationships with the rest of the personality, functioning somewhat independently."

In MPD cases, an individual manifests two or more different identities. One personality may take over the body during an interval of time, and the next one to assume control may not have any idea what actions and behaviors the body has acted out during that time period.

Bennett Braun is a Chicago psychiatrist in private practice. He is also on faculty at the Rush University department of psychiatry and at the University of Illinois, Chicago, department of psychology. In 1983, Braun told *Brain/Mind Bulletin* that during therapy, when patients relive their early traumatic experiences, striking physiological effects are often recreated.

Physical Changes

For example, one of Braun's female patients developed a red, raised region of skin when she was manifesting a child personality. She had had a hot iron pressed against her by her mother (also a sufferer from MPD), supposedly in an effort to teach her about "hot." Warned by her mother not to scratch the itching injury, she developed yet another personality to absorb the itch. The symptomatic area disappeared after therapy.

When another patient reexperienced her memories of family members' putting out cigarettes on her skin, her body showed red dots shaped like the end of a cigarette. The marks lasted up to ten hours after each therapy session and came back with the return of that personality.

In another case, the marks from a bullwhip—an early trauma—appeared with a specific personality.

The study of the psychophysiology of multiple personalities will probably change traditional views of medicine, he pointed out. If varying personalities in one body/mind have varying allergies, their responses to medications may also differ. They may be sensitive to a drug in one state and require large dosages in another. Because of the amnesia between personalities, it is easy for multiples to overdose.

RESOURCE

Bennett Braun edited *Treatment of Multiple Personality Disorder* (American Psychiatric Press, 1986), a collection of papers by Braun and numerous colleagues and experts, discussing the state of the art of psychiatry's understanding of MPD and its treatment.

In his own essay, "Issues in the Psychotherapy of Multiple Personality Disorder," Braun points out two distinguishing characteristics of MPD patients:

"1) an inborn biological/psychological capacity to dissociate that is ususally identified by excellent responsivity to hypnosis, and

"2) repeated exposure to an inconsistently stressful environment."

Child abuse is a common factor, particularly if the abuse is inexplicably mixed with affection. Writes Braun, "The child who has been abused starts to have pleasant and unpleasant memories of his or her parents. After continuous exposure to inconsistently abusive situations, the patient with dissociative capacity begins to file the memories of these traumatic events separately, and they begin to take on a life history of their own."

The Hidden Observer

As early as 1976, evidence for an intelligent "someone else" operating alongside normal consciousness came from the hypnosis laboratory of Ernest Hilgard, a noted Stanford University psychologist who discussed his research at a seminar at the Neuropsychiatric Institute at UCLA that year. He calls this parallel consciousness "the hidden observer."

Hilgard described his first encounter with the hidden observer for *Brain/Mind Bulletin*. "We first found the phenomenon in a young man—a blind subject who had achieved hypnotic deafness. At one point one of the students said, 'How do we *know* he isn't hearing anything?'

"So I asked him to raise his finger if he could hear what was being said. The finger went up. Then the subject said, 'Would you mind bringing me out so you can tell me what just happened—what caused my finger to lift?'

"I then told him that when I placed my hand on his head, I wanted to be in touch with the part of him that had lifted the finger. As soon as I placed my hand on his head, I was able to get from him descriptions of what had been said, how many times I had clapped the wooden blocks together, and so on. When I lifted my hand, he reverted to the earlier hypnotic state and said, 'The last thing I remember, you told me I would talk to you when you placed your hand on my head. Did I say anything?'

"We also learned from him that while the tests for hypnotic deafness had been going on, he was working on a statistical problem for another class. He had been dwelling on statistics when he felt his finger lift. As you can see, this indicates a truly parallel processing capability!"

Here are some remarkable examples:

• A male patient studied by Braun was allergic to citrus juices in all personalities but one. Switching personalities was as effective for him as taking an antihistamine.

• Seven of Braun's patients were examined by Chicago-area optometrist Kenneth Shepphard, who measured their vision as they switched personalities. He found "remarkable changes."

• Another patient of Braun's, severely allergic to cats, developed a rash, runny eyes, and bronchial congestion—except in one ego state, in which she could play with them for as long as she wished with no symptoms.

MPD patients also appear to have extreme fluctuations of pain thresholds. Most have headaches and symptoms that resemble those of migraine sufferers. A high percentage abuse alcohol, which may help them rationalize the mysterious gaps in their lives.

Self-hypnosis

MPD patients are unaware of the self-hypnosis that leads to the formation of multiple personality, Braun said. "Self-hypnotic trance may be the outward equivalent of putting in the clutch when shifting gears. It enables the individual to shift from one physiological state to another."

Because hypnosis offers the most efficient access to the various ego states, some skeptics say that suggestion, in fact, *creates* the phenomenon. Braun said that of the 23 cases he treated and the 59 he diagnosed between 1980 and late 1983, only four were hypnotized prior to diagnosis. "In some cases I waited for as long as three years to verify my suspicion. Now I use hypnosis when indicated—and save time."

Changes in MPD patients, Braun noted, are not as bizarre as they may seem if compared to the physiological shifts achieved in non-MPD subjects through hypnosis.

Fusion

How can MPD patients become unified? Braun explained that treatment, which may take years, usually starts when the therapist explains to the patient's personalities the nature of their mysterious amnesic episodes. Therapy for an MPD patient is automatically "group" therapy.

The therapist becomes the good, consistent parent the multiple never had. Most clinicians treat multiples with hypnosis for two reasons: they are easily hypnotizable and a simple hypnotic cue can become the access code for each personality.

As the therapist gathers histories from each personality, patterns emerge. If new personalities appear during treatment, the therapist tries to reintegrate them as quickly as appropriate and possible.

Most of the personalities resist this fusion into one self because they fear that they themselves will die. Ironically, sometimes multiples commit suicide because one of the personalities decides to kill another, not understanding that they share the same body.

The moment of fusion can be dramatic. When New York therapist Armand DiMele was attempting the final integration of one of his patients, the last personality—a holdout—became angry. "In her anger, she started to cry," DiMele told *Brain/Mind Bulletin* in 1983. "I knew then that we were going to make it. This personality had always been too tough to cry. If she could feel, the boundary was already broken."

After fusion, most adult multiples require about two years of therapy. During this time they gather up the scattered memories of their once-split selves.

Child Abuse and MPD

In an interview for *PragMagic,* Bennett Braun reiterated that the vast majority of multiple personality disorder patients began as child abuse cases—over 97% of the thousand-plus cases that have been studied to date. "The mind's ability to cope is overwhelmed by this abuse," Braun explains. "It just can't cope." The emergence of different personalities offers a means of coping.

"Females are more likely to be abused than males," he said. "In this particular population, and I'm not talking about the population as a whole, about 23% of females had incestuous relationships with their mothers. And so we find that more women are sexually abusing children than anybody thought."

As a hopeful development Braun cited the 1987 opening of the first unit specifically built and staffed for treatment of dissociative disorders at the Rush Presbyterian–St. Luke's Medical Center in Chicago, where treatment is a primary goal. Research and teaching are strong second-ary interests. "It's the only one of its

COMMENTARY

Ernest Hilgard told *Brain/Mind Bulletin* in 1976 that multiple personalities are probably more common than has been believed.

"In the days when hypnosis was popular, before psychoanalysis, multiple personality seemed more prevalent because people looked for it. Psychoanalysis has not been particularly friendly to aspects of multiple personality. If a person went off in that direction, it was the analyst's responsibility to bring him back immediately.

"It may be that now—with so many people looking within—aspects of multiple personality are emerging more often. Certainly we all have multiple *sides*. It's easy to divide the personality in hypnosis, to give each part a name, and get them to converse. This can be dangerous. You have to be very careful not to *produce* a multiple personality.

"As Erik Erikson has said, our personalities include many identifications from childhood. Usually, in the true cases of multiple personality, you find that the individual has been unable to join together these fragments of identity. A child who is cruelly treated and can't identify with a parent may transfer that identification to a grandparent or other adult; then the grandparent dies or leaves. These kids can't achieve a consistent identity."

EXERCISE: EVERYDAY MULTIPLICITY

Multiplicity affects even those of us who do *not* suffer from multiple personality disorder. Who among us can claim to be a single, unified person? Each of us contains a "cast of characters," so to speak. Consider these common examples of routine multiplicity:

- Did you ever write a seemingly crucial and insightful memo to yourself, only to read it later on and have it make no sense whatsoever?

- Did you ever enthusiastically make a commitment—perhaps to attend a social get-together or lend somebody money—only to regret your commitment a day or two later?

- Did you ever excitedly purchase something only to consider your purchase a waste of money soon afterward?

- Did you ever write and mail someone a letter, then almost immediately wish you could take it back?

Doubtless, you can think of many examples like the ones above. We usually respond to such situations by asking ourselves, "Why did I do that?" But we might just as easily ask, *"Who did that? It couldn't have been me!"* These are moments when we eerily suspect that we are not altogether alone in the seeming privacy of our own minds. Consider these other common forms of multiplicity:

- Is the "you" which has a cup of coffee in the morning a different person from the "you" which has not?

- Are you a different "you" among strangers than among friends or family?

- Is the worried "you" a different person from the carefree "you"?

- Is the "you" which has had a few cocktails at a party a different person from the sober, workday "you"?

"I'm not myself today," goes the old cliché. But like all clichés, it contains more than an element of truth.

kind in the world," says Braun. This center is a particularly remarkable accomplishment, due to the limited funding for research in this area.

What Does MPD Mean to Us?

What are the implications of multiple personality disorder in all our lives? Braun points out that "multiple personality represents a fascinating natural laboratory to look at psychophysiological interactions—in particular, psychosomatic medicine," citing such remarkable physiological occurrences as changes in eye color, insulin requirements, and blood pressure among different personalities.

The lessons may also include the vastness of human possibility. "Multiples may be the most important route to understanding and gaining access to the untapped skills and potential we all have," Brendan O'Regan, vice president for research of the Institute of Noetic Sciences in San Francisco told *Brain/Mind Bulletin*. O'Regan quotes the Portuguese poet Fernando Pessoa: *In every corner of my soul there is an altar to a different god.*

"Through sensitive study of multiples," O'Regan said, "maybe we can learn to light the candles on all of those altars. Maybe we can learn to unify minds that are split and expand to their full potential those that seem limited."

The Dreaming Multiple

When we dream, who does the dreaming? Is it a separate personality? New York psychotherapist Armand DiMele told *Brain/Mind Bulletin* of a discovery he made while treating a patient whose previous multiple personalities were now fused. "She had been having nightmares. I was concerned that a new personality might be forming ... so I hypnotized her and asked to talk to the sleeping self.

"Then I tried to fuse the sleeping personality with the waking one. Later the client called, almost in desperation. She couldn't sleep at all!"

As an experiment he hypnotized a non-MPD subject and attempted to fuse the waking and sleeping personalities. Again, the result was profound insomnia.

Then DiMele called on the sleeping personality of the former MPD patient. The sleeper explained that it is, in fact, present during normal consciousness, but in a half-asleep state. It does not look through the eyes but "sees in darkness."

*Just as we tend to assume
that the world is as we see it,
we naively suppose that
people are as we imagine
them to be.*
*In this way everyone creates
a series of imaginary
relationships based
essentially on projection.*

—C. G. Jung
"General Aspects of Dream Psychology"
in *The Collected Works of C. G. Jung*
(Princeton University Press, 1954–79),
quoted in *Projections*

The idea of the sleeper as a distinct personality may make sense in terms of a phenomenon sometimes reported by those in the reverie between sleeping and waking: a remembered continuity of dream life, including people and places familiar only during sleep. "This possibility raises other interesting questions," DiMele said. "Does it make sense to interpret dreams as if they belong to the waking personality? They may, in fact, belong to another order of consciousness."

Projections

Why are we deeply disturbed by some people who have unpleasant qualities and much less bothered by others? Why is it that some people are not particularly upset by problems or weaknesses in others?

Psychologist James Halpern and anthropologist Ilsa Halpern say that "the answer lies in the fact that we are most affected—irritated or fascinated—by people who exhibit those very qualities we too possess, whether or not we are aware of it." In their book, *Projections: Our World of Imaginary Relationships* (Seaview/Putnam, 1983), the Halperns define projection as "the blurred perception of another person that arises because we are seeing an aspect of ourselves rather than the other."

Projection is not abnormal or disturbed except when it is carried to an extreme. It is part of our daily lives. But if we are not aware of our tendency to project attributes on others, we may have repeated problems in our relationships.

The Halperns discuss three levels of projection:

• *Parallel projection,* the most superficial level, in which we tend to see others as we see ourselves.

• *Unconscious projection,* which corresponds to Freud's ideas, means both the repression of one's own painful or unacceptable feelings, and seeing those feelings in others.

• *Mythic projection,* related to Carl Jung's theory of psychology, involves our projection of powerful archetypal images onto others.

Parallel Projections

We use parallel projection to make the world seem less threatening. We feel more comfortable when we can assume that those we meet have similar needs, interests, or emotional responses to life. We also use parallel projection to defend ourselves. For example, if we cheat on taxes, we like to believe that everyone does it—or at least, wants to do the same thing. We feel that we aren't so bad if we're just like everyone else.

A common case of parallel projection can occur when a parent assumes that a child is "a chip off the old block." Sometimes this turns into an expectation that the child will desire the same career or lifestyle as the parent, regardless of what the individual child actually wants.

Parallel projection is, of course, also found in romantic relationships. Lovers often believe they have discovered someone who thinks and feels just like they do, who wants all the same things from life. Later, the lover may be shocked to discover another quite separate human being, who has many desires different from the lover's own.

Unconscious Projection

Unconscious projection arises out of a habit of repression—the denial of something in ourselves. We can use up a lot of energy in an effort to protect ourselves from things we don't want to face. In extreme cases, defined as paranoia, a person might avoid self-criticism but imagine severe and constant criticism coming from others.

The Halperns say that one tragic result of a parent's projecting unconscious material on a child can be child abuse. Parents, often under severe stress, may want to be taken care of, to be parented, to be children themselves. They have unrealistic expectations of the child and unexamined resentments. They strike out at what seems to them to be the cause of their own distress.

In love relationships we may unconsciously project a parental image on our partner. We may look for a mate who is just like a parent, or one who is just the opposite. In either case, the projection obscures the real person.

Myths and Archetypes

Jung believed that we will project our own mythic "shadow" side on the world when we are not conscious of it in ourselves. Although people have difficulty acknowledging any evil in themselves, those who are unaware of their shadow sides will have difficulty understanding and accepting themselves and, therefore, a hard time understanding and accepting others. Such people lack the humility and tolerance so necessary for human relationships

---

RESOURCE

Part of our diversity may be based on certain innate archetypes. In *The Hero Within: Six Archetypes We Live By* (Harper & Row, 1989), Carol Pearson maintains that we perceive the world from within the the roles we play. Pearson lists the six that have the greatest influence on our development and growth: Innocent, Orphan, Martyr, Wanderer, Warrior, and Magician.

We live out heroic adventures as we move from one of these archetypes to another. Each archetype offers its share of opportunities for growth and evolution, and its limitations and pitfalls as well.

The Innocent lives in a nourishing, Edenic state, which inevitably gives way to worldly disillusionment. At this point, the Orphan—the archetypal "disappointed idealist"—appears, looking desperately for easy solutions and the "quick fix." If one doesn't become perpetually stuck in this mode, one of two archetypes is likely to take over: the Wanderer or the Warrior. The Wanderer may seem cowardly in trying to escape the world's problems, but also courageous in facing the unknown alone. The Warrior, of course, stays and fights things out—but may really be only the Orphan in disguise, "covering fear with bravado."

At some point, the Martyr is likely to surface. The Martyr must learn "to distinguish between transformative sacrifice and mere suffering caused because we are too cowardly or too unimaginative to think of a more joyous way to live."

The culminating archetype is the Magician—whom Pearson insists we all really are, and must discover that we are by means of the hero's journey. The Magician, she says, realizes that the universe is in the process of being constantly created and that we are involved in that creation.

INVENTORY: THE WORLD OF PROJECTIONS

In *Projections: Our World of Imaginary Relationships* (Seaview/Putnam, 1983) James and Ilsa Halpern give some clues for recognizing projections, although they say there are no foolproof answers. The degree of our own obsession or irritation is one indicator. They also suggest checking our reactions against those of friends to see if we are overreacting to someone. The following inventory is excerpted from their "thumbnail sketches to assist the reader in recognizing projections."

Parents and Children

Do you overestimate the similarities between yourself and your child? Are you able to see *differences* between you? What are the differences? If you cannot clearly articulate the differences, you may be using parallel projection.

Can you acknowledge that there is conflict between yourself and your spouse? If everything in the family seems wonderful except for one troublesome child, he is probably being scapegoated. He is likely to be receiving unconscious projections from the whole family.

Can you see weaknesses in your child? If you are overwhelmed and speechless by his beauty and brilliance and cannot speak about anything else other than your child's miraculous accomplishments, you may be projecting the mythic magical child.

Couples

When a couple relationship is formed, one of the first projections to break down is parallel. If you live with a person, it is almost impossible not to recognize differences after a short time. If you meet someone and believe that you are of one soul and one mind, you are using parallel projection.

During periods of stress, do you find yourself getting angry with your partner? When you are under pressure, do you look to your partner to anticipate your needs or your moods? It is often under these circumstances that we project parental images onto our mates, expecting them to take care of us and feeling angry or disappointed when they refuse to contain this projection. . . .

When we can find no specific reasons for why we feel "head over heels in love" with someone, projection of the animus (dream boy) or anima (dream girl) is often operating. If our world feels magical, if our lover seems too good to be true—he probably is. The feeling of unreality is quite accurate.

On the Job

Do you feel a spirit of comradeship with your coworkers? Do you feel that your relationships with your peers at work are the most satisfying aspect of your job? Do you think that they would support you if you were in trouble, just as you would support them? This is a sign of parallel projection.

Does your boss always make you uncomfortable? Do you see him consistently as extremely impressive and as knowing what is best for you, your coworkers, the company? . . . On the other hand, are you usually angry or dissatisfied with the boss? These reactions are triggered by the projection of parental images.

Is there someone at work who really annoys you? Has there always been someone at work you find irritating? . . . If such a person leaves or is fired, does another extremely annoying person emerge to make your life miserable? These are all indications that the shadow is being projected.

and growth. According to the Halperns, "If we are unconscious of the shadow, we will see it in our neighbor, or in communists, capitalists, blacks, or Jews. We may take drastic action to destroy this evil."

They point out that we may also project certain mythic images that seem to be common to humans in all cultures. Jung called these the archetypes of the collective unconscious. Such images, found in dreams, myths, religions, fairy tales, and the arts, include the hero, the savior, the trickster, the wise old man, the dream boy (animus), and dream girl (anima).

Parents who have lost their own childlike nature may project the myth of "the magical child" on a real child. Their conviction that their child is wonderful and special may give the child self-confidence and self-esteem. But, the Halperns remind us, "there is a real danger that children who are seen as small gods may simply be spoiled."

We tend to project our internal image of a dream boy or dream girl on our lovers. These archetypes generally include positive characteristics that we have never actualized in ourselves—representing our own undeveloped potentials. Our longing for another, the Halperns say, "may symbolize our desire for wholeness and completion."

And similarly, we may assign roles to people at work who seem to be like ourselves, or to fit our internal images of father or hero. Or the nurturing, protective, powerful boss may become a mother figure to her younger protégé.

We can become quite emotionally involved with celebrities we identify with unconscious or mythic images. This includes politicians as well as entertainers and athletes. Indeed, the Halperns say that "beyond our intellectual interest in politics and other world events, we have an interest in and fascination with political figures because they are good targets for the projection of two basic and important mythic images—the hero and the shadow." Well-known figures often retain popularity exactly because they learn to play the roles we project on them.

Recognizing Projections

Cynicism is an important first step in recognizing our projections—but it is not the final one, according to the Halperns. Cynicism can be based in our desire to break down our illusions, to see people clearly. We become skeptical of our own heros and of the claims that others

(Continued on page 104)

COMMENTARY

Our Future Selves

Our *future selves* constitute another kind of multiplicity. We should never stop asking ourselves that primal childhood question: "What do I want to be when I grow up?" It's a question that keeps the future alive and flexible.

Obviously, we have many future selves to choose from—selves that make different choices along the way, and consequently become, in a sense, different human beings. Thinking ahead to a year from now, how is the self who asks for a raise going to be different from the one who does not?

In an interview for *PragMagic*, movement psychologist Stuart Heller pointed out one of the most obvious difficulties of choosing one's future self and attempting to become it: *The self you want to become may not have the same past as you do now.* Your desired self may have had different educational or career opportunities, have been in different relationships, have made different decisions along the way. It is likely that this desired self has not made the same mistakes you have made.

"That person," explains Heller, "could not have a lot of my past, because my past would not extrapolate into that future."

How do we keep the fact of our past from limiting our future possibilities? How do we become the future self we want to be? "I look at the question of what kind of past that person would have had, to lead to that future," says Heller. "Then I begin to practice my new history."

In other words, by behaving *as if* you had the same past as the person you wish to become, you gain a certain psychological advantage.

EXERCISE: AS OTHERS SEE YOU

Each of us is somebody else's fiction.   These fictions are everywhere. Each person you know can be said to perceive a different "you." There is a risk in not paying enough attention to these "other yous" and your actual relationship to them—a risk of losing part of your freedom and identity.

Quickly bring an acquaintance to mind. You may gain the most dramatic insights from thinking about someone you don't know very well, whose information concerning you may not be as complete as that of an intimate friend. Make a list of the preconceptions you believe this person holds about you, along the following lines:

• What faults does this person think you possess?

_____
_____
_____
_____

• What virtues does this person think you possess?

_____
_____
_____
_____

• What likes, desires, and dreams do you think this person would ascribe to you?

_____
_____
_____
_____

• What dislikes, aversions, and fears do you think this person would ascribe to you?

_____
_____
_____
_____

• How would this person sum you up as a human being, if describing you to somebody else?

_____
_____
_____
_____

EXERCISE, continued

At this point, stop and consider *your points of disagreement* with the person—whether they concern favorable or unfavorable perceptions.

• In what ways do you think your acquaintance is mistaken about you?

_____
_____
_____
_____
_____
_____
_____
_____
_____
_____

• How do you think your acquaintance came by this faulty understanding?

_____
_____
_____
_____
_____
_____
_____
_____
_____
_____

From this information, you can get some idea of the differences between the "you" this other person believes in, and the "you" that you, yourself, perceive. Whatever your own feelings about the matter, both "yous" are quite real, each in their own way; the perceptions other people hold about you can affect your life in very tangible ways, regardless of what you believe about yourself.

Also consider this: In the act of doing this exercise, you may have contributed to making a fiction out of your *acquaintance*. Would your acquaintance agree or disagree with the guesses you have made?

To some degree we are constantly creating fictions about ourselves. Sometimes other people's information about us may be more reliable than our own. Did you gain any surprising insights, any new points of information about *yourself* as a result of considering other people's observations of you? Our interpersonal fictions are literally inescapable, and demand a close look.

*The routine of our daily work
has too often served as
deep, dumb, deaf sleep,
a refuge from two of life's
most crucial states of being—
keen awakedness to the
needs of others and
equal awakedness to the
transcendent, which only
comes in some state of
loitering, dallying, tarrying,
goofing off.*

—Francine du Plessix Gray
"In Praise of Idleness"
Harper's, April 1990

make about themselves, about their magical children and perfect parents and lovers.

But there is more to dissolving projections than that. What we see in others may be illusions, but their effects on us are very real. If we do not recognize the images that we project, skepticism alone will not prevent us from continuing to find new candidates for the roles we have created.

Learning to recognize the hidden images and feelings in ourselves can be hard work, but it is only when we get to know our projections that we can see beyond them. Then we can begin to respond to something more real in the people we meet. The unpleasant projections can dissolve and we can own and participate in the desirable ones instead of attaching them only to other people.

How can we tell, then, when we are projecting something on others or seeing what is really there? It is through interaction with others, rather than isolation, that we are able to work through to this kind of self-realization. James and Ilsa Halpern, like Jung, say to be on guard for moments when someone seems to cause the most intense emotional reactions in us. That's when we should ask whether we are actually responding to that other person or to something in ourselves.

Working

One of the most intriguing relationships we have is our relationship to our work. We may even choose to think of our work as a living entity, with whom we contend and communicate daily.

And of course, work can be a setting for other relationships. For many of us, our workplace is one of our main sources of interactions with other people. We meet people who are not family and might never become friends, but we must cooperate with them to get the job done.

In the workplace, we will need to give consideration to our projections and our many selves just as in any other relationship. In the last section, we listed several workaday symptoms (such as projecting the role of mother or father on a boss or coworker) which James and Ilsa Halpern warned could indicate problems arising from our own projections.

In assessing our relationship with our work, it is important to consider our relationship with success. Are we fond of success? Do we invite it? Or do we display a fear of success that holds us back from our full potential? How motivated are we as workers? If we seem super-motivated, is it sincere and productive, or neurotic and compulsive? Is there really such a thing as a workaholic?

Whether we have a job or not, each of us is part of a larger organization—in our families and society as a whole. As members of families and small groups, we can often benefit from some of the lessons learned in the workplace.

Fear of Success

What is "fear of success"? Where does it come from? What are its consequences? Katherine Garner of New York University, Peter Gumpert of the University of Massachusetts, and Donnah Canavan of Boston College presented experimental reports at a symposium on the neurotic fear of success at a 1978 meeting of the American Psychological Association.

They said that a person who seems to fear success is actually ambivalent about succeeding. Success-fearers are not exactly self-destructive; they don't do things that guarantee failure. A success-fearing individual draws back from the brink of success, but does not want to fail, either, and will work hard if it appears that failure is uncomfortably close. He or she wants to be good but not *too* good. Paradoxically, the success-fearer has an exaggerated sense of competition.

Fear of success is as prevalent among men as women, and it has been demonstrated in children. The syndrome seems to begin in family relationships. Psychologists say it may begin when a child reaching out for mastery and independence repeatedly gets negative reactions from a parent. Then a sensitive child may become anxious whenever mastery appears at hand.

RESOURCES

The Success-Fearing Personality by Donnah Canavan, Katherine Garner, and Peter Gumpert (Lexington Books, 1978) is a study of a phenomenon the authors say is surprisingly widespread: the neurotic fear of success.

In *Fear of Success* (Lexington Books, 1990), Donnah Canavan gives an overview, up-to-date research data, and implications for future research on the problem.

Canavan gives the following examples of typical success fearers:

• One student who had been evaluated as doing poorly in a Ph.D. program got the top grade on her qualifying exams. But then she left all the copies of her dissertation in an elegant briefcase in an unlocked car—and lost them to a thief. "The student was shocked that anyone could have been so cruel as to steal all the copies of her dissertation. She simply did not see that she had virtually invited the theft of the briefcase, which from the thief's point of view happened to be stuffed with paper."

• A dieter successfully lost all the pounds she needed to lose in order to fit into her ideal-size jeans. But when she could just close the zipper, "she was inexplicably seized by an uncontrollable desire to raid the local bakery."

RESEARCH

Work Environment and Stress

Psychologist Margaret Chesney reported a clue to job stress in a 1983 issue of *SRI Journal*. The ideal work environment for certain individuals may be a drastic mismatch for other people. Stress on the job may mean one thing to some managers and another to others. People trying to reduce workplace health risks cannot rely on single solutions.

Researchers at SRI International were seeking the risk factors of heart disease, the nation's number one killer. High blood pressure, cholesterol, and smoking had been firmly established. However, even when all these are taken together, along with a family history of the problem, fewer than half of the cases can be predicted.

In a study of 400 "Silicon Valley" managers, Chesney and her team at the Menlo Park, California, think tank discovered that neither physiological risk factors such as high blood pressure or heart rate, nor the nature of specific jobs, were sufficient alone to explain risk. Rather, the combined fit of individual style with environmental demands determined the outcome.

For example, Type A managers—known to be more competitive and high-strung—prefer autonomy on the job. In an environment that encourages independence, they are less at risk than others, as evidenced by lower blood pressure.

Type B people on the other hand prefer structure. They showed higher blood pressure when given greater independence.

The researchers also reported in *The Success-Fearing Personality* (Lexington Books, 1978) on studies of the behavior of parents of success-fearing children.

In one case, children were attempting to make words from larger words. The parents of success-fearing children tried to "help" their children more than other parents, as if they did not trust the child's ability.

"When the child had stopped actively making words and seemed stuck, he or she may have been thinking of additional ways in which words could be made with the letters available. Thus the parent's verbal or nonverbal hints probably interfered with the child's thinking . . . and made it seem that the parent's thoughts about the task were richer, more useful or more important than those of the child."

Overall, the experiments suggested that a parent's *actions,* rather than intentions, lead the child to feel that the parent is not comfortable with the child's attempts to do well without help. And at the same time the child sees that the parent considers the task important. So, it must be done well—but it is dangerous to do it on one's own. The anxiety that results becomes a lifelong, unconscious pattern. It arises whenever the person is thrust into a situation where independence or mastery are important.

Response to Praise

Canavan, Garner, and Gumpert discussed results showing that, in interactions with coworkers, success-fearers do not respond the same as those who had no such fear. For example, research has shown that success-fearers do not respond the same as control subjects when they are given randomly determined positive or negative feedback. For those *without* fear of success, performance improved when they were given positive feedback or told their performance was average. If they were told they had done poorly, their subsequent performance worsened.

Typically, if success-fearers were told they had done well, their performance worsened. If they got "failure feedback" or "average feedback," they improved. This was confirmed in experiments with elementary-age children, high school students, and college students. The fearing and nonfearing groups were identified by means of questionnaires based on identified traits of success-fearers.

Success-fearers may work hard for success from a safe distance, but become anxious and sabotage their own performance whenever it appears that they may actually be successful.

According to the researchers, when the success-fearer is progressing well, "he is likely to belittle himself and create in his imagination a great chasm between himself and his competitors. He rejects favorable information as flattery or as produced by chance."

If he makes good progress, he refuses to concede that he is anything near a success, yet reverses cause him exaggerated fear. Success-fearers "have strong motives both to succeed and not to succeed." Their ambivalence usually relates to a sense of competition with persons important in their lives.

Commitment and Workaholism

Why is it that some people are enthusiastic about their work and others are not? How does a company find highly motivated workers or manage to motivate the ones already employed? Is the person who has an overpowering drive to achieve a "workaholic," whose behavior is damaging to health and relationships, or is he or she a gift to society? Is "workaholic" an unfair description of those who thrive on their work as Marilyn Machlowitz believes (see sidebar)? In 1980, *Leading Edge Bulletin* reported on the opinions of several business consultants about workaholism and motivation.

According to Christopher Hegarty, a California business consultant and nationally recognized authority on job stress, workaholism is a neurotic relationship with a job.

Hegarty said that "a highly motivated worker works out of a sense of commitment. For many there is a certain form of joy that can only come from hard, productive, risk-taking labor." Where the healthy motivated worker is committed, Hegarty pointed out, the workaholic has a compulsive sense of duty.

Long hours and hard work do not make a workaholic, Hegarty said. "It's the anxiety and stress the person attaches to a job that determines whether you're a workaholic." Workaholics "appear to be busy every moment, but actually they're often nonproductive. They're running away from a massive fear of failure."

RESOURCES

In *Workaholics: Working With Them, Living With Them* (Addison-Wesley, 1980), Marilyn Machlowitz comments, "Workaholics love their work. They live their work. Contrary to the stereotype, the workaholic need not be narrow, negative or tyrannical, but someone with a zest for work that spills over into other areas."

Anne Wilson Schaef and Diane Fassel say in *The Addictive Organization* (Harper & Row, 1988) that behavioral addictions affect companies and the people who work for them.

John D. Adams, editor, designed *Transforming Work: A Collection of Organizational Transformation Readings* (Miles River Press, 1984) to illuminate the burgeoning interest in Organizational Transformation—as opposed to the Organization Development of the 1960s. To compare the two, Adams draws on a Ken Wilber metaphor: "He likens translation (development) to moving the furniture around on the floor and transformation to moving the furniture to a new floor." The essays are wide-ranging and thoughtful.

T. G. I. M.: Making Your Work Fulfilling and Finding Fulfilling Work is by Charles Cameron and Suzanne Elusorr (J. P. Tarcher, 1986). T.G.I.M. stands for "Thank God It's Monday." Cameron and Elusorr cover the full range of needs, desires, and dreams of anyone looking for satisfaction in the workplace—including the delicate and elusive business of "underwriting your true work."

The Joy of Working: The 30 Day System to Success, Wealth, & Happiness on the Job, by Denis Waitley and Reni L. Witt (Dodd, Mead, 1985), is an attitude-lifter and self-described "do-it-yourself daily life guide." Upbeat and inspirational.

RESEARCH

Work Spirit

Sherrie Connelly, an Arlington, Virginia, business consultant, spent several years interviewing people about their experience of meaningful work. She presented her findings at a 1983 New Hampshire conference on organization transformation.

Connelly described a quality she calls "work spirit"—the subjective experience of "Everything goes right!"

She cited, as an example, her first meeting with conference organizers Frank Burns and Harrison Owen:

"Harrison was hurriedly feeding conference brochures into a postage machine. Frank was pushing them rhythmically into a mailbag. No difficult task, of course, but both of them were smiling as their movements merged into one continuous aesthetic act."

Experiences of work spirit reveal in the actors a high degree of focus or unity of direction. They are typified by:

• A driving focus or ordering principle
• A feeling of contribution
• An element of risk or challenge
• A sense of not knowing—but knowing that things will turn out well
• A sense of destiny—of doing the work one is meant to do

Connelly believes that peak performance akin to that of athletes can be fostered in organizations.

Where is the boundary between work and play? Do managers have a milder sense of work spirit than entrepreneurs? Can it be used for team-building?

"I hope to gain a better understanding of joy in work and the potential contribution of work spirit to formal organizations," she said.

Commitment to Work

Other psychologists defined the hard worker differently. Psychologist Eugene Jennings of Michigan State University, an advisor to blue-chip corporations, said that those we call "workaholics" carry the load in American business. "They are the achievers, the excellers."

Others don't like them, he said, because they have no time for cocktails and small talk, and so they "make us feel we're not as good." He added, "We're not."

Studies show that highly motivated workers generally blur the distinction between work and pleasure. If it is true that superworkers are motivated by enjoyment of their role, then the real problem of business is finding ways to transfer this kind of commitment to other employees.

Ron Medved of the Pacific Institute, a Seattle-based training organization, observed that "commitment is tied to decision-making. The executives, as the decision-makers, have all the 'goodies' in a motivational sense. There is supernutrition at the top of the hierarchy and malnutrition at the bottom."

The whole issue, Medved said, is complicated by the fact that we all grew up in hierarchies. So many of our familiar relationships—families, schools, the military, companies—all are structured like pyramids. "Life is all about arriving at the pinnacle. Now men and women who have worked all their lives to acquire power and prestige are being asked to share it. It's called participatory management—and while it's difficult for some, it works."

He listed some options which companies use so that employees can take part in decision-making:

• Flextime, which allows workers a choice of hours, common in Europe and now used by hundreds of American companies and government agencies
• Companies in which employees help design their jobs and work in teams
• Workers voting on pay raises for each other
• Workers and managers forming nonhierarchical "quality circles" to identify and solve production-line problems

4.
LEARNING MAGIC:
Sharpening Our Wits

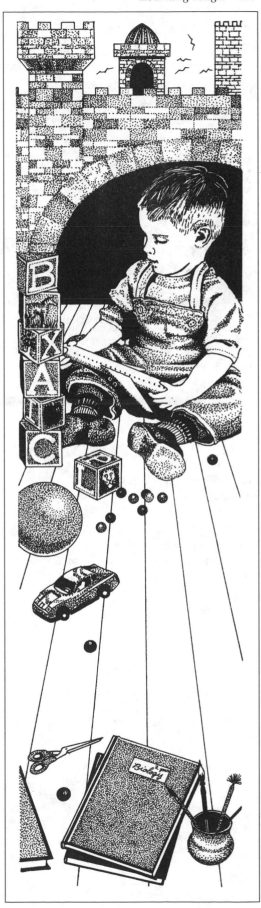

You are likely to have heard the news that the Industrial Age has come to an end and the Information Age has begun. What does this mean to us as learners—and as teachers? Does it simply mean that there's a lot more information and more knowledge to be taken in and processed in the same old ways?

Quite the contrary. Learning itself has become a very different commodity than it was before. We're rapidly learning more and more about learning itself. Intelligence is proving not to be the fixed, unchanging entity we always thought. "Wrong answers" are taking a more exalted place in the learning process. Teaching methods such as Suggestology have demonstrated the role of relaxation in learning. And neuroscience is painting a picture of learning as a tremendously fluid process.

What is thinking? What is intelligence? How do we "learn to learn"? These questions are being tackled from a variety of perspectives—by teachers, educational researchers, philosophers, brain researchers, and social critics.

In this section, you will find information to help you deal with such questions and ideas as:

• new definitions of intelligence, and the limitations of "IQ" as a test of intelligence

• efforts to enhance learning, here and abroad

• how we learn—and how we *learn* to learn

• how your determination to learn may be more important than innate intelligence

• what multiple-choice testing may really tell you about yourself

Rewards Help Kids Raise Scores on IQ Tests

Some children gained as much as 14 points on an IQ test when they were promised rewards for improved scores, Margaret Lloyd and Theresa Zylla of Drake University said in *Psychological Reports* (63). Their work was reported by *Brain/Mind Bulletin* in 1989.

The researchers divided preschool children who had taken an initial IQ test into high- and low-scoring groups. Half of each group was then randomly assigned to receive tokens—redeemable for prizes—for correct answers on a second, equally difficult test.

Those who were promised tokens for correct answers on the follow-up IQ test four weeks later did considerably better than children of apparently equal ability who were not rewarded.

Both high and low scorers who received tokens performed better than the children who did not. Among the low scorers, all eight who were given tokens improved their scores, whereas only three nontoken children did.

Half of the token-rewarded high-scoring children did better the second time. Their gains far outweighed the small declines of others. By contrast, improvement was measured in only one of eight children who did not get tokens.

- how you "think about thinking" early in life
- alternative learning techniques
- what brain research can tell us about learning
- how to enhance your memory
- how to cultivate a "beginner's mind"

Both research and experience suggest that learning and teaching aren't separate processes at all, but part of the same continuum. Most of our lives, we are doing both. The arrival of the Information Age might seem very threatening if it were not for this thrilling influx of information about learning itself.

Intelligence

Most of us have been faced with the long-enduring mystique of the IQ score. Perhaps we took IQ tests as children and grew up with the understanding that our childhood scores reflected fixed and unchanging measures of innate intelligence. Intelligence has long been regarded as something that can be tested and measured in terms of an "intelligence quotient."

IQ scores have proved to be somewhat reliable in predicting how well a student will do in school, and so we tend to equate IQ with learning ability. But IQ scores have serious limitations. For example, racial and cultural differences can make standard intelligence tests unreliable.

Perhaps we should follow the lead of innovators around the world who seek to *enhance* intelligence rather than just break it down into components of measure.

Intelligence Testing

At a 1987 convention of the American Psychological Association, intelligence theorist Robert Sternberg of Yale University said that tests usually account for "between 5 and 25% of the variance in scholastic performance—rarely more." Yet, he noted, "school administrators and teachers sometimes fail to recognize just how limited the validities of the tests are."

Sternberg identified criteria for intelligence testing that might make the practice more worthwhile. These include a reformulation of the basic theories of intelligence along with an increased emphasis on practicality, ability to cope with novelty, and creative thinking.

In the premier issue of the journal *Questioning Exchange* (1987), Sternberg wrote: "In requiring only the answering of questions, IQ tests are missing a vital half of intelligence—the *asking* of questions."

Cultural Differences and IQ

"Psychologists should stop saying that IQ tests measure intelligence," J. R. Flynn of the University of Otago in New Zealand told *Brain/Mind Bulletin* in 1987. "They should say they measure an abstract problem-solving ability that sometimes correlates with intelligence. Within homogeneous groups, the correlation is high, but between groups, it can actually be negative."

He said that there can be no measure of real intelligence on an isolated basis, without accounting for factors such as motivation, cultural context, values and incentives, or group and environmental characteristics.

"This is not to suggest we cannot test for something with a high correlation to intelligence," Flynn added. But he pointed out that current IQ tests are only useful within homogeneous groups with shared living and learning experiences.

Flynn described his "lively correspondence" with Arthur Jensen, a proponent of the idea that blacks have inherently lower IQs than whites. "Jensen admits that IQ comparisons cannot be made between generations," he said. Flynn maintains that cultural distance, even more than the mere passage of time, makes the comparison of scores useless.

COMMENTARY

Predicting Infants' Intelligence

Marc Bornstein of New York University and Marian Sigman of UCLA reported in *Child Development* (57) and *Proceedings of the National Academy of Science* (82) that, by observing a four-month-old baby, the child's intelligence at age four can be predicted with moderate success. This is based on two factors:

• Visual and auditory attention, which indicates how quickly the baby becomes interested in a new object and then loses interest

• The time the mother spends pointing out objects and events in the environment

Attention seems to represent speed of information processing. How quickly does a baby notice something new in the environment and how quickly does it move on?

Babies who show efficient attention also tend to prefer complexity, to explore their environments rapidly, and to play in sophisticated ways.

The researchers say that attention may, in fact, reflect an innate drive rather than general intelligence. The alert child is driven to explore new environments, which may affect the testing situation. "The child with strong motivation to explore . . . and to perform during testing might persist longer during learning situations and intelligence assessment."

This drive or motivation may also reflect the mother's level of interest. Mothers' behavior in calling attention to the environment tends to be consistent over time, which could account for a steady unfolding of intelligence.

Brain/Mind Bulletin reported on the research in 1987.

Outgrowing Low IQ

The effects of childhood deprivation on intelligence may not be as irreversible as many have believed, according to a 1982 report by Norwegian researcher Dagmund Svendsen in the *Journal of Child Psychology and Psychiatry* (1).

Brain/Mind Bulletin reported on the research in 1982.

A study of 28 Norwegian students who had gone to schools for the educable mentally retarded revealed that they had made significant gains in IQ between childhood and 27–33 years of age. More than one-third were no longer considered retarded.

Interestingly, those who ceased to be retarded as adults had experienced the most serious problems in childhood, including alcoholic or criminal parents, an unwed mother, severe neglect, or an institutional upbringing. Only those who had experienced few or no such problems as children declined in IQ.

The study supports a growing body of evidence that "adverse living conditions in childhood do not set unalterable limits on human development," Svendsen said.

IQ and Intelligence

In 1987, Flynn reported in the *Psychological Bulletin* that test results from 14 nations indicated massive overall IQ gains, ranging from 5 to 25 points in a single generation. However, after careful analysis of the tests and scores, he concluded that IQ tests do not really measure intelligence.

Flynn argued that "IQ differences between groups cannot be equated with intelligence differences." Norwegian data—like American data—was contradictory, indicating that IQ could go up while academic achievement went down. Dutch data suggested the existence of unknown environmental factors "so potent that they account for 15 of the 20 points gained."

Flynn also pointed out that the very large body of literature contrasting IQ between Asians and Occidentals demonstrates the futility of many cross-cultural comparisons. While IQ scores for Japanese Americans and Chinese Americans are often lower than their white counterparts, Americans of Asian descent outperform and outachieve their peers in all other indices of intelligence in the "real world."

A study by Hiroshi Azuma of Shirayuri College in Tokyo, reported in *Japanese Psychological Research* (29), revealed major differences in how Japanese and Americans define intelligence. The research was reported in a 1987 issue of *Brain/Mind Bulletin*.

Male and female college students and mothers of the female students were asked to choose among 67 items to determine what they considered to be the qualities of an intelligent person. Azuma concluded that Japanese associate "social competence" with high intelligence. "Ability to take other points of view," "listens well," and "sympathetic" were among the descriptors used to identify an important factor called "receptive social competence."

In Azuma's study, young Japanese males were inclined to attribute greater problem-solving ability to other males, while most females did not show any tendency toward sexual stereotyping.

An Intelligence Program

A unique, high-level government department operated in Venezuela for five years: the Ministry for the Development of Intelligence. Its purpose was the develop-

EXERCISE: A LEARNING JOURNAL

"How intelligent are you?"   We may sometimes find ourselves speculating about—and perhaps doubting—the intelligence of others as well as of ourselves. We see intelligence as a possession rather than a process. We're often so distracted by intelligence as some sort of a *commodity* that we fail to notice the magical gifts our own intelligence brings us in daily life.

Try this method of journal-keeping to keep track of what you learn, the rewards of your intelligence.

Keep a simple journal that you turn to at the end of each day—a journal in which you write down the answer to three simple but valuable questions.

The first is this:
- *"What did I learn today that I didn't know before?"*

It is important to be selective. This is not a place to keep inventory of all the random bits of information you pick up during the course of each day. What did you learn today that really *fascinated* you? What did you learn today that you found truly *magical* in some sense? Was it a new word, a historical fact, a recipe, a recent event, a bit of trivia?

The second question is this:
- *"How did this new knowledge make me feel?"*

Did you feel delight, curiosity, anger, or the simple pleasure of learning something for its own sake? If you can't identify a feeling of some sort, it is probably not worth jotting down your new knowledge.

The third question is this:
- *"What do I expect this new knowledge to add to my life?"*

Perhaps there is some way that this new knowledge will actively enrich your work, relationships, recreation, etc. Or perhaps the value of this new knowledge is simply the joy of having it—which is reason enough.

A tip in carrying out this journal: Think about this practice from time to time during the day. Ask yourself now and again, *"Have I found tonight's journal entry yet?"*

If evening starts closing in, and your magical new knowledge has not yet shown itself, consider ways of seeking it out. Should you buy a magazine, randomly open an encyclopedia, watch a television special, go to a museum? Even in the last remaining minutes of your waking day, it's not too late to learn something really intriguing. A magical piece of knowledge is often right at your fingertips—as close by as the nearest book or radio.

"You learn something new every day," the clichéd saying goes. Like most clichés this may well be true, but too often we miss out on the sheer joy of what we learn. We don't even notice when we do learn things. Keeping this journal steadily over a period of time is likely to produce an interesting effect. You may well find yourself appreciating your capacity to learn for what it brings to your life, rather than trying to measure it against that of others around you.

In any circumstance, "stupidity"
is a curable "disease."
It is not a situation to be endured
with resignation; it is a social
problem that can be combatted. . . .
Genius is rare because the means
of becoming one has not been
made commonly available.
A "genius" ought not be seen
as one endowed with
extraordinary faculties.
A genius is not a superman,
but a normal man or woman.
The rest of us are infranormal.
We are called to reach the
genius level.
And, in the future, to surpass it.
Today's exception will be
tomorrow's rule.
Intelligence is only natural.
Stupidity requires explanation.

—Luis Machado in
The Right to Be Intelligent
published in Spanish in 1978
and English in 1980
(Pergamon Press)

ment of greater intelligence and creativity of Venezuelans through the educational system and the mass media.

In 1983, Luis Machado, minister of that department, told *Leading Edge Bulletin* that it is the prime responsibility of government to create world peace through increased global intelligence. "Education is a tool for peace and freedom. The development of human beings can lead their nations out of underdevelopment."

The Family Project

With the aid of video programs, often illiterate Venezuelan mothers were helped by volunteers to learn to stimulate their infants' brains through sensorimotor exercises. They used sound, smell, touch, and visual aids with their children, from birth to age six.

The mothers also learned how to sense their babies' needs and interpret their cries, to make toys from common household items, and to involve the whole family in the infants' development.

Dee Dickinson, director of New Horizons for Learning in Seattle, visited the largest maternity hospital in Venezuela. She told *Leading Edge* that the most vital part of the learning process involves instilling in the mother a pride and confidence in the potential of her child and the knowledge to create a positive, stimulating environment.

"Research studies indicated that these children were quite different from their siblings and came into school with very different abilities and interest in learning," she said. According to administrators and teachers involved in the program, Dickinson said, these babies are unusually alert, curious, and eager to learn.

The Learn-to-Think Program

In 1979, Edward DeBono, a noted teacher of thinking (see sidebar page 116), trained 30 Venezuelan teachers to instruct students in analyzing all kinds of situations, seeking a variety of solutions and openly exchanging opinions. These teachers trained others, and by 1983, 42,000 teachers were ready to instruct 1.2 million children between ages 9 and 14. By 1985, 120,000 teachers had been trained in seminars to teach specific cognitive skills.

Visual Education and Other Enrichments

Based on the work of French artist Jacob Agram, Venezuelan preschool children began at age three learning to identify a "visual alphabet" composed of geometric shapes, lines, and primary colors, which serve as a foundation for learning to read. "This also trains visual acuity, coordination of visual and thinking processes, and creative expression," Dickinson said.

These Venzuelan programs ranged from chess for seven- to nine-year-olds—to teach problem-solving strategies—to enrichment programs for children and classes for adults, including military personnel and civil service employees.

Although political changes have curtailed many of the programs that extended beyond the schools, those that are part of the educational system remain available, Dickinson said. The Venezuelan initiative reminds us that we can all increase our individual capacities to learn.

How We Learn

If IQ is not the firm indicator of ability that we may have thought, what do we know about how we learn? Determination, perseverence, and a healthily evolving learning environment may be more important than innate ability. Moreover, leaps forward in learning take place not when we avoid making mistakes, but when we pay attention to what our mistakes teach us.

We have to reverse certain long-held assumptions. Teaching no longer means imposing information from the outside but getting inside the experience of the learner. And good learning may demand a healthy focus on what one does *not* know.

RESOURCES

Beyond I.Q. by Robert Sternberg (Cambridge University Press, 1985) presents the Yale psychologist's "triarchic" theory of human intelligence.

Intelligence, as he sees it, involves three major elements. *Context* has to do with adaptation to the present environment, shaping of it, or finding a better one. *Experience* is another element. *Components,* the third element, are the structures and mechanisms that underlie intelligence.

Sternberg sees insight as a key to so-called giftedness. Major scientific, artistic, and philosophical accomplishments involve intellectual insights. What is important is *how* you think—a quality of thought—not what you know or how much you know or how much you can take in.

Rationality and Intelligence by Jonathon Baron (Cambridge University Press, 1985) discusses the implications of his belief that rational thinking can be taught. "Intelligence is the set of properties . . . that make for effectiveness, regardless of the environment the person is in." Intelligence, in other words, is whatever works.

RESOURCE

DeBono's Strategies for Becoming a "Masterthinker"

Masterthinker's Handbook (International Center for Creative Thinking, 1985) demonstrates author Edward DeBono's longtime interest in "lateral thinking" and the learning of thinking skills. The teaching of thinking is a very hot area, both in education and in the training industry. DeBono, a veteran teacher, has boiled down what he knows even further.

In his new "body framework," he shows how the thinker can direct attention to one aspect of a matter at a time to avoid confusion. He looked for strategies that are "very simple, easy to remember, and easy to use."

He defines a masterthinker as someone who has developed thinking skills to such a high degree that he or she can direct thinking to any subject whatsoever, just as a master carpenter can take on any carpentry task.

Masterthinkers have no interest in proving themselves right and others wrong. Rather, they explore objectively. They are confident but never conceited, constructive rather than destructive, cooperative and eager to share ideas.

They value feelings and use them in decision-making. They know that thinking is the ultimate human resource, one on which the future of the world depends.

Topics: the "intelligence trap" (stuck thinking that can overtake some smart people), active and reactive thinking, "bones" (discovering the conceptual skeleton of the problem), "muscle" (the force of the idea or argument), "nerves" (for linking things up), "fat" (that which gives only bulk and does not add to the solution), "skin" (presentation).

The book itself, with its streamlined format and direct statements, exemplifies the points it makes.

Perhaps most of all, we should beware of "how-to-do-it" instructions, and try to find things out in vital and exciting ways.

The Unfolding of Learning

"Almost everyone can learn what anyone can learn when provided with favorable learning conditions," advises eminent educational researcher Benjamin Bloom. With a team of researchers at the University of Chicago, Bloom conducted his five-year study of America's top performers in six fields: concert pianists, Olympic swimmers, sculptors, tennis players, research neurologists, and mathematicians. He published his findings in *Developing Talent in Young People* (Ballantine, 1985).

Bloom found that given a creative and supportive environment, it is a child's determination—not innate gifts—that predict success.

To discover how potential becomes achievement, the team interviewed the talented individuals, their families, and the teachers of people whose talents had reached a recognizable peak. They expected to find stories of children whose gifts were seen at an early age. Instead, they heard tales of unrelenting dedication.

The concert pianists, for instance, invested an average of 17 years in studying and performing (because they started at five to six years of age), the other high achievers at least a decade.

The development of talent is an extremely long process, Bloom concluded. "How do children maintain a commitment to learn at that level?" he asked. "Certainly schools aren't set up to reward such a long-term study."

Patterns of Learning

Bloom discovered a pattern to the learning years:

• *Phase 1.* The early phase was playful, filled with immediate rewards. Children were exposed to a chosen field of study "more by circumstances than by personal choice." If the fit was good between the child's traits and the talent field, progress was rapid.

• *Phase 2.* Then, between the ages of 10 and 14, the children became "possessed." They saw themselves as "pianists" or "swimmers" and began a prolonged study of technique.

• *Phase 3*. Between ages 16 and 20-plus, they shifted emphasis from technical precision to personal expression. With the guidance of a master teacher, the activity became a combination of work and play, a "calling." Motivation arose from within.

During each period, a different kind of teacher was called for: in the first phase, a neighborhood instructor would do; for precision, students needed a higher-level person. Finally, a master teacher was called in. "Our schools do not take this evolutionary process into account," Bloom said.

At each stage, too, the parents' role was crucial. Most encouraged questioning and curiosity. Parents tended to build a "child-centered" environment. And in every case, they emphasized doing one's best.

But these were not overbearing parents, Bloom pointed out. "If parents press too hard or too early, the children turn off." There seems to be a self-regulating mechanism that works when the timing is right.

The children who "made it" were not always the ones considered to be the most talented, parents reported. In many cases siblings were originally considered more gifted. "Only a few had progressed far enough by age 11 or 12 for someone to make confident predictions that they would be among the top in the field by age 20 or 30."

Rather, they were the offspring with the most persistence and eagerness. These qualities, according to Bloom, are learned from parents, teachers, and peers. "They can be learned only rarely if others devalue or scorn them."

The Beginner's Mind

At one time or another, we all assume that we know more than we actually do. What we may not realize is how this affects our ability to learn new things. Huntington communications expert Elizabeth Berry suggests that an attitude of not knowing, comparable to the Zen idea of "beginner's mind," can help unlock learners' minds.

Everyone has an idea about what qualifies as good writing, for example. Those very notions, they say, can interfere with learning how to write.

Acting *as if* we don't know how to perform a particular task or have never seen a familiar object before can help us maintain openness to new possibilities.

RESOURCES

Learning How to Learn by Joseph Novak and Bob Gowin (Cambridge University Press, 1984) sets out a straightforward theory "of how children learn and, therefore, how teachers and others can help children think about science as well as other topics."

Schooling, they say, offers few intrinsic rewards because the instruction is rote, arbitrary, and verbatim. Students who seek meaning in such instruction often fail.

The authors disagree with the view that learning is synonymous with a change in behavior. They aim for a change in the meaning of *experience*.

The best teachers seem to be the best learners as well. *Growing Minds: On Becoming a Teacher* (Harper & Row, 1984) by Herbert Kohl is about teacher as apprentice and craftsman.

Kohl's relatives were builders. "As a teacher, I've always thought of myself as part of the construction business. All of us are in different stages of completion or renovation." The teacher, he says, has to become a construction expert, someone who knows how to help draw together skills and resources to create a harmonious functioning whole or how to renovate a structure that is dysfunctional or damaged.

Kohl, who is also author of the bestsellers *36 Children* (New American Library, 1967) and *The Open Classroom* (NY Review/Random House, 1970), weaves compelling stories through this account of the self-education of an educator.

EXERCISE: BEGINNER'S MIND

How can we practice a more open attitude to learning, sometimes described as "beginner's mind"? We might start by considering something we do each day, a skill that we employ regularly at home or on the job. Think of an everyday activity that requires a reasonable degree of skill, but that is also something you've mastered, something you believe holds no more surprises. Perhaps it's using a computer program, working in the garden, or preparing a meal you've made many times before. It should be part of your routine, not something you feel you're in the process of learning.

Try this little role-playing game. The next time you go about this seemingly routine activity, pretend as vividly as you can that you've *never* done it before in your life.

To use George Leonard's phrase, "Play the fool." Go through the imaginary process of having to learn the whole thing from scratch. If it's a computer program, allow yourself to stumble through it making whatever mistakes a beginner might make; you might even go back and work through the tutorial, or at least part of it. If it's a recipe, methodically follow the instructions, trying to understand them as if for the first time. Find yourself exploring every aspect, every nook and cranny of the activity, just so you can get its rudiments. In any case, *allow yourself to be clumsy, naive, and unskillful.*

Once you've done this, ask yourself the following very revealing question: *Did I learn anything I didn't know before?* Jot down your observations.

_____

_____

_____

_____

_____

_____

_____

_____

_____

_____

As comically incompetent as you may have felt while attempting this exercise, there's a good chance you picked up some new scrap of knowledge. Was it something you were likely to have learned sooner or later, with or without this exercise? Or was it something you were subtly blocked from learning—blocked by your conviction that you'd "mastered" your activity?

The point is not that you have to feign complete ignorance in order to learn anything. But the *sensation* you may have experienced of a newness and freshness about a task is something worth cultivating. If you can bring it into your daily life voluntarily, it may help you to learn things you might otherwise overlook.

How to Be a Learner

George Leonard, contributing editor of *Esquire,* and former senior editor at *Look,* is another proponent of the beginner's mind. At a 1986 "New Visions" conference in Lincoln, Nebraska, he recounted an occasion when he was put on the spot by a sculptor who asked, "How can I be a learner?" Without thinking it out consciously, Leonard answered, "It's simple—to be a learner you've got to be willing to be a fool."

Leonard said that he did a double take a couple of months later, realizing that the statement was more important than anything he had written in his book *Education and Ecstasy* (Delacorte Press, 1968). Being a fool doesn't mean being dumb, he said, or even unlearned. The fool in the Tarot deck is the number zero, without which we could not do mathematics. Being a fool means having openness, as if we were seeing things for the first time.

He used the example of a baby's learning to talk. The baby babbles; out of the sounds comes the syllable "da" and daddy goes crazy. The baby babbles on, but enthusiastic reinforcement leads to the more frequent production of "da" sounds and then "da-d" and "da-dee." The baby becomes "the most awesome learner on this planet" because it is allowed to babble, to be a fool.

If traditional educational methods were applied, Leonard said, the child babbling "da" would be told that the sound was wrong and would be given repeated examples of the "correct" word: "Now repeat after me." The child would never learn to talk or would, at least, have a severe learning disability. "What things might we do if we were allowed to be fools?" Leonard wondered.

Wrong Answers

A "beginner's mind," of course, produces a lot of wrong answers as it searches for the solutions that work best. Some research suggests that those *wrong* answers should not only be allowed to happen, but that they should also receive more positive attention.

Because the emphasis of our educational system is on the storage of facts, J. C. Powell of the University of Windsor in Ontario believes we have ignored a more human dimension—the evolving capacity to think. *Leading Edge Bulletin* reported in 1981 on Powell's careful study of wrong answers and development of an instruc-

> *The transforming teacher senses readiness to change, helps the "follower" or student respond to more complex needs, transcending the old levels again and yet again. The true teacher is also learning and is transformed by the relationship. . . . A closed teacher—a mere "power wielder"—is not a true teacher.*
>
> —Marilyn Ferguson
> *The Aquarian Conspiracy*
> (J. P. Tarcher, 1987)

COMMENTARY

Kids Think About Thinking

Contrary to previous opinion, children appear to think about thinking from a very early age. According to University of Michigan psychologist Henry Wellman, they have a rich internal life, which they can distinguish from the "real world."

"Young children do *not* confuse the external world with what they are imagining or thinking about," Henry Wellman told *Brain/Mind Bulletin* in 1983.

Children two and a half years old already can distinguish between inner and outer realms, according to studies from the early 1980s. The children try to explain mental phenomena by comparing them to physical events, Wellman said. Thinking is "like talking" and dreams are "like movies." But they know the difference.

In conversations, Wellman studied the natural speech of many young children. Some start at two to make contrasts: "That's not real, I'm just pretending."

One three-year-old, while drinking hot chocolate, told his mother: "I peed in the hot chocolate.... Not really. I was just tricking you, but you didn't know that." He could imagine both his and her internal responses, the researcher said, and he could describe them for her.

If they were merely externalizing, he said, they would not differentiate the brain from the head. But children report that the brain is invisible and inside the head. They also know a doll does not have one.

When asked what the brain does, children described mental activities—thinking, remembering, dreaming—instead of external ones such as talking. "Knowing what children think about their minds will give us clues about how they use them. This will help us understand how they learn—and how we do."

tional approach that dramatically accelerates learning.

A student who fails to choose the "right" answer on a multiple-choice test receives a zero for that item—and valuable information is lost. Educators have always assumed that the student was guessing.

Teachers listen *for* the expected answer rather than listening *to* the answer they get, Powell said. In conventional teaching "the child who cannot frame his or her ideas the way the teacher does very quickly *learns* to be a failure."

Sometimes the answers are not wrong at all but contain useful information. A teacher asked her class to draw "seven blue robin's eggs in a nest." One child drew only five eggs because he had learned elsewhere that robins never lay more than five.

Other researchers, Powell noted, have observed that "profoundly informed people often read more ambiguity into a question than had been intended."

We no longer need people as information retrievers, Powell pointed out, but we still educate by that model. This emphasis has helped create "our devastatingly impersonal society, in which we seek black-and-white answers." The effective problem-solver is flexible, he said.

Powell discovered that when students learn to detect the errors in their own processes they move ahead very quickly. They become "self-instructional." "Once I started to teach them from the point of view *they* were using, a surprising thing happened. Both their enthusiasm and their performance made a large jump upward."

In two algebra classes, formerly average students performed a full standard deviation above those in the school's other five classes. A sixth-grade class's average reading scores increased sixfold over the prior year. One child gained 20 IQ points.

Memory

We have long thought of memory as a container or receptacle, a kind of "storage shed" of the mind. This model is on the wane as researchers confirm that memory is a creative process, not a passive accumulation—a skill, not a lucky trait. Babies may remember far earlier experiences than we imagine.

Then how can we remember better? Research indicates that memory is linked with feeling and emotion, suggesting that we can use our feelings as tools of memory. Even smiling or frowning might serve as keys to specific memories.

Memory is proving to be at once vastly more sophisticated and vastly more simple than we imagined. Ancient mnemonic techniques and other memory "tricks" notwithstanding, the most crucial key to memory is one simple word: *attention*.

Mood and Memory

Gordon Bower and his coworkers at Stanford University discovered that the mood we are in when we read a narrative or study a set of words influences what we learn. They reported their findings in *American Psychologist* (36) and *Journal of Experimental Psychology: General* (110). *Brain/Mind Bulletin* reported their work in 1982.

Hypnotic suggestions were used to put subjects into happy or sad moods, during which they read stories that described a mixture of happy and sad events. The subjects were later tested for recall while in a neutral mood. Those who had been happy when they read the story recalled somewhat more happy than sad events from it; those who had been sad recalled more sad than happy events. Thus,

RESEARCH

Infant Memory

Brain/Mind Bulletin reported in 1985 on a study by Carolyn Rovee-Collier of Rutgers, showing that infants have a much greater ability to remember than had previously been thought. Infants as young as 8 to 12 weeks have long-term memory, Rovee-Collier said, and context is a key.

After studying 1,500 infants in their homes over a five-year period, she found that young babies can remember the details of a mobile two weeks after they first played with it. They would refuse to play with a new mobile or even the original mobile if it contained only one different object.

If they were tested in a crib with a bumper-pad different from when they first learned to play with the mobile, they would not play.

"Infants don't remember a mobile out of context, much as you and I might not recognize our dental assistant in a movie-theater line," Rovee-Collier said.

COMMENTARY

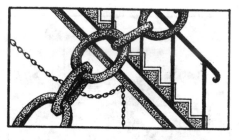

Memory: Chain and Stairway

Our emotions lead to attention, then attention and experience lead to understanding, making something easy to remember, explains Edmund Blair Bolles in *Remembering and Forgetting: An Inquiry into the Nature of Memory* (Walker and Company, 1988). He describes the elements of memory as being linked together like parts of a chain.

"We remember what we understand; we understand only what we pay attention to, we pay attention to what we want.

"This chain gives us memory. When memory fails, the problem lies in some inability to move along the chain."

There are other metaphors that can be used. Bolles says that he usually prefers the image of a staircase. "Along with a sense of connection, this idea includes dependence. A step on a staircase depends on the steps below."

one's mood while reading causes one to pay more attention to—and learn more about—material that agrees with that mood.

On the other hand, if subjects were in a neutral mood as they read the original narrative, they did not selectively remember its happy or sad events even when they were placed in one of those moods just before the recall test.

Bower also found that, when asked to recall events from their childhood, people will remember predominantly happy events if they are temporarily happy, and predominantly sad events if they are temporarily sad. Bower refers to this phenomenon as mood-state dependent memory. "It is as though the two states constitute different libraries into which a person places memory records," he said. "A given memory record can be retrieved only by returning to that library, or physiological state, in which the event was first stored."

Bower also pointed out that this might explain the difficulty of recalling infant experiences. When the maturing brain changes state, memories of the infant state become inaccessible in normal consciousness. And people with multiple personalities may associate their different "selves" with distinct emotional states, none of which they can recall while in another mood.

Facial Expressions Affect Memory

Evidence from studies by James Laird and others in the psychology department of Clark University also suggests a strong link between emotions and memory. They reported their findings in *Journal of Personality and Social Psychology* (42). *Brain/Mind Bulletin* reported their work in a 1983 issue.

In one study, subjects read either humorous selections by comedian Woody Allen or anger-provoking editorials. The Allen material later was recalled best if subjects were smiling; editorials were recalled best while frowning. Inaccuracy was greatest when the opposite facial expressions were assumed.

In a second study involving three negative emotions, accuracy of recall was associated with the corresponding facial expressions for anger, sadness, and fear.

The relationship between facial expression and recall is dramatic in some individuals. One subject who participated in earlier experiments told Laird: "When my jaw was clenched and my brows down, I tried not to be angry, but it just fit the position. I'm not in an angry mood, but

EXERCISE: EXPRESSION AND MEMORY

Try this simple test of the link between memory and facial expression. Sit quietly by yourself. Think of an emotion-charged incident from the fairly distant past—something sad first of all.

Smile. And while smiling, try to describe the incident in writing as fully as you can.

_____
_____
_____
_____

How successful were you? Did the flow of memory come easily, or did you have to strain for details?

Now frown or use a sad expression and see if any new information comes.

_____
_____
_____
_____

Is a sad incident more easily recollected smiling or frowning?

Think of an emotion-charged *happy* incident. *Frown* or look sad and describe it.

_____
_____
_____
_____

Now smile and describe it further.

_____
_____
_____
_____

Most people find happy incidents more easily recollected while smiling and sad incidents more easily recollected while frowning or looking sad. Is this true for you?

If you monitor the correlation between your moods and your ability to remember things, you can develop memory tactics of your own. For example, you may choose not to struggle to remember unhappy incidents while happy, or vice versa.

Or you may choose to subtly alter your mood state with a simple change of facial expression.

COMMENTARY

Greek Memory Arts

Merle Wittrock of UCLA's Graduate School of Education has done impressive work increasing the literacy of U.S. Army recruits. He was inspired in part by the kind of ancient imagery systems discussed by Edmund Blair Bolles in *Remembering and Forgetting* (see main text). He discussed his work with *Brain/Mind Bulletin* in 1988.

Wittrock noted that Simonides, a Greek lyric poet who lived around 500 B.C., taught orators to remember their content and sequence for many hours of extemporaneous speaking. In both ancient Greece and Rome, people mentally located image-clues in various parts of remembered buildings and courtyards. This system "was centrally important to the classical art of memory."

In the eleventh and twelfth centuries people such as Thomas Aquinas and Albertus Magnus encouraged the revival of the ancient memory techniques.

Wittrock cited the hypothesis of Francis Yates (*The Art of Memory,* 1966) that medieval painting, sculpture, and architecture were influenced by the rules of classical memory. The bizarre, vivid imagery embodied in art and architecture may have served to aid memory.

Modern psychologists may have misunderstood the medieval mind. Perhaps people did not naively "believe in" grotesque and fanciful figures but rather used them as provocative reminders of religious teachings about vices and virtues.

Despite the interest of individual scientists, philosophers, and statesmen, memory systems declined in influence after the Renaissance.

I found my thoughts wandering to things that made me angry."

For other people, however, change of facial expression has no noticeable effect on recall.

Remembering and Forgetting

One of the most comprehensive reports on memory is *Remembering and Forgetting: An Inquiry into the Nature of Memory,* by Edmund Blair Bolles (Walker and Company, 1988). Bolles demonstrates that memory is not so much storage but a creative, constructive act. Remembering is "a living product of desire, attention, insight and consciousness."

Instead of saying so-and-so has a great memory, implying a passive accomplishment, "we come closer to the mark in saying so-and-so is a great rememberer. Remembering well is like running well or playing well. It is not for the lazy and not for the fearful."

Artificial Memory

In a chapter on "The Remembrance of Things Personal," Bolles cites evidence that memory is constructive rather than an archive. In ancient and medieval times, he points out, people had no printing presses, computers, or index cards. Respecting the fragility of memory, they revered it as the font of art and learning.

The ancients developed and taught techniques of "artificial memory." For example, they organized and recalled facts by arranging scenes in an imaginary space. (See Merle Wittrock's work in sidebar.)

By the end of the 1300s the availability of paper made it possible for people to make memoranda. As reliance on paper prevailed, artificial memory was eclipsed. Although scientists such as Galileo and Descartes were intrigued by artificial memory, the new "rational" viewpoint leaned toward abstract systems. And the Puritans believed it dangerously exciting to the imagination.

"Artificial memory died like a healthy old man who had lived so long people forgot he was mortal until one day he sneezed and was gone," Bolles says.

EXERCISE: ARTIFICIAL MEMORY

The ancient art of "artificial memory" emphasized associations between *space* and *images*. If a person is trying to remember a series of images, these images can be mentally distributed throughout an imagined space—perhaps a familiar house, building, or courtyard. If they are arranged in novel, even incongruous ways, they can easily be "found" there at some later time.

We often carry out a watered-down version of this technique without thinking about it. For example, suppose you go grocery shopping one day and forget to bring your shopping list. What kind of mental process do you use while roaming confusedly up and down the aisles? In all likelihood, you take a mental tour of your house, trying to visualize what's missing in various places. In your mind, you open the refrigerator door; you hold the milk carton in your hand to see how full it is; you count the eggs; you check to see if the vegetables are fresh. Then you go over to the pantry, open it up, and perform the same operation.

Doing this in a rather haphazard way is likely to produce many mistakes. And the associations you're making between space and images may be uninteresting. An important key to artificial memory is to keep associations weird, incongruous, bizarre—even crass or vulgar. Try this activity:

Don't keep a shopping list this week. Instead, whenever a needed household item crosses your mind, mentally place it somewhere in your living room. Take particular care to create preposterous circumstances. For example:

• Are you out of ice cream? In your mind, carry a full, new carton of ice cream into your living room and place it squarely on the furnace grate. Of course, it starts to melt all over the grate very quickly.

• Are you out of toothpaste? In your mind, remove the cap of a brand-new tube of toothpaste and place the tube under the corner of your living-room rug—right where it is most likely to be stepped on and to squirt toothpaste everywhere.

• Are you low on eggs? In your mind, take a fresh, full carton of eggs into your living room, climb up on a chair, and shove it into the ceiling light-fixture. Take care that it hangs precariously, liable to fall at any second.

• Are you out of cat food? In your mind, open up a brand-new can of cat food in your living room and dish it out into one of your potted plants. Your cats quickly rush in to devour the food, making a sad mess of your plant while they're at it.

The list, of course, goes on. Every time you add an item to your list, take a moment to remind yourself of already present hazards. By the time you go shopping, you've created an imaginary obstacle course. While you're in the store, pause and take a mental tour of your living room. You shouldn't have much trouble remembering your grocery list. In fact, you may be quite surprised at the number of items you can keep in your head.

When you return home and put your shopping items away, mentally clean up your living room as you do so. When you put your eggs in the refrigerator, rescue the eggs you left in the light fixture. When you put the ice cream in the freezer, remove the ice cream from the furnace grate, taking care to wipe up the sticky mess. And so on.

Now you have a nice, clean living room to make a mess of for next week's shopping.

Or—you can go back to keeping an old-fashioned shopping list!

The Discipline of Remembering

In an interview for *PragMagic,* Edmund Blair Bolles pointed out that we should carefully weigh the ever-present, underlying danger that our remembering may become completely self-serving. Given the elaborateness of memory, this can happen without our even knowing it.

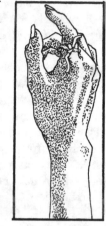

"For example," he said, "there are some politicians and public figures of national stature who don't learn a thing from experience; they simply forget about anything which denies their assumptions."

In *Remembering and Forgetting,* Bolles painstakingly examined the Watergate testimony of John Dean, finding extraordinary, self-serving inaccuracies. Said Bolles, "I don't believe that Dean could have recalled or remembered the conversations which took place between him and Richard Nixon if his life had depended on it. That's because of the way he had lived his whole life."

Perhaps we should all learn a lesson from this, said Bolles. "I think it's very important to develop the discipline of paying attention to those things which deny your assumptions." He has become increasingly aware of a pervasive societal imperative to "pay no attention; that doesn't matter"—an attitude particularly prevalent in public relations work. Too often, "we remember things the way our prejudices say they happened."

Bolles cites Charles Darwin, who wrote down every fact that contradicted his theories so that he wouldn't forget them. "I think that's a good discipline," he said. "I think that is something kids should learn."

Bolles maintains that honest and responsible remembering is a product of a lifetime's practice. It doesn't just happen; it demands commitment.

The Process of Memory

For years, researchers assumed that memory was "stored" somewhere in the brain, and the quest of researchers was to locate just where. Such attempts have failed. Bolles cites recent laboratory evidence that the organ of memory is the neuron itself: "Memory uses no storage; the neuron merely begins to behave in a new way." Memory is a truly creative effort, carried out by versatile neurons picking up new habits and working together in teams.

For this reason, it is a mistake to compare computer "memory" to actual human memory. Computer memory is passively stored, not actively generated. The fact that memory is not clearly distinguishable from thought, notes Bolles, is "probably the greatest surprise of memory research."

Ordinary Forgetting

Bolles suggests that formal introductions are a key to remembering names. If you can remember the voice of a third party telling you the person's name, you are likely to bring back the name itself.

Of course, formal introductions are becoming a rarity, leading Bolles to "wonder if the widespread problem of learning names partially arises from society's increasing informality."

Ordinary forgetting, Bolles comforts us, "does not imply stupidity, creeping senility or even not caring. . . . You forget your keys because you did not notice where you put them."

Next time, he says, notice that you are setting them down. "As I put something down, I would notice, 'I'm putting this here,' and, by Jove, it works."

To remember more, "digest more, and then fill the world with reminders."

Recall and Recognition

Remembering arises out of an interplay between *recall* and *recognition.* Recall, Bolles says, is the production of a memory; it produces information. Recognition has to do with understanding significance, being able to identify that information.

They are hard to distinguish, Bolles said in an interview for *PragMagic,* because they often work together. The distinction becomes clearer when they fail to connect. Suppose you're trying to remember the name of the President of the United States. If the name "George Washington" comes to mind, you know that's not correct. In that instance you've recalled something, but you've failed to recognize it.

At the other end of the spectrum, you might be walking down the street and see someone you know you've met somewhere before, but the person's name eludes you. In that instance, you've recognized something but have failed to recall information needed to identify it.

EXERCISE: EVOKING A CASUAL MEMORY

Where did I leave my wallet?

Did I turn off the coffeemaker?

Did I lock the door before I left?

We all know and dread such questions, and almost invariably feel helpless and stymied when they arise. We feel foolish for not having paid better attention in the first place. And too quickly, we fly into a mild panic, thwarting clear memory altogether.

Suppose you wrote down an important phone number, only to discover the next day that you had misplaced it. What should you do? "The best thing to do is relax," says Edmund Blair Bolles, "maybe even in a dark room, and just think about it."

He suggests you retell the *story* of your writing down the number and putting it someplace. But don't just do it passively. Really evoke and relive it. Use poetic images if you can. Let pertinent details float into recollection: "I was on the phone . . . so-and-so was in the kitchen cooking potatoes . . . I could smell the potatoes . . . a fire engine went by . . . the siren was shrill."

Explains Bolles, "The deeper you get into this experience, the fuller and more productive your memory is likely to be." You may evoke a detail that will serve as a specific reminder.

Richness and Remembering

Seen as a creative process, memory might seem disturbingly relative. (See sidebar commentary.) For example, you might remember something with absolute certainty, yet still have that memory prove to be inaccurate. On the other hand, you might be very doubtful about a memory, and yet have it prove to be absolutely correct. "There is no correlation between your confidence and your correctness," Bolles said.

What kind of experiences are easiest to remember? Richness seems to be a key. By "rich," Bolles does not

---

COMMENTARY

Memory and "Objective Truth"

Does the discovery that memory is a creative process suggest that memory is less accurate than we had hoped and believed? Edmund Blair Bolles told *PragMagic* that we should not be alarmed, but added, "I think it should promote prudence." And he described his experience on the jury for a murder trial.

The testimony produced many contradictory statements. The memories of the witnesses and the defendant didn't match very well. "And to some of the jurors, that was very suspicious," said Bolles. They were frustrated by the apparent impossibility of arriving at a clear-cut account of what had actually taken place.

Bolles didn't find it necessary to completely discount conflicting statements. To the contrary, he was concerned about one detail upon which all the witnesses were consistent. To him, they had obviously fallen into a pattern of agreement and were not in a process of active remembering.

When he watched witnesses testify, he was relatively unpersuaded by witnesses who blandly recited what they remembered. He was more convinced by those who seemed, in spirit, to be "right back at the scene of the event." He sensed they were more actively involved in the act of remembering—and their testimonies *felt* more persuasive.

The trial demonstrated the role of interpretive memory, and reinforced what he had already learned from his research, that "we're now to be forever disappointed in the hope of ever discovering the 'objective truth' of the past."

More recently, he found himself reading about the battle of Waterloo. It struck him that our knowledge of that battle itself was based on the rather frail accounts of a few generals, "all based on memory of very hectic times. I suddenly realized we probably have only a very scanty idea of what happened at Waterloo."

RESOURCE

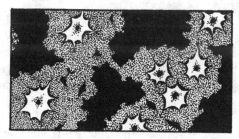

Memory as "Group Effort" of Cells

In *The Invention of Memory* (Basic Books, 1988), Israel Rosenfield describes the case against storage as the mechanism for memory.

Rosenfield, a neurologist, proposes that the most reasonable alternative is Gerald Edelman's model: memory as recategorization. Edelman, who won the 1972 Nobel prize for his discovery of the antibody molecule, described the theory in *Neural Darwinism* (Basic Books, 1987).

The immune system has to fabricate antibodies to invaders it has never seen before. It cannot rely on "memory" as we conceive of it. In Edelman's model, the brain does not learn or remember in the sense of establishing a central library of information. Rather, a variety of maps, the first of them established in the embryo, "speak" to one another to create categories of things and events.

In the Edelman model, cells develop and relate to one another in dynamic context, establishing "neuronal groups." The group is the fundamental unit of selection. Because the neuronal group alters with history and changing context, it would be an unreliable storage unit. However, in concert the groups can create categories. By matching and overlapping categories, they can place a new stimulus into an appropriate context. In other words, the "memory" is assembled.

---

mean chaotic. When things are chaotic, your senses are overloaded; you get confused as to what is going on. "A rich experience is one in which there is a lot going on but it's all in harmony."

Suppose you're trying to remember something that happened at a party. Perhaps there was music. You can use such details as reminders. A lack of details can make memory difficult. "I think austerity makes it hard to remember," says Bolles, reiterating the importance of reminders in the memory process.

"I came to this work not as a psychologist by academic training, but as a literature major," he said. For this reason, *Remembering and Forgetting* represents a kind of personal, philosophical triumph. During his 20 years of professional writing, Bolles has been interested in making the humanistic argument against the mechanistic argument, always with an underlying faith in the humanistic view. "Although this book is not a work of propaganda, it reflects that my faith was justified."

Bolles says that the creative model of memory has affected his perceptions of other people. "In an odd way, I'm much more tolerant of their humanity," he said. He is more patient with people's frailties, with their apparent lapses of attention and remembrance. "It's become clear to me that learning or understanding is real work, that it's not passive."

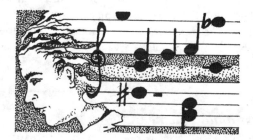

Learning Alternatives

It seems that we all need to learn more these days—and to learn it faster. But what does this require of us and our children? Does it mean mental drudgery and rote memorization? To the contrary, successful learning programs employ imagery, music, recitation, and games—an overall sense of creativity and play. They are increasingly learner-centered, breaking down the age-old mystique of the teacher.

Given the extraordinary developments in recent years in our understanding of learning, intelligence, and memory, it seems reasonable to expect the advent of vastly improved teaching methods. The success of some privately run learning centers challenges our public schools to seriously rethink the process of learning.

Accelerated Learning

For years, some educators have claimed that mental imagery dramatically aids learning. But their efforts were considered frivolous by their more mainstream colleagues. According to a study conducted by David Meier, director of the Center for Accelerated Learning in Lake Geneva, Wisconsin, this internal technology has passed a test with flying colors. *Brain/Mind Bulletin* reported on the study in 1984.

Meier found that college students using mental imagery performed 12% better on immediate recall than students learning the same material without mental imagery. Furthermore, those using the practice performed 26% better on long-term retention tests than those not using it.

The year-long study included 268 students from the University of Wisconsin, El Paso Community College in Texas, Lake Forest College in Illinois, and the Milwaukee Area Technical College. Mental imagery eased learning regardless of students' school, class, age, sex, ethnic group, or preferred learning style. It also stimulated more positive attitudes toward learning.

"If internally generated images are superior to externally generated ones in the learning environment, then we need to give mental imagery the same attention we are giving to sophisticated, computer-driven audiovisual learning devices," Meier said.

"After all there is no device, no matter how sophisticated, that can equal the power, flexibility, and ease of use of the human imagination. We all possess the world's finest multisensory teaching machine right inside our own heads."

A Master teaches essence. When the essence is perceived, he teaches what is necessary to expand the perception. The Wu Li Master does not speak of gravity until the student stands in wonder at the flower petal falling to the ground. . . . He does not speak of mathematics until the student says, "There must be a way to express this more simply." In this way, the Wu Li Master dances with his student. The Wu Li Master does not teach, but the student learns. The Wu Li Master always begins at the center, at the heart of the matter.

—Gary Zukav
The Dancing Wu Li Masters
(Morrow, 1979)

RESEARCH

Test Gauges Thinking Style

A nonverbal test of "thinking style" is being used to determine useful educational and work experiences for individuals with learning problems. "With this assessment tool," said educational consultant Dorothy Davis, who designed the test, "we have uncovered a myriad of hidden talents and abilities that had gone unnoticed by other measurement devices."

The New Columbus Agency, a Tucson, Arizona, counseling center for delinquent or "incorrigible" youths, uses the test to tailor its approach to the learning biases of its clients. Claire Norwick, a therapist at New Columbus, said that the "Relational Thinking Styles" test "gives us new insight into why these children operate the way they do."

The diagnostic test has theoretical roots in research on the specialization of the brain's hemispheres; it assumes that people habitually use either a "left" or "right" mode for processing in a particular situation. Davis believes that rapidly switching from right- to left-hemisphere processing styles ("lacing") enhances overall learning. She has designed exercises for such integration.

The test is commonly used for children deemed hyperactive, "lazy," emotionally handicapped. They have normal IQs, but their learning styles don't fit normal classrooms.

Three to five individuals in the same age range manipulate and arrange a variety of materials. No questions are asked, and there is no reading or writing. "We watch the operation—not what they do but how they do it."

The test evaluates the ability to set goals, view alternatives, make judgments, and visualize the future—abilities vital to learning, Davis emphasized.

She maintains that schools place too much value on verbalness. "The real process of organizing, of putting meaning to the world, is probably a nonverbal system. We verbalize it in order to share it."

Multisensory Imagining

The Center for Accelerated Learning has successfully used its training methods with corporations such as Bell Atlantic. Although imagery has continued to be important in Meier's work, he has found that other senses also provide powerful tools.

In *Training and Development Journal* (May, 1985), he wrote: "The more senses involved in the image or episode, the more useful it is, because the brain codes information more efficiently in multisensory images than in words alone. I teach people the order of the planets by having them relax, close their eyes and, with all their senses, experience an episode involving a Mercury automobile, the goddess Venus, a Mars candy bar, the cartoon dog Pluto and so forth."

Imagining yourself in a story can help you to recall aspects of a process, a system, or a piece of equipment: "The movie *Fantastic Voyage* took the audience on a trip through the human body. Trainees can do the same thing

---

INVENTORY: TWO LEARNING MODES

The following list, compiled by Chuck Price of AT&T and based on Accelerated Learning ideas, offers an overview of two learning approaches:

TRADITIONAL LEARNING tends to:	ACCELERATED LEARNING tends to:
emphasize separateness	emphasize wholeness
confuse uniformity with unity	welcome diversity
trivialize the individual	exalt the individual
dull the creative spirit	nurture creativity
be EITHER/OR	be BOTH/AND
emphasize ONE BEST WAY	be purposefully eclectic
be competitive	be collaborative
restrict	liberate
block human energy	release human energy
be static & rigid	be dynamic & flexible
be linear & hierarchical	be geodesic & mutual
be single-pathed	be multipathed
feel UNnatural	feel natural
be audio/visual	be multisensory
be hard work	be joyful
be a process	be a state of mind

—from *The A.L. Network News* (Summer 1984)

by mentally miniaturizing themselves and traveling through a computer, a processing system, a paperwork flow, or a satellite system. The training manager of a large paper manufacturer has an interesting way of orienting new employees to the business. He has people imagine themselves as wood fiber in a tree, and he takes them through the whole paper-making process until they roll out of the mill as a finished product."

In an interview for *PragMagic,* Meier emphasized that the Center for Accelerated Learning employs many techniques, including a relaxing environment, high-energy involvement, music, games, role-playing, songs, team projects, positive suggestion, and humor.

Explained Meier, "We try to reconstruct a total environment, and it involves a lot of components. They all affect each other. It's hard for me to say which is the controlling component." Learner-centeredness, as opposed to the teacher-centeredness that marks typical learning environments, is another important element of the program.

Mind-Mapping

Mind-mapping is a technique of putting down information in nonlinear, nonserial format. "You start in the middle of the page with the name of the topic," said Meier, "and then you branch out into the components, using key words. You keep branching and building from one idea to another, making doodles to represent your ideas together with the word."

Variations on the mind-mapping technique are described in Peter Russell's *The Brain Book* (Hawthorn, 1979).

Collaboration

Collaboration is another crucial component of Accelerated Learning, Meier said. "We design the training so that, within the first hour or two, we bring about bonding among the learners. This way learners very quickly lose the traditional assumption of individualism in the learning place.

"This has a number of effects. The threat level goes way down, so learning becomes a joyful activity rather than a punishing activity. It's not judgment day, it's fulfillment day when collaboration is in the air and you know that everyone is helping everyone else to master the subject matter of the course. We try to let all of our training

---

RESOURCE

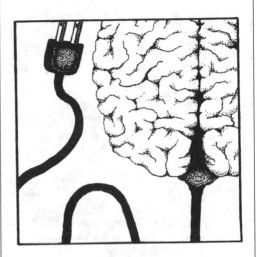

The Whole-Mind in Book Publishing

An introductory text on computers has been developed with both sides of the brain in mind.

"The book recognizes the specialization of the cerebral hemispheres in human information processing," author William Taggart, Jr., told *Brain/Mind Bulletin.*

The book—*Information Systems: People and Computers in Organizations* (second edition, Allyn and Bacon, Inc., 1986; distributed by Wm. C. Brown)—alternately stimulates the cognitive modes of the left and right hemispheres.

"All illustrations for the text were prepared before the narrative was written," said Taggart, a professor of management. "This forced the traditional linear mind to consider the subject holistically before its expression in linear verbal form. The result is a conscious presentation of the content in two modes: words and patterns."

THEORY

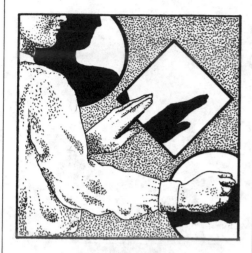

Modeling behavior

Theoretically, say NLP practitioners, any human ability or quality can be modeled and learned. In a 1982 interview with *Brain/ Mind Bulletin,* Leslie Cameron-Bandler explained that NLP seeks to model behaviors that reflect competence and excellence.

Techniques they use include:

• Mirroring and pacing—matching one's own patterns and rhythms to those of the listener, to establish rapport.

• Response sensitizing—detecting the expectations of the listener.

• Changing history—viewing one's own past from a different perspective.

• Reframing—transforming undesired situations and sensitivities into strengths by changing perspective.

• Anchoring—linking a desired response (courage, relaxation, fearlessness) to a repeatable stimulus (specific feeling, memory, gesture).

techniques foster collaboration and get out of the parent/ child mode of instruction."

Philosophically, Meier believes that "learning should be natural, like it is for a child; it should be playful, it should be nonpunishing. It should involve the total mentality of people, not the closed-down sort of thinking we carry around with us as adults."

Neuro-Linguistic Programming

Neuro-Linguistic Programming was initially developed by linguist John Grinder and mathematician and computer scientist Richard Bandler. They began by observing the nonverbal behavior and language patterns of successful therapists such as Virginia Satir, Milton Erickson, and Fritz Perls. They then devised techniques for making certain abilities available to others.

Neuro-Linguistic Programming places ultimate responsibility for clear communication on the sender, Leslie Cameron-Bandler told *Brain/Mind Bulletin* in a 1982 interview. She pointed out that communication can occur even without intent—any utterance, gesture, or pause may get a response. "If you are misunderstood and don't want to be, you have to be flexible and reconstruct your message until it has the desired impact," she said. "You just have to be sensitive enough to your receiver."

In NLP training, people learn to pay attention to the styles of their listeners. For example, they may speak in terms of the receiver's predominant sensory mode: "I see what you mean," "I hear you," "I can grasp that."

INVENTORY: THE CODE OF THE EYES

A well-known code used by NLP practitioners is eye "accessing cues," a list of nonverbal cues that theoretically signify the mental process being used. These apply specifically to right-handed persons:

• Looking to upper and horizontal left signifies recall of previous experience—upper left, of visual memory; horizontal left, of auditory memory.

• Looking to upper and horizontal right signifies new processing—upper right, construction of visual images: horizontal right, putting impressions into words.

• Looking to lower left signifies attention to internal auditory dialog; to lower right, accessing feeling states.

"You limit your ability to communicate when you insist on your own style of presentation," she said. "Flexible behavior can get the response you want. The most flexible member of any system always has the greatest potential influence."

EXERCISE: TURNING UP THE LIGHTS

NLP promotes visualization techniques that make use of submodalities, which are subcategories of our five senses. These include brightness and shape for sight, pitch and rhythm for sound, pressure and texture for touch, etc. In the following basic exercise, Richard Bandler vividly demonstrates the use of the submodality of brightness to alter your perception of a past experience:

Think of a past experience that was very pleasant—perhaps one that you haven't thought about in a long time. Pause for a moment to go back to that memory, and be sure that you see what you saw at the time that pleasant event happened. You can close your eyes if that makes it easier to do. . . .

As you look at that pleasant memory, I want you to change the brightness of the image, and notice how your feelings change in response. First make it brighter and brighter. . . . Now make it dimmer and dimmer, until you can barely see it. . . . Now make it brighter again.

How does that change the way you feel? There are always exceptions, but for most of you, when you make the picture brighter, your feelings will become stronger. Increasing brightness usually increases the intensity of feelings, and decreasing brightness usually decreases the intensity of feelings.

How many of you ever thought about the possibility of intentionally varying the brightness of an internal image in order to feel different? Most of you just let your brain randomly show you any picture it wants, and you feel good or bad in response.

Now think of an unpleasant memory, something you think about that makes you feel bad. Now make the picture dimmer and dimmer. . . . If you turn the brightness down far enough, it won't bother you anymore. You can save yourself thousands of dollars in psychotherapy bills.

I learned these things from people who did them already. One woman told me that she was happy all the time; she didn't let things get to her. I asked her how she did it, and she said, "Well, those unpleasant thoughts come into my mind, but I just turn the brightness down."

—from *Using Your Brain—For a CHANGE*
by Richard Bandler
(Real People Press, 1985)

RESOURCES

Selected books on Neuro-Linguistic Programming:

Change Your Mind —And Keep the Change by Steve Andreas and Connairae Andreas (Real People Press, 1987).

The Emprint Method by Leslie Cameron-Bandler, David Gordon, and Michael LeBeau (Real People Press, 1985).

Frogs into Princes by Richard Bandler and John Grinder (Real People Press, 1979).

Know How: Guided Programs for Inventing Your Own Best Future, by Leslie Cameron-Bandler, David Gordon, and Michael LeBeau (Real People Press, 1985).

Magic in Action by Richard Bandler (Meta-Publications, 1985).

Reframing: Neuro-Linguistic Programming and the Transformation of Meaning by Richard Bandler and John Grinder (Real People Press, 1982).

Solutions: Practical and Effective Antidotes for Sexual and Relationship Problems by Leslie Cameron-Bandler (Real People Press, 1985).

Tranceformations: Neuro-Linguistic Programming and the Structure of Hypnosis by Richard Bandler and John Grinder (Real People Press, 1981).

Using Your Brain—For a CHANGE by Richard Bandler (Real People Press, 1985).

RESEARCH

Computers as Partners

Robert Dilts, one of the originators of Neuro-Linguistic Programming, launched a new company, Behavioral Engineering, to design NLP-based software. He says that his new programs "change the computer from a dispassionate machine into a partner sensitive to an individual's internal reactions. It learns to read you—and show you your responses."

The user rests a hand on a device about the size and shape of a computer mouse, which measures skin perspiration, mimicking lie-detector technology. The device can also be attached to the fingers with Velco wraps.

In one game, when the user thinks of something exciting, a spaceship takes off. When he thinks of something relaxing, it returns. "It's an entertaining way to learn stress management," Dilts noted.

But more than that is going on. The computer stores users' responses and compares them to others. "It keeps learning your most important variables, increasing your sensitivity to internal changes," he said.

Other programs reveal the user's "brain music"—the range of tones that fit each person's relaxed, alpha state, for instance. A spelling program helps students gain access to visual or auditory cues to remember how to spell words.

Another product, called Neuro-Link, measures heart rate, body temperature, and differences generated in the body by the two brain hemispheres. In one software program, the user brings a graphic of broken halves of the planet Earth together by balancing the two brain hemispheres.

Cameron-Bandler is especially interested in the abilities of people who rise above adversity and enrich the lives of others. "I am moved by human beings and how they change. I am fascinated by the way people are able to go through strife and trauma and come out of it more loving, generous, and creative."

Reading Behavior

NLP practitioners infer internal states and mental processes by "reading" the outward forms of behavior—content and tone of language, gestures, eye movements, changes in facial coloration, lip size, jaw placement. Effective behaviors are then "coded" in notation systems so that others may learn them.

Increasing Options

Without awareness of their options, Leslie Cameron-Bandler said, people tend to evolve according to what they can't do rather than to what they can. They avoid what they don't want rather than going after what they do want. "NLP helps us go for the positive. Any desirable behavior can be learned. We can choose our evolution."

The purpose of NLP, she said, is to increase a person's options. For example, instead of attacking unwanted problems such as smoking, overeating, or shyness, NLP offers people an opportunity to choose their own alternatives.

Success with NLP depends on the intensity of one's objectives. "You can have what you want. Is it worth what it takes to get it? There is no question of whether or not, merely a question of how."

Optimalearning®

Ivan Barzakov, president of the Barzak Educational Institute in San Rafael, California, and creator of Optimalearning, told *Brain/Mind Bulletin* in a 1982 interview that "all things in the environment—colors, sounds, textures, rhythms, shapes, objects, other persons, the appearance and syntax of a text—are significant in the learning process.

"The mind does not perceive just bits and pieces but is constantly weaving a large pattern from our experiences. If you feed your brain properly, there is practically nothing it isn't capable of learning."

Optimalearning programs engage participants with art, classical music, literature, visual design, games and other group processes, techniques of suggestion, and traditional instructional materials for "full-brain learning" and personal mastery. Through a combination of experiences in sensory awareness, relaxation, imaging, and other mental focusing activities, they seek to teach people how to evoke their best performance on any task.

Optimalearning builds on Suggestology, an accelerated method of learning foreign languages that was developed by another Bulgarian, Georgi Lozanov (see sidebar). After becoming a leading teacher of Suggestology methods, Barzakov, who holds several degrees and speaks nine languages, became convinced that they should be utilized worldwide.

Barzakov also began to experiment and to develop his own methods. Unlike Suggestology, which always depends upon a teacher, Optimalearning includes self-study and exam-taking, and teaches all subjects at all levels.

Relaxation and Visualization

In an interview for *PragMagic,* Barzakov said that he and his associates have learned much about the role of relaxation. For learning, he does not recommend progressive relaxation (in which one relaxes one part of the body after the other) or artificial relaxation (which can involve attention to breathing). Instead, visualizations are used to create a relaxing scene. "In visualization," he explains, "it is very important to create safe conditions, very personal conditions." The instructor tries not to impose too much. The learner is free to choose a scene, ranging from some lovely natural locale to his or her own room.

Barzakov does not attempt to teach information while the student is in the midst of a visualization. "We work with the border zone," says Barzakov, the state that arises immediately after the learner has come out of a visualization. In the border zone, students are still "very receptive, very relaxed, eyes open and ready to learn. That is the optimal time."

Learning States

Barzakov and his associates have worked a great deal with the spectrum of learning states. For example, he points out that expectancy plays an intricate role in learning. "Expectancy is a strong belief that something is really about to happen. As you get results, there is a growing

COMMENTARY

Suggestology

In the early 1970s, a Bulgarian approach toward accelerated learning aroused considerable curiosity in this country. The phenomenom was Suggestology, created by Bulgarian psychiatrist Georgi Lozanov.

But a number of factors stymied its adoption, among them a delay in getting adequate translations and the Bulgarian government's proprietorship of the method. In 1976, a Des Moines, Iowa, conference/workshop sponsored by SALT (Society for Suggestive and Accelerative Learning and Teaching) revealed how Suggestology produces vast acceleration in learning:

• A relaxed ambience is essential. Most students bring an ample supply of anxiety into the classroom, the result of years of stress, fear of failure, and humiliation in school.

• Change of pace is important. A lively presentation of material—e.g., a foreign language vocabulary presented in skits—may be followed by a later session in which classical music is played.

• The teacher—performer, instructor, supporter—is authoritative yet never threatening. Body language and tone of voice are considered as important as verbal content.

• The teacher never criticizes, never specifically tells the student he is wrong. Corrections are made obliquely, for example, by giving a correct pronunciation of a word in the context of another sentence.

• Music, dramatic skits, and games are seen as stimuli to engage the right- and left-brain hemisphere processes as well as the brain's emotional centers simultaneously.

• With frequent ungraded tests to corroborate the effectiveness of the learning, the individual often experiences success for the first time in his academic career. It is not uncommon for some students to achieve 100% scores on vocabularies of several hundred words.

Music for Learning

One of the most widely-known components of Optima-learning is "Reading With Music," in which the learner studies information while listening to music, typically from the baroque period. Music of many different kinds and tempos is used to assist in different kinds of learning.

The Barzak Educational Institute has introduced a series of music cassettes called The Optimalearning Classics. One cassette focuses on slow movements by Pachelbel, Handel, Manfredini, Scarlatti, and others, "tailored for learning terminology, facts and figures, technical data and language vocabulary, with high retention."

Another cassette offers a variety of different movements by Corelli and Albinoni: "Corelli's characteristic alternation of slow-fast-slow-fast movements creates the rhythmical pattern highly conducive for absorption of all sorts of material in the long-term memory, storytelling, presentations, child rearing."

Other music is offered for imagination and creativity, and to accompany a variety of activities, such as: writing; problem-solving and decision-making; alleviating depressed moods; and "healing one's soul." Excerpts from romantic and post-romantic composers are appropriate for these purposes.

Two other cassettes consisting of a unique combination of baroque with post-baroque music are designed to make driving in congested traffic and long distances more enjoyable and productive. They facilitate athletic and physical activity as well as housework and daily chores.

sense of anticipation, which becomes a belief." Barzakov distinguishes expectancy from an expectation of a specific learning goal. "I'm not against goal-programming," he says, "but when it comes too prematurely, it may inhibit the process and you may limit yourself."

A familiar learning state is an outwardly relaxed but inwardly alert condition in which one can absorb information with seeming effortlessness. It is a state of tranquil receptivity.

Barzakov has discovered a symmetrically opposite state he calls "dynamic equilibrium." He explains, "It's a state in which you appear to be dynamic and excited, and yet you're relaxed at the same time. Let's take an example from life. Try to remember playing a favorite game, either as a child or later in life. You may have been outwardly

INVENTORY: RECEPTIVE STRATEGIES

Barzak Educational Institute director Ivan Barzakov told *Brain/Mind Bulletin* that he strives to teach his students a state of "childlike openness and receptivity." The strategy for inducing this state is threefold: enlarging awareness, inviting best performance, allowing the "deep self" to function.

• *Enlarging.* "Be a sponge," Barzakov tells workshop participants. "Open your senses and your mind to all the possibilities in this environment. Be willing to try new experiences. Judge only in retrospect." Multiple stimuli are used to increase attention, interest, and the capacity for simultaneous awareness.

• *Inviting.* "Do not chase the bird of best performance; invite it," Barzakov admonishes. "Leave all expectations aside. Do not learn on purpose. Drop all concern for how anything applies— don't try to see what it means. Suspend your belief that you must be aware of what you are learning in order to learn it, and that knowing is being able to explain. Trust your mind and flow."

The workshop facilitates a relaxed but alert state of mind that heightens receptivity.

• *Allowing.* "The more you allow the creator within you to express itself, the more easily you will learn whatever you want and need to know.

"Go with whatever emerges spontaneously and lightly from within you," Barzakov urged. "The way that things come easiest from you is the clue to your best performance. They come from your deepest self and express your inner priorities." He believes that our best learning and performance come from the hidden teacher/artist within each individual.

excited while playing it, and at the same time internally relaxed."

He says that dynamic equilibrium, as opposed to tranquil receptivity, lends itself to problem-solving in mathematics and physics, and to other kinds of decision-making. "There are a variety of situations in which an active cognitive state is required, in which one's state of mind appears to be predominantly excited."

Barzakov pointed out that "recent studies confirm that most productive learning only occurs when a variety of brain-wave states are induced." He prefers to alternate passiveness with dynamic equilibrium.

Speeding Up Learning

Barzakov and his chief associate and senior cotrainer, Pamela Rand, believe that Optimalearning can fulfill needs not met by most schools. Rand has developed Optimalearning-based language programs specifically for children. The tapes and booklets offer parents and children a chance to explore languages together. They were developed from studying children raised to speak two or three languages.

Barzakov says that Optimalearning is used to help professionals of all kinds communicate more efficiently, using both the conscious and the unconscious mind. This concerns not only business executives and trainers, but also health professionals, who learn how to establish optimal rapport with patients and also how to eliminate counterproductive stress in their work and daily life.

An interesting coincidence underlies Barzakov's tremendous interest in increased learning. In Bulgarian, the word "barzak" means "rapid" or "accelerated."

RESOURCE

Culture, Communication and Cognition: Vygotskian Perspectives, edited by James Wertsch (Cambridge University Press, 1985), is an overview of Lev Vygotsky's rich contribution to the psychology of learning.

Vygotsky, a Soviet psychologist who died at 38 in 1934, is taking on the stature of a William James. His theories once directed avant-garde Soviet research, then went underground after his death for several decades when he was considered anti-Marxist. His works are increasingly available in the Soviet Union and are attracting international attention.

Vygotsky did not have a single overarching theory as did, say, Pavlov, Jung, or Freud. He generated a repertoire of interactive ideas. But one idea stands out—an observation that may shed more light on education than any idea in recent history. His Zone of Proximal Development (ZPD) is what we might call a concept of potential.

Our models of learning have been involved in a kind of catch-22. When we encounter a learner, the learner can only show us readiness based on past experience. We assume that the learner is only so good because of present performance—and we have no idea what the person can do given optimal instruction. So we pitch our teaching to the current level of attainment rather than experimenting with the learner's capacity to learn.

In other words, we treat people as if they will always be as bright or capable as they are now, without taking their history into account. The most tragic victims of this assumption are the disadvantaged. Their ZPD—the gap between what they are doing and what they could do—is greater than the ZPD of those who have had more teaching, coaching, or exposure. If we see people as less capable than they are, we bore them by our teaching methods. They are not engaged or challenged. They lose interest in their education.

NOTES:

5.
LIVING MAGIC:
Your Good Health

We would have preferred calling this chapter *"Healthing Magic."* But that would look like a misprint.

Still, we no longer think of health as a static, passive condition. So doesn't the word "health" have a right to be a verb, and not a mere noun? We always talk about health—and about healing—at the oddest possible moment: after we've become sick.

Disease isn't our topic here. It certainly demands our attention when it comes into our lives, as do its emotional equivalents, depression and despair. Our real topic is *living:* something we do daily, in sickness and in health, in stress and in relaxation—living *well,* in body and in mind. Disease assumes less control over our lives when we make health a full-time concern.

This section will deal with:
• How hostility and cynicism can be dangerous to your health
• How depression is on the increase in our culture
• Whether you're a Type A or Type B personality—and the latest news as to what that means for your life
• How Post-Traumatic-Stress Disorder affects veterans and children
• How the immune system and the nervous system interact
• Ways of coping with depression and with stress
• How environmental stress can affect your health
• New perspectives on the mind-body connection in addictions

RESOURCES

In *Who Gets Sick: How Thoughts, Moods, and Beliefs Can Affect Your Health* (J. P. Tarcher/Peak Press, 1988), Blair Justice, an award-winning medical writer and science editor, has assembled a highly readable but encyclopedic volume on sickness and treatment.

Justice has divided the book into five major sections: Germs and Stress, Neurotransmitters, Coping, Vulnerability, and Self-repair. His application of brain research to health is unprecedented in its depth and simple usefulness.

The humor is a bonus. Among the large-type quotes heading chapter sections:

Rule No. 1: *Don't Sweat the Small Stuff.* Rule No. 2: *It's All Small Stuff. And if you can't fight it and you can't flee, flow.*

And: *A pessimist is someone who, when confronted with two unpleasant alternatives, selects both.*

In *Love, Medicine and Miracles* (Harper & Row, 1986), physician Bernie Siegel says that for certain patients "every thought and deed advances the cause of life." These exceptional patients "manifest the will to live in its most potent form."

Siegel describes how patients who have focused on what's wrong with their *lives* as opposed to their *bodies* demonstrate remarkable healing. He notes that "neglect of the mind-body link by technological medicine is actually a brief aberration when viewed against the whole history of the healing art." Not only in tribal medicine, but also in Western practice from its beginnings, "the need to operate through the patient's mind has always been recognized. . . .

"Contentment used to be considered a prerequisite for health."

Responsibility for your health begins with you. But lest the word "responsibility" sound threatening, let's spell out the good news: You've got as much to say about *healthing* as any doctor. *To your good life!*

What Is Health?

It hasn't been long since health was considered a purely physical concern—a matter of body and not mind. Now there is more and more talk about a body-mind connection, and about the role of attitude in healing.

This makes sense in a very brass-tacks way. After all, if you have a good self-image, you'll take good care of yourself; and if you take good care of yourself, you'll be healthier. But the real connection may be deeper, more mysterious—and more wonderful.

A positive sense of your own individualism and worth may play an important role in healing. Cynical, suspicious, and negative outlooks may be harmful.

Health is an integral aspect of daily living. No longer limited to the concept of getting well after a disease or disability has struck, health is now seen in a larger context. It means being well. It also means a state of well-being.

Healing and Wholeness

"You need to heal people's lives . . . the *byproduct* is physical," said Bernard Siegel, Yale surgeon and author of the best-selling *Love, Medicine and Miracles,* at a 1988 conference in Kalamazoo, Michigan. "The issue is not really avoiding death. The issue is: Are you enjoying living and what it does to your body?"

The conference, "Helping Heal the Whole Person in the Whole World," was sponsored by the John C. Fetzer Foundation. The participants were primarily medical and health-care professionals, educators, and foundation executives.

Siegel recalled being inspired by a patient who asked how to live between office visits. "What an incredible, wonderful thing!" he said. "By pursuing this question, I realized I could practice medicine with success as its orientation, not simply avoidance of death.

"Get a bunch of people together and teach them about living, and something absolutely incredible happens. Many have their diseases reversed." Siegel told of a landscaper, diagnosed with terminal stomach cancer five years ago, who refused to stop "making the world beautiful" for treatment. The result has been a complete remission, with the man going strong at age 83.

In addition to outward protection given us by our usual five senses, Siegel proposed that the body has a sixth "healing sense." "Would our creator have gone to all that trouble to protect our outside and done nothing for our inside?" he asked.

"We once defined 'fitness' as survival long enough to reproduce," said physiologist Harold Amos of Harvard Medical School. "Today, we clearly need a broader definition."

INVENTORY: THE PESSIMISM CONNECTION

Pessimism may be hazardous to your health (see sidebar, this page). Christopher Peterson of the University of Michigan listed several factors that seem to relate pessimism to illness:

• Pessimism may be linked to poor problem-solving ability and therefore to serious problems—hence, vulnerability to illness.
• Pessimism may lead to social withdrawal, behavior also associated with illness.
• Pessimism-related helplessness may affect the immune function.

Peterson cautioned, however, that optimism is as likely to be a symptom of good health as a cause.

"I think they work together," he said. "But combining optimism with hard work is still the best way to improve your health. A smile button alone isn't going to ward off an epidemic."

RESEARCH

Pessimism and Illness

A young man's style of explaining bad events—optimistic or pessimistic—may be a predictor of health in middle age.

This finding is based on a 35-year follow-up of Harvard graduates first interviewed in 1946. The study was authored by Christopher Peterson of the University of Michigan and colleagues, who reported in the *Journal of Personality and Social Psychology* (55); *Brain/Mind Bulletin* discussed their work in 1989.

Subjects matched for age and health were queried about difficult experiences in World War II. Some offered cheerful explanations, others were glum or guilty.

Researchers categorized the negative accounts as global ("It will ruin my whole life"), stable ("It will never go away"), or internal ("It was my fault").

As predicted, those with negative interpretations were consistently sicker than their peers.

The disparity appeared to have peaked around age 45, though substantial differences existed from age 35 onward. The authors speculated that the effect of psychological outlook on health is greatest in early middle age. In later years, general physical problems may take on greater importance.

"The finding reinforces common sense," said Peterson. "The way you explain an event is a particularly good indicator of your level of helplessness, your likelihood of attacking problems head-on.

"While there are many ways pessimism might lead to poor health, I believe it's most strongly linked to behavior. A pessimistic person is less likely to quit smoking, refuse extra dessert, or get the most appropriate medical attention."

RESEARCH

Depression to Become Epidemic?

In 1987 *Brain/Mind Bulletin* reported on a variety of developments relating to depression:

• *Depression is on the increase.* *Science* (233, 235) offered statistics about this onslaught of depression. Teenagers, elderly males, and those from 18 to 34 years of age are singled out as depression-prone groups. In addition, an estimated four out of five people don't report their depression to doctors.

• A study of 20,000 adults in five U.S. cities found that 15% had suffered mental disorders or addiction problems within a six-month period.

• According to the National Institute of Mental Health, the rate of diagnosed depression has increased greatly among those born after World War II. The average age of the onset has declined from around 40 in 1945 to the midtwenties.

At the Michigan conference, endocrinologist Leonard Wisneski of George Washington University said that, at one point in medical school, he suddenly saw how completely body and mind were interconnected—a notion that seemed to run counter to his training. "I had been forced to look at the lay of the 'land' only; to see footprints, deformities. I was a body mechanic, trained to look at the sea and the land as completely different and separate. Suddenly I realized that the water, land, and air were all related—something medical school had never addressed."

Others touched on similar themes. Norman Cousins, author of *Anatomy of an Illness* (Bantam, 1981) and a faculty member at UCLA Medical School, recounted how an announcement of possible food poisoning at a football game caused hundreds of people to become ill. When the announcement was repudiated, the illnesses vanished. "Because we are fearful and prone to panic, those emotions are translated into an exaggeration, an intensification, of illness. If I could give one gift to people, it would be to liberate them from their fears . . . because fears create illness."

Naomi Remen, medical director of Commonweal Cancer Help Program in Bolinas, California, said, "Health is not an end—it is a means. It enables us to serve a purpose in life, but it is not the purpose of life.

"Healing is not a matter of mechanism: it is a work of spirit."

Depression

If you're depressed, or have recently been depressed, don't feel alone. Depression, often called "the common cold of mental health," is more common than ever. It may even be becoming an epidemic.

This is hardly surprising. We are living in a difficult and confusing time.

Depression has been called the best understood of the mental disorders. A vast array of antidepressant medications have been developed, along with other treatments, but there is still no psychiatric consensus about diagnosis, causes, or treatment. There is some concern that it is a catchall diagnosis.

However, as depression becomes a focal point for investigating the interaction of mind and body, it may provide insights into many other illnesses.

How can we deal with common depression? There seems to be a paradox at work. On one hand, a makeshift cheerfulness, a too rigorous and inflexible insistence on "positive attitude" may not be appropriate; remember the dangers of alexithymia, discussed in "Being Magic" (pages 36–41). On the other hand, a certain amount of "unrealistic" optimism may actually be conducive to mental health.

What does this mean? Maybe we should be aware of our darkest feelings, even as we act on our most optimistic thoughts. *Attention* and *action* may be the keys to combating depression in an era rife with uncertainty and despair.

Self-Focus

Randy Larsen and Gregory Cowan, researchers in the Purdue University department of psychological sciences, reported in *Motivation and Emotion* (12) that too much self-consciousness in relation to unfortunate events may be a hallmark of depression. *Brain/Mind Bulletin* reported on their work in 1989.

Larsen and Cowan studied 62 college students who kept records of events and moods for 56 days. The students rated daily happenings for negative or positive impact, and judged whether or not they had been at all personally responsible for what had happened. They also took tests to measure their levels of depression and self-consciousness.

The researchers found that depressed subjects were quick to blame themselves, but not to take credit. They held themselves more accountable for *negative*—but not *positive*—events than their more stable counterparts.

Depressed people, they said, also seem unable to evaluate the importance of everyday occurrences. Their

Lincoln suffered bouts of melancholy all his life. So did William James. And Winston Churchill, who called his "the black dog."

Yet as a society we have not rewarded leaders (such as Jimmy Carter) who were candid about being uncertain, much less unhappy. Thomas Eagleton was bumped from the Democratic national ticket after admitting that he had once undergone electroshock therapy for depression. Edmund Muskie, a leading presidential contender, became an also-ran when he wept in front of an audience.

Brain/Mind Bulletin, 1987

INVENTORY: SYMPTOMS OF DEPRESSION

Are you depressed? All of us are at one time or other. Most of the time, our depressive episodes are brief and transitory, but major depressive episodes can last for a couple of weeks or longer.

How do we know when we're depressed? The question sounds simple. But there is a phenomenon called "masked depression," in which a person doesn't recognize his or her own condition. Sometimes friends, workmates, and family may be more likely than you to notice that you're depressed. They might perceive a clue as simple as a perpetually sad facial expression.

Although the clues to major depression are many, texts and experts tend to agree on the following symptoms:

- *Loss of interest or pleasure.* You may lose interest in pastimes and activities that you normally enjoy. You may withdraw from friends, or experience a loss of sexual drive. If asked to describe your mood, you might just say, "I don't care anymore."
- *Appetite disturbance.* This can take the form of loss of appetite or compulsive eating, leading to either weight loss or weight gain.
- *Sleep disturbance.* Insomnia is common, particularly during the early morning hours. Sometimes, however, there is an increase in sleep. You may feel particularly low when you wake up in the morning.
- *Physical agitation.* You might find it difficult to sit still; you might pace a lot or pick up nervous mannerisms. On the other hand, your movements might slow down noticeably.
- *Changes in speech.* Your speech might be marked by slowness, pauses before answering questions, or monotony. Perhaps you are increasingly prone to complain or raise your voice.
- *Decreased energy.* You may feel unexplainable fatigue even if you haven't exerted yourself.
- *Negative feelings.* You may have feelings of worthlessness or guilt. You may tend to remember past events in a negative way, or be unnecessarily hard on yourself for minor weaknesses. You may take a nihilistic view of things, and express pessimistic points of view. You may be perpetually sad and gloomy.
- *Concentration problems.* Your attention span might be shortened and limited. Perhaps you find it difficult to make decisions.
- *Morbid thoughts.* You may become preoccupied with, or afraid of, death. Or you may wish yourself dead and make suicidal plans.

Not all of these symptoms will necessarily be present when major depression occurs. And although depression is distinct from grief, anxiety, or anger, some of its symptoms may overlap with these other conditions. Examples include sleep and appetite disturbances, loss of sexual drive, prevailing guilt and inadequacy, chronic fatigue, and suicidal thoughts or actions.

Major depression is a likely diagnosis if you have experienced two of the following symptoms for more than a month: apathy, joylessness, lack of energy.

mood shifts tended to be out of proportion to the effect of the negative things that happened to them.

"Not only do depressed people tend to magnify bad events, they also don't seem to feel much excitement over things that are objectively good," Larsen told *Brain/Mind Bulletin*. "If they are given compliments that would make most other people happy, they might look instead for ulterior motives."

The power of "nonnegative thinking" was pointed out by researchers. They said that it may be more important to avoid association with negative situations than to associate yourself with good ones. They noted that disassociating oneself from a bad event appears to be a normal human response, probably designed to protect self-esteem. In depression, this response process fails to function correctly.

Realism and Mental Health

Accumulating evidence challenges the notion that mental health depends on a realistic view of oneself. In fact, Shelley Taylor of UCLA and Jonathon Brown of Southern Methodist University observed in *Psychological Bulletin* (103) that what we often describe as a realistic attitude may be conducive to depression. *Brain/Mind Bulletin* reported on their work in 1988.

"Decades of psychological wisdom have established contact with reality as a hallmark of mental health," said Taylor and Brown. "In this view, the well-adjusted person is thought to engage in accurate reality-testing, whereas the individual whose vision is clouded by illusion is regarded as vulnerable to . . . mental illness. Taylor and Brown said that it now appears that normal people do better when they have some assumptions that seem "unrealistic" when compared to observers' views of their performance. Then, they have optimism and self-confidence.

It is depressed people who tend to be "realistic" about life: they remember both positive and negative things about themselves; they blame themselves and others for the negative things that happen. They are actually relatively unbiased in processing information about themselves, the researchers said.

Contrary to expectations, "the mentally healthy person appears to have the enviable capacity to distort reality in a direction that enhances self-esteem, maintains beliefs

RESEARCH

Depression in Small Children

Preschoolers can have depressionlike states, according to Javad Kashani of the University of Missouri in Columbia and his colleagues. They reported their research in the *American Journal of Psychiatry* (143); *Brain/Mind Bulletin* discussed their work in 1987.

An initial study, based on parent questionnaires, found no evidence of depression among preschoolers. Later, however, working directly with teachers, the investigators rated the mood and behavior of 109 young children. The children were judged on activity, interaction, physical complaints, and play.

The nine who were rated as depressed had undergone significantly more stressful life-events than their age-mates. Unlike older depressives, they tended to be more irritable than sad.

Only one was judged as having a major disorder—a five-year-old who talked about wanting to "kill myself and die."

INVENTORY: HELPFUL ILLUSIONS

Following are some of the common but possibly adaptive misperceptions summarized by Shelley Taylor and Jonathon Brown:

• *Unrealistically positive views of the self.* Not only do mentally healthy people tend to credit themselves with far more positive than negative traits, but they may have difficulty remembering negative information.

Even when people admit their own negative aspects, they may dismiss them as inconsequential. People tend to think of their inabilities as common, their talents as "rare and distinctive."

They also tend to think of things they are not good at as less important than the things they do well.

• *Illusions of control.* In experimental gambling situations involving chance, mentally healthy people tend to think they have control or are applying skill. For example, they think that they have greater control if they personally throw dice than if someone else does it for them.

Both mildly and severely depressed individuals seem to be less likely to have the illusion of control.

• *Unrealistic optimism.* Most people say that they are oriented toward the present and the future or primarily toward the future—as opposed to the present or past only. They think optimistically about the future, believing that the present is better than the past and that the future will be even better.

Most young people estimate their chances at liking their first job, getting a good salary, or having a gifted child as higher than the chances of their peers. They think they are less likely than others to have an auto accident, be the victim of a crime, or have trouble getting a job.

• *Happiness or contentment.* Most people report being happy most of the time. In surveys of mood, 70 to 80% of respondents report that they are moderately to very happy. Most believe that others are average in happiness, and 60% believe that they are happier than most people.

People who consider themselves happy tend to have higher opinions of themselves and an exaggerated belief in their ability to control what goes on around them.

• *Ability to care for others.* Optimism may improve social functioning. One study found that people with high self-esteem and an optimistic view of the future were better able to cope with loneliness at college than were individuals who did not have these tendencies.

• *Capacity for creative, productive work.* "There may. . . be intellectual benefits to self-enhancement." Memory seems to be organized so that people recall information relating to themselves well.

in personal efficacy, and promotes an optimistic view of the future." Although these opinions of the self may be illusions, they seem to foster mental health—including the ability to care about the self and others, the ability to be happy or contented, and the ability to engage in productive and creative work.

People can change through a desire for growth and variety in their lives, rather than because of negative conditions. For example, an individual may think that a new career direction will be even more rewarding than a current one. Positive illusions may inspire people "to make changes that might be avoided if the uphill battle ahead were fully appreciated."

Illusions may also help people put unavoidable negative experiences in the best light.

Although positive illusions can also be harmful, as when people pursue careers for which they are not suited, even these illusions may be offset. A man who does poorly at a job may not acknowledge that he is doing a poor job, but may conclude that he does not like the job and therefore leave.

Positive illusions, the researchers say, can help "make each individual's world a warmer and more active and beneficent place in which to live." Taylor and Brown are authors of *Positive Illusions: Creative Self-Deception and the Healthy Mind* (Basic Books, 1989).

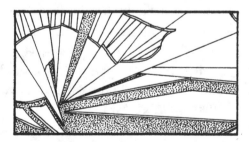

Stress

An even more complex example of the mind/body/feeling interaction is the area of stress. The term includes physical, mental, and emotional pressures. There is plenty of stress in day-to-day existence. How you respond to stress may have to do with your behavior type—whether you are a Type A (driving, dominant) or Type B (calm,

Sustained Exercise Reduces Some Symptoms of Anxiety, Depression

Barry Ledwidge of Simon Fraser University psychology department, Port Coquitlam, B.C., reported in the *Canadian Journal of Behavioral Science* (12) that sustained physical exertion can moderate anxiety. *Brain/Mind Bulletin* discussed his research in 1980.

Anxious persons tend to be frightened by the typical symptoms of their anxiety: racing heart, fatigue, breathlessness. Their alarm, in turn, often intensifies those very symptoms.

Ledwidge observed that when anxiety sufferers experience these same symptoms as a result of vigorous exercise, they are not frightened because they attribute the effects to physical activity. Regular exercise makes them more comfortable with such symptoms, even when they recur in anxiety-provoking circumstances. Sustained exercise also moderates anxiety by relaxing muscles and promoting sound sleep.

Ledwidge pointed out that vigorous exercise increases production of the brain chemical norepinephrine, which is notably deficient in depressive persons. Other symptoms of depression reduced by such exercise are chronic fatigue and abnormal sleep.

To produce the results cited by Ledwidge, exercise must be aerobic, which increases the body's ability to process oxygen. Aerobic exercise brings the heartbeat to about 140 beats per minute, which is about 70% of maximum. Running, swimming, cycling, walking, rowing, handball, cross-country skiing, and jogging are common aerobic exercises.

Signs of Stress in Class of 1992

The freshmen who entered American colleges and universities in 1988 were the most anxious and emotionally unstable ever measured. A 23rd annual survey, reported in *The American Freshman: National Norms for Fall 1988,* was conducted jointly by the American Council of Education and UCLA. More than 300,000 students entering 585 schools participated.

• Only 60.1% seek "a general education" from college, down from 70.9% in 1977. Seventy-two percent reported that "making more money" was a big reason for pursuing a degree, compared with only 50% in 1971.

• More than 10% reported depression, and 21.5% said they felt "overwhelmed" by their responsibilities, up from 8.2% and 16%, respectively, in 1985.

• More than 57% reported copying someone else's homework during the previous year, and 36.6% admitted cheating on an exam.

• For the first time in 22 years, the number of freshmen saying they smoke regularly increased from the previous year. More than 10% were smokers.

Among other data reported by the survey: An all-time high of 21.8% described themselves as politically conservative, though only 18% reported discussing politics during the previous year. As a whole, student opinion remained fairly liberal on such issues as abortion and the environment, but fewer students than ever opposed the death penalty (23%) and 70% favored drug testing by employers.

laid-back) personality. There is evidence to indicate that your response to stress may have a dramatic effect on your health.

And there is increasing interest in post-traumatic-stress disorder. PTSD sufferers seem to be caught in a state of chronic emergency, with exaggerated physiological responses to even minor stresses. Although the disorder was first diagnosed among combat veterans and other victims of war, it has also been identified in children who have witnessed violence.

Then there's the issue of environment—not just on a global, ecological scale, but our immediate everyday surroundings as well. Physical habitats, whether home or work, are sources of comfort or of stress. Such commonplace factors as sound and electromagnetic fields affect us more than we tend to realize.

In short, stress concerns all of us in many different ways. One kind of stress can cause another, as well as interact with a broad range of symptoms. But what, exactly, is the relationship of stress to health? Should we be more concerned with stress itself, or our tactics in dealing with stress? The answers are subtle and complex—but they reveal some new strategies for living.

Type A Behavior

Perhaps the most familiar form of stress is that connected with what physicians call Type A behavior. The basic traits of Type A men were identified in 1959 by cardiologists Meyer Friedman and Ray Rosenman as speed-impatience, ambition-competitiveness, hostility-anger.

Classically, the so-called Type A person has been seen as driving, dominant, tense, and likelier to develop coronary disease than the more calm, patient, laid-back Type B person, who lacks these driving characteristics.

Cynicism and Type A Behavior

Cynicism may be hazardous to your health. A number of studies on Type A behavior and heart disease revealed that attitudes can trigger severe physiological responses. And in the case of heart attack, scientists have cited the culprit mental state: distrust of other people—cynicism.

Before this discovery, personality tests of Type A people typically measured their hostility levels. But this turned out to be imprecise, according to Redford Williams and his colleagues of the Duke Medical Center Psychiatry Department, Durham, North Carolina. They reported their findings in *The Sciences* (September/October, 1984); *Brain/Mind Bulletin* discussed their work in 1984.

"Cynicism, better than any other single word, captures the toxic element in Type A personality," Williams said. If a more trusting attitude can be learned, he said, help for heart patients may be on the way.

In a series of experiments, Williams and his colleagues focused on "hostility" because, as Williams reported, "it has no redeeming value." These were their findings:

• According to psychological tests, the "hostility" scores of Type A people were significantly higher than those of Type B.

• High scorers were 50% more likely to have coronary artery blockages than were low scorers.

• This was one of the first Type A studies to include women. Results suggest that hostility may do its damage without regard to gender.

Another study confirmed these findings: More than 200 male physicians took the hostility scale 25 years earlier. Among those with high scores, rates of coronary illness and death were five or six times higher than among those with low scores.

Only the hostility factor linked Type A behavior with hardening of the arteries. When Williams statistically removed it from the study, the link disappeared.

Having isolated a damaging element, Williams wanted to be sure "hostility" characterized it correctly. Some of the items on the hostility scale—"I think most people would lie to get ahead," "Most people make friends because they are useful to them"—do not directly reflect hostility, he said.

After analyzing the responses of 1,500 people to 50 items, Williams found a more concise unifying theme: cynicism, a contemptuous distrust of human nature and motives.

Trusting Hearts Last Longer

Speaking at a 1989 American Heart Association meeting in Monterey, California, Redford Williams suggested that suspicious people can be taught to have more trusting hearts. "Certain biological characteristics seem to make hostile people good candidates to die earlier," he

RESEARCH

Student Stress Lowers Immunity

On the day of a final exam, college students showed lower levels of an important antibody for fighting infection, compared with the days before and after the exam, John Jemmott and Kim Magloire of the Princeton University psychology department reported in the *Journal of Personality and Social Psychology* (55). *Brain/Mind Bulletin* reported on their work in 1989.

Jemmott and Magloire measured the concentration of secretory immunoglobin A (S-IgA) in the saliva samples of 15 undergraduate students, who were tested five days before their final exam, on the day of the exam, and two weeks after it.

S-IgA levels were considerably lower during the exam period, which was rated by students as unusually stressful. "We're getting closer to understanding the relationship between stress and disease," Jemmott told *Brain/Mind*.

Students were also asked to rank themselves on two scales: the amount of love and support they *received* and the amount they *needed*. Although those reporting strong support scored higher overall than those with low support, each person's individual need appeared to be the key factor. Students who had the smallest perceived disparity between the amounts of love and support needed and received showed the highest levels of S-IgA.

"Self-perception, as usual, appears to play a key role," Jemmott said. "If people feel they have high support, they probably have smaller stress reactions."

RESEARCH

Stress, Personality, and Mortality

A psychological measure of suspiciousness predicted survival in a sample of 500 older men and women whose health was followed for approximately 15 years. High scorers on the suspiciousness index were significantly more likely to die when compared to others of the same age, sex, functional health, and lifestyle patterns (cholesterol, alcohol intake, smoking).

John Barefoot and colleagues at Duke University reported their research in *Psychosomatic Medicine* (49); *Brain/Mind Bulletin* discussed their work in 1988. The researchers said their findings add to growing evidence that hostile or cynical attitudes undermine health. In an earlier 25-year study of physicians conducted by Barefoot, those scoring high on a hostility index had a premature death rate 6.4 times higher than those with low scores.

Those in the present study were white, middle-class adults drawn from the subscriber lists of a health-insurance plan. When they became part of the study in 1968–70, they were 46 to 71 years old, with a mean age of 58.9 years.

Of the 330 who were employed, 102 were semiskilled or unskilled, 108 were skilled, clerical, or sales workers, and 120 were professionals or managers. Sixty-one percent were high school graduates. At the beginning of the study 85% of the subjects were married.

said. "However, personality and environment are also very important. By working to change your outlook on life and reducing the stress of confrontation, you can improve your chances."

INVENTORY: THE TRUSTING HEART

Redford Williams offers these 12 steps toward achieving a trusting, healthier heart. This list is adapted from his book, *The Trusting Heart: Great News About Type A Behavior* (Times Books, 1989).

1. *Monitor your cynical thoughts.* Williams recommends keeping a log of situations in which you respond cynically and attempting to evaluate them from a different perspective.

2. *Confess that you recognize your own hostility.*

3. *Force yourself to stop cynical thoughts in progress.*

4. *Examine situations reasonably.*

5. *Put yourself in the other person's shoes.*

6. *Learn to laugh at yourself.*

7. *Learn to relax.* Techniques such as yoga and meditation can be very useful.

8. *Practice trust.* Make a special effort to place trust in someone, even if in an unimportant matter.

9. *Learn to listen.*

10. *Learn to be assertive.* When difficult situations arise, assert your point of view calmly rather than reacting aggressively.

11. *Pretend today is your last.* Williams reflects that after people experience major illnesses their hostility is often reduced.

12. *Practice forgiving others.*

Stress and Illness

Although there is little argument that stressful events tend to trigger illness, the tie between personality types and specific diseases is less clearly established. However, patterns are emerging from work at several research centers. One group of findings seems to indicate that antiemotional people are more prone to cancer, overemotional to coronaries.

Stress and Strain

A well-known British personality researcher, H. J. Eysenck, has summarized a group of European studies that also indicate a striking difference between the personality types that will later develop either heart disease or cancer. Eysenck, of the University of London Institute of Psychiatry, published his data in *British Journal of Medical Psychology* (61). *Brain/Mind Bulletin* reported on the work in 1989.

Eysenck emphasized the importance of distinguishing between "stress" and "strain"—as is done in physics. Stress is the outside force, strain the reacting of the object under stress. Personality is the variable that varies the strain in reaction to stress. "Many types of stimuli . . . impose more of a strain on emotionally unstable than emotionally stable people," Eysenck observed.

European Studies

Eysenck referred to the findings of three long-term studies—one in Yugoslavia (1,353 subjects) and two in Germany (872 and 1,042 subjects). The investigation, conducted by Ronald Grossarth-Maticek, found dramatic correlations between personality style of individuals not yet ill and later rates of premature death from cancer or heart disease.

The Yugoslavian subjects ranged in age from 59 to 65 when tested. In Germany, most were between 40 and 60. Grossarth-Maticek and his coworkers then recorded the number of premature deaths in each group over the next 13 years.

They found that individuals who tended to repress their emotions in the face of stress were far likelier than others to die of cancer. Those who rated high on emotional frustration and aggression had a high rate of cardiac-related deaths.

RESEARCH

Stress Linked to Temporary Female Infertility

Human and animal studies, summarized in a report in *New Scientist* (17), revealed that both physical and psychological stress can disrupt the female reproductive cycle.

Brain/Mind Bulletin discussed these findings in 1985.

Fertility clinics report that up to 80% of their cases can be attributed to "psychosocial stress."

On the physical side, female athletes exemplify the stress-infertility link. They often suffer from irregular or abnormal menstrual cycles during intensive training periods.

Recent findings also suggest that the brain's natural opiates—endorphins and enkephalins—are involved. Women on difficult training schedules exhibit higher levels of endorphins and enkephalins in the bloodstream.

Administration of enkephalin to normal volunteers lowers the production of pituitary hormones LH and FSH. The result: menstrual abnormalities and eventual infertility.

The effects of strenuous exercise appear to be temporary. They are reversed as soon as women complete their training regimens. Also, they can be reversed by an opiate blocker, naloxone.

Stress also affects the male reproductive capacity. Sperm banks report dramatic reductions in sperm counts in students during final exams. High levels of cortisol, another hormone released during stress, inhibit sperm production in the testicles.

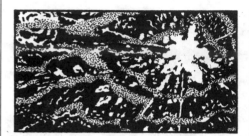

Post-Traumatic-Stress Disorder

Symptoms of PTSD include jumpiness, nightmares, sleeplessness, difficulty in concentrating, fear of recurrence of traumatic events, and attempts to avoid feelings. It is typified by emotional constriction and physiological hypersensitivity.

John Helzer and coworkers in the Washington University School of Medicine Psychiatry Department reported on the syndrome in the *New England Journal of Medicine* (317); *Brain/Mind Bulletin* discussed their work in 1988.

One study found PTSD in the following:

	%
veterans wounded in Vietnam	20
general population	1
civilians exposed to physical attack	3.5
noninjured Vietnam veterans	3.5

Mental-health researchers in Los Angeles studied 159 children a month after a fatal sniper attack on their elementary-school playground. One child and a passerby were killed and 13 children injured in the 1984 siege, which lasted several hours.

The number of PTSD symptoms was directly related to the children's proximity to the violence, Robert Pynoos of UCLA's Neuropsychiatric Institute and coworkers reported in *Archives of General Psychology* (44); *Brain/Mind Bulletin* discussed their work in 1988.

Personality variables were more predictive than smoking in the occurrence of lung cancer, for example. Smoking was virtually a prerequisite for getting lung cancer, but of the smokers only the emotionally repressive types (Type 1 in following inventory) seemed to get the disease.

INVENTORY: PERSONALITY AND ILLNESS

The personality types established by Grossarth-Maticek were based on personality profiles developed from the answers participants gave to detailed questions about their emotional life. The researchers broke subjects down into four types:

• *Type 1, or underaroused,* tended to have one valued person or object as their emotional focus. Because their well-being was profoundly involved in this person or object, they became strained or depressed if they experienced loss, distance, or separation. They were found likelier to get cancer.

• *Type 2, or overaroused,* were also focused on one emotional object but were more susceptible to a breakdown of any kind and not just loss. They tended to react with frustration and anger rather than depression. These emotionally frustrated individuals were found to be likelier to develop heart disease.

• *Type 3, ambivalent,* responded with depression on some occasions, anger and frustration at other times.

• *Type 4, autonomous,* were emotionally well adjusted, healthy, and self-reliant.

Neither of the latter two groups was predicted to have high risk in any area.

In these studies the prediction of risks for each personality type proved remarkably accurate.

	% died of cancer	% died of heart disease
Yugoslavian		
Type 1 subjects	46.2	8.3
Type 2	5.6	29.2
German		
Type 1	17	1.8
Type 2	5.9	13.5

In a second German group, all of whom were selected on the basis of being ranked as "highly stressed" by friends and relatives, the pattern was the same—that is, a far greater percentage of Type 1 people died from cancer and Type 2 people died from heart disease.

The overall death rate was 40% greater for stressed than random subjects.

Therapy for Behavior

Eysenck and Grossarth-Maticek reported that behavioral therapy has an impressive preventive effect. For 50 people in Germany, it starkly reduced the number of deaths. After 10 years, 45 of the 50 who had participated in behavioral therapy were still alive, but 31 of a control group of 50 had died. None of those in the first group died of cancer, compared to 16 in the second group.

The therapy was designed to help individuals whose personality was predictive of either cancer or heart disease to achieve greater emotional autonomy.

Responses to Stress

An earlier study of former medical students at Johns Hopkins University also indicated that individual styles of stress reaction may predict the type of illness likely to occur in later life. This research was reported in 1980 by Caroline Thomas and Lee McCabe in *The Johns Hopkins Medical Journal* (147). They had been following the lives of 1,337 medical students who attended the school from 1948 to 1964.

Healthy individuals and those who later developed specific illnesses had different stress-response patterns:

• *Healthy status.* Those who remained healthy tended to react to stress with generalized tension or increased activity. They seldom showed exhaustion, depressed feelings, sleeping difficulties, anger, loss of appetite, or irritability.

• *Coronary.* Students who later became coronary patients showed early patterns of reacting to stress with depression, general tension, and anger. Other characteristic responses included the urge to sleep (in those who were depressed) or sleeping difficulties, and the urge to be alone.

• *Cancer.* Perfectionism was highest in the group that later developed cancer. They also reported early patterns of depressed feelings and loss of appetite in the face of stress. This was the only group that had not shown health concerns in their student days. The cancer victims were also less likely to make a philosophical effort to resolve their stress or to feel the urge to confide in others.

Harvard Tests Mother Theresa Effect

Even a secondhand experience of a loving attitude may spur the immune system, judging from experiments at Harvard reported in *Advances* (Spring 1985).

David McClelland, known for studies of human motivation, showed movies of Mother Theresa, the Nobel Prize–winning nun who cares for the sick in India, to undergraduates. McClelland wanted to see if a film could transmit the experience of loving care that would in turn boost immunity. Immune responses were measured by a change in the saliva associated with a defense against colds.

About half the group said Mother Theresa was a wonderful inspiration; the other half were skeptical. Immunity increased even in some who intensely disliked her.

"Perhaps she was contacting these consciously disapproving people in another part of their brains," McClelland said, "and that part was still responding to the strength of her loving care."

If so, he added, belief in the healer may not be necessary for healing.

Furthermore, those whose immunity improved reported a motivation to serve or to do something positive for someone else. They typically wanted to serve yet were not too interested in a personal outcome.

The AIDS Book: Creating a Positive Approach (Hay House, 1988) draws from author Louise Hay's work with AIDS patients and others who have attended her weekly meetings in Los Angeles and other major cities. Many participants in the "Hayrides" reported a recovery of immune function or the diminishing of other symptoms—due in part, they believe, to Hay's emphasis on love, forgiveness, and self-acceptance.

The many case histories in the book reflect her circumspect approach to AIDS. She emphasizes nutrition but no particular diet, encourages openness to alternative therapies, but also urges patients to follow their medical regimens.

As Hay sees it, most of the people afflicted with AIDS feel oppressed and hopeless. "I am not a healer," she says in the introduction. "I do not heal anyone. I am a very simple lady who knows and teaches the power of love; that's all I do." People who feel loved and who can love, she says, may create their own healing.

Healing AIDS Naturally (Human Energy Press, 1987) by Laurence Badgley is about AIDS and our fear of AIDS. Badgley is a physician who has synthesized treatment technologies from all parts of the world. His bias, if it can be called that, is evident in the dedication page: "To all the courageous practitioners who are attempting to understand the natural laws and to incorporate these laws into the efforts they make for those they help."

Using his understanding of these natural laws, Badgley treats a whole spectrum of diseases, including AIDS, ARC, herpes, candida, and cancer. He explores the use of specific nutritional supplements (vitamins, minerals, herbs). He also uses "energy medicine" such as acupuncture and crystals to treat diagnosed energy imbalances.

There is no cure for disease, he says. "In all cases, the body heals itself."

• *Mental illness.* This group had reported the greatest tendencies toward exhaustion, exhilaration, anxious feelings, urge to eat, or nausea under stress. They were also likely to make a philosophical effort to resolve their stress.

• *Suicide.* Students who later committed suicide had the highest rate of increased activity, sleeping difficulty, loss of appetite, urinary frequency, and desire to be alone. This group had the lowest tendency to be angry or to make an effort to resolve their stress philosophically.

In 1989, Caroline Thomas told *PragMagic* that the researchers were still following the same subjects.

AIDS and Hope

Laurence Badgley, author of *Healing AIDS Naturally* (see sidebar) and director of the Foundation for Research of Natural Therapies (FRONT), was one of the sponsors of the 1989 Advanced Immune Discoveries Symposium in Los Angeles. Badgley offered a new model of the AIDS disease process. "The virus, upon entering the body, is 'put to sleep'—but later, cofactors like drug abuse, alcohol, poor nutrition, and stress wake it up."

Other speakers agreed, emphasizing the role played by peripheral influences. George Solomon of UCLA and the University of California, San Francisco, who coined

INVENTORY: SURVIVING AIDS

Lydia Temoshok, then a psychologist at the University of California at San Francisco (now at the Henry M. Jackson Foundation, Walter Reed Army Medical Center), described to *PragMagic* several common characteristics derived from her own observations of long-term AIDS survivors. Among them:

• Acceptance of the diagnosis, combined with refusal to consider it a death sentence. "There are many patients who have not died and are doing well," she said. "We can't merely describe it as a terminal illness. There is more to it than that."
• Perceiving the physician as collaborator.
• Having "unfinished business" to attend to—strong motivation to survive. One patient vowed not to die until he finished adding rooms onto his house; at last check, he had obtained bank loans and was almost to the edge of his property.
• Taking personal responsibility for the disease and healing.
• Being in tune with one's own body and feelings and acting accordingly. Those who are in tune stop and sleep when tired and can say no when they don't want to do something.
• Having a spiritual feeling of something beyond the "self."

the term "psychoimmunology" in the 1960s, reported that three factors can generally predict the speed of declining immune function in an HIV-positive person:

- Number of lifetime sexual partners
- Number of sexual diseases
- Number of friends who have died

All those factors, as well as the stress Solomon considers unavoidable in being homosexual, can attack the immune system. The majority of adults suffering from AIDS are homosexual and bisexual men.

"Good copers likely will do better with AIDS," Solomon told the audience. "Why do women, whose immune systems are normally stronger, reportedly have less success surviving?" His answer: Most female AIDS victims studied have been drug abusers, who by their very nature are not copers.

"AIDS does not inevitably lead to death, especially if you suppress the cofactors that support the disease," said Badgley, quoting AIDS virus discoverer Luc Montagnier of Paris's Pasteur Institute. "It is not the virus that has changed its basic configuration but the behavior of its host."

Some Environmental Questions

We are all aware of widely publicized public concerns about the ozone layer, air and water pollution, pesticides, and radon in our homes. But it also appears that there are more ambiguous sources of possible stress from our environment. *Brain/Mind Bulletin* has reported on research indicating that our homes and offices may be dangerously polluted by electromagnetic waves as well as by certain levels of noise and vibration.

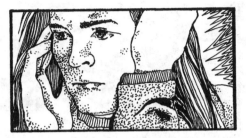

Noise and Vibration

Noise and vibration can trigger a temporary loss of hearing. In a Finnish experiment reported in the *International Archives of Occupational and Environmental Health* (57), simultaneous exposure to both caused a significantly greater raising of the hearing threshold (requiring sounds to be louder in order to be heard) than either alone.

Olavi Manninen said his findings, reported in a 1987 issue of *Brain/Mind Bulletin,* supported other studies showing a deterioration in reaction times, and changes in heart rates and blood pressures in people exposed to noise, vibration, or heat.

As a practical example of the effects of combined noise and vibration, Manninen cited "... the high risk of coronary heart disease among bus drivers reported by Norwegian researchers," which he said would be associated with the conditions under which they work.

COMMENTARY

Living in Electromagnetic Fields

In an article in *Archeus* (2:1) entitled "Living in Magnetic Fields," biophysicist Otto Schmitt noted that people have been living in a magnetic field of half a gauss (the standard unit of measure for such fields) for generations. This has long been assumed an acceptable level of exposure—or in the jargon of the Food and Drug Administration, GRAS (Generally Regarded as Safe). *Brain/Mind Bulletin* reported on Schmitt's work in 1988.

However, Schmitt said, "we have been eating up our margin of safety at an appalling rate. If we maintain the present exponential rate of escalation of such field strengths ... we can reliably predict serious trouble before the end of the century." It is becoming cheap, easy, and useful to incorporate magnets and stray electromagnetic field sources into our everyday devices, Schmitt said. For example, there are laser devices that read tags in supermarkets, loudspeakers with large lumps of strongly magnetic material, bed vibrators, "even small hand-held hair driers [that] pour out fields of 40 gauss or more."

When the researchers conducted an experiment to see if university students could recognize the presence of such fields, half the subjects spontaneously reported having some kind of headache.

"We have not yet developed a folklore to protect technically uninformed people, as we have in the case of red-hot coals, unidentified snakes, and razor blades," Schmitt said.

Noise and Environmental Stress

Controllable and uncontrollable noise were used as stressors by Baltimore researchers hoping to learn more about the mechanism involved in "learned helplessness." People were little affected by noise they could turn off during a 30-minute period, but the same amount of noise left them upset and neurophysiologically affected when they were unable to control it.

Alan Brier of the Maryland Psychiatric Research Center and his coworkers reported their work in the *American Journal of Psychiatry* (144); *Brain/Mind Bulletin* discussed the research in 1988. Brier and his colleagues were investigating a sense of helplessness that is believed to play a part in depression.

People in good mental health had to listen to a loud (100 decibels) tone in two different settings. First they were able to turn off the tone by pushing a button. In the second situation, button pushing had no effect, but the subjects did not know that. Twice during the session they were handed notes urging them to "continue to try hard."

Subjects reported their moods before starting each session. After the uncontrollable noise they reported an increase in depression, helplessness, anxiety, and tension.

"Lack of control over even a mildly aversive stimulus" can produce significant changes in healthy subjects, the researchers concluded.

The Electrical Environment

In 1989, *Brain/Mind Bulletin* reported that the California Public Utilities Commission issued a review study and held public hearings on risks from electromagnetic (EM) fields. The California report conceded that evidence of health risks is strong, although it maintained that knowledge was insufficient to justify specific legislation.

"Well-designed studies show significant associations between indicators of exposure to above-average electric and magnetic fields and increased incidence of specific health problems," the report said.

The study cited various forms of cancer and reproductive problems as areas most needing investigation.

What Are EM Fields?

"There are electric and magnetic fields wherever there is electric power," Carnegie Mellon University professor Granger Morgan points out in *Electric and Magnetic Fields from 60 Hertz Electric Power: What do we know about possible health risks?* (Carnegie Mellon University, 1989). Morgan's booklet describes our electric current, the fields it generates, and discusses scientific research on the possibility of dangers associated with these fields (see sidebar on page 158 and inventory on page 159).

Morgan reminds us that the current used in North American homes and offices alternates its flow 60 times each second. It is called 60 hertz (Hz) power. Certain fields are associated with 60 Hz power: electric and magnetic. "These fields are created by electric charges. Charges produce two kinds of fields: *electric fields,* which result just from the strength of the charge, and *magnetic fields,* which result from the motion of the charge. Taken together these are often referred to as electromagnetic fields."

The strength of electromagnetic fields can be measured with special instruments or calculated according to formulas from physics and electrical engineering. The effect of these fields gets weaker as you move away from them. Several fields can add together or they can cancel each other out.

Although they are all forms of electromagnetic energy, Morgan says that 60 Hz fields are not really much like X rays and microwaves. "The energy carried by the X rays is so large that it can break molecular bonds. It can actually break apart DNA, the molecules that make the genes. This is the way X-ray exposure leads to cancer. However, the energy carried in 60 Hz fields is *much* too small to break molecular or chemical bonds." Microwaves are also too weak to break chemical or molecular bonds, but they set up strong currents that cause heating.

For a long time it was believed that 60 Hz fields could not produce significant biological changes or effects because they do not break molecular or chemical bonds and do not produce significant heat. Morgan notes that "this argument has turned out to be incorrect because there are other ways in which fields can interact with individual cells to produce biological changes. Whether these changes can lead to health risks remains unclear."

RESOURCES

Electromagnetic Man: Health and Hazard in the Electrical Environment (J.M. Dent, London, 1989) by Cyril Smith and Simon Best covers the history of our understanding of EM fields from ancient times through modern breakthroughs, basic concepts, the electrical aspect of human biology, medical uses of EM, the connection between allergy and electrical sensitivity, pollution and danger from EM fields (including military installations).

Smith is the researcher who initiated the first undergraduate course in medical electronics at a British university. Best is an outstanding medical journalist specializing in the effects of EM fields.

The Body Electric by Robert Becker and Gary Selden (Morrow, 1985) is a definitive book, a first-person account of bioelectrical research. Becker's work, along with that of others in the field, sheds light on mysteries of cancer, acupuncture, and psychiatric disorders. It also discusses possible modalities for psi and collective consciousness.

"I sing the body electric . . ." wrote poet Walt Whitman. For Becker, too, life is electricity. The orthopedic surgeon spent his research career outlining a neglected portion of biology—electromagnetic fields and healing.

Becker describes fields within fields: Each cell is pulsing within the body's larger field, which beats in tune with the Earth's magnetic field. Health, Becker says, depends on a narrow range of frequencies.

Low-frequency fields, long thought to be too weak to affect human beings, are now known to interfere with bodily cycles.

"These discoveries presage a revolution in biology and medicine," Becker says. "One day they may enable the physician to control and stimulate healing at will.

"This new knowledge will also turn medicine in the direction of greater humility, for we should see that whatever we achieve pales before the self-healing power latent in all organisms."

Prudence and Health Risks

"In our private lives we exercise prudence all the time when we face an uncertain risk. In public decision making we may have more trouble being 'prudent' about uncertainty. Public risk management activities tend to treat things as either dangerous or safe, with no middle ground. It may take some guts for a regulator to adopt a 'prudent avoidance' strategy.

"Prudence means 'exercising sound judgment in practical matters.' It means being 'cautious, sensible, not rash in conduct.' How, for example are people prudent about cancer in their private lives? They don't smoke. They eat diets with little charbroiled food and lots of fiber. *But* prudent people do not: refuse to go to an important business meeting because one of the participants occasionally smokes; go without breakfast when all that is available on the menu is regular cereal rather than their usual high fiber cereal; or, order lobster for their children because it is the only food on the menu that isn't charbroiled. Prudence means you take steps to control risks but at a modest cost. You keep some sense of proportion and you don't go overboard."

—from *Electric and Magnetic Fields from 60 Hertz Electric Power: What do we know about possible health risks?* by Granger Morgan and others Published by the Department of Engineering and Public Policy Carnegie Mellon University

The Effects of Electromagnetic Fields

Strong electric fields can produce a slight tingling sensation by vibrating hairs or by triggering various sensors in the skin. People generally cannot sense the presence of magnetic fields. Morgan points out that "while these 'perception' effects are interesting, and have received quite a lot of research attention, few people ever spend time in fields that are strong enough to be felt."

He feels that "potentially more important results come from experiments which show that under certain circumstances fields can interact with the surfaces of cells and trigger changes inside these cells . . .

"While the details remain unclear, a variety of experiments have shown that fields, even fairly weak fields, can interact with the cell surface, or with some of the receptor molecules in that surface, and produce changes in how the cell operates. The fields contain very little energy. In some way the cell surface or its receptors act as an amplifier to send a signal into the cell that can change things like the rate at which the cell makes hormones, enzymes and other proteins. These chemicals play roles in the operation of the cell and in signaling to other cells and tissues."

Morgan discusses specific laboratory findings, most of which did not find any differences between animals or tissues exposed to fields and those not exposed to fields. He adds, "The few studies that did find interesting changes have been followed up with more detailed experiments. Effects that have been reported include: changes in various chemical messengers including chemicals like melatonin that are important in daily biological cycles called circadian rhythms, and chemicals called neurotransmitters which send signals between nerves; changes in the rate at which the genetic material DNA is made and in the rate of errors when RNA is copied from it; changes in the amount of calcium found inside or on the surface of cells."

He also says that studies of people exposed to fairly strong fields in special exposure rooms have reported effects on heart rate and reaction time and that studies of people sleeping with electric blankets report changes in the level of the hormone melatonin. "There is some indication that some people respond more than others."

Morgan points out that it is not clear if these effects have significant implications for people's health. Studies have found a statistical association between increases in field exposure and increased cancer rates, although no

INVENTORY: MANAGING RISKS

Granger Morgan, head of the Department of Engineering and Public Policy and a professsor of electrical and computer engineering at Carnegie Mellon University has commented on the possible health risks of electric and magnetic fields. Research on possible risks from exposure to 60 Hz electric and magnetic fields and the problems of communicating about these risks has been supported at Carnegie Mellon by the U.S. Department of Energy, the Electric Power Research Institute (EPR), and the National Science Foundation (NSF). The brochure from which these items were taken was supported by a grant from the National Science Foundation.

"How could prudent people manage their risks from 60 Hz electric and magnetic fields if they wanted to?" Morgan asks. He continues, "Not by tearing all the wiring out of their house. That would be extreme."

The following suggestions are from his booklet:

- Put away your electric blanket (or electrically heated water bed) and go back to using regular blankets. Or, use the electric blanket to preheat the bed, and then unplug it before going to bed (the magnetic field disappears when the blanket is switched off; the electric field may remain as long as the blanket is plugged in.)

  There may be a few people, such as those who have circulatory problems, for whom an electric blanket is very important. For these people the cost of going without an electric blanket may be too high to make this a prudent step.

- Small electric motors produce strong magnetic fields. If you want to reduce your field exposure you might look around for small electric motors that you are close to. For example, a motor-driven electric clock on your bedside table may produce a fairly strong magnetic field by your head. If you want to practice prudent avoidance, you could move it to a dresser across the room or replace it with one of the newer digital clocks or with a travel clock or windup clock.

- If you are buying a new home, it might be prudent to consider the location of distribution and transmission lines as one of many things you consider. However, remember that even if fields are ultimately demonstrated to pose a health risk, things like traffic patterns in the streets and radon levels in the house are likely to be more important for your own or your children's overall safety than anything related to fields. If you are already in a home, moving in order to get away from existing lines goes beyond what we would consider prudent.

—from *Electric and Magnetic Fields from 60 Hertz Electric Power:*
What do we know about possible health risks?
by Granger Morgan and others, published by the
Department of Engineering and Public Policy,
Carnegie Mellon University

Electromagnetic Fields and Crib Death

British researcher Roger Coghill told a Tucson, Arizona, international congress that high EM levels may play a key role in infant crib death. In 1989 he also described to *Brain/Mind Bulletin* a large-scale British survey of sudden infant death syndrome (SIDS) cases that found higher-than-normal electric fields in every instance.

SIDS (called "cot death" in Britain) is the sudden and seemingly inexplicable death of healthy babies, usually during sleep. Most of the 70 infants studied in London had slept in electric fields at least 10 times the average ambient fields in the city. Among the conditions causing the high levels were nearby power lines and electric subway tracks.

In addition, Coghill said, in 6 of 34 cases studied in Sweden, infants who died were wrapped in electric blankets.

"Sudden infant death is the most frequent cause of infant mortality," he said. "The number of cases has risen by 50% in the past five years."

The mechanism through which EM rays could damage human health is not yet established, Coghill said.

cause or contribution has been identified. "Depending on the study and the type of cancer, the incidence of cancer in exposed populations may be up to two to three times higher than that experienced by unexposed or less exposed populations." He points out that, in contrast, "cigarette smoking increases the risk of lung cancer by 20 to 60 times."

Reports of Growing Concern

The growing concern over the potential dangers of ordinary EM fields was highlighted in three June 1989 issues of *The New Yorker*. "Annals of Radiation: The Hazards of Electromagnetic Fields," by Paul Brodeur, provided a three-part historical summary of suspicions and investigations.

Brodeur chronicled an alarming tale of slow governmental response, dubious scientific pronouncements, and finally—as the specter of EM risk came into focus—attempts at cover-up. He reviewed a large body of evidence, mainly accumulated over the past 10 to 15 years, suggesting that EM fields in sufficient quantity may endanger physical and psychological health.

Countering longtime industry arguments, Brodeur explained that emissions from power lines and other continuous sources are much more potent than those of common household appliances, which are used sporadically, and whose fields drop off sharply in strength beyond a few inches. The notable exception is electric blankets, which have circumstantially been implicated in health dangers.

Brodeur gave considerable attention to concerns that frequencies used in certain radar systems have been demonstrated to suppress immune function in mice and have also been associated with increased incidences of cancer.

Brodeur reported that investigators have uncovered evidence that visual display terminals, widely used with computers, can have negative effects on pregnancies. Researchers' attention was drawn to a potential problem by reports, beginning in the late 1970s, of clusters of miscarriages and birth defects among women working in offices using VDTs.

Addictions

The issue of addictions is fraught with rhetorical phrases, such as "the war on drugs" and "just say no." While this flood of concern and consciousness raising is undoubtedly healthy, the combative myth that presently surrounds addictions may not be helpful.

We need to think of addictiveness in a larger context. People become addicted to *licit* substances as well as *illicit* ones. They also become addicted to work, sex, hobbies—a whole range of nonsubstances.

We perceive a workaholic on his way up the corporate ladder in a very different light from a heroin addict. But how real is the difference?

One question is crucial. Why do people become addicts? Answers from some therapists suggest that the addict is not so different from everyone else, but an unwitting victim of yearnings common to all of us—yearnings that can as readily be directed toward healing and wholeness as toward addiction and illness.

Toward a New Model of Addiction

"The current model of an addictive personality isn't very useful," physician-author Andrew Weil told participants in a 1986 Brookridge Institute conference. "Addiction proneness is a fundamental aspect of being human."

Weil is a professor of addiction studies at the University of Arizona and the author of *Natural Mind* (Houghton Mifflin, 1986) and *Chocolate to Morphine* (see sidebar, page 162). Weil and others explored new approaches to substance abuse at the session "Addiction and Consciousness," in Burlingame, California.

Addiction is a side effect of a natural human drive, the search for more satisfying mental states, many of the

Alcoholics are people first and alcoholics second. People are complex, organic systems, and not all people grow at the same pace. All have potential to grow physically, mentally, emotionally and spiritually. . . .

For some this means going beyond existing [treatments] because that's where they happen to be in their growth. Not because other treatments are wrong, inferior or anything else—all work perfectly well for some of the people some of the time, but none at this current time work for all of the people all of the time.

—Shirley Burton in the *Addictions and Consciousness Journal* (September 1988)

RESOURCES

Beyond Addictions, Beyond Boundaries, edited by Shirley Burton and Leo Kiley (Brookridge, 1988) is the proceedings of the first year's conference, compiled by the co-founders of Brookridge.

Drug, Set and Setting: The Basis for Controlled Intoxicant Use by Norman Zinberg (Yale University Press, 1984) argues against oversimplification of the causes, patterns, and outcome of drug use. Investigating addiction in the 1960s, Zinberg, a clinical professor of psychiatry at Harvard Medical School, wondered why some users do not abuse such substances. He concluded that they limit their use of substances to specific occasions, settings, or purposes.

Chocolate to Morphine: Understanding Mind-Active Drugs (Houghton Mifflin, 1972), by Andrew Weil and Winifred Rosen, is a comprehensive, illustrated encyclopedia of mind-active drugs.

speakers said. Some abusers are seeking transcendence, others just relief from chronic discomfort.

"This is a drug-using culture," said Weil. Chocolate, coffee, and tobacco are among our favorite drugs. Cigarette addiction dwarfs all other public health problems, he said, but the habit is considered psychological, not physical. "The distinction is meaningless.

"Addiction is not so much a pharmacological problem as a spiritual one," Weil said. He urges clients to divert their drive in healthier directions—for example, exercise rather than smoking. Like a number of therapists at the Brookridge conference, he recommends meditation and techniques that focus on breathing. "But there's no instant solution. Inner work—a restructuring of personality—is essential."

Most addicts are trying to experience greater wholeness, he said. Research and treatment approaches that don't acknowledge this hunger are doomed to failure. "The prevailing materialistic model of medical science, which denies the importance of consciousness, can't treat addictive behavior any more than it can understand it."

Substance abusers, according to Arizona physician David Hawkins, are seeking a better frame of mind—an effect, not a substance. "They don't have to be ashamed of their goal just because the method doesn't work."

Speakers emphasized that addiction does not necessarily begin simply as pleasure-seeking or escape from responsibility. It may be a failed attempt at a legitimate goal: exploration of creative possibilities, a more positive attitude, greater social ease, self-understanding.

Too many treatment models, they noted, have been based on guilt; addicts are treated as weak willed, unable to face life without the aids others can forego.

Most addictions, Weil noted, are more socially acceptable than substance abuse. Other speakers noted that compulsive behavior is less frowned upon in the areas of food, sex, relationships, work, hobbies.

Alternative Therapies

Many abusers are attempting to self-medicate depression, anxiety, or metabolic problems that make it hard for them to achieve positive states naturally. Janice Phelps, a Seattle physician, introduces dietary changes and nutritional boosts, including intravenous vitamins, to correct biochemical imbalances in addicts. When that is not enough, she said, antidepressants seem to help.

Santa Monica, California, psychiatrist Alan Brovar said, "The first priority is to get them clean and sober, without diversions or discussions of mysterious techniques." He has used a wide variety of methods: breath counting, movement, yoga, walking, light therapy to relieve seasonal depression, negative-ion generators, cranial electrotherapy stimulation, subliminal audiotapes, and medication.

However, Brovar told *PragMagic,* "a long menu of possibly effective approaches with their quasi-technical explanations may prove to be a misguided distraction (if not an outright danger) to the recovering addict or alcoholic." He emphasized the individualization of treatment—tailoring a combination of methods to the individual client.

Rick Irons, a Seattle, Washington, addiction specialist, teaches patients to describe their struggles metaphorically, in heroic terms. He uses specific settings and rituals to intensify the effects of therapy. Modern culture, he said, lacks rites of passage. He uses such rites to transfer power symbolically from the substance to the client.

Naomi Remen, a private practitioner of behavioral medicine in Sausalito, California, said that patients' attention should be directed to their healing rather than their

---

INVENTORY: A HEALING ATTITUDE

At the 1986 Brookridge conference, therapist Lee Jampolsky pointed out that we have been trying to cope with drugs and addictions in terms of a "disease model" instead of a "consciousness model." He said, "The disease model is a useful metaphor, especially in the early part of treatment, when you begin to reduce guilt and blame. But it is damaging to stop there. Just changing behavior to 'not using' is not recovery."

Jampolsky recommends an approach he calls "attitudinal healing," based on the well-known *A Course in Miracles.* Several of the basic assumptions include:

- There is nothing outside of you that will make you happy.
- Peace is an attribute in you.
- Addiction is the result of external searching that can really be seen as a form of spiritual search.
- Health is inner peace; healing is to let go of fear.

Says Jampolsky, "The disease model takes an avoidance approach. A spiritual, transpersonal approach points out the blocks but focuses on the good."

RESEARCH

Belkin Reports Soviet Interest in Peptides, Alternative Therapies

Aron Belkin is the director of the giant National Center for Psychoneuroendocrinology in Moscow, which has branches in 16 Soviet republics. He is a specialist in addiction research. In 1987, *Brain/Mind Bulletin* interviewed Belkin about the state of addictions research in the USSR.

Belkin said that the key issue is "the mind/body connection and the expanding field of psychoneuroimmunology itself. To say mind and body are one is almost a platitude. . . . The ancient Greeks knew as much. The key is the interaction. We are investigating how an immaterial thought creates such dramatic repercussions in the body."

In the USSR, "we're starting to regard the brain as a large endocrine gland, secreting hormones and regulating itself with peptides. . . .We are particularly interested in how the peptides relate to emotional states."

Belkin said that "yoga therapy, meditation, and psychedelics are all being studied," as therapeutic possibilities in altered states. "We're interested in alternative approaches because of our focus on diabetes and alcohol addiction."

He also said that the Soviets are interested in breathing therapies in general and Stanislav Grof's work in particular. "There may be some philosophical and methodological differences, but the techniques and empirical content are very appealing. Many of us will be promoting this kind of work in the USSR."

In *Intoxication: Life in Pursuit of Artificial Paradise* (Dutton, 1989), Ronald Siegel, a pharmacologist at UCLA, proposes that alteration of consciousness is a primal drive.

Human beings and many animals change their mental states through intoxicants. Robins get drunk on berries, moths consume the hallucinogen datura, and cockroaches eat opium.

No human society, Siegel maintains, has ever eliminated drug use or drug smuggling. Given that organisms all seem to possess what he calls "the fourth drive" (after sex, food, and water), Siegel proposes a concerted research effort to develop drugs that could intoxicate in a more manageable way, without addiction or toxic side effects.

pain. She asks clients, "Can you remember the moment you healed as clearly as you remember the moment you broke?"

According to many therapists, even relapse can be part of the healing process. David Hawkins calls it "relapse of consciousness." Andrew Weil believes that relapse brings us to the root of the problem.

Tobacco

Andrew Weil and other therapists have pointed out that tobacco is the single most addictive drug known. In addition, because injections are diluted, inhalation is a far more potent means of ingesting than intravenous injection, Weil said at the Brookridge conference in 1986.

Before the Civil War, smokers did not inhale because tobacco was too harsh. But afterward, the tobacco plant was improved and new curing methods permitted inhalation. Studies indicate that habitual nicotine use may cause a true drug dependency. In an effort to find out why 50 million Americans are smoking, despite overwhelming evidence of health hazards, researchers have also come up with evidence of the "benefits" of nicotine.

Jack Henningfield of the National Institute of Drug Abuse said that nicotine meets the technical criteria of an addictive drug in laboratory studies, *Brain/Mind Bulletin* reported in 1986. At a University of Kentucky conference on the neurobiological aspects of tobacco smoking, Henningfield said that nicotine affects brain-wave function, alters mood, and serves as a biological reward for both lab animals and human volunteers. The conference was covered in *Science News* (129).

Smokers who quit for ten days showed significantly slower and poorer test performance—reduced concentration, short-term memory, and other cognitive skills. Smoking or nicotine gum restored the skills.

"The effect is real—it's physical," Henningfield said.

The *Bulletin* also noted a British study of 1,000 smokers that found a 15% improvement in concentration during smoking. Another study of 30 smokers and 30 nonsmokers found an 8% improvement in both groups right after smoking or taking nicotine tablets. Keith Wesnes of the University of Reading, one of the researchers, said cognitive improvements persisted up to 30 minutes after smoking.

Caffeine

The average American drinks some 32 gallons of soft drinks and 28 gallons of coffee a year, making caffeine "the world's most popular drug," according to a 1988 editorial in the *British Medical Journal* (295).

In addition, caffeine is an ingredient in many prescription and nonprescription drugs. It is widely used to treat respiratory problems. The editorial also noted that an estimated 95% of American women consume coffee during their pregnancies.

Subjectively, caffeine produces a feeling of alertness, increased interest, endurance, reduction of fatigue, and delay of sleep.

Caffeine is one of the drugs banned for use by Olympic athletes. In addition to stimulating the central nervous system, it affects heart and skeletal muscles, kidneys, respiration, and possibly, the adrenals. It has been linked to heart attack, arrhythmia, insomnia, anxiety, and irritability.

In a New Zealand study, pregnant rats fed high levels of caffeine were more energetic than those with no caffeine exposure, but their pups were roughly half as active as the other groups. They remained less active and more emotional throughout their lives. No differences were observed between litters or mothers fed less caffeine, or none at all, R. N. Hughes and I. J. Beveridge of the psychology department, University of Canterbury, Christchurch, reported in *Psychobiology* (15); *Brain/Mind Bulletin* discussed their work in 1989.

RESEARCH

Coffee and Heart Disease

In a 19-year study of the role of coffee drinking in fatal coronary heart disease, Dan LeGrady, who was at Creighton University at the time of publication, worked with colleagues at Northwestern University's Department of Community Health and Preventive Medicine. They reported their findings in the *American Journal of Epidemiology* (126). *Brain/Mind Bulletin* discussed their work in 1989.

The researchers found that those who drank six or more cups per day were 71% likelier to die prematurely from coronary heart disease than all other groups. The subjects of the study were 1,910 white male employees of Western Electric Company in Chicago, who were 40 to 56 when the project began in the 1950s.

Of those who drank six or more cups daily, nonsmokers were more likely to die of coronary disease than smokers.

There was no apparent connection between coffee drinking and alcohol use. Those who drank six or more cups of coffee a day, however, smoked twice as much as the zero- to one-cup drinkers.

NOTES:

6.
CREATING MAGIC:
The Art of Life

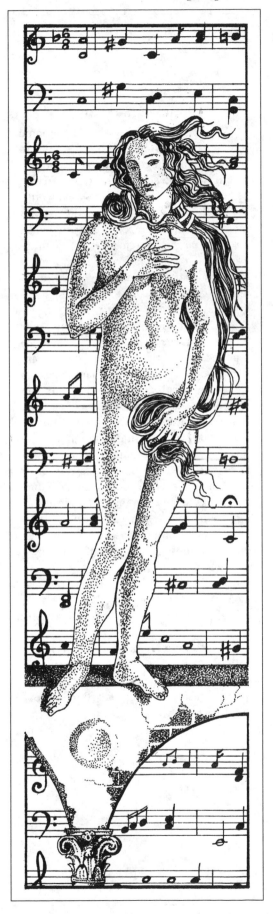

The subject of creativity sometimes seems to have been clouded by a deliberate conspiracy of mystification. To begin with, there is the assumption that creativity is solely the province of artists of one kind or another—poets, novelists, playwrights, sculptors, painters, composers. We see these people as strange and separate—and often tortured and unhappy.

This myth leads us to believe that creativity has nothing to do with everyday people in the everyday world—nothing to do with science, business, politics, schools, family, or anything that really matters.

But creativity and creative solutions are very much needed in many different fields—and in everyday life. And creativity can be learned. Everybody can enjoy being more creative.

In this section, you will find information on:
• how certain musical tones can energize your nervous system
• how the concept of beauty may be in our genes
• how music communicates, and what it tells us about emotion
• how to enrich your aural experience of the world
• why scientists and artists need similar creative skills
• the logic of intuition, and why it is important to top business executives
• the relationships between creativity and mood disorders
• how you can encourage and teach creatively gifted children
• how to enrich your own creativity

There is a common theme in all this information: Hard-and-fast conclusions about creativity are not to be had. The study of creativity is, itself, in a process of creative change.

The Restorative Power of Music and Chant

Why are some sounds considered sacred throughout the world? From the Aum to lullaby, from Gregorian chant to modern choral song, the spiritual exercise of voice brings a serenity and power beyond words.

French physician Alfred Tomatis has long studied the therapeutic effect of chant. He found that high frequencies appear to energize and recharge listeners. Sounds in the low frequencies can "discharge" or tire listeners. This is the secret to chant—high frequencies.

The sound of Gregorian chants falls within the range of recharging sounds, he reported. In addition, they are like a "respiratory yoga." Those who chant appear to slow their breath and induce listeners into their own state of tranquillity.

Tomatis has visited Benedictine monasteries worldwide to study the monks who practice Gregorian chanting. At one retreat in France, a young abbot was reforming tradition. He severely cut back on the time the monks spent chanting and noticed that they soon began to grow sluggish and sleep more. A consulting physician put the men on a conventional diet, and matters grew worse.

Tomatis was called in. He reintroduced their lengthy chanting schedule. Soon, he said, they were sleeping less, working more, and feeling better.

"Some sounds are as good as two cups of coffee. Gregorian chants are a fantastic energy source. I work with them as background music and sleep only three to four hours each night."

The Arts: A Hidden Agenda

"What is beauty?" is an age-old question. The answer is still elusive. What makes a melody or a picture pleasing? Why do we find the arts enriching?

Research during the last few years suggests remarkable, if tentative, answers. Sounds prevalent in music from baroque and classical periods have been demonstrated to "recharge" the nervous system. The relationship between music and emotion has been studied with astounding results. And the most pleasing of all visual proportions is present in DNA itself.

There seems to have been a "hidden agenda" to the arts all along. Far from being merely diverting, the arts have long played a crucial but barely recognized role in our emotional, spiritual, and even physical well-being.

The Ear as an Organ of Consciousness

Our ears may be important in regulating both the body's overall energy level and the quality of our speech.

French physician Alfred Tomatis reported at a 1984 symposium that the human body can be "charged" by particular frequencies accessible to the middle ear (see sidebar).

According to Tomatis, the ear is not merely an organ for hearing and maintaining equilibrium. The middle ear transmits sound to the cortex of the brain in the form of a charge of energy. The cortex then distributes this energy charge throughout the body, "toning up the whole system and imparting greater dynamism to the human being."

This cortical charge, he said, is channeled to various parts of the body—larynx, pharynx, lungs, heart, stomach, liver, kidneys, and intestines.

Since the middle ear contains more "receivers" for high- than for low-frequency sounds, high frequencies have the greatest charging effect. Low-frequency sounds provide insufficient energy to the cortex to compensate for the body's energy use, Tomatis said, and in the absence of high frequencies can have a discharging effect. Prolonged exposure to low frequencies can be physically and mentally exhausting.

Depressed individuals and others who listen to music with high frequencies experience increased dynamism, motivation, and competence, Tomatis said. They also report reduced fatigue and improved attention, concentration, and memory.

EXERCISE: GREGORIAN CHANTS

You can test the ideas of Alfred Tomatis for yourself if you have a pocket cassette player with headphones. Buy a recording of Gregorian chants at any classical or New Age record store. As Tomatis explains, the range used in such chants can have a powerful energizing and recharging effect upon your nervous system.

Play the tape as much as you like. Keep the volume low, so it doesn't interfere with your daily activities. Remember, the idea is not to *pay attention* to the sounds, but merely to benefit from their distinctive range. A very low, unobtrusive volume is quite sufficient—a volume over which you can easily hear the conversation of others.

Monitor your own reactions. Do you feel more alert, tranquil, and energized over time? Judge for yourself how much listening is helpful to you.

Hearing Defects

The quality of one's speech and singing—usually attributed to the larynx—is also regulated by the ear. "If the hearing changes, the voice also changes."

The ear is adapted to hear particular frequencies at varying levels of intensity. Tomatis maintains that a

---

COMMENTARY

On Mozart, Music, and Language

A Toronto psychologist attributes the almost universal popularity of Mozart's music to the fact that he began playing and composing in early childhood. *Brain/Mind Bulletin* reported the theory of Paul Madaule (then of The Listening Centre) in 1984.

Madaule said that Mozart incorporated his own physiological rhythms into his music before linguistic ones were imprinted. Because physiological rhythms are more universal than any particular language or ethnic heritage, Mozart's music is imbued with fundamental human familiarity.

The importance of music in the development of human speech is critical, Madaule noted. "Music has prelinguistic value because it introduces language. We know, for example, that children approach the verbal world largely through nursery rhymes and dances, which make possible the neuronal integration of rhythm and linguistic melody.

"Music responds to a vital human need by touching the deepest roots of the psyche and by opening the doors to the world of verbal communication. Therefore, the ability to listen to it is of utmost necessity."

Madaule, Timothy M. Gilmor, and Billie Thompson are editors of *About the Tomatis Method* (The Listening Centre Press, 1989), in collaboration with Tim Wilson.

RESEARCH

The Golden Section

An experiment by John Benjafield and his associates at Brock University in St. Catharines, Ontario, Canada, suggested that human beings may naturally make divisions in the ratio known as the Golden Section. They reported their findings in the *Canadian Journal of Psychology* (34). *Brain/Mind Bulletin* reported this work in 1981.

The Golden Section is a proportion gotten by dividing a line so that the smaller section has the same ratio to the larger that the larger has to the whole line. In algebra: $a/b = b/(a+b)$. This proportion may have been used in the Great Pyramid, some Greek Temples (see Parthenon in illustration) and Gothic cathedrals. It is often used by artists.

Experimental evidence suggests that the so-called Golden Rectangle, with sides in this proportion, may be the most aesthetically pleasing of all rectangular forms.

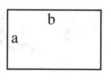

Benjafield and his coworkers asked 32 students to divide a five-centimeter (two-inch) line into various proportions: one-half, two-thirds, three-fourths, and the Golden Section. They approximated one-half and the Golden Section ratios almost equally well and much more accurately than two-thirds or three-fourths. In fact, the largest number of "direct hits" was scored on the Golden Section.

Asked to rate a set of their acquaintances as positive or negative, subjects tended to consider 62% of their friends as positive—a proportion that approximates the Golden Section.

hearing defect in any portion of the sonic frequency range produces specific problems relating to music.

• Defects between 500 and 1,000 cycles per second make it impossible for a person to appreciate music.

• Defects between 1,000 and 2,000 cycles per second prevent one from singing in tune.

• Defects above 2,000 cycles per second preclude the harmonic and other tonal qualities that make the voice pleasant or melodious rather than flat and unattractive.

The right ear is the "leading ear" for vocal regulation, Tomatis said. In one experiment, he had opera singers perform while monitoring their voices through headphones. When the channel to the right ear was tuned out, their voices lost harmonic quality, they sang off-key and off-time, and they also experienced fatigue. When only the left-ear channel was tuned out, they improved their overall performance.

Violinists and actors wearing headphones experienced comparable losses of performance capability when the right-ear channel was tuned out, he said.

Treating Hearing

Tomatis maintains that many individuals have tuned out their own hearing when they experienced traumatic incidents at critical stages of their physical development. His sonic therapy repeats the ear's developmental stages.

Patients begin by listening to filtered vocal or musical frequencies comparable to those experienced by a fetus. They then listen to the sudden change of frequencies experienced during birth. Next they are exposed to the "prelinguistic" sounds, such as Gregorian chants, lullabies, cradle songs, and nursery rhymes. Finally, they are asked to imitate syllables and other linguistic sounds.

Tomatis said that high frequencies are emphasized because they are important in regulating vocal and body dynamics. He considers Mozart's music the most beneficial in therapy because it is both vitalizing and calming.

Not all hearing problems are organic. Tomatis discovered that hearing can be affected by the listener's personal objectives. In one survey, individuals who valued activity and performance heard much better than those more concerned with reward and compensation.

He has devised a psychological "listening test" to measure the effect of personal tendencies. He found that some people classified as deaf by physiological tests nevertheless are able to hear by paying close attention. Others whose physical hearing is perfect are "hard of hearing" because of selective inattention.

The Art of Listening

Alexandra Pierce, a professor of music and movement at the University of Redlands, has taught courses in listening for both music and nonmusic majors for 21 years.

A highly trained musician and composer herself, Pierce explained that her interest in listening began when she realized she was hearing the music she played in her mind, "rather than really listening to the sounds each time they were played." By anticipating sounds a certain way, they came out that way—and no better.

So she spent years teaching herself to listen. But she didn't stop with music. She began to pay greater attention to sounds in her entire environment.

In her workshops, she teaches others to do the same—collaborating with her husband Roger, a movement educator and writer. Nonmusicians take the course for a variety of reasons, including consideration for others and self-improvement. "We make a lot of noise unnecessarily," she explains. People can learn to move more silently and gracefully.

Or they may be interested in getting a larger context, "the big sound picture." People enjoy learning "to get a sound to be its best self—like the best possible sound of a key going into a lock." They learn how sound triggers feelings and start to notice the vitality, range, and rhythm of their own speech.

Why We Don't Listen Well

Just as we are somewhat blind to the visual environment, Pierce says, we are relatively deaf to our aural environment. These are some of the possible reasons:

• *Indifference and lack of training:* "We are slovenly in how we listen," Pierce said. "We do not exercise our ears. We distort words and meaning."

The loss of hearing in old age may be, in part, a result of this indifference. Pierce cited a Stanford report that Masai warriors of Eastern Africa show no decline in hearing with age.

• *Resistance to unpleasant sounds:* People are put off by certain sounds, like toothbrushing. We put up a wall to keep from hearing someone chew on celery.

RESEARCH

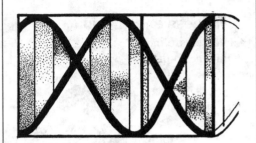

Beauty Is in the Genes of the Beholder

Two Israeli mathematicians and a chemist at the Weizmann Institute of Science in Rehovot, Israel, proposed that "beauty is in the genes of the beholder"— that the proportion known as the Golden Section (see sidebar at left) is inherent in the DNA itself.

D. Harel, R. Unger, and J. L. Sussman reported in *Trends in Biochemical Sciences* (11). *Brain/Mind Bulletin* reported their work in 1987.

Structurally, DNA is a double helix, two chains coiled around the same axis. Relationships within DNA include the external *width* of the double helix, the *length* of each turn configuration (the "pitch" or height of a representative slice), and the vertical *offset* of one helix from the other, which forms the minor groove.

Recent high-resolution X-ray studies of long chains of B-DNA showed that these internal relationships of the DNA fit the Golden Section. Other DNA structures show similar relationships.

The Golden Section has also been seen in some phenomena in nature, as in the degree of spiral curvature in some seashells and in the ratio in some plants between the number of leaves and their spiraling around the stem.

Blindness and Imagination

Adolescents blind from birth performed better than sighted adolescents on a test of their imagination designed by E. Paul Torrance, a leading researcher in childhood creativity. The study was conducted by Roger Johnson of the College of Education, Old Dominion University, Norfolk, Virginia. He reported his findings to an annual meeting of the American Psychological Association in New York City.

Words that imitated natural sounds—*ouch, groan, jingle, zoom, fizzy*—were used to stimulate the imaginations of 91 blind and 91 sighted adolescents aged 10 to 21. The study took place in a "nontest" atmosphere in which the subjects were encouraged to enjoy themselves by "letting their imaginations run wild."

Their verbal responses were analyzed according to the similarities they found between two otherwise unlike things.

The blind adolescents scored significantly higher than the sighted ones in terms of creative imagery, Johnson said. By adolescence, the blind are "certainly not imaginatively inferior" to the sighted.

"Since the blind adolescent does not have sight to rely on," Johnson said, "out of necessity he must depend more on other senses—including imagination. When [he] is called on to give imaginative responses, it must be remembered that he has had years of experience in using his imagination in order to adjust to a sighted world. Being blind may, in fact, be an advantage on a creative imagery task."

We close out unpleasant sounds in the same way that we close out unpleasant emotions. For example, people may recall certain sounds from their childhood in a negative light, like the turbulence preceding a divorce: doors crashing, sudden cries, explosive sounds, sounds associated with arguing.

"The particular type of sound becomes a unifying motif around which people organize their other hearing," she says. "But they can learn to open to conflictual sound without trauma."

• *Cultural bias toward the visual:* Our very language emphasizes the visual. We talk about vision and visionaries, but we have no term for inspired hearing. "What is the auditory counterpart of 'insight'?" Pierce asked.

• *Hearing abstractly rather than directly:* Just as people have difficulty in art because they try to draw what they *remember* and not what they *see*, we tend to describe an associated *object* rather than the *sound*. When we are asked what we hear, we are likely to say "keys" rather than

---

EXERCISE: FIRST STEPS IN LISTENING

Alexandra Pierce and her husband, Roger, lead workshops in which "generous movement" aids listening. These are the initial steps they take their students through:

1. Notice that you are surrounded by subtle sounds: breathing, coughing, doors closing, distant passing cars, birdsong, hum of fluorescent light.

2. Put your attention on in-and-out breaths. As the body feels quieted, subtle hearing becomes second nature.

3. Limit other sensory modes. That is, close your eyes or avoid touching, to heighten your awareness of sound.

4. Listen to sound in parts:
   • Bend—the line a sound makes. Does it go up and down, as in the voice of a singer, or straight, like a motor? The word "bend" itself has a bend.
   • Height—tops and bottoms of bends.
   • Grain—roughness and smoothness of sound. The grain of a rotating concrete mixer is rough. The grain of flute music is smooth.
   • Volume—loudness or softness.

Paying attention to these qualities in speech makes you aware of your own speech. "You convey fewer double messages."

EXERCISE: BEING MOVED BY SOUND

The Pierces emphasize that the body has natural, spontaneous responses to sound, as dramatized by the following tips and activities. Try them, and explore your relationship with the world of sound.

• Lift up your voice in song. There's a great inhibition about singing, even among articulate people. "We're afraid of our own voices."

• Listen to animal "voices." We anthropomorphize the sound of animals (think of a dog's bark as angry) and thus miss a wide range of possible meanings.

• Limit other sensory modes. Close your eyes or avoid touching. This will heighten your awareness of sound.

• Take responsibility for what you hear. The ear participates by inferring meaning. We may distort, for example, by hearing a scolding tone when none was intended.

• Hear your words and mean them differently. Say "the blackbird flew over the house" with various inflections. As you listen to yourself, you enrich your relationship with words.

• Take a sound history. Return to sit in the same place several times during a day; notice how the sounds change.

• Make a sound map. Mark your location on a large piece of paper. As you hear sounds, map their locations. Show barriers that alter the sound. Your "sound envelope of surrounding space" will enlarge.

• Take a vow of silence. You can carry a note saying that you have vowed silence until a certain time. Carry a pencil and paper so you can respond to questions.

• Think about and discuss sounds you like and don't like. Consider the bend, grain, and so on. Listen to "junk sounds" such as chairs scraping.

• Go to a "hi-fi" location. A campground or forest has relatively few sounds to weed out from one another. Imitate the sounds you hear. Respond with sounds of your own.

EXERCISE: ORGANIC MUSIC

In her book *Self-Transformation Through Music,* pianist and music therapist Joanne Crandall offers many useful observations and exercises relating to music and sound. To begin, she deals with the most primal element of music: rhythm. She tells of the role of rhythm and pulse before and after birth, and throughout our lives: "Our bodies are rhythm instruments. . . . Rhythm involves repetition: it is the base, the ground from which all else emerges."

Try the following exercise from her book:

1. Sit quietly in a relaxed, comfortable position, breathing gently. Place your fingers on your pulse at the neck or the wrist until you become familiar with the feel of your own heartbeat.

After a few moments of quiet attention, begin moving softly, gently, nodding your head, rocking from side to side, any movement that seems simple and appropriate. Use your heartbeat as the underlying rhythm for the movement. Observe without judgment the flow of your body as it is orchestrated by your heartbeat. You might imagine your heartbeat emerging from the floor, providing a ground, a base, for your movement.

2. Turn your tape player on record. After a few moments of quiet attention, begin playing or singing, using your heartbeat as the underlying rhythm for the music. Continue playing until you feel the inner signal to stop.

Now play back what has been recorded. You may wish to move or dance to the music, feeling the connection between your heartbeat and your body through the channel of your own music. Again, observe without judgment the flow of your movements that has been orchestrated by your music. You might imagine your heartbeat emerging from the floor, providing a ground, a base, for the music and your movements.

3. During the day, in the midst of your activities—walking, talking, listening to or playing music—pause for a moment. Place your fingers on your pulse. Feel your heartbeat describing the rhythm of your body, connecting you to the rhythm of life around you.

—Joanne Crandall
Self-Transformation Through Music
(Theosophical Publishing, 1986)

describe the rattle in our pockets, or to say "refrigerator" rather than describe the rumble of the motor or the swish of the door, opening. When musicians are asked to describe music they're hearing, they tend to name a specific instrument—a violin, clarinet, or piano—rather than describe the music itself.

• *Personal issues:* The biggest single block to hearing may be a fear of the truth—"the same thing that limits seeing." People fear the implications of what they hear because they may have to take action, so they block out perception.

"People experience intense emotions regarding sound," says Pierce. "Sound is very 'hot.' " Pierce predicts that sound will increasingly become a socio-political issue. She talks of "sound imperialism," the intrusion of loud motors, lawn mowers, and amplified music. And those who are forced to work or live in noisy environments can suffer considerable hearing impairment. The noise level next to a busy freeway can damage the hearing apparatus in less than eight hours, she said.

As a group, musicians are "the poorest listeners," Pierce said. "Many conservatory graduates say they are disturbed because they can't hear certain things." As they have become ever more specialized and "expert," they have come to expect—and produce—certain sounds.

Typically this makes for lifeless notes and joyless performances. But by listening more carefully and imagining more richly, they can create more multifaceted sounds. The usual training of musicians, Pierce said, leads to "formulaic playing"—perfect but uninspired. "I help musicians get the true sound from their instruments. I try to take them from performance into communication."

She feels that "if music were more about inner listening and communication, it would regain its ritualistic value." Pierce's training, one graduate student said, teaches "gratitude for life."

The Code of Musicality

Why do we say that a piece of music is "sad" or "happy"? What emotional structures in human beings resonate with musical expression?

Neuroscientist/concert pianist Manfred Clynes has answered long-standing questions about how music derives the power to change states of mind. And he explains

---

RESEARCH

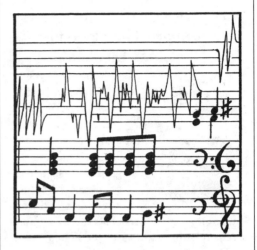

The Composer's "Signature"

One of Manfred Clynes's most remarkable discoveries is a "pulse" characterizing the works of individual composers since the second half of the eighteenth century. Clynes demonstrated this pulse by having musicians such as Pablo Casals and Rudolf Serkin mentally rehearse several works by the same composer. As they played the music inside their heads, the musicians "conducted" through finger pressure on the sentograph (a device that detects the "shape" of a musical pulse).

"We can speak of a Mozart pulse, a Beethoven pulse, a Schubert pulse, a Brahms pulse," Clynes told *Brain/Mind Bulletin.* "They apply to the entire work of the composer, to both slow and fast movements and to different meters.

"As handwriting or a brushstroke of a painter can, the pulse reveals aspects of the intimate, personal nature of the composer, his unique point of view. A Mozart piece played with Beethoven pulse sounds bizarre. But it is not a matter of style—even Haydn and Mozart have different pulse forms. In the absence of the composer's characteristic pulse, any of his compositions sound unauthentic and unconvincing. It's as if his presence has been withdrawn."

RESOURCE

Essentic Forms: A Shape Language for Human Emotion

Manfred Clynes's book *Sentics: The Touch of Emotions* (Prism Press, 1989) explains how the "shapes" of joy, anger, love, sex, hate, grief, and reverence have been determined through experiments involving hundreds of subjects in various cultures.

These shapes take about two to ten seconds to express. As Clynes views it, they are a property of the central nervous system. Their purpose is the communication of feeling.

Essentic forms are common to such sensory modes as touch and sound—and are perhaps more primary. "Essentic form is biologically given and appears to be genetically preserved," he said.

We perceive emotional qualities in music if we are attuned to the "language" in which they are embodied. This is not unlike the way the tone of voice in speech reflects essentic form, and is easily understood by everyone in a culture.

The way in which essentic form is embodied in the musical fabric tells a story. It is its "tone of voice."

why some musicians transcend their more technically skilled colleagues in engaging the listener. Clynes discussed his research with *Brain/Mind Bulletin* in a 1985 interview.

Clynes holds degrees in neuroscience and engineering from the University of Melbourne, a master's degree in music from the Juilliard School in New York, and has done graduate work at Princeton. Born in Vienna, he toured the major cities of Europe as a teenage pianist. As a musician, Clynes studied with Pablo Casals and Sascha Gorodnitzki. He is head of the Research Centre, New South Wales Conservatorium of Music, and professor of neuropsychology and Sugden Fellow at the University of Melbourne.

Using what he learned from decades of experiments, Clynes programmed a computer so that it could play "any melodies by Mozart, Beethoven, and Schubert with sensitivity and subtlety."

In order to do this, he found a predictive relationship in the *melodic contour* of each single note—so that from the shape of the present tone we can intuit what is to follow.

This might be compared to the relationship between the dramatic story line of a novel and the varying intensities of images. If the novel works, if it is "moving," the reader experiences a connection between the intention of the author in telling the story and the choice of words that establish the tone.

The Shape of Human Emotions

Clynes earlier had discovered a phenomenon he calls *essentic forms*—meaning primary emotional responses. Subjects exerted finger pressure on a sensitive device called a sentograph to express emotions. Distinct forms were found for anger, love, grief, sex, reverence, joy, and trust.

When he mathematically translated the pressure pattern of an emotion into an actual sound shape, Clynes found that experimental subjects could identify the original emotion from nothing more than that sound.

The phenomenon was cross-cultural. Aborigines listening to the sound could name the emotions originally produced by middle-class city-dwellers.

Subtleties of amplitude and duration give music its meaning, Clynes said. Music sounds dead and uninteresting without this "microstructure."

This microstructure seems to be almost as unconscious as breathing, yet a musician cannot mechanistically impose it. Clynes compared it to speaking when we don't think of the words we are going to say—they just come out, each word introducing the next.

The Creative Person

Who is creative? What—if anything—makes an artist, composer, or poet different from other people? Perhaps very little. There is evidence that the most successful scientists and businesspeople use the same creative thinking tools that artists use.

Is profound creativity inevitably linked to great suffering? Is it inevitably individualistic?

Research has demonstrated a link between emotional disorders and literary creativity. But even writers who suffer from mood disorders are most creative when they are in relatively stable states of mind.

Clearly, we should be cautious about romanticizing creative suffering, real though it may be. Indeed, we should be cautious about any assumption that places creativity beyond the pale of everyday existence.

Scientists as Artists

"It's time the contributions of the fine arts to science and technology are recognized and used," science historian Robert Root-Bernstein told *Brain/Mind Bulletin* in 1985. "The fine arts are specifically useful, not merely sources of values or modes of expression."

Root-Bernstein, author of *Discovering* (Harvard University Press, 1989), is a professor of physiology at Michigan State University. He believes that a correlation exists

RESEARCH

Music and Emotion

According to Manfred Clynes's findings, emotion can be seen as a pattern that exists in the nervous system.

"The constructive use of generalized emotions" can be triggered without association with a person or event, he told *Brain/Mind Bulletin.* Joy, sadness, or love can be felt with no reason other then the shape of the musical phrase.

When the shape (or essentic form) of the emotional quality is expressed purely, it communicates most powerfully.

The greatest music may ennoble us by eliciting emotion without an object. By experiencing joy or sadness without content or association, we gain another perspective: Music may train us to become more peaceful and rational in the face of strong feeling.

Emotions are tied to general thinking patterns that make up our worldviews, Clynes said. By generating a sequence of generalized emotions, music potentially touches on all facets of life.

These thinking patterns tied to generalized emotions are not to be confused with specific events or associations. For example, Clynes mentioned a recent series of experiments that demonstrated an inherent link between love and trust.

Observing a repeated sequence of expressions of love and anger, Clynes found that even a small, insignificant lie temporarily tended to block the experience of love. The same lie did not block anger—and in some instances even enhanced it.

The current cultural split lies not between scientists and everyone else but between those who innovate or create and those who do not. Innovators and the process of innovation must become the focus of study. Innovation is the lifeblood of cultural change.

—Robert Root-Bernstein
in *Daedalus* (1984)

between scientific eminence and creativity in the fine arts. "The connection was first proposed in 1878 by J. H. van't Hoff, the first Nobel laureate in chemistry," he said. "I'm attempting to verify his thesis by studying the lives of important scientists since 1800."

Root-Bernstein sees the creative process as the unifier of art and science. He asks: What are the correlations between scientific imagination and other forms of creativity?

"Our greatest scientists are generally skilled in non-verbal thinking," he said, "yet we usually discourage science students from studying artistic subjects. Unless we reverse this trend, they will continue to be cut off from thought processes that lead to creative breakthroughs."

Most imaginative scientists are also artists, poets, musicians, or writers, he found. For example, Louis Pasteur and C. G. Jung painted; Max Planck and Albert Einstein had an intense interest in music.

Physicists Murray Gell-Mann (poet), Victor Weisskopf (pianist), and Robert Wilson (sculptor) say that scientific and artistic problem-solving involve a similar process.

Mathematician Ralph Abraham has proposed that music may model complex systems in which events occur in parallel. Music trains the mind to see how complexity, as in a Bach fugue or a physiological process, results from simple rules and patterns.

Mitchell Feigenbaum, who developed the mathematics of catastrophe theory, studies paintings to see how artists perceive clouds and streams. Ilan Golani was able to analyze animal movement by adapting dance notation to the needs of neurophysiologists.

Nonverbal forms of thought, especially visual thinking, are more important to scientists than verbal forms, Root-Bernstein said. "Experiments alone cannot produce conceptual breakthroughs. . . . One must first be able to imagine that which is to be tested and how to test it."

The ability to imagine new realities is correlated with making analogies, with playing, modeling, abstracting, idealizing, harmonizing, pattern forming, approximating, extrapolating.

"Creativity may be the ability to take a problem—How do mountains form?—and translate it into another form, such as an analogy, a model, or picture, that is more easily manipulated mentally. Then it can be translated back into some verbal or mathematical form."

It is not just that a scientist is an artist, he said, but that he works as an artist when he does science.

The Logic of Intuitive Decision-Making

"Intuitive decision-making is logical," says Weston Agor, who teaches organizational management in the public administration program at the University of Texas at El Paso. Agor is the author of *The Logic of Intuitive Decision Making* (Greenwood Press, 1986) and *The Role of Intuition in Leadership* (Sage Publications, 1989). "Top executives say that the failure to heed intuition is their greatest regret," he told *Brain/Mind Bulletin* in a 1986 interview.

Agor has studied thousands of managers in his exploration of intuitive decision-making. He finds that, because intuitive managers don't like to be told how to do things, they often underestimate the amount of direction someone else might need. They can also be impatient with people who don't grasp their vision quickly.

"Some learn to say, 'This is what I think, give me reasons why it isn't so.' "

Sometimes what "feels" right proves wrong. What happened? "They say they became too closely identified with a person involved in the decision 'on an emotional beam.' For example, they saw the person not as he was but as how he would *like* to be." Or they were fatigued. "Don't decide when you're tired," they conclude.

Another factor is the emotional sensitivity that is a part of their gift. It may lead them to please others rather than follow their "real" intuitive sense.

Top executives have what Agor calls an integrated style; they can function both intuitively and analytically.

He has also developed tests for pure intuitive talent. The "pure intuitive" can function well in certain settings: new product ideas, trend identification, fashion.

A cosmetics executive told him, "A Harvard MBA would be lost here—we make most of our decisions based on intuition." Intuition is crucial in areas such as marketing, intelligence work, sales, and emergency-care nursing.

People who use intuitive strategies generally "tripped into them by accident," Agor told *Brain/Mind Bulletin*. They find they can ground and fine-tune their intuition simply by noticing how it functions.

The Art of Entrepreneurship

"I've always thought of entrepreneurs as being the more artistic members of the business community," said Bernard Goldhirsh, founder of *Inc.,* on the occasion of the magazine's tenth anniversary. "For them, business becomes a medium of creative expression."

In the anniversary issue (April 1989), 29 contributors discussed how the past decade had changed the way they thought about business.

"What I learned when the world takes a tilt from being left brain to right brain," said John Sculley, president of Apple Computers, "is that you have to really focus on the creative side if you want to gain productivity. People are going to be most creative and productive when they're doing something they're really interested in. So having fun isn't an outrageous idea at all. It's a very sensible one."

COMMENTARY

A New Creativity

"The cliché of the driven (and, frequently, alcoholic) artist is not only common, but actually a kind of cultural ideal . . . ," writes author and social critic Morris Berman. He discusses creativity's historical context in an essay in *The Reality Club* (Lynx Books, 1988), and in his book, *Coming to Our Senses: Body and Spirit in the Hidden History of the West* (Simon & Schuster, 1989).

Berman says that this idea ignores the possibility that the creative process evolves. "Future creativity might be a very different animal from the one that it is now."

Berman adapts a model of three types of creativity from a little-read essay by Sigmund Freud.

Freud identified a dwarfed creativity he called Type I. It appears when parents thwart a child's sensual explorations of his/her surroundings. The child's curiosity often shuts down, and no further explorations are made.

Type II creativity comes about if the child is able to overcome this repression, but is plagued by a resulting psychic upheaval, which turns its creativity into a "contemporary form of exorcism." Post-medieval Western art is almost wholly of this category, and the "tortured artist" is its perpetual image.

Type III creativity emerges when the child manages to avoid the trauma of repression altogether; its sensual curiosity survives and matures without neurosis.

Type III is marked by an absence of conflict. But does such a serene form of creativity really exist in our culture? Berman cites examples of medieval and oriental art, and lists a few Western artists in our century: poet Wallace Stevens, sculptor Henry Moore, and minimalist composers Philip Glass, Steve Reich, and Terry Riley.

But he also cautions that hopes of an easy transition "may be premature." Our culture may have to complete its fascination with pain and conflict before it can achieve truly transcendent modes of expression.

Agor first became interested in intuition 20 years ago when he was working in Procter and Gamble's international marketing division. "I noticed that some of the executives could make these intuitive calls.

"Later I worked for William Milliken, governor of Michigan—a highly intuitive guy. In the political setting the skill was prominent—the business demanded it."

INVENTORY: TOOLS OF IMAGINATION

The Creatively Gifted Child: Suggestions for Parents and Teachers by Joe Khatena (Vantage Press, 1978) offers parents and teachers information on how to identify exceptionally creative children, and also suggestions on how to nurture and encourage that creativity. (See related exercise, page 183.) Citing the work of J. P. Guilford and E. Paul Torrance, he lists four creative thinking abilities used in the measuring of creativity:

• *Fluency:* "the ability to produce many ideas for a given task." To measure someone's fluency, you might ask them to list a number of unusual uses for a brick. "The more ideas a person produces," writes Khatena, "the higher his fluency ability is."

• *Flexibility:* "the ability to produce ideas that show a person's movement from one level of thinking to another, or shifts in thinking relative to a given task." If two of the uses listed for a brick are "use it as a paperweight" and "use it to hold down a pile of clothes," this shows fluency but not flexibility, since "in both cases the brick acts as a weight, and there is no shift in thinking." But consider these ideas: "throw it at someone, coat it with chocolate and give it to someone as a birthday cake for a joke, and warm it in a fire and iron a shirt." These represent distinctly different uses, and demonstrate flexibility.

• *Originality:* "the ability to produce ideas that not many people think of or that are unusual, remote, and clever."

• *Elaboration:* "the ability to add details to a basic idea produced." A person might be given a number of squares and told to draw a variety of different objects based on those squares. One square might be used to represent a door. But how many details are used to portray the door? "If a person decides to add such details like hinges, decorative structure, extensions to the length, a nameplate, a peephole, and so on, he is elaborating on the basic idea of door."

Above all else, Khatena stresses the responsibility of teacher and parent. "You have it in your power to cause creativity to happen and flourish before your very eyes. Be the catalyst of the mystery and magic of existence, for in the creativity of your child may lie a magnificent future for all."

Agor has worked with such clients as Hawaii Telephone, the National Security Agency, the City of Phoenix, and Tenneco. He says he is encouraging high executives to come out of the closet about their use of intuition. "Particularly women. A lot of women in business are suppressing their intuitive skills, trying to be more macho than men." One female manager, he said, talks about "dressing her intuitions in data clothes."

"American business is at a crossroads," he said. "As we move into more complex situations, intuitive skills will become more important. Leadership will have to pay as much attention to the 'imagineers' as they do now to the 'engineers,' or our economy will be in deep trouble."

Mood Disorders and Creative Writers

The "madness" of creative writers may have more to do with feeling than thinking, judging from a recent study. An Iowa study revealed that 80% of well-known creative writers suffered severe depression or manic-depressive illness, compared to 30% of other professionals matched for age, sex, and income.

Nancy Andreasen, a psychiatrist at the University of Iowa Medical School, studied 30 writers who had served as visiting faculty of the prestigious Univeristy of Iowa Writers' Workshop, among them Philip Roth, Kurt Vonnegut, John Irving, John Cheever, Robert Lowell, and Flannery O'Connor. Two writers committed suicide during the 15 years covered by the study.

The writers were four times likelier than the other professionals to be alcoholic, Andreasen reported in the *American Journal of Psychiatry* (144). Schizophrenia had not occurred in either group. *Brain/Mind Bulletin* cited this study in 1987.

In a similar study, psychologist Kay Jamison found a 30% rate of depression among 47 top British artists and writers. The rate was highest among the poets and playwrights. Kareen and Hagop Akiskal of the University of Tennessee, Memphis, have found a high incidence of cyclothymia—nearly 70%—in an ongoing study of 20 French artists, writers, and musicians. The mood swings of creative people usually started in their teens or twenties.

(Continued on page 185)

RESEARCH

The Creativity of the Emotionally Disturbed

Creativity researcher E. Paul Torrance and his colleague Shaker Kandil reported high creative potential among emotionally and socially maladjusted children.

Fifty children in grades one through five in special public school programs for emotionally disturbed and behavior-disoriented children "showed unusual strength in fluency and originality, but not in flexibility," Kandil and Torrance said. Their report appeared in the *Journal of Creative Behavior* (12). *Brain/Mind Bulletin* reported this work in 1979.

The children, tested individually with the Torrance Tests of Creative Thinking, were compared to the national norms. Eighty percent of the disturbed and disordered children scored above average on fluency, one-fourth ranking in the upper two percent on national norms. On originality, seven-eighths were above average, and nearly half were in the upper two percent.

These findings verify other reports that socially and emotionally maladjusted children often have higher creative potential than their normally adjusted counterparts.

Special programs for these children ought to capitalize on their originality and fluency and "strengthen their flexibility in solving problems," the investigators said.

INVENTORY: SATORI SKILLS

In *The Search for Satori and Creativity* (Creative Education Foundation, 1979), E. Paul Torrance says that the word "satori" describes the moment of creative breakthrough, but transcends the common American concept of "aha." Satori includes the long practice, devotion, and discipline that precede insight or inspiration.

Torrance discusses creative skills—how they have been studied and measured, and how they can be developed.

The following are just a few examples:

• *The problem*—At the very outset, all truly creative effort depends on one's awareness of a problem, and the ability to define it.

• *Be original*—The United States Patent Office has a concept of "inventi-level," which measures degrees of originality.

• *Be aware of emotions*—Emotions must be recognized and understood for creative breakthroughs to take place. Creative commitment may even be said to be an act of love.

• *Put your ideas in context*—According to R. Buckminster Fuller, children start off wondering about the universe and we respond by teaching them ABCs. As they grow, they forget the big questions of life.

• *Visualize it—richly and colorfully*—There is an increasing emphasis on imagery in our culture. This is fortunate; our images of the future can motivate and enable us.

• *Visualize the inside*—We need to get inside internal "black boxes" in which we have concealed aspects of a problem that have resisted solution.

• *Breakthrough—extend the boundaries*—When we get stuck in a problem, we may well need to rethink that problem, redefine it. (See related exercise on page 183.)

• *Let humor flow—and use it*—Humor is inherently creative; it depends upon surprise and incongruity. It is sadly neglected in problem-solving.

• *Get glimpses of infinity*—"Creativity is infinite," writes Torrance. "It is shaking hands with the future. And genius is a creative mind adapting itself to the shape of things to come."

EXERCISE: EXTENDING BOUNDARIES

In *The Search for Satori and Creativity,* educator and researcher E. Paul Torrance discusses what happens when you become bogged down in a creative problem. Perhaps you look at it over and over again and don't know what to do about it. Or perhaps the solution seems obvious, but doesn't work when you try to implement it. In this case, carrying out an inappropriate solution in "bigger and better" ways won't do any good.

To help sort through such creative dilemmas, Torrance introduces the concept of first- and second-order change. In first-order change, you try to find a solution inside the boundaries of a problem. In second-order change, you *extend the boundaries* of the problem.

To demonstrate this principle simply and concisely, Torrance offers the following activity:

I believe that this concept might be understood more effectively by experiencing or reexperiencing the old nine-dot problem, an excellent analogy of first- and second-order change. If you already know one solution to the nine-dot problem, see if you can think of a different solution.

Your problem is the very straightforward and simple one of connecting the nine dots pictured in the figure below by four straight lines without lifting your pencil or pen from the paper. Take time out and try it.

Were you able to solve the problem? If so, how were you able to break free of the shackles of the natural tendency to see the nine dots as making a square and thinking of the solution only in terms of this square? Once you can do this, numerous solutions become possible. Otherwise, you could try 1,000 solutions without success. If you were unable to find a solution, you will find one of the most common solutions on the next page.

This is symbolic of the problem of first- and second-order changes. Most people assume that the nine dots contain a square and that the solution must be found within the square, a self-imposed condition. One's failure does not lie in the impossibility of the task, but in the attempted solutions. A person will continue to fail as long as he attempts only first-order change possibilities. Solutions become easy once one breaks away from the image of the square and looks outside of the nine dots. The solution is a second-order change which involves leaving the "field" (the square).

EXERCISE, continued

Look at the most common solution of the nine-dot problem as given on the previous page. Asks Torrance, "Now that you have 'broken or extended the boundaries,' can you think of another solution?"

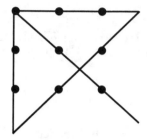   

Torrance also proposes a problem-extending exercise that bears more directly on daily life:

List some of the most persistent and bothersome problems you encounter in your family, place of work, contacts with city or state government, or the like:

_____

_____

_____

_____

_____

Then select the one that seems to you to be the most persistent and bothersome. What has been the usual definition of this problem?

_____

_____

_____

_____

How can the boundaries of this problem be extended and the problem redefined in such a way as to bring about a second-order change?

_____

_____

_____

_____

—E. Paul Torrance, *The Search for Satori and Creativity*
(Creative Education Foundation, 1979)

The Akiskals also found a correlation between artistic leanings and strong mood swings in 750 psychiatric patients in Memphis. The common denominator, however, may be success in general rather than just the arts. Individuals distinguished in business and leadership may have similar mood changes.

Many questions remain. Does this suggest that people might have a genetic predisposition for creativity? What is the cause-and-effect relationship between affective disorders and creativity? Does creativity result from emotional conflict, or does creativity *produce* emotional conflict? Or is it an interactive combination?

Nancy Andreasen treats those questions with caution and respect. In an article in *Comprehensive Psychiatry* (29), she warned that her data is anecdotal and should be understood as such.

In "Genius and Insanity Revisited," coauthored with Arthur Canter and published in *Life History Research in Psychopathology* (University of Minnesota Press, 1975), Andreasen discusses the possibility that the creative act itself may bring about intense shifts of mood: "I think, inevitably, when people write, they sort of drive a shaft into themselves and, in the process, peer down into the abyss. That may be a contributing factor."

But perhaps there is a need to experience the emotional depths of depression "to enhance the creative individual's understanding of the human condition." The works of writers such as Virginia Woolf and painters such as Munch, Rembrandt, and van Gogh might suggest this. "On the other hand," she writes, "creative work is also (and probably most often) produced during periods when the person is not suffering, perhaps as suffering 'recollected in tranquillity.' "

Episodes of moderate mood elevation may serve as incubation periods "during which ideas are developed that can then be explored when the mood is more neutral and the mind more rational." Though mood swings might enhance creativity, it is nevertheless important to keep in mind that writers tend to be most productive in comparatively stable states.

RESOURCES

Frank Wilczek is one of those rare scientists who are devoted to understanding the creative process. In *Longing for the Harmonies: Themes and Variations from Modern Physics* (W. W. Norton, 1989), he and science writer Betsy Devine draw the reader into the harmonies and even the humor of his vocation.

"One of the inspirations for this book was the idea that practicing scientists could learn from the great composers about making beauty accessible." They set out to develop ten major themes of physics, "showing through a series of variations how one simple idea can give birth to a logical but delightfully surprising series of interpretations."

The Creative Brain (Applied Creative Services, Lake Lure, North Carolina, 1988) is a handsome, large-format book, rich in illustrations and cartoons. "I wanted the book's design to reflect everything I knew about individual perceptual styles," author Ned Hermann told *Brain/Mind Bulletin.*

The book includes a copy of a brain-dominance test that Hermann designed to identify learning styles for the reader to fill out and send in for a scoring.

He has conducted seminars and workshops for many Fortune 500 companies, with a special emphasis on matching learning style to job. A mismatch between one's natural abilities and one's work, Hermann maintains, is the major cause of personal unhappiness.

RESOURCES

In *Drawing on the Artist Within* (Simon & Schuster, 1986), Betty Edwards, author of the immensely successful *Drawing on the Right Side of the Brain,* says that drawing is a language, potentially as important as reading, capable of framing a problem for new insights.

Edwards points out the fallacy of our attitude toward drawing: We make materials available to youngsters and hope they'll make the most of the situation. But they are rarely given any guidance. If we taught reading that casually, who would read?

Human expression through drawing, as Edwards sees it, is not necessarily to produce "art" as a product but to learn to see and understand.

Edwards believes that any normal person is capable of drawing well. The great art of the cave man suggests that human beings are naturally equipped to capture what they see—if they are not too hampered by what they think they know.

Drawing With Children by Mona Brookes (J. P. Tarcher, 1986). Brookes, whose Monart method of drawing instruction has attracted wide attention among educators, spells out her technique in this richly illustrated volume. Despite the title, the book is for everyone who has ever wanted to draw. Brookes has included pairs of pictures done by children and their novice parents.

Students learn a basic alphabet, "five elements of shape"—dot, circle, straight line, curved line, angle line. As they identify and reproduce these elements, they focus on what they see. This focus engages the attention, foiling the self-criticism that too often paralyzes artistic effort.

As she began training teachers in California schools, Brookes started getting feedback on effects of the method: improved concentration and visualization, problem-solving skills, shape discrimination that aided reading. Composition of elements helped teach numbers. Of course, success in drawing inevitably enhanced self-esteem.

Enhancing Creativity

Surely the most important questions about creativity are: Can it be learned? Can it be used in everyday problem-solving—in the workplace and in the home? The answer to both questions is yes. Not only has creativity been studied and measured, but techniques to raise our creative horizons have been developed.

And as we learn more about everyday creativity in our own lives, we can learn how to nurture the creativity of our children as well.

What Fosters Creativity?

Where does creativity come from? Most researchers say that it can be found in all of us.

John Briggs is an associate professor of English at Connecticut State University in Danbury and also teaches classes at the New School for Social Research in New York City. In his book, *Fire in the Crucible: The Alchemy of Creative Genius* (St. Martin's, 1988), Briggs investigates the question through lively biographical material, scholarly research on creativity, some neuroscience, and interviews with researchers.

Wondering about the variety of things that capture the attention of creators, Briggs says, "It's plausible to maintain that because each of us is different, each is endowed by those differences with a special sensitivity to some subtle dimension of reality that others overlook."

Probably every child is drawn to seek hidden meanings, he says. Those who turn the quest into a life's work seem unusually capable of intense absorption and unusually sensitive to ambivalences and contradictions.

Omnivalence

They are also attracted to a state of mind Briggs calls "omnivalence"—a coined word that comes from "ambivalence." Omnivalent people have discovered that there are many ways of perceiving things, that they may feel many different ways about something. Briggs believes that it may be this capacity for omnivalence, learned early, that fosters interaction between talent, passion, and cultural fit that leads to genius.

Brilliance is less important, he says, than obsession and dedication. "I know quite certainly that I myself have no special talent," Einstein said shortly before his death. "Curiosity, obsession and dogged endurance, combined with self-criticism, have brought me to my ideas."

Child Prodigies and Late Bloomers

Briggs reminds us that most child prodigies develop a single talent. Relatively few make outstanding contributions as adults—possibly because things are too easy for them. They fall quickly and easily into a groove already worn by the culture.

Others, typically not prodigies, have to create their own grooves. They struggle to find a language to describe their sense of omnivalence. If they do find it, they may become recognized as creative geniuses.

Triggering Creativity

But if creative work is largely a product of diligence and persistence, what initially triggers creative experiences? In *Brainstorms & Thunderbolts* (Macmillan, 1984), authors Carol Orsag Madigan and Ann Elwood say that creativity may be triggered by supernatural experiences, intuitive flashes, intense emotional responses, chance happenings, or self-induced drug states.

The following examples are adapted from their book:

• On his honeymoon, cartoonist Walter Lantz was disturbed by a persistent woodpecker. While chasing the noisemaker, Lantz got the idea for his famous cartoon character, Woody Woodpecker.

• Young Sam Clemens (Mark Twain) caught a scrap of paper—a page from a history of Joan of Arc—swirling in the wind as he walked home from work. The incident awakened him to the delights of history and literature. Forty-six years later he published *Personal Recollections of Joan of Arc,* which he considered his finest work.

(Continued on page 190)

RESEARCH

Compliments Help Creativity

Researchers Terry Greene of Murray State University and Helga Noice of Rutgers said in *Psychological Reports* (63) that a good mood may encourage creativity. *Brain/Mind Bulletin* reported their work in 1989.

Greene and Noice divided 22 rural Kentucky middle-schoolers into two random groups. Upon arrival for testing, those in the first group were complimented on their clothing, hair, and/or jewelry and given packages of chewing gum. The second group received nothing.

Each group then took two tests of creative ability. In one, subjects were required to mount a candle using a box and tacks so that wax did not drip on the floor. The other simply asked that students generate names of fruits and birds.

Seven of the 11 complimented children solved the candle problem, compared to only 2 of the other 11. The specially treated group also did far better on a word-generation test, averaging 29 words each in the allotted time versus only 15.6 for the other group.

EXERCISE: ENCOURAGING CREATIVITY IN CHILDREN

What can you do to encourage your child's creativity? In his book *The Creatively Gifted Child: Suggestions for Parents and Teachers* (Vantage Press, 1978) educational psychologist Joe Khatena offers valuable advice to parents and teachers. The following activity is a useful exercise in "restructuring":

> We are often faced with something whose parts are put together or structured in a certain way to give it an identity. If we are able to pull apart these elements and recombine them or restructure them in a different way, we are very likely to come up with something having a new or original identity. It really needs creative energy to free oneself from the bonds of the old order for the purpose of bringing about a new order.

1. *Restructuring Using Nonverbal or Figural Materials*

To teach your child to use this strategy with figural materials you may start with constructing an 8 x 12 inch flannel-board, and make cutouts of say 3 geometrical shapes such that you have 10 of each kind. I have preferred to use black flannel to cover the board, and some brightly colored, lightweight paperboard for the geometrical shapes like the semicircle, triangle, and rectangle. If you like to use these shapes, make circles one inch in diameter and squares that have sides one inch long. By cutting the circles in two you will get semicircles, and by cutting the square into four parts you will have rectangles; in addition you can make two right-angled triangles by cutting across the diagonal of a square. These shapes are relatively versatile and allow for all kinds of manipulations and combinations. When you have all these pieces cut, put them in a little plastic bag or envelope ready for use. You should make two sets so that you can freely work with your child on the materials.

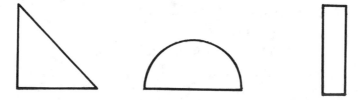

Now that these pieces are ready and the flannel-board prepared, give them to your child. Tell him that you are going to construct a figure on the flannel-board and get him to watch what you do. You may begin by constructing a *human figure:* a triangle for a hat, two semicircles for the face, two triangles for the body, two rectangles for the arms and two more for the legs, and two semicircles for the feet. All this requires the use of 3 triangles, 4 semicircles and 4 rectangles, making a total of 11 pieces. Encourage your child to do the same giving him whatever help he may need at the time. Then pull apart the pieces you used to make the human figure and reconstruct them into an *automobile,* making sure that only the same 11 pieces are used.

EXERCISE, continued

The four semicircles can now serve as the two wheels. Place one rectangle on one wheel and a second rectangle on the other so that the long sides of the two rectangles are on the wheels and the short sides are side by side. Then place two triangles in the shape of a square upon the rectangles on the rear wheel, and the remaining two rectangles upon the one that was first placed on the front wheel. Finally put the remaining triangle against the short sides of the three rectangles above the front wheel so that its base is against them and the apex of the triangle is pointing forward. The car is now ready. Let your child do the same and once again help him to build the car. When he has done this, tell him to pull apart the same 11 parts of the automobile and rearrange or restructure them into another object. Of course with a little practice you will see him producing scenes as well. Your child may try to persuade you to allow him to use some of the pieces in the bag, but do not let him. Encourage him to use his imagination and work within the restrictions of the strategy.

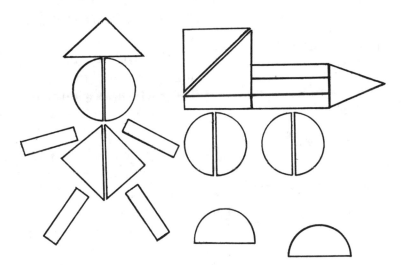

2. *Restructuring Using Verbal-Figural Materials*

Restructuring can also be used to encourage your child to be more creative with words. For instance, you can show him a picture . . . and encourage him to ask questions about it which cannot be answered by merely looking at the picture, guess why events in the scene are taking place, and the consequences of these events, as warm-up activities. This may then be followed by getting him to restructure three elements of the picture . . . into an unusual and interesting story.

*If you take any activity,
any art, any discipline,
any skill, take it and
push it as far as it will go,
push it beyond where it
has ever been before,
push it into the wildest
edge of edges,
then you force it into the
realm of magic.*

—Tom Robbins
quoted in *Silver Departures*
edited by Richard Kehl
(Green Tiger Press, 1983)

• In bed with a toothache, the renowned mathematician Blaise Pascal had an uninvited flood of thoughts about the cycloid, a curve generated by a point on the circumference of a circle that rolls on a straight line. For the next two years he pursued his major work, *A History of the Cycloid*.

Creativity and Learning

The relationship between high IQ, creativity, and apparent learning style (left or right brain, integrated, or mixed) was examined in several experiments by creativity researcher E. Paul Torrance of the University of Georgia Department of Educational Psychology and his coworkers. A 1979 issue of *Brain/Mind Bulletin* cited their findings, reported in *Journal of Creative Behavior* (12) and *Gifted Child Quarterly* (23).

They found that:

• People can change their preferred styles of learning and thinking through brief but intensive training.

• Those who have a left-hemisphere style of processing information score lower on tests of creative thinking ability and show fewer creative traits than their peers.

• Gifted students with a predominantly left-brain style have greater difficulty than their peers in seeing the implications of new knowledge and skills and apply their learning less.

Torrance and Cecil Reynolds exposed 200 "gifted and talented" high school students to a diverse range of learning methods. Students were shown clear relationships among information from different disciplines. Another group of 68 graduate students were given specific training in methods associated with the right hemisphere, including brainstorming, imaging, and metaphorical thinking.

The high school students tended to become more integrated in their styles, using right and left hemisphere modes in a complementary way. The graduate students shifted significantly to a right-hemisphere style of functioning.

Right-Brain Thinking

Torrance and Salah Mourad found that creative ability in adults with superior intelligence is associated with learning styles that rely heavily on right-hemisphere processes (holistic and spatial thinking, imagery, intuition) or an integration of left- and right-brain modes.

A study of students in the Georgia Governor's Honors Program, conducted by Torrance and Orlow Ball, found that "right-brain" or "integrated" students were significantly better able than the left-brain students to see the relevance of what they learned in the program and to find ways to apply it. The authors concluded that "deliberate methods of training might be used with gifted students having a left-hemisphere style of learning to make better use of their learning in special programs for gifted and talented students."

The lunatic, the lover and the poet
Are of imagination all compact:
One sees more devils than vast hell
* can hold,*
That is, the madman: the lover, all
* as frantic,*
Sees Helen's beauty in a brow of
* Egypt:*
The poet's eye, in a fine frenzy
* rolling,*
Doth Glance from heaven to earth,
* from earth to heaven;*
And as imagination bodies forth
The forms of things unknown, the
* poet's pen*
Turns them to shapes and gives to
* airy nothing*
A local habitation and a name.

—William Shakespeare
A Midsummer Night's Dream

NOTES:

7.
CHANGING MAGIC:
Life's Many Transitions

In a sense, life *is* transition. As we discovered in "Being Magic," we all go through yearly, monthly, and even daily cycles. We also experience the great cycle of human aging and maturity, and cultural and evolutionary transitions as well. New ways of looking at birth and death—surely the most dramatic transitions of all—are proving to be most revealing, with "near death" and other metaphysical experiences dramatically altering many a life.

Transition is a constant fact of life. We are never at some plateau waiting for the next big change but always experiencing the process. When change seems forced upon us, it can feel uncomfortable. We may even try to deny that our world is changing, or that we are. But new examinations of the nature of things tell us that we aren't unvariable entities moving through life; we *are* processes of change.

And never has the need for understanding our individual and cultural transformations been greater than it is today.

This section contains information about the many kinds of transition we're all faced with in our own lives and in our culture:

• seeing birth as a continuum, rather than a single and often traumatic event
• how we can experience the positive side of aging
• difficulties in defining death
• how the near-death experience has transformed some lives
• how the paranormal appears to be becoming normal

*Real death is not a source
of terror for the ordinary
intelligent, sensitive being.
It is living death that is the great
nightmare. Living death means the
interruption of the current of life,
the forestalling of a natural death
process. It is a negative way of
recognizing that the world is really
nothing but a great womb,
the place where everything is
brought to life. . . .
Actually, there is nothing but a
steady stream of activity,
a movement toward or away
from life.
All that we really know is
becoming, the endless change and
transformation. Things are
constantly being recreated.
The real fear, the real terror,
lies in the idea of arrest.
It is a living idea of death.
Some people are born dead.
Some people impress us as only
half alive. Others again seem
radiant with energy.*

—excerpt from Henry Miller's
Wisdom of the Heart
(New Directions Books, 1941)
from an essay,
"The Enormous Womb,"
written in the early years
of World War II

• successful experiments in remote-viewing and out-of-body experiences

• how new stories in the sciences are changing our ideas about the nature of reality itself

• how cultural changes may be producing new types of human beings and a new society

• discovering the potentials of personal transformation

Becoming aware of the powerful forces of change at the scientific and cultural levels can help make our personal transitions productive and graceful.

Lifetime Changes

We tend to pay attention to life's obvious transitions—the ones we meet in the full light of consciousness. We ask questions like: When does one become an adult? Exactly what is middle age? How old is old enough?

Lately even more baffling questions have arisen, such as: What do we really mean by birth and by death? And what do they tell us about what happens in between?

Birth is only one of our transitions. Once we are here, we are still in for a lifetime of change. Reports of "near-death experiences" stir up that long-standing question of whether death really is an end, or just a transition.

And there is considerable evidence that physical and mental vitality can be prolonged into later years. Your experience of growing older may depend heavily on the possibilities you see, the stories you tell yourself, and the activities that you undertake as a result of your beliefs.

Prebirth Memories

We are not born all at once. Birth is more than the physical contractions of the uterus and the propulsion of the fetus from womb to world. Each birth is a continuum of events that begin during gestation and continue through a period of postnatal bonding. Birth is both physical and psychological.

Viewing childbirth as just such a continuum was proposed at a 1982 conference, "The Perinatal Period: Interface of Biology and Behavior," sponsored by the Esalen Institute and the Ergos Foundation of Vancouver, Canada. The two dozen participants included specialists in neurobiology, neuroendocrinology, neuropsychology, anatomy and physiology, obstetrics and gynecology, clinical psychology, hypnotherapy, psychiatry, and philosophy.

Several participants discussed awareness in the fetus and its persistence in memory after birth. Under the influence of hypnosis and psychotropic (mind-altering) drugs, many people have recalled prenatal and birth experiences. These memories often correlate with current physical and psychological problems: headaches, respiratory disorders, phobias, depression, anxiety. Recalling the experiences often relieves or eliminates the symptoms.

Thousands of clients in LSD and other therapies have relived the trauma of near-suffocation that can result from constriction of the umbilical cord or from contractions of the uterus constricting blood in the arteries, said Stanislav Grof of the Esalen Institute. Physical and psychological rigidity, shallow breathing, anxiety, and other symptoms often disappear when birth trauma is reprocessed.

The ability to recall the details of one's birth under hypnosis is uncanny, obstetrician David Cheek said. His patients can correctly indicate which arm freed first during delivery and which way the head turned as it emerged. He has verified the accuracy of such reports by checking them against obstetrical notes made during delivery.

Remembering What Was Said

San Fransisco therapist Jack Downing reported that, while under hypnosis, a client "relived" a painful fetal memory. He seemed to recall that, when his mother said she was pregnant, his father was upset and wanted her to get an abortion. He said, "I've been saving to buy a Chrysler." A bitter argument followed.

RESEARCH

Birth Trauma a Self-fulfilling Prophecy

Thinking of birth as labor tends to define it as a painful trauma fraught with danger to the well-being of mother and infant. Yet, the stress of delivery can be anticipated, lived, and remembered as a positive transformational experience for both mother and child, said Peter Levine, co-organizer of the 1982 Esalen conference, "The Perinatal Period." (See main text.)

"It is not birth that is traumatic," said Arizona physician Lewis Mehl, "but traumatic birth that is traumatic."

And traumatic birth may be a self-fulfilling prophecy. Physicians and nurses tend to have complicated pregnancies and births, and physicians often encounter the very obstetrical complications they most fear and expect.

When birth complications were no longer discussed in an ongoing class for expectant mothers, said Berkeley therapist Gayle Peterson, their occurrence decreased. She also recommends making use of hypnosis and the therapeutic relationship to create positive expectations.

Bonding and communication between the mother and the fetus results in a decrease in premature labor for women who are considered to be at risk, Peterson said.

Excessive use of drugs was criticized by many. "It's more scary for the newborn when the mother is not conscious," Mehl said. To the extent that infants are directly affected by drugs, Stanislav Grof said, "we may be programming a drug-dependent society by giving newborns a cellular memory of countering stress with drugs."

RESEARCH

Hypnotized Children Recall Birth Experiences

Children under hypnosis accurately report their birth experiences, as verified by their mothers' detailed recollections, also obtained by hypnosis.

With few contradictions and much dovetailing, a child's recall—as late as age twenty-three—corresponds to the mother's recounting of specifics, such as her hairstyle, the obstetric instruments used, conversations in the delivery room, the character and behavior of nurses and doctors, and the mother's own emotional and physical state.

These findings were made by San Diego psychologist David Chamberlain of the ATC Research Foundation. He reported at a 1980 meeting of the American Society of Clinical Hypnosis in Minneapolis. His study included ten mother-child pairs. He reported that "infants note who is nervous, careless, tired, crying, smiling, or angry. They sense when fathers are uninterested, afraid, or friendly. They 'get the message' from what is going on around them without the need for formal language skills."

He pointed out that his findings overcome the usual objections to the validity of birth memories: that they are guesswork, hallucinations, or fabrications.

The experiment also contradicts another criticism. "The theory that all these 'memories' really came from the mother in the form of hints and bits of information over the years does not account well for the extremely personal feelings and thoughts that are characteristic of birth reports, or for the homely details that no mother would bother to communicate to a child."

Chamberlain draws on hundreds of purported birth memories in his book, *Babies Remember Birth: And Other Scientific Discoveries About the Mind and Personality of Your Newborn* (J. P. Tarcher, 1988), and has concluded that "the usual rituals of obstetrics, parenthood, education, and other social systems are in urgent need of humanization."

The client wondered if his current feelings of insecurity had something to do with his father's rejection. But he found the memory hard to believe because his parents had never argued in his presence. When he questioned them, they reluctantly acknowledged the incident. The confrontation had so upset them that they agreed never to argue again.

Fetal perception of such events is taken very personally, Downing said. "The knowledge involved in such prenatal conditioning is extremely literal."

In a 1989 letter to *Brain/Mind,* David Cheek, now retired, wrote that "I have found that many grown-up kids have misinterpreted the information they received or thought they received before they were born."

Cheek, formerly president of the American Society of Clinical Hypnosis, said that "the supersensory openness to impressions apparently is active as early as the moment a mother realizes she is pregnant—maternal hormones go right through the placenta, but I feel sure from my hypnosis research that maternal thoughts are picked up by the embryo. "It occasionally even seems possible to verify the impression of a hypnotized person, through the mother's recall of the event, that the embyro 'heard' when the doctor told its mother she was pregnant. This is hard to fathom, since the nerve mechanisms for hearing aren't completed until the fifth month of gestation."

Helpful Strategies

The Esalen conferees discussed a number of remedies for problems associated with prebirth memories:

• *Renegotiating memory.* "Memories can be negotiated," Grof said. "If you consciously reconstruct and complete your experience of a physical trauma, you can be rid of its psychological effects."

• *Changing attitudes.* "Many mothers are worried that birth will be traumatic for their child," said Arizona physician Lewis Mehl. Cheek said a link may exist between such anxiety and spontaneous abortions. Using hypnosis to determine the unconscious attitudes of expectant mothers, Cheek discovered that many have a great fear for themselves or their babies.

Women who habitually miscarry often have troubled sleep, Cheek said. He suggested that their dreams may provide clues to their fear, which can then be resolved during counseling or hypnotherapy.

• *Conscious gestation.* Positive imaging of the birth experience can prevent or minimize birth trauma, according to several conferees. "What we imagine and dream in our hearts, we create in our subsequent experience," Mehl said. "A healthy fantasy in advance can compete with contrary experience."

Mehl, Downing, and therapists Gayle Peterson and Ian Mcnaughton all stressed the importance of "conscious gestation" in which parents communicate directly to the fetus. In addition to assuring the fetus of parental love, concern, and joyful anticipation of its birth, the pregnant woman can also provide specific communications. For example, if she becomes upset with her partner, Mcnaughton said, she can assure the unborn child, "It's all right, I'm not mad at you."

Peterson makes use of hypnosis to create images of the baby inside the womb and to allow for dialogue to take place between mother and unborn child. "Body-centered hypnosis not only takes the focus off of possible birth complications," Peterson told *PragMagic,* "but actually changes body memory on a neurophysiological level, accounting for the increase in healthy, normal deliveries that have been noted in my childbirth preparation classes."

• *Professional sensitivity.* "Documenting the existence of long-term memory of the birth experience would change the way birth takes place," said conference co-organizer Stephen Porges of the University of Maryland Institute for Child Study/Department of Human Development. Until very recently, newborns were believed to have no memory for procedures that are physically or psychologically traumatic. For example, circumcision is commonly performed without analgesia. "Physicians would certainly use analgesia if they thought the baby's pain was unconsciously remembered with potentially long-term consequences," Porges commented. "Because we live in a period of high technology, we have arrogantly assumed that we also live in a period of wisdom. But anyone at the top of his field realizes how little is known."

Aging and Maturing

"If there is growth throughout life, human beings may be psychologically at their most highly developed state when they are very old," Marion Perlmutter, a gerontologist at the University of Michigan told *Brain/Mind Bulletin* in 1989.

RESEARCH

"If I'd known I was going to live this long, I'd have taken better care of myself"

It's no joking matter. Judging from a study of aging men reported in *Experimental Gerontology* (22), keeping fit may delay the sensory decline associated with growing old. *Brain/Mind Bulletin* reported on the study in 1988.

Researchers Wojtek Chodzko-Zajko and Robert Ringel said they hope to learn why some individuals are resistant to the usual consequences of aging. Although sensory scores usually decline with age, they found great differences among men of the same chronological age.

Breath capacity, cholesterol, body weight, and blood pressure were measured in 70 male subjects aged 40 to 84. Men who scored high on these fitness measures also had faster reaction time, more lens accommodation, better vocal qualities, and stronger scores in hearing and tactile sensitivity than their less-fit contemporaries.

The data supports theories that people need not age passively but can choose to delay sensorimotor and cognitive loss by improving the quality of nutrition, exercise, and other aspects of their lives.

Age Wave by Ken Dychtwald and Joe Flower (J. P. Tarcher, 1989) is a vigorous, incisive look at the changing demographics of America and the world.

Dychtwald, who has researched the aging movement since the early 1970s, notes that in the 1986 elections the oldest demographic group (over 65) outnumbered the youngest (18 to 24) for the first time.

Some of the many facts and figures that Dychtwald and coauthor Flowers present:

• More than half of all people who have ever lived to age 65 are alive today.

• A century ago, the median age of Americans was 21 years. By 2000 it will be 36.

• The average American retiree at age 61 can look forward to an average of 15 healthy, active years.

• People over 50 control 70% of the total net worth of American households.

Dychtwald also sets out to retire prevailing myths about aging:

• People over 65 shouldn't be dismissed as "old." Age 65 came into use as a mandatory retirement age in the late nineteenth and early twentieth centuries. At the time, 65 was significantly longer than the average life expectancy. By the same standards, Americans today would retire at well past 100. As we age more slowly, retirement will be postponed longer and longer.

• Most older people are not ill. Only 5% of people over 65 are in hospitals or institutions, and the average age of patients admitted to nursing homes is 80.

• Our brains degenerate less than we think as we grow older. Only 10% of those over 65 have any significant memory loss, and less than 5% have any serious mental impairment. Most of these people are extremely old, and many of the causes—depression, lack of exercise, drug-induced confusion—are reversible.

Perlmutter is studying people over eighty. Although they number only one percent of the population, they are the fastest-growing age group in the U.S.

Aptitudes of the elderly are generally measured by tests designed to evaluate the young, she said. But old people differ in experience and skills.

When children become more thoughtful and less impulsive, we say they are maturing; when elderly people spend more time in thought, we call them senile. But Perlmutter reminds us that they may show more wisdom and insight because of slower thinking.

"Often mental decline reflects poor health, not aging *per se*." Society would benefit from realizing that mental decline is not a natural result of aging, she said. "Growing older is not different from growing up."

INVENTORY: LIVING IN THE AGE WAVE

How do your life plans and prospects take the future into account? The growing numbers and improved health of older people are likely to affect our personal lifestyles as well as business and government. With the coming of the "Age Wave" (see sidebar), Ken Dychtwald projects changes such as these:

• Advances in science, medicine, and especially personal fitness will help people live considerably longer. An estimated 80% of older people's health problems are preventable or postponable with better self-care.

• Perceptions of family life, including a person's relationship with parents and children, will be altered.

• The physical environment will be changed somewhat to better accommodate the elderly—from better lighting to easier-to-open medicine and food containers.

• A person may choose not to retire or may work at various occupations after initial retirement. Among other pursuits, seniors will enjoy enormous opportunities to work as volunteers. Age discrimination, retraining, and other workplace issues will gain importance.

• Older people will continue learning later in life. Even today, 45% of all college students in America are over 25.

Aging—Another Self-fulfilling Prophecy

"Old people become crazy for three reasons," gerontologist Alex Comfort said in an address to the 1980 assembly of the American Academy of Family Physicians: "Because they were crazy when they were young, because they have an illness—or because we drive them crazy."

Comfort, author of *A Good Age* (Crown, 1976) and *The Joy of Sex* (Crown, 1972), proposed that the last reason is the most common. He estimated that 75% of the so-called "aging" in the United States is a self-fulfilling prophecy that "our folklore, prejudices, and misconceptions about age impose on 'the old.'

"If we insist that there is a group of people who, on a fixed calendar basis, cease to be people and become unintelligent, asexual, unemployable, and crazy, the people so designated will be under pressure to be unintelligent, asexual, unemployable, and crazy."

Comfort noted that geriatrics is the one major medical resource generally unavailable to American patients. He said the neglect results from ageism, including assumptions that "the old are naturally infirm, their infirmity is biologically ordained, their intellect shares in the decline, they are medically uninteresting to active practitioners, and—until Medicare—they were financially unprofitable."

INVENTORY: YOUTHFUL AGING

Compared with others your age, how do you feel?
- ❏ Older
- ❏ Younger
- ❏ About the same

This question was asked of 150 persons 65 or older by researchers Margaret Linn and Kathleen Hunter of the Veterans Administration Medical Center in Miami, Florida. Their report appeared in *Journal of Gerontology* (34) and was described in *Brain/Mind Bulletin* in 1979.

Those who perceived themselves as younger were markedly better off in their psychological functioning. The most crucial variable was the extent to which they saw themselves as controlling their own lives, the factor psychologists term "locus of control."

Those who felt younger also had greater self-esteem, more life satisfaction, were of higher social class and in better health. The overall trend was for females to view themselves as younger than males, whites as younger than blacks. Higher scores on the WAIS, an intelligence test, also correlated with a younger self-perception.

Because a sense of being in control is such an important factor, the researchers said, those working with the elderly should support their efforts to control their environment. Feeling younger than one's age-mates may be a denial of reality but "may be necessary for good psychological functioning."

RESEARCH

Religious Involvement Helpful to the Elderly

A large-scale study of elderly residents of New Haven, Conn., indicated that those who reported "public religious involvement" (attending church or synagogue) were less likely to be functionally disabled or to show signs of depression, researchers reported in 1987 in *Social Forces* (66).

Ellen Idler of Rutgers University also analyzed the relationship of nonpublic religious experience in the health of the New Haven subjects, 1,139 men and 1,617 women. She used as the index of private religiousness two items in the survey:

Aside from attendance at religious services, do you consider yourself to be:
1) deeply religious
2) fairly religious
3) only slightly religious
4) not at all religious

How much is religion a source of strength and comfort to you?
1) none
2) a little
3) a great deal

Among men, incidence of disability or disability-associated depression was less likely in those who reported "private religious involvement."

RESOURCES

In *Mindfulness* (Addison Wesley, 1989), Ellen Langer, a psychology professor at Harvard, points out that our habitual inattention costs us dearly. "We build our own and our shared realities, and then we become victims of them—blind to the fact that they are constructs, ideas."

Langer talks about what she calls "premature cognitive commitment"—jumping to conclusions. This leads us to believe certain things about aging, for example. Our beliefs directly affect why we age.

She cites a study done in the 1970s in which the experimenters created a 1959 retreat environment for two groups of 75- to 80-year-old men. Members of one group were asked to reminisce about the year 1959, whereas the other had to re-create the year vividly, even in their casual conversation.

Members of the experimental group were shown pictures of each other as they had looked 20 years earlier. By the second day these men became more active and independent, serving themselves from the retreat kitchen and cleaning up afterward.

Within four or five days the experimental group had, in effect, grown younger. Among the "biological markers" affected were increased finger length, sitting height, improved manual dexterity, and improved right-eye vision. They also outscored the comparison group on a reaction-time test that involved identifying famous faces of 1959, perhaps because the celebrities seemed more contemporary to them.

Mindfulness alone—remembering to pretend—could be a major factor in the youthening effects, Langer pointed out.

Maximum Life Span by Roy Walford (W. W. Norton, 1983) proposes that undernutrition without malnutrition is the key to extending lifespan. Gerontologist Walford predicts cultural changes to come about as a result of people living healthfully for 120 years.

Comfort's assessment was supported by National Institute of Mental Health research that estimated that half the hospitalized elderly over 60 have depressive illness—which is treatable but unrecognized. Similarly, the President's Commission on Mental Health reported that more than 100 reversible syndromes mimic senile dementia (loss of physical and mental abilities resulting from organic brain dysfunction).

Attributing these syndromes to brain deterioration, the commission said, obscures the fact that "sick old people are sick because of illness, not because of old age." Until medical practitioners discriminate illness from aging, "we will continue to warehouse older people in nursing homes instead of preventing the conditions that [sent] them there."

Misuse of antihypertension and antianxiety drugs often induces or heightens depression. In such cases, the drugs can cause pseudosenility, Carl Eisdorfer of the University of Washington told the 1980 meeting of the American College of Physicians. He said 35% of dementia patients with reversible conditions are misdiagnosed as incurable because of drug-induced depression, alcoholism, metabolic disorders, and other problems.

Existential Love

Dean Rodenheaver of the University of Wisconsin–Green Bay and the late Nancy Datan have challenged the myth of geriatric asexuality, both at the APA meeting and in a paper included in R. Weg (ed.), *Sexuality in the Later Years: Roles and Behavior* (Academic Press, 1983). Noting that "the supreme triumph of our humanity over our biology is that we not only make babies but we also make love," they described two seasons of love.

"Generative love" of family and home often sacrifices the present for the sake of the next generation. "Existential love," which comes with full maturity and old age, celebrates the present in poignant awareness that "life is the more precious because it is fleeting."

Datan and Rodenheaver, considering existential love to be one of maturity's greatest gifts, said it is the source of "the unique patience so often seen in grandparents—who know how brief the period of childhood is, since they have seen their own children leave childhood behind them." They defended the sexual expression of existential love as being no less natural than sexuality in generative love.

Defining Death

Just as we can consider birth a continuum and life a process of evolving, we are also finding it more difficult to pinpoint a moment that can be called death. Doctors must deal with complex questions about what brain death is and when a patient has a right to die.

When is a person dead? Modern medical technology makes any answer seem arbitrary.

At a 1981 meeting of the American Psychological Association, Bernard Towers, professor of anatomy and psychiatry at UCLA, remarked on the simplicity of the earlier criteria for determining death: "We listened for a heartbeat, we felt for a pulse, we checked for breathing with a mirror or a wisp of cotton wool placed before mouth and nose. We looked into the eyes, those windows of the soul. If anything moved, then the patient was still alive. When nothing moved, we folded the corpse's arms and pulled the sheet over the face."

Electronic equipment now monitors internal signs— neural reflexes, neurohormonal activity, cortical evoked potentials—that once were invisible. And complex life-support systems can sustain for an indefinite period those who are irreversibly unconscious.

"Death occurs in stages and by degrees," Towers said, "and not necessarily in the same order for everyone. There is death of cells, of tissues, of individual organs of the body, of complex organ systems; and there is death of that organizing principle that integrates the parts on behalf of the whole body." Towers's paper on the topic was published in 1982 in *Death Education* (6).

A federal commission recommended that death be defined as "irreversible cessation of all functions of the entire brain, including the brain stem." Towers termed this a "conservative definition" designed to be noncontroversial. "At least it allows for and even requires the turning off of the machines even though the rest of the central nervous system (the spinal cord) may be intact, as also might be most or all other organs of the body."

But the definition does not satisfactorily address the ultimate concern: "How much of medulla or pons or midbrain is needed for 'personhood'. . . that with which we think and feel and relate to our surroundings? If that part is irretrievably destroyed, can we legitimately say that the patient as person is 'gone' and should be declared dead?"

RESOURCES

Who Dies? (Anchor, 1989) by Stephen Levine provides a classical spiritual perspective for contemporary readers.

Survival? Body, Mind and Death in Light of Psychic Experience by David Lorimer (Routledge & Kegan Paul, 1984) reviews the historical and clinical evidence suggesting the continuation of consciousness after death. It includes recent scientific theories of David Bohm, Rupert Sheldrake, and Ilya Prigogine.

Childhood and Death by Hannelore Wass and Charles Corr (Hemisphere Publishing, 1984) discusses the attitudes of dying and suicidal children with ideas for helping them and their parents.

The Last Dance by Lynne DeSpelder and Albert Strickland (Mayfield, 1983) is a massive review of cross-cultural and historical attitudes toward death, how health care systems handle it, how children and survivors cope, medical ethics, and life after death.

Working It Through by Elisabeth Kubler-Ross (Macmillan, 1982) recounts her workshops for those touched by death: the terminally ill, the doctors, nurses, and clergy involved, and the survivors.

RESEARCH

NDEs Reported

Students at Wichita State University produced audio- and videotapes of people who have undergone near-death experiences and offered them to health professionals and faculty teaching death-and-dying courses. "With all the evidence we have, the typical nursing curriculum across the country still doesn't cover the subject," Dr. Howard Mickel, then-chairman of the Wichita State religion department told *Brain/Mind Bulletin* in 1984.

He cited Gallup Polls showing that one in three people on the brink of death reported features of the NDE. More than eight million people reportedly have traveled out-of-body, moved through a tunnel, or felt a sense of transcendent peace.

"Because medical science still calls these experiences hallucinations, we read about them in the *National Enquirer,"* he said. "They should be in the 1,500 death-and-dying courses across the country."

Mickel has since retired from Wichita State but told *PragMagic* that he continues his research and tours the country with an exhibit of photography, artwork, and commentary on NDEs. "Typically, after a presentation, at least four people come out of the closet. We help them overcome embarrassment about their experiences."

He said that his most recent research shows that "there is not a single type of NDE, but a *variety* of types around the planet and through history."

Revival From Coma

The definition of death is a question that is not easily resolved. "Too many families are led by professionals to give up on comatose relatives," Associate Director Robert Phillips of the International Coma Recovery Institute in Garden City, N.Y., told *Brain/Mind Bulletin* in 1983. "Now we know this is not a closed issue—significant improvement is possible in a large percentage of patients."

Under the Institute's program, families learn to stimulate patients' senses. They bombard the coma victims for 11 to 14 hours a day with light, noise, pressure, taste, and smell. They also stimulate their limbs with alternating movements. Phillips looks for initial signs of learning: "If we tell them we're going to touch them with something cold, for instance, they may start to withdraw. This means they got our message and awareness has returned."

Ninety-two percent of patients at the Institute are aroused from coma. Of those, 35% resume normal functioning. People who had been in a coma for up to 18 months have progressively recovered with this program, Phillips said.

Patients and their families are demanding more control over the decisions made about defining death and prolonging life.

Near-Death Experiences

Thousands who have narrowly escaped death have reported leaving their bodies, seeing a life review, traveling through a tunnel, meeting deceased friends and relatives, encountering a being of light, and then reentering their bodies. Such experiences are common, but their causes and meanings are uncertain.

Are near-death experiences (NDEs) merely the "toxic psychosis" of a rapidly deteriorating brain deprived of oxygen? Or are they glimpses of a realm of consciousness that follows physical death? Growing interest in such questions brought a large audience to a symposium at the 1981 American Psychological Association convention in Los Angeles.

Cardiologist Michael Sabom, formerly of the Emory University School of Medicine and now in the private practice of cardiology, cited six cases in which physically unconscious persons near death later accurately described—from a viewpoint outside of their bodies—

attempts to resuscitate them. These and 100 other near-death cases are described in his book, *Recollections of Death: A Medical Investigation* (Simon & Schuster, 1983).

More documentation of such experiences is necessary, Sabom said, to warrant any conclusion that consciousness can function separately from the body. Whatever the research shows, he cautioned, "these experiences are occurring near death, not at death, and thus cannot be said to represent scientific evidence either for or against the existence of an afterlife."

Denying that a single explanation of near-death experiences is possible, Glen Gabbard of the Menninger Clinic observed that neurobiological, psychological, social, and transpersonal/spiritual factors all converge in NDEs. None of these, he said, can fully explain what may be a "successive series of discrete states of consciousness" with distinct causes. Gabbard called for "openness to other frames of reference with the understanding that one's own paradigm may not contain all the answers."

Gabbard concluded, "We must be willing to acknowledge the mysterious quality of these phenomena. . . . As Einstein said, 'The most beautiful thing we can experience is the mysterious. It is the source of all true art and science.'"

University of Virginia psychiatrist Raymond Moody's 1976 book, *Life After Life* (Stackpole), sparked public and clinical interest in near-death experiences. He told *Brain/Mind Bulletin* in 1981 that research is vital to the mental health of those who have such experiences. "It is important to be able to say to such people that they are not alone, that many others also have these experiences."

Despite the many books now available on the subject, said Moody, "most people who have a near-death experience aren't aware of how common it is until they share it." Patients should be informed that medical doctors have no authority to explain NDEs, he added. He tells patients, "This is something we don't understand, so ultimately it's up to you to put it together. But we can assure you that the experience is not unusual."

Moody does not consider NDEs proof of an afterlife. "Many people assume that I have a particular understanding of these experiences. I don't 'understand' them, one way or another. I'm just curious."

COMMENTARY

The Classic NDE Experience

 Based on in-depth interviews with those who had experienced NDEs, Kenneth Ring created a composite version of the classic near-death experience. A psychologist at the University of Connecticut, Ring summarized his work in his book *Life at Death* (Coward, McCann, 1980).

No one reported all of these elements, but they occurred often enough to be hallmarks.

The experience begins with a sense of profound peace and well-being that culminates in joy—the emotional ground against which other features of the experience unfold. There is no pain, no bodily sensation. The person feels that he is dying or has died.

Next he finds himself outside the physical body, perhaps looking down at it. He sees and hears acutely. He feels drawn into another reality, often floating through a soft black void or a tunnel. He suddenly becomes aware of a presence that seems to induce thoughts in him, stimulating a life review. There may be a rapid, vivid visual playback.

Time and space seem to be meaningless. The individual is no longer identified with the body. "Only the mind is present, and it is weighing—logically and rationally—the alternatives that confront him at this threshold . . . to go further into this experience or return to earthly life. Usually the individual decides to return on the basis . . . of the perceived needs of loved ones."

Sometimes he floats "through the dark void toward a magnetic and brilliant golden light from which emanate feelings of love, warm and total acceptance." He may enter the world of light and meet loved ones who died earlier.

Usually the experience is abruptly terminated after the decision to return, sometimes with a jolt.

Glen Gabbard of the Menninger Clinic in Topeka, Kansas, published a series of case histories in *With the Eyes of the Mind,* co-authored with Stuart Twemlow (Praeger, 1984).

In one, a two-year-old boy who bit into an electrical cord had no heartbeat or respiration for twenty-five minutes. When his mother later asked him what he remembered of the incident, he said: "I went into a room. . . . It had a very bright light. . . . There was a very nice man who asked me if I wanted to stay there or come back to you. . . . I wanted to be with you and come home."

A twenty-nine-year-old woman vividly recalled an experience she had at age seven. While deathly ill, she had heard a soft, barely audible sound: "the most beautiful sound . . . like a chorus of soprano voices." She felt a sense of peace, weightlessness, and freedom. She found herself floating above her physical body, aware that she had two distinct bodies in different positions, one asleep, one hovering above.

Other beings in the room with her appeared as stars or sparks of light floating around her. Then she perceived a blackness at the beginning of a tunnel. She "moved through it, as if magnetically drawn, to the exhilarating sound of rushing wind." At its end she saw tiny, bright pinpoints of light toward which she moved. A bearded man appeared in a long white robe. She asked the "Christ figure" if she could go and play in this beautiful place and was granted permission. There she met loving people, but eventually she found her way back and reported to the man that some of the people would not communicate. "It is time to go home," he told her. She experienced the return to her physical body.

The figures found in these experiences reflect the developmental level of the child, Gabbard believes.

NDEs of Children

Children also report near-death experiences that are much like those of adults, but apparently less life-altering, detailed, and dramatic. Five physicians at the University of Washington School of Medicine interviewed 40 children, 29 of whom had had serious illnesses and 11 of whom had nearly died. They reported their findings in the *American Journal of Diseases of Children* (140). *Brain/Mind Bulletin* reported their work in 1983.

Seven whose lives had been threatened reported NDE-type experiences. Those who were not seriously endangered had no unusual experiences. This suggests that the phenomenon is associated with the brush with death rather than being a product of any particular pathology or imagination. Six of the survivors reported being out of the physical body, five said they entered darkness, four described a tunnel, and three remembered deciding to return to the body.

Seattle pediatrician Melvin Morse, one of the researchers, told *Brain/Mind Bulletin* in 1987 that he first became fascinated by the phenomenon when one of his young patients described an NDE. In contrast to adults, who usually report detailed NDE experiences, all but one of the children described only short fragments of concrete

How do the near-death experiences of being out of one's body compare to similar experiences when the possibility of death is not a factor? The *Journal of Nervous and Mental Disease* (169) reported that deep feelings of peace, a panoramic life review, and contact with a barrier beyond which the subject could not go were common to out-of-body experiences under all circumstances. (See following pages for more on OBEs.) The findings appeared in *Brain/Mind Bulletin* in 1981.

Compared to other OBEs, near-death experiences were more often perceived as profoundly meaningful, spiritual, and life-changing. No single component of the experience was exclusively associated with nearness to death. But several were most often reported when life was endangered.

• Hearing noises during the early stages of the experience
• Traveling through a tunnel
• Seeing one's physical body from a distance
• Encountering nonphysical beings, especially deceased loved ones
• Encountering a brilliant white light that evoked a deep sense of affinity

memories. They reported no life review, time alteration, or detachment. None of the children verbalized the sense of mission expressed by some adults. Adults typically report meeting dead friends and relatives, whereas children see their teachers or living classmates.

The findings were consistent with the adult studies showing a typical (core) NDE. The core childhood NDE includes a feeling of leaving the physical body, seeing the body from a vantage point above it, perception of darkness, traveling through a tunnel, and an abrupt return to the body.

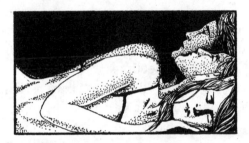

The Paranormal

What do the near-death experiences described in the previous pages tell us? Do they offer a glimpse of the continuation of life after death, or are they merely hallucinations? And what does it really mean when we call a phenomenon "merely hallucination"? Is there a sense in which even hallucinations tell us something "real" about reality?

Such questions abound when we discuss the paranormal, phenomena that include remote viewing, telepathy, precognition, psychokinesis, and synchronicity—collectively known as "psi" or psychic phenomena. Like most of these phenomena, out-of-body experiences and past-life memories are difficult to test by the ordinary methods of science, and so are surrounded by tremendous controversy. They are also gaining tremendous public attention.

The extreme camps of the debate are zealous indeed. True believers and debunkers alike occasionally behave with equal abandon, dogmatism, and irrationality—either blindly accepting phenomena without foundation or evidence, or dismissing all evidence without sufficient cause.

RESEARCH

Is the Paranormal Becoming Normal?

The paranormal may soon be reckoned normal, judging from survey results published in *Brain/Mind Bulletin* in 1987. A survey conducted by the National Opinion Research Center of the University of Chicago found a steep increase in psychic experiences. The center, which has polled Americans on their spiritual life since 1973, gave the following comparisons of people who say they have experienced specific paranormal incidents:

	1973	1987
Extrasensory perception	58%	67%
Contact with the dead	27%	42%
Visions	8%	29%
Déjà vu	59%	67%
Clairvoyance (remote viewing)	24%	31%

Various Gallup polls in the 1980s found increased reporting of a variety of mystical experiences:

Those who had an unusual spiritual experience	43%
Those who had a near-death experience	15%
Those who are convinced there is life elsewhere in the universe	46%
Those who believe in reincarnation	23%

Ingo Swann, the artist-writer and laboratory subject who helped pioneer the experimental design for "remote viewing" research, offers a simple and useful perspective on extrasensory experiences in *Natural E.S.P.*(Bantam, 1988). It's real, natural, and universal, he says. You can develop it; you can even repeat and refine your experiments.

Swann shows us the strategies for his telepathic "picture drawings," and examines the analytical side of creativity, as he sets out the historical case for mind-to-mind communication. He points out, explains, describes; he doesn't argue.

Jon Klimo launches his ambitious volume *Channeling* (J. P. Tarcher, 1988) with an overview of the overpromises, fraud, and mental-health risks historically associated with trance channeling.

Klimo attempts to find the gold among the dross. He reviews the history of the phenomenon, describes a variety of contemporary examples, then focuses on what he calls "open channeling" techniques that facilitate attunement and creativity.

In *Afterlife: An Investigation of the Evidence for Life After Death* (Doubleday, 1988), Colin Wilson says in the first chapter, "This book is not an attempt to convince anyone of the reality of life after death. It is simply an attempt to present the facts in an orderly manner. At the end the reader should be in a position to make up his own mind."

This wide-ranging history is entertaining, even enlightening, but Wilson is at his philosophical and storytelling best in the last chapter and postscript.

"Most of us have allowed the subconscious to become messy and untidy, like a disused playroom that has become a repository for old junk. . . . Every time we catch a glimpse of the mess through the half-open door, we shudder and hurry past. Yet it would only take half an hour with a broom and mop to make it one of the nicest rooms in the house."

A new kind of skepticism may be needed—a skepticism that is critical *and* open in equal measures, a skepticism that dismisses nothing out of hand. And there may be a question even more fundamental than "Do such things really happen?" Rather, perhaps we should ask: "Can such experiences be of personal benefit to me?" There is only one way to find out; we are our own best laboratories.

Out-of-Body Incidents

In 1981, *Brain/Mind Bulletin* reported on a detailed survey by Kansas psychiatrist Glen Gabbard, Stuart Twemlow, and psychologist Fowler Jones. The group of 339 persons reporting out-of-body experiences (OBEs) was described as "highly representative of the general population." The researchers described their findings at a series of professional meetings.

Subjects who reported having "an experience where you felt that your mind or awareness was separated from your physical body" were tested for evidence of psychosis, hysteria, death anxiety, danger seeking, and attention absorption (the capacity for daydreaming and fantasy). Ninety percent were not near death at the time and 79% were both physically relaxed and mentally calm immediately before the experience.

No distinctive psychological profile emerged from the survey. The group's educational level was higher than the United States average. Their age at the time of OBE was evenly distributed from 2 to 65. The group had only a few more females than males.

OBEs Reported

Following are some of the experiences that were described, and the percentage reporting each:

Reported having more than one OBE	66%
Described experience as "more real" than dreams	94%
Reported seeing their bodies from a distance	51%

Found themselves in a different environment, from which their body was not visible	33%
Said that the experience was remarkably pleasant	85%
Said that "serenity" predominated	72%
Said they experienced "joy"	55%
Felt fear at some time during the experience	35%
Questioned their own sanity	5%
Considered the experience religious in nature	55%
Became more convinced of an afterlife	66%
Reported lasting benefits	75%
Said their lives were changed	60%
Said it was the "greatest thing that ever happened to them"	43%
Wanted to repeat the experience	89%

Overall, subjects characterized the experience as integrating and positively transforming, not disorienting or fragmenting. In the OBE, "there is no clouding of consciousness as is reported in dream states," the researchers said. "Subjects are absolutely certain that they were not dreaming."

"Those who were calm had more detailed and vivid experiences than those who were fearful," Twemlow said. They were also likelier to report a dramatic and lasting impact on their lives. Fearful subjects were less likely to interpret the experience spiritually or religiously.

Although more than half of the group did consider the experience spiritual or religious in nature, their previous and current religious affiliation was not significantly affected—unless the OBE occurred near death.

COMMENTARY

Extended Abilities Without Sight or Hearing

Keith Harary and his colleagues at the Institute for Advanced Psychology (see main text) have conducted experiments with handicapped individuals, including the congenitally blind and deaf. He called the preliminary results "highly suggestive" although he is careful not to make unfounded claims. Nevertheless, he says, "we have not found handicapped people to be any less capable of using their extended abilities (ESP or remote viewing) than people who are not disabled. There may even be compensatory abilities."

Since the congenitally blind do not have a visual experience at all, it may come as a surprise that their extended perceptions seem no less potent than the sighted's. So there is a possibility that so-called ESP may be more than a matter of mere perception; it may constitute a kind of *communication*.

Because of the mutual exploration involved, Harary thinks of his handicapped colleagues as friends rather than subjects. He told *PragMagic* that he has gained skills and insights. "I'll drop something in the dark," he says, "and I'll find myself going to right where it is and picking it up. I don't even think for a moment about turning on the light. It's just become automatic to listen to where it landed and walk right to it, because I watch my [blind] friends do it so much."

The Influence of Imagery

William Braud and Marilyn Schlitz of the Mind Science Foundation in San Antonio reported in *Journal of Scientific Exploration* (3) that subjects were able to affect the physical state of other subjects by using mental imagery. *Brain/Mind Bulletin* reported the research in 1990.

Braud and Schlitz employed over 300 volunteers for their tests. They placed subjects in separate, distant rooms and instructed one to try to physically calm or activate the other's nervous system through mental imagery.

The recipient of the imagery was isolated from contact with the influencer and was not told when the attempts at calming or activating would be made. His or her physiological state was monitored by measurements of galvanic skin response.

The influencer attempted to use imagery to create the desired nervous system response in intermittent 20-second periods. Influencers variously tried:

• To create the desired state in themselves mentally and transfer it.

• To create the effect from the other person's point of view.

• To imagine graph readings showing the change they were seeking.

Braud and Schlitz said that in 13 carefully designed preliminary tests, one person's imagery coincided with another's physiological state vastly more often than chance or known bodily rhythms would predict. In 321 sessions, the receiving subject's physical state corresponded to the imagery 57% of the time.

The overall effect seemed strongest, Braud and Schlitz said, when generated by people with interests in healing or received by subjects likely to benefit most from having their mood changed (such as those high in stress).

Since the subjects were "essentially a well-adjusted group of people with relatively little alcohol abuse and few psychosomatic disturbances," Jones said, "it would seem unwise to categorize OBEs as delusional, hallucinatory, or drug-induced." Drug or alcohol use by the group was strikingly low, and only four had been using psychedelic drugs (LSD) or marijuana at the time of the OBE.

Is It Genuine?

How do you determine whether someone has had a genuine OBE? At this point, Gabbard said, "The subject himself is the best person to know if he had the experience." Whatever OBE subjects report, "it is not possible to *prove* that something—e.g., 'mind'—separates from the body."

OBEs do not, of themselves, call for psychiatric treatment, Gabbard said. Such treatment might be harmful. Education about the experience and reassurance that others have shared it are "far more therapeutic than conventional psychiatric intervention."

Readers may want to experiment with the excerpt from Keith Harary's "How to Have an Out-of-Body Experience," reprinted from *Omni* in the Appendix of *PragMagic*.

The Study of Psi

Many established scientists and researchers believe that any serious research into the paranormal is impossible. Even those who acknowledge the existence of psi may believe that such phenomena are too ephemeral and unpredictable to be tested. Why is it *important* to study extended abilities? What experimental methods are required? Are the experiences themselves anything more than an oddity, without any application in the real world?

In 1986, noted psi researcher Keith Harary and colleagues—including his wife, Darlene Moore—founded the Institute for Advanced Psychology in San Francisco. The Institute has since moved to Los Angeles, a modest operation with an interdisciplinary team, composed of psychological consultants, physicists, biologists, and communication experts.

Harary, who holds a Ph.D. in clinical counseling and experimental psychology, discussed some of these difficult questions with *PragMagic*.

EXERCISE: HOW TO HAVE A MYSTICAL EXPERIENCE

In December of 1988, Keith Harary published an article in *Omni* entitled "How to Have a Mystical Experience." "Mystical experiences," he wrote, "are not necessarily extraordinary events that happen only to extraordinary people such as dedicated meditators or peyote eaters. You may deliberately induce a mystical state by paying attention to subtle feelings and ideas lying just beneath the layers of everyday awareness."

The following exercise, entitled "Imagine," is excerpted from the article. Although neither this nor other exercises will *guarantee* a full-blown mystical experience, Harary says, "You probably will become aware of feelings, thoughts, and questions about your place in the universe—the subtle stuff we daily ignore or are not even conscious of. You cannot change what you will not accept or even look at about yourself—and that willingness to scrutinize yourself is the peephole to an altered state of consciousness, a mystical view of life."

Objective: To understand who you've become (your identity) by pretending your memories are merely a product of your imagination; to ask yourself, Is there a more basic and immutable part of my identity beneath the superficial roles I assume? Is there some aspect of my life—a particular experience or another person—that is impossible to imagine as an illusion?

Setting: Choose a place where you're completely alone for a couple of hours. (You may also practice this exercise if you're alone among a group of strangers—on an airplane or in a movie theater.)

INSTRUCTIONS

1. Sit in a comfortable chair, close your eyes, and take a deep breath. As you continue to breathe slowly, let your life pass before you: childhood events, adolescent experiences, major life accomplishments or mistakes, memories of family members and friends. Don't become analytical about past relationships or get stuck on particular experiences. Just let your impressions come and go. How does it feel to be the person you've become?

2. Take another deep breath. As you exhale, concentrate on how alone you are at this moment. Pay attention to your physical environment and your body's sensation. Continue to breathe slowly.

3. Now imagine that your present situation and immediate surroundings represent the whole of reality. Everything you remember about the world and your life, the people and events in it, is imaginary. In fact, you've just come into existence in the past few moments. If you are surrounded by strangers, imagine that they are also experiencing their lives as an illusion.

Benefits: With regular practice you may begin to experience everyday reality in a different way—not as boring, habitual, or conflicted. You may feel freer to consider more satisfying careers, start creative projects, or ask potentially threatening questions like, What do I want out of life? Ask yourself who you might be if all you remember about your life is an illusion.

RESEARCH

Remote Viewing: Soviet Healer 'Sees' U.S. Target

In a startling remote viewing experiment, reported in *Brain/Mind Bulletin* in 1984, a Soviet healer described two different target locations more than 10,000 miles away.

In the experiment, Djuna Davitashvili, healer to former president Leonid Brezhnev, sat with her eyes closed, cleared her mind, and described her impressions of the San Francisco site where American team member Keith Harary would be six hours later. Meanwhile, Harary used a die to randomly select his site—the merry-go-round at Pier 39. No one else was aware of it.

The healer's description "had many unique and striking correspondences with the target," said American physicist Russell Targ. She described a rectangular plaza at the end of a road. She saw a round structure, low buildings with pointed roofs in a long line, a "profile of an animal's eye and pointy ears," and a "white couch or divan."

"It was apparent that we had created a bridge of consciousness between our two countries," Targ said.

The Soviet Academy proposed continued collaboration toward an understanding of the physics and psychology underlying this phenomenon. Targ proposed that this ability might one day be used to help verify nuclear proliferation treaties.

"We don't use the terms 'remote viewing' or 'ESP' anymore. We call what we're looking at 'extended perception and communication.' It's a term which doesn't imply any value system, or even any conclusion about what's happening. In shorthand, we call it 'extended abilities.' "

Rigorous experimental methods are required for the study of psi, Harary said. There must be "no leakage of information," no possibility that the experimenters are giving unconscious hints to their subjects. Double-blind methods are used, so that even the researchers don't know what the target is when the experiments are in progress. All phases of the process are recorded on videotape.

The Institute's current research with the blind, deaf, and handicapped uses two basic approaches: he allows loosely controlled training sessions not recorded in the actual data, to "help a person to deal with certain kinds of inner experiences, and get hands-on experience," but he also insists on the tightly controlled gathering of experimental data.

"We tried a whole bunch of methods," said Harary, "but the one that we found that was most effective and most controlled was to simply not have the answer exist in present time." So the answer is randomly chosen *after* the viewing has been attempted (see example in sidebar).

Why Study Psi?

But why study these phenomena at all? One major theme of this research is *connectedness*—at all levels. "Personally," Harary said, "my whole approach to this work has become much more socially oriented, much more involved with such issues as where we're going as a culture and as a society. I don't see the work I'm doing on subjective human experience and human potential as being in any sense separate from ecological and political questions. We don't have the luxury right now of going off and doing things that we find psychically amusing. We don't have that luxury *at all*. We have to do things that motivate people to make positive global changes."

Harary has written exercises for *Omni* (1988) entitled "How to Have a Mystical Experience" and "Eight Ways to Have an Out-of-Body Experience" (see page 209 and Appendix respectively). "We're not going to answer what out-of-body experiences are through a purely psychological analysis. We can't. But people can find out what it means to them in their own lives without our telling them."

Harary says he writes articles on how to have mystical experiences "because if you make that normal and acceptable for people, something you can do at the bus stop and in your living room, then it's no longer unattainable, out there in the void—no longer an excuse not to expand your awareness.

"Politically and socially, it's crucial that we not deny that aspect of ourselves that reaches out toward the unknown, toward connectedness and meaning. When you get totally caught up in a mundane, materialistic view of reality in which everything that can possibly be known or invented already exists, then you have free reign to basically lead a meaningless life. You're not connected with the rain forests, you're not connected with the rest of humanity, and you feel no need to worry about the destruction of the planet."

Synchronicity

Synchronicity refers to the striking, apparently meaningful coincidences first discussed scientifically in 1919 by biologist Paul Kammerer in *The Law of Seriality,* and defined by C. G. Jung and Nobel physicist Wolfgang Pauli in 1955.

Examples of synchronicity include: the unexpected encounter with an individual one needed to see very much; or a sudden and improbable sequence of related words and symbols in a brief period, like a day in which one receives a gold object, a call from someone named Gold, the announcement of a golden wedding anniversary. These events sometimes seem to involve the whole spectrum of psychic phenomena—psychokinesis, telepathy, precognition, clairvoyance.

A theory relating to synchronicities—how to detect these meaningful coincidences, how to read their meaning, and speculation on their possible purpose—provoked strong interest at a 1979 meeting of the Parapsychology Association at St. Mary's College in Moraga, California. The conference proceedings were published in 1980 by Scarecrow Press.

The convention of professional researchers may also have marked a turning point for methodology and approach: speaker after speaker urged that investigators supplement classical scientific procedures with more imaginative approaches to the elusive phenomena.

RESOURCE

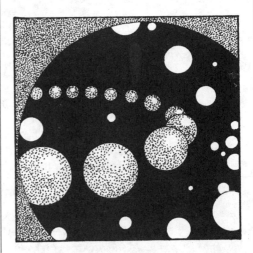

Synchronicity—the meaningful convergence of events—is given a new context in *The Tao of Psychology: Synchronicity and the Self* by Jean Shinoda Bolen (Harper & Row, 1979). Jungian psychiatrist Bolen suggests that significant coincidences represent an unfolding from the Tao—the underlying unifying principle of the universe given various names by various spiritual traditions. In the Eastern religions this unfolding is expressed in the saying, "When the pupil is ready, the teacher will come."

Bolen concedes that there are no rational explanations for the ways in which thoughts, dreams, or inner psychological states coincide with external events. For instance, a woman dreams that her sister's house is afire and calls in time to awaken her and save her life.

She quotes Jung's observation: "The understanding of synchronicity is the key that unlocks the door to the Eastern apperception of totality that we find so mysterious." Seeing synchronicity at work in our lives establishes a sense of connectedness to other people and the universe, she suggests. It promotes psychological growth and a sense of meaning in one's life.

Bolen, like several other psychotherapists and psychoanalysts, sees a correlation between increased mental health and a growing awareness (or incidence) of meaningful coincidence.

EXERCISE: KEEPING A SYNCHRONICITY DIARY

How can we study synchronicities in our own lives? Diary-keeping is a useful tool. Barbara Honegger discussed her own diary with *PragMagic,* one in which she recorded both daytime events and dreams. You may wish to do the same.

> Keep a small watch handy—preferably of the small, plastic, digital variety that can be stuck to the inside of your notebook. Use it to note the exact time of your entries. As you're going about your day, if there is something that strikes you as "uncanny, odd, numinous, synchronistic," write it down and note the time. For example, perhaps while you're driving one day, a word or a name will come to mind. Soon after, the same word turns up on a sign or billboard, in a conversation, or on the radio. Just the act of jotting such things down will draw your attention to odd events and coincidences you might otherwise not notice.
>
> It's also a good idea, during the course of your day, to jot down a certain number of *normal* events as well. Underline or highlight the unusual incidents. The next morning, record the dreams you have had during the night.

Speaking of her own practice, Honegger said, "I learned that *over time,* there was a pattern amongst the highlighted or underlined events. And they, in turn, related to the underlying (or linguistic) 'deep structure' of the dreams."

Honegger cautions that not everyone's experience will be like hers. "I can't really teach people to get specific results. I can only show them what I do, and if they decide to do it and they find out the same thing, fine."

> After a month or two of keeping the diary, you might put it in a drawer and after another month or two, come back to it. Honegger found that it gave her a renewed objectivity to look at the "free-associational structure amongst those highlighted or underlined numinous events. . . . They didn't necessarily have meaning at the time—but meaning became more apparent *across time.*"

> After about a month or two of diary-keeping, you may want to try this: In a separate notebook, write down only the highlighted or underlined portions of your diary in chronological sequence, "so that you kind of collapse out everything that isn't highlighted. This way you get a purely numinous account of the last month or two months or whatever." When you look at it, you may find that it "has the structure of a dream—a *single* dream, except drawn from the numinous aspects of your daily existence over a period of time."

John Palmer, then president of the Parapsychology Association, suggested that the old "transmission" models, which focus on how mind can transmit thought or energy, may be less fruitful than approaches that treat psi simply as correspondences between life events. Among the provocative new approaches cited by Palmer was the synchronicity theory proposed by Barbara Honegger of Washington Research Institute in San Francisco.

Synchronicity and the Right Brain

Honegger suggested that synchronicities are the strategy of the intuitive right hemisphere of the brain to communicate unconscious needs and proposed solutions to the left hemisphere through symbolic language: events, objects, "coincidences."

She maintained that the right hemisphere has a rich and subtle understanding of language but is thwarted by its neurological inability to control speech and writing in the normal everyday awake (NEA) state. Therefore it alerts the left brain—the "conscious" mind—by psi or involuntary attention to certain objects or information.

If you keep a diary of coincidences and also note when your attention is drawn to something for no apparent reason, you may find that these events add up to a kind of metalanguage over a period of weeks, a free-associational string of words and symbols much like the string of associations that emerges from dreams.

Honegger proposed that synchronicities occur and are detected in a waking state that is the counterpart of REM sleep. Just as most people don't recall their dreams, most people either don't notice synchronicities or forget them right away. Honegger, who has kept her own diary of such events for many years, has led workshops and seminars on synchronicity catching.

Synchronicity Catching

"Contrary to popular opinion, synchronistic events are not rare but quite common," she said. "Just as low dream-recallers report increased dreaming when they are awakened during REM sleep, those 'synchronicity blockers' whose synchronicities are pointed out to them while they are still in progress often express disbelief that such striking coincidences could have gone unnoticed."

Her use of the diary (see exercise on facing page) offers a new experimental approach to the phenomena and possibly a technique for interpreting them. However, she

COMMENTARY

The Hologram as Metaphor

"I believe we're in the middle of a paradigm shift that encompasses all of science," Karl Pribram said at a 1977 Houston conference on health care. He went on to spell out a powerful multifaceted theory that could account for sensory reality as a "special case" constructed by the brain's mathematics but drawn from a domain beyond time and space, where only frequencies exist.

Pribram, a renowned brain researcher, has accumulated evidence for a decade that the brain's "deep structure" is essentially holographic. He has published a number of papers on the topic.

Pribram's conversations with his son, a physicist, led him to the recent theories of David Bohm (see opposite sidebar). To his great excitement, he found that Bohm speculated that the nature of the universe might be more like a hologram, a realm of potentialities underlying an illusion of concreteness. Bohm pointed out that ever since Galileo, science has objectified nature by looking at it through lenses.

Pribram was struck with the thought that the brain's mathematics might be "a cruder form of a lens. Maybe reality isn't what we see with our eyes. If we didn't have that lens, we might know a world organized in the frequency domain. No space, no time—just events. Can that reality be 'read out of' that domain?" Transcendental experience suggests that there is access to the frequency domain, the primary reality. Phenomena of altered states of consciousness may be due to a literal attunement to the invisible matrix that generates "concrete" reality.

Pribram pointed out the extraordinary insight of mystics and early philosophers that preceded scientific verification by centuries. "Every once in a while we have these insights that bring us back to the infinite," he told his audience. "Whether it will stick this time or we'll have to go around once more will depend on you. The spirit of the infinite could become part of our culture and not 'a little far out.'"

acknowledges that her theory does not explain how synchronicities are accomplished, especially those that require the interaction of events in the lives of several individuals.

"We can begin to uncover some of the rules, perhaps," she told *Brain/Mind Bulletin*. "We can learn to see correspondences. But the mechanism itself will probably remain occult—literally, hidden."

What do the sciences say in response to the increasing plausibility of the paranormal? Is the universe quite the tidy mechanism Newtonian physics assumed it to be? If not, how should that concern us in our daily lives and as members of human society?

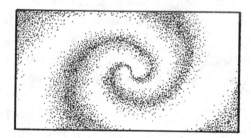

New Stories in Science

What is real?

This is one of those demanding questions that we constantly expect science to answer for us. And whether we recognize it or not, the answers science gives us can affect our very lives. They can make us feel either liberated or enslaved. They can make us feel empowered to change ourselves and our society—or they can leave us in a state of helplessness and despair.

After all, how free can we hope to feel when science tells us that our universe is a clocklike mechanism, moving along deterministically despite our efforts? And how free can we feel when science tells us that our ancestors were engaged in a tooth-and-claw struggle for survival—a struggle we are doomed to repeat?

But science is changing its mind about these and other issues. At this point, we need to pay close attention to two concepts: the paradigm and the hologram.

In *The Structure of Scientific Revolutions* (University of Chicago Press, 1970), a paradigm is defined by science historian Thomas Kuhn as "the entire constellation of beliefs, values, techniques, and so on shared by the members of a given community." The current scientific paradigm is going through a drastic change—but toward what?

Perhaps you have seen a hologram. It is made when an object is photographed onto a glass plate by means of a laser. The photographic patterns appear meaningless and chaotic when viewed in ordinary light. But a laser makes sense of those patterns, producing an illusion of the original three-dimensional object. If you break the plate, the image can be reconstructed—*using any piece of the hologram.*

The hologram may be a metaphor of a new way of looking at the universe—and the role of mind in the universe.

Science is, indeed, telling astounding new stories about the nature of reality, and about our evolution, past, present, and future. An overall theme is interconnectedness and cooperation.

The Tendency Toward Disorder

How do order and complexity emerge from the tendency toward increasing disorder in the universe, which is called entropy? This riddle has plagued science for decades. In 1977, Ilya Prigogine, a Belgian physical chemist, was awarded the Nobel Prize in chemistry for his theory of dissipative structures, which explains how new order can arise *from* entropy, rather than despite it.

Prigogine is now connected with the Center for Studies in Statistical Mechanics, the University of Texas, Austin, and the Service de Chimie Physique, Université Libre de Bruxelles, Belgium. He is the author of *From Being to Becoming* (W.H. Freeman, 1980) and coauthor of *Order Out of Chaos* (Bantam, 1984). Prigogine discussed his theories with *Brain/Mind Bulletin* in 1979 and again in 1984.

His theory of dissipative structures showed that open systems (which includes all living systems) are "perturbed" by energy fluctuations due to their interaction with the environment. These perturbations eventually cause the systems to fall apart. The resulting chaos allows new interactions and recombinations, so the system "falls together" again at a higher level of order.

Fluctuations in Society

The theory of dissipative structures has been related to the traffic flow on freeways and to the perturbations of local socioeconomic systems caused by changes in interstate highways. Prigogine has been called on as a consultant by the United States Department of Transportation on several occasions.

In a dissipative structure, small fluctuations can suddenly change an entire system, just as a creative minority in a society can cause it to shift to a new order.

"The analogy with history is so obvious—fluctuations, behavior of a small group of people, can completely change the behavior of the group as a whole," according to Prigogine.

Cultures are perhaps "the strangest of dissipative structures." Some innovations succeed, but others are suppressed by the surrounding "medium," the dominant society.

A critical number of advocates of change can create a tendency to change toward a new "preferential direction."

Prigogine believes that societies now have the opportunity, because of their size and density, to become more diversified and pluralistic.

A book, a rock, a cup of cold coffee, are closed structures. They are not taking in or putting out energy. But dissipative structures are open; they exchange energy with the surrounding environment. Hot coffee is an example.

A dissipative structure can be a chemical solution, a seed, a dynamic pattern in the brain—or even a society. Prigogine likes to use the town as an example. The town takes energy from the surrounding environment and converts it or dissipates it (as when a factory sends forth its products).

The more complex a dissipative structure is, the more energy it needs to maintain all that complexity. This may make the system highly unstable and subject to sudden change. If the fluctuations reach a critical size, they can drive the whole system into a new state. The new state occurs as a sudden shift, much like a kaleidoscope shifts into a new pattern.

Prigogine's predictions about the role of fluctuations in producing new structures were sometimes confirmed by computer simulation. Unlike Einstein, who reportedly did not even bother to open the telegram informing him that his theory had experimentally been confirmed, Prigogine said he always feels "somewhat astonished" when he turns out to have been right, when everything falls into place.

Being Driven by the System

Large fluctuations organize new order through *nonlinear* processes. As an example of nonlinearity, Prigogine mentions freeway traffic. If there is very little traffic, you are able to drive more or less as you choose, with minimum slowing or lane-changing as the result of other cars. You are in a linear mode.

But if traffic begins to thicken, you are not only driving but being *driven by* the system. All the cars are now affecting each other. You are in a nonlinear process.

Human society also serves as an example: as individuals in a dense society become acquainted with other individuals, each soon has points of contact with more friends and friends of friends throughout the entire system. The more interactions that occur, the greater the potential for change.

As society grows less stable because of the increasing complexity, this interaction can create a new organization. Therefore, nonlinear systems are said to be self-organizing.

At every level of reality there are transformations of this kind: evolution, chemical phase shifts, brain shifts, social and behavioral change.

The Changing Universe

If we think of the universe as unchanging, or if we see change only in terms of decay, we fail to see that periodic chaos can lead to new order. Prigogine and his associates propose that change is positive and constructive, that entropy produces new patterns.

Apparently, then, the universe has a tendency to reorganize, as well as a tendency toward disorder. Even in everyday life, there may be a time to let things fall apart and regroup naturally. Although we can't individually control the particulars of a nonlinear process, Prigogine's theory indicates that we may be on the brink of a higher level of organization—even when all we can see is chaos.

"We really have an open universe," Prigogine says. "There is the feeling that we live in this world of innovation, creativity, that we are at a very exciting moment, perhaps a turning point."

Morphogenetic Fields

If substantiated, a startling hypothesis introduced by a respected British scientist could overturn many of our basic ideas about nature and consciousness. Plant physiologist Rupert Sheldrake is the former director of studies in cell biology and biochemistry at Cambridge University, and a research fellow of the Royal Society. His "hypothesis of formative causation" proposes that the universe functions not so much by immutable laws as by "habits"—patterns created by the repetition of events over time.

In his book *A New Science of Life* (J. P. Tarcher, 1981), Sheldrake proposed that all systems are regulated not only by known energy and material factors but also by invisible organizing fields. These fields have no energy but serve as blueprints for form and behavior. His 1988 book, *The Presence of the Past* (see sidebar) further explains his theories.

Sheldrake calls the invisible organizing field, or matrix, a "morphogenetic field," from *morphe* (form) and *genesis* (coming-into-being). *Brain/Mind Bulletin* popularized the abbreviated term "M-field." Whenever an atom, molecule, cell, organism, or other morphic unit

---

RESOURCE

The Presence of the Past by Rupert Sheldrake (Times Books, 1988) further develops his theory of morphogenetic fields.

Even with some experimental evidence, Rupert Sheldrake's hypothesis of formative causation will continue to be controversial, and not only because it represents a break with past thinking. It also undermines materialist philosophy and even challenges the very foundation of the scientific method.

Sheldrake says that the structure of morphic fields is not determined by either "transcendent ideas (in the Platonic sense) or timeless mathematical formulae, but rather results from the actual form of previous similar organisms."

This evolutionary "memory" depends on what he calls morphic resonance, based on similarity. The more similar an organism is to previous organisms, the greater their influence on it by morphic resonance. And the more such organisms there have been, the more powerful their cumulative influence.

Sheldrake says that, ordinarily, we simply regard the origin of the universe and its creativity as an impenetrable mystery and leave it at that. "If we choose to look further, we find ourselves in the presence of several long-established [religious] traditions. . . .

"In all these traditions we sooner or later arrive at the limits of conceptual thought and also at a recognition of these limits. Only faith, love, mystical insight, contemplation, enlightenment or the grace of God can take us beyond them."

RESOURCE

A Brief History of Time: From the Big Bang to Black Holes (Bantam, 1988) by Stephen Hawking is the author's gift to non-physicists. "What do we know about the universe, and how do we know it? Where did the universe come from, and where is it going? Did the universe have a beginning, and if so, what happened before then? What is the nature of time? Will it ever come to an end?"

Hawking is generally regarded as the leading theoretical physicist of our time. His standing is all the more remarkable given that he has been crippled since youth by Lou Gehrig's disease. Although he is also mute, he continues to hold Newton's chair as a Cambridge lecturer. (He "speaks" by operating a computerized device.)

Recent physics breakthroughs, he says, suggest answers to some of these long-standing questions. Topics include the Uncertainty Principle, black holes, elementary particles, and the unification of physics.

Any complete theory should eventually be understandable in broad principle by everyone. "Then we shall all, philosophers, scientists, and just ordinary people, be able to take part in the discussion of the question of why it is that we and the universe exist. If we find the answer to that, it would be the ultimate truth of human reason—for then we would know the mind of God."

first comes into being, it generates an M-field that affects all later units of the same type.

According to this hypothesis, whenever one member of a species learns a new behavior, the causative field for the species is changed, however slightly. If the behavior is repeated long enough, its "morphic resonance" affects the entire species.

Evolution reflects the emergence of new M-fields. A change originally made slowly or with difficulty becomes easier and easier to make, as more and more members are added to the field.

Sheldrake's hypothesis may account for some of the puzzling phenomena that have been observed in research. For example, although it is difficult to crystallize an organic compound for the first time, later crystallizations of the same compound are much easier to produce.

"The conventional explanation," Sheldrake said, "is that fragments of previous crystals that serve as 'seeds' get carried from laboratory to laboratory to laboratory on the beards or clothing of migrant scientists. When the effect still happens in the absence of any such identifiable carrier, seeds are usually assumed to have traveled around the world as microscopic dust particles in the air."

Sheldrake's theory suggests that the very existence of the first crystallizations eases the difficulty of those that follow.

M-fields and Learning

When change occurs in one unit, the effects are translated by means of its M-field to all its counterparts. Since the nervous system is also governed by M-fields, Sheldrake's hypothesis has powerful implications for learning theory. "If a number of rats, for example, learn to carry out a task that rats have never done before, then other rats everywhere else in the world should be able to learn the task more easily, in the absence of any known type of physical connection or communication."

In fact, there is evidence that such learning resonance occurs. In Harvard experiments beginning in 1920, psychologist William McDougall found a significant increase in the rate at which successive generations of rats learned to escape from a specially designed water maze. Even when he bred only the slowest-learning rats from each generation, the effect persisted.

When two other research groups repeated the experiment, their first generations of rats learned the maze almost as quickly as McDougall's last generation. Some rats learned the task immediately, without error. The phenomenon was never explained.

Paving the Way?

The hypothesis of formative causation, Sheldrake acknowledges, "involves such a radical departure from the currently orthodox way of looking at the world that it is unlikely to be accepted unless supported by convincing evidence. But if there turns out to be something to it, it will have revolutionary implications."

Perhaps we should all consider the possibility that when we, as individuals and in groups, learn new habits and change our own lives—we might actually be making it easier for others to do the same.

A "Living Systems" View

What do our new scientific stories have to teach us about how to heal our planet? Can we use nature itself as a guide for cultural change?

In 1986, physicist Fritjof Capra discussed these questions at a Nebraska conference, "New Visions: A New You, A New Universe." He says that there is an emerging recognition that the problems of our time, including the threat of war, poverty, and starvation, are but different facets of one crisis, "a crisis of perception." Capra teaches physics at the University of California, Berkeley, and is the author of *The Tao of Physics* (Shambhala, 1976), *The Turning Point* (Simon & Schuster, 1982), and *Uncommon Wisdom* (Simon & Schuster, 1988).

"Most of our social institutions subscribe to the concepts and values of an outdated perception," Capra said. That set of beliefs, which we now call the old paradigm, originated in the seventeenth century with the scientific revolution.

"The French mathematician and philosopher René Descartes purported a division between the realms of mind and matter, and described the material universe as a machine, including the human body. Descartes used the metaphor of a clockwork, likening the healthy body to a well-made clock. The universe and all living systems consisted of 'basic material building blocks.' "

This metaphor, Capra noted, is still the basis of contemporary medicine. And, he said, we still make unfortu-

RESOURCES

The Turning Point: Science, Society and the Rising Culture, by Fritjof Capra (Simon & Schuster, 1982). Capra, author of *The Tao of Physics*, delineates the social implications of the discoveries of the new physics. He uses systems theory to create a new language and approach to understanding living systems.

As a system approaches a critical point— "the turning point"—it "decides" which way to go. This decision determines its evolution. As our cultural turning point approaches, Capra says, our greatest hope for the future is the realization that historic, evolutionary changes cannot be stopped by short-term political action.

Green Politics: The Global Promise, by Fritjof Capra and Charlene Spretnak (E.P. Dutton, 1984), examines the controversial "post-liberal" party. Upon their founding in West Germany, the Greens often asked provocative questions in simple, direct language: How is one's personal life a political statement? What are the social implications of systems thinking? How is grass-roots decision-making implemented at the national level? How can we achieve a lasting peace without radically restructuring the economy?

The principles behind these questions are spelled out in a preliminary way in the Greens' federal program, say Capra and Spretnak. "We represent a total concept, as opposed to the one-dimensional, still-more-production brand of politics. Our policies are guided by long-term visions for the future and are founded on four basic principles—ecology, social responsibility, grass-roots democracy, and nonviolence."

nate divisions between such areas as economy and social environment. For example, decisions of economic policy are usually made without any consideration for social and environmental costs or consequences. "In the past few decades," said Capra, "these assumptions have proven severely lacking and limited."

"The rising culture," a term Capra borrows from British historian Arnold Toynbee, is based on a more holistic vision—that is, emphasizing the whole rather than mere parts. It is an ecological worldview based on the theory of living systems that has emerged during the last 20 years.

"All living organisms are living systems," explained Capra, "from the smallest bacterium, through the wide range of plants and animals to human beings. Parts of our

---

INVENTORY: OF MACHINES AND SYSTEMS

Fritjof Capra listed certain concepts of the receding paradigm:

- The idea of the material universe as a mechanical system
- The idea of the human body as a machine
- The idea of life in society as a competitive struggle for existence
- The belief in unlimited material progress through economic and technological growth
- The belief that a society in which the female is everywhere subsumed under the male is one that follows natural law

Capra also discussed concepts of the new systems view:

- The systems view looks at the world in terms of relationships and integration.
- Systems are integrated wholes whose properties cannot be understood by taking them to pieces and understanding them in terms of smaller units. They are wholes whose specific structures arise from the interaction of parts. The nature of a whole is always different from the mere sum of its parts.
- Living systems are intrinsically dynamic; their forms are not rigid structures, but flexible manifestations of underlying processes.
- Self-organization is a key pattern in living systems. A living system organizes itself, and therefore has a certain autonomy vis-à-vis its environment. This pattern applies to systems of all kinds: cells, organs, people, families, communities, and ecosystems.

—adapted from Fritjof Capra's talk "A Crisis of Perception" at the 1986 "New Visions" conference

bodies are living systems: the heart, the liver, the kidney, and other organs, down to individual muscles and cells."

We should think of social systems in the same way, including family and community. These are "ecosystems in which a variety of individual organisms are linked together in a web of exchanges and interactions. All these systems are *wholes* whose specific structures arise from the interaction and interdependence of their parts."

Living in a New Paradigm

Capra pointed out that in ecosystems—the natural systems of the earth—everything moves in cycles. He stated two important rules for living in ecosystems.

• Remember that growth is not necessarily progress. "When you do something that is good, more of the same will not necessarily be better." In society as in nature, there is such a thing as harmful, pathological growth—a fact seldom recognized by economists and politicians.

"The strategy is not to maximize but to *optimize*. The question of scale becomes very important. There is an appropriate scale for every organization, every city, every community." Capra quoted Hazel Henderson: "Nothing fails like success."

• Recycle. "The more a society and its economics are based on the continual recycling of its natural resources, the more they will be in harmony with the surrounding environment. The air we breathe, the soil we stand on, the food we eat, and the water we drink consist of the very same molecules that have been continuously recycled for about 3 billion years."

The Rising Culture

When we observe our society in a static way, it may seem that all of the old paradigm beliefs are still in power. Capra recommended that we look at our culture through "an ecological perspective," a fundamental change in worldview that he said is, in fact, emerging in social movements and in science.

A living system is always evolving, and when our culture is seen as a living system, Capra said, you can see that the old worldview is declining and a new one is rising to take its place. This is "an evolutionary change of a magnitude that cannot be prevented by short-term political activities." This must not take the form of violent revolution, he stressed, but of nonviolent transformation.

RESOURCES

In *Previews and Premises* (Morrow, 1983), Alvin Toffler expands his views on "info-politics," economics, work, the role of women, the influence of media, and the impact of computers.

According to Toffler, change comes in waves that sweep across society, cutting through class, race, and special-interest groups. The waves are chains of associated trends that reinforce one another, speeding up change and moving society in a new direction. The main ingredients are diversity and accelerated change. "It's the convergence of many internal and external forces that builds up the pressure for a revolutionary restructuring of economies. The result: a higher, far more complex level of development, which is far more dependent on information."

In *Walking on the Edge of the World* (Houghton Mifflin, 1988) by George Leonard, the time, more or less, is the 1960s and '70s. The setting, in a way, is a moving current, dominated by the high waters of the civil rights and human potential movements.

Personal moments fold naturally into historical drama, such as the march of civil rights protesters to Selma, Alabama, and the assassination of a president.

Leonard talks about the experiences that led him to write about the need for deep educational reform. He describes his first encounter with Michael Murphy, cofounder of Esalen, and his excitement at discovering aikido, a martial art he now teaches.

EXERCISE: PLAYING WITH THE PARADIGM

Sit quietly and briefly reflect on the following highly unlikely premises. Suppose you wake up one morning and you read the following item in the newspaper:

> • It has been discovered that our universe is actually contained inside a gigantic ball, painted blue on the inside. Gigantic creatures live on the outside of that ball, as we live on the earth. That ball is contained inside another gigantic ball, painted red on the inside. Apparently, there are an infinite number of universes contained inside an infinite number of balls—all painted primary colors on the inside.

Suppose you are quite certain that the news item is not a joke. How might you respond? Doubtless, your view of "how things are" will be badly shaken. Is it possible that your life will go on in much the same way it always has? Perhaps.

But more likely not. Certain concepts and ideas run deep enough in the collective psyche to affect the very nature of life and society. When such sweeping ideas change, it is sometimes called a "paradigm shift." Such shifts have happened from time to time during human history—and no doubt even before recorded history. Such changes are hard to understand intellectually. It is best to use one's imagination—to *feel* the change rather than try to comprehend it rationally.

Now we suggest that you sit quietly again and reflect on the following premises. Imagine yourself in the historical situations described below. Don't intellectualize or verbalize too much; just get a sense of your gut reaction.

> • A NEW CENTER: It is A.D. 1512. You and almost everybody else have always believed that the earth stood firmly in the center of the universe. You have just finished reading Nicolaus Copernicus's *Commentariolus,* which vividly and convincingly explains that the earth and the other planets move around the sun. How does it *feel* to have your entire universe redefined? Does it feel strangely different to be human?

> • A NEW HISTORY: It is A.D. 1830. You have never thought much about the age of the earth. Like most people, you have assumed that Mosaic calculations were correct, and that the earth was but a few thousand years old. You have just finished reading *Principles of Geology* by Charles Lyell, a history of the evolution of the earth's crust, describing eons of gradual change. Lyell has made it startlingly apparent that the earth is literally billions of years old. Like most people in your culture, you have never considered the possibility of so much time, of such an old earth. How do you suddenly *feel* about your position in history—about the nature of time and progress?

When your way of looking at the universe changes, the universe itself changes in a way that is often difficult to define.

EXERCISE, continued

Newtonian physics was a keystone in an earlier paradigm, conceiving of time as separate from space; Einsteinian physics, with its paradoxes of space and time, contributes to our present paradigm. Somehow it makes our world different.

Sit quietly again and reflect on the following premises:

- A NEW MEDIUM: Most of us, at one time or another, try to imagine what it would have been like to be a primitive human. We tend to think of such a life with certain stereotyped images—living in a cave, killing mastodons for food, painting great cave murals, and the like.

But imagine something a little different. Imagine that you are not human, but a very advanced ape. Imagine that the land has been ravaged by a volcanic eruption; there is no food to be found. To save yourself and your fellows, you have to go into the water to search for food—something that creatures of your kind have never done. You wade into the water for the first time. It is a strange sensation. To your own surprise, you find yourself walking more upright.

According to the "aquatic ape" hypothesis, such a creature may have been an ancestor to all of us. An aquatic habitat may have spurred human evolution. Can you *feel* any change in your sense of genetic identity at this thought?

- A NEW CONNECTEDNESS: Imagine the farthest object in the universe that can be seen. It can be whatever you want—a star, a hunk of rock, a flying saucer. This object is at least several billion light years away—a distance so great that it will take countless lifetimes for the light currently emanating from that object to reach you.

Now imagine that the very same object is exactly as far away as you originally conceived it to be—and yet, very paradoxically, despite unimaginable distances, imagine that you and the object occupy the same space.

Certain ideas in modern physics, including David Bohm's "implicate order," suggest that everything in the universe is connected at a mysterious level more fundamental than time and space. Like a hologram, each piece contains the information of the whole. Or as Groucho Marx once said, "Any closer and I'd be standing behind you!"

How does this make you *feel* about time and space—and more importantly, about *relationships* of all kinds?

- A NEW NOTION OF LEARNING: Imagine yourself in the act of learning something. Can you think of something at school or at work that you are soon going to have to learn and expect to be difficult? Maybe it's a computer program, the contents of a textbook, or shorthand. As you imagine yourself laboriously studying, also think of the many people who have learned the same material before you. What if, in some mysterious way, *their* having learned it makes it easier for *you* to learn?

This is one of the implications of morphic resonance. Perhaps it seems naive to assume that we could consciously tap into an M-field and suddenly know what we want to know. But how does the idea of a collective field of memory make you *feel* about the act of learning?

RESOURCES

Megatrends: Ten New Directions Transforming Our Lives (Warner Books, 1982) by John Naisbitt asserts that the U.S. is undergoing major cultural shifts.

His ten megatrends include an all-embracing change from an industrial society to one based on information. He forecasts a more human balance for our high-tech environment, which he calls high-touch. Other trends include shifts to decentralization, world-based economy, long-term planning, participatory democracy, networking, multiple options, self-help, and population shifts to the West, Southwest, and Florida.

In *Megatrends 2000* (Morrow, 1989) Naisbitt introduces his updated list of ten cultural shifts.

The major cultural trends he predicts are: a global economic boom during the 1990s; a renaissance in the arts; the emergence of free-market socialism; the development of global lifestyles and cultural nationalism; the privatization of the welfare state; the rise of the Pacific Rim; the rise of women in leadership positions during the next decade; a new focus on biological sciences; a religious revival during the third millennium; and the triumph of the individual.

Cultural Change

Physics and the other sciences are describing an increasingly interconnected and interdependent universe. *"But,"* you may ask, "what does that have to do with how I live my life?"

Remember the aphorism we proposed earlier in *PragMagic:* "Holism means never saying 'but.' "

Let's keep the thoughts of Fritjof Capra and our other scientists in mind as we look at transformations taking place in our culture. After all, civilizations behave in accordance with how the cosmos is thought to work. As scientific discoveries and personal intuitions create new priorities, societal structures shift to fit those ideas.

How often have you thought about some problem in society—whether locally or globally—and felt as though you could see a solution with crystal clarity?

And how often have you then shaken your head sadly and said, *"It doesn't matter what I think"*? A sense of futility comes easily these days. It won't go away in an instant. And yet . . .

One of the messages of the new stories of science is that it *does* matter what you think. Thought and meaning themselves are intimately connected to the universe. Our very observations change the way things are. Reminding ourselves of this from time to time may make purposeful action in the culture less intimidating.

And a sense of cultural responsibility doesn't have to make us feel as lonely as it used to. A number of trackers of social change have said that enormous revisions are taking place in our culture. Self-interest and materialism may be on the wane. Self-motivation is becoming more common, and altruism may be coming in style.

Changing Attitudes

The late Arnold Mitchell was a social economist and director of the first SRI International Values and Lifestyles Study (VALS). He was the author of *Nine American Lifestyles* (Macmillan, 1983), a long-range study on the role of values in social change based on VALS and on other surveys. In a 1983 interview with *Leading Edge Bulletin,* Mitchell discussed the shifts he saw developing in American attitudes.

Mitchell described a move toward authenticity, directness, and simplicity in all areas. The developing

---

INVENTORY: LIFESTYLES

In *Nine American Lifestyles,* Arnold Mitchell described a "double hierarchy" in which the psychological evolution of consumers proceeds along two tracks—one for those who are goal-driven and materialistic, the other for those who are idealistic and conserving.

Some consumers are categorized as need-driven—those who want but cannot have. Beyond that level, consumers who gain buying power split into:

• *Outer-Directed,* those who buy with an eye to appearance or peer pressure. These include Emulators, who strive to be like those whose success they admire, and Achievers, who are geared to success and expend much of their wealth and energy on the "good things of life." Achievers are competitive, self-confident, well educated, affluent, and generally influential within their professions. They set the trends for Outer-Directed consumers.

• *Inner-Directed,* idealistic, conservation-oriented persons who value the artistic and spiritual. These include those categorized as Experiential or Societally Conscious.

Experiential consumers seek direct experience, deep involvement, intense personal relationships, and a rich inner life. Their interests are likely to include backpacking, gardening, handcrafts, meditation, volunteer social work.

Societally Conscious people emphasize social issues and responsibilities and embrace a "Spaceship Earth" philosophy.

At the top of the hierarchy, both tracks converge into a new consumer type who integrates selected values from both camps. The Integrated consumers rely on an inner sense of what is fitting, self-fulfilling, and balanced. They know what they like and dislike. Their global perspective makes them mature, informed, and ecologically alert. Despite their relatively small numbers, their living pattern sets the standard for Inner-Directed people.

Mitchell predicted an increase in people holding Inner-Directed values in the 1990s, although he said the Outer-Directed group will be in the majority even in 1990.

COMMENTARY

Naisbitt: A Renaissance in the Arts and Other Trends

John Naisbitt spoke of ten new trends for the 1990s in a talk sponsored by the Greater Orlando Chamber of Commerce, *The Orlando Sentinel* reported in 1988:

• An increase in higher-paying managerial and professional jobs—defying the myth of declining pay as we move away from an industrial society.

• The arts and "spirituality" will be on the upswing during the nineties: "Science and technology will not tell us what life means."

• The decline of cities. More Americans are moving to rural areas than to cities.

• The end of the welfare state and the death of socialism. Nations are learning from the example of the failed Soviet economy; care for the needy and helpless will come under increasing private control.

• The emergence of English as the world's first universal language.

• The increasing importance of individuals in the global economy. People are increasingly networked by information technology.

• A shift in international economic influence from the Atlantic to the Pacific Rim. America will trade with Asian nations more than with Europe.

• A decline in political parties. Individuals will assume greater control over political processes.

• The blossoming of worldwide agriculture. A permanent oversupply of food will remove limits on population growth.

• Free trade and a unified global economy. Trade deficits will become meaningless: "It's the surest road to lasting world peace."

U.S. "Mid-life Crisis" and New VALS Typology

The *SRI Journal* (July 1989) described a new typology of U.S. consumers, built on psychological dimensions the researchers saw emerging for the 1990s. According to *SRI,* "a variety of demographic and economic forces have precipitated a 'mid-life crisis' of values in the United States." They cited declining national strength and influence in the face of aggressive foreign competition as one of the causes.

Edward Flesch, director of the VALS study, said, "For individuals and families, questions about the meaning of life, work, personal and community roles, and life-styles are likely to intensify in the next ten years." He added, "Today, while values still play a role in shaping choices, economic, educational, and other constraints have limited people's ability to freely express their values as consumers."

The VALS study group became convinced that the Inner- or Outer-Directed framework had become too general for understanding social interaction. For example, they said, "Affluent outer-directed consumers have embraced some of the attitudes about health and the environment that once were clearly in the domain of inner-directed people.

"Similarly, economic circumstances are forcing inner-directed people to pay more attention to the material aspects of life."

From a two-year program of national surveys of thousands of consumers, the researchers produced a new report, VALS 2, which divides consumers along two key dimensions:

• Self-orientation—"the patterns of attitudes and activities that help people reinforce, sustain, or modify their social identities"

• Resources—"the range of psychological and material resources that enhance or constrain a person's ability and motivation to act according to his or her self-orientation"

turn toward significant work and significant relationships, he said, "could mean the beginning of a new ideology—a view of what is real and important—that has credibility deep and wide enough to engage the core values of most Americans."

Some characteristics of the new ideology include: a sense of national pride expressed through individual action, decentralized decision-making, recognition of the contributions of others, acceptance of many viewpoints, and attention to the spiritual and artistic aspects of life.

Global Solutions

World problems don't persist simply because there are no answers, Anthony Judge, editor of *The Encyclopedia of World Problems and Human Potential* (see opposite sidebar) told *Brain/Mind Bulletin* in 1987. Rather, the solutions appear to be competing. At the moment, as Judge sees it, "we're in a kind of gladiatorial arena in which each answer is supposed to beat up the others and come out triumphant."

"It's kind of a wave/particle problem," he said. "We need to shift from the notion of one idea *versus* another."

He compared the more sophisticated view to the depth of a stereoscopic picture. "The perspective of alternating and multiple solutions can get us out of the paradigm of asking which is better. Our answers can coexist.

"What's exciting for me is seeing that there are creative ways of responding to disagreement," Judge said. "In the past 20 years people have been trying to move toward consensus. Now we can see the value of competing views. In fact, if you strip disagreement from any creative work, you have something so flat no one will respond to it."

In walking, he said, "we alternate feet. You don't say that your left foot disagrees with your right. It's just the walking process. If we can grasp the dynamic of differing perspectives, we can embody them in a new understanding."

Government or corporate policy may run in natural and mutually corrective cycles, he said. "Take the environmentalist and industrial lobbies. We could have cycles in which each has priority. This helps to correct for aberrations or excesses. Such cycles occur in nature."

Judge cited the example of "natural correctives within a family. If either parent dominates for too long, or if a single parent uses only one approach to child-rearing, you have not only a monotonous situation but an unbalanced one."

He said that business moves in cycles, but business-people try to avoid them instead of investigating them and working with them. Most people are stuck in part of a learning cycle, "locked into a particular phase. Most institutions represent only a single phase of a learning cycle. They don't know how to shift to the next phase."

INVENTORY: EMERGENT IDEAS OF SOCIAL CHANGE

What significant international social shifts have emerged from the 1980s? *Brain/Mind Bulletin* put this question to Anthony Judge. Some of his choices were:

• Social innovators and change agents are increasingly *wary of each other*.
• *Positive forces seen as having feet of clay.* "Just as we once decided that there are no bad guys, we have to recognize that there are no good guys, either. Most people are wearing hats of gray, not black or white."
• A major *strategic sense* of worthwhile projects. People are asking, "Where should I be putting my energies?" (An example: Leaders in Britain's peace movement decided that they should work out long-term strategies. This offended some followers who consider strategy "just for eggheads.")
• Growing realization that there is a large *pool of potential enthusiasm* for serious social issues, as evident in the popular support for the Band-Aid recording, *Live Aid Concert,* and so on.
• An increasingly *informed body of potential change agents.* "People are less naive than they used to be. They have skills and see the importance of applying them if something meaningful is to happen."
• Growing recognition that *even reactionary forces have a role to play.* They impose a kind of discipline that is part of the dynamic—a balance for experimental freedom.
• *Recognizing our roles.* "You know the old saying—you're either part of the solution or part of the problem. We have to recognize *how* we are part of the problem if we are to understand the nature of the solution required."

RESOURCE

The Encyclopedia of World Problems and Human Potential (K.G. Saur, 1986; 3rd ed., spring 1990), edited by the Brussels-based Union of International Associations, is the most extensive "expert" networking tool to date. The book identifies 13,000 world problems—political, social, and economic. It includes everything from natural disasters and trade barriers to poverty, disease, and torture.

The volume also identifies thousands of available tools with which to combat the problems and achieve greater human satisfaction. Examples include cultivation of community, conservation practices, and the transcending of national boundaries. Some categories address personal-growth concepts, such as the "flow" experience in sport. The index, with 25,000 cross-references, reveals an overview of issues that have to be addressed in the context of social evolution.

"Collective strategies" include profit-sharing, land reform, and cooperative ventures. "Individual strategies" include the activities of tourists, consumers, "informers," homemakers, even beggars. The book offers techniques for "transforming conferences" and approaches to interdisciplinary thinking.

The power of metaphor, symbols, and patterns is illustrated by hundreds of specific modes of human communication. Among them: advertising, folklore, lectures, graffiti, cartoons, maps, and music.

Problem-Solving Versus Transformation

Transformation is more difficult than anyone imagined, "more subtle and full of traps," Jacob Needleman told *Brain/Mind Bulletin* in a 1978 interview. Needleman is the author of a number of books , including *The Heart of Philosophy* (Knopf, 1982) and a novel, *Sorcerers* (Mercury House, 1986), which deals with the search for the inner self.

"We speak of obtaining freedom from the linear mind. When that happens, however briefly, it is extraordinary, certainly one of the most powerful elements of the transformative experience. But freedom from conditioning is not easy to achieve, although it is sometimes made to sound that way.... In many ways the culture has co-opted language of the spiritual disciplines without facing their real challenge."

Needleman pointed out that deep growth and learning is different, and more difficult to achieve, than mere psychological adjustment. "Therapy may make an individual better adjusted, more creative, happier. Transformation, on the other hand, refers to the birth of a new entity, a change at a different level." Our culture itself does little to encourage the transformational process, but is, instead, "problem-solving in its approach. The individual may resolve a problem having to do with job or marriage or something else—and close off the larger 'question,' not touch upon it at all.

"The spiritual traditions deepen the question, pull you further into it. The question may not have answers in the ordinary way. It may be necessary for the whole self to become the question at some point."

New technologies don't make the problem easier; instead, they pull us outward. "The problem is how to balance the needs of the inner self with the outward pull. But in a sense the art of living in all times and places has been the balance between our mystical nature and our active, worldly nature. We are both."

Transformation

What *is* transformation?

It's a good question to ask, since "transformation" is getting to be a catchall word these days. With all the literature, workshops, and authorities of one stamp or another trumpeting an agenda, there is a real danger of learning the terminology and not getting the real thing.

Transformation is quite different from mere problem-solving; it is much more fundamental. When an individual or a culture transforms, a kind of rebirth is taking place; the universe becomes a subtly different place.

In her book *The Aquarian Conspiracy* (J. P. Tarcher, 1987), *Brain/Mind Bulletin* editor/publisher Marilyn Ferguson speaks of transformation in terms of the "passenger" mind and the "pilot" mind.

"A mind not aware of itself—*ordinary* consciousness—is like a passenger strapped into an airplane seat, wearing blinders, ignorant of the nature of transportation, the dimension of the craft, its range, the flight plan, and the proximity of other passengers.

"The mind aware of itself is a pilot. True, it is sensitive to flight rules, affected by weather, and dependent on navigation aids, but still vastly freer than the 'passenger' mind."

And so transformation is a kind of movement from the role of "passenger" to "pilot." But how do we undertake such a movement?

This question brings us back to one of our recurring themes, the importance of story—and of myth. We delude ourselves when we say that something is "just a myth." Nothing is "just a myth." A myth has enormous power to bind or to liberate, to limit or to transform.

Many of our old myths are showing wear and tear. They suggest that, while individual problems may be

EXERCISE: LUCID WAKING

The transformative process can be helped along through subtle shifts of viewpoint. In "Being Magic," we were introduced to the concept of lucid dreams—those fascinating episodes in which *we know* that we are dreaming. This is as good a time as any to introduce a new concept, an obvious corollary to lucid dreaming: *lucid waking*.

This suggestion is not entirely tongue-in-cheek. We pay less attention to our waking states than we might suppose. A whole new universe crept upon us while we were drowsing. Too often we wander through the waking world in exactly the way a nonlucid dreamer wanders through the world of sleep: helpless against random events, unaware of the true nature of things, and oblivious to the possibilities for experimentation and adventure. Perhaps it's time to rub the sleep out of our eyes and take a better look around. But how can we practice lucid waking?

Try the following steps:

• The first, not surprisingly, is also a lucid dreaming tactic. Ask yourself, with some frequency throughout the day, "Am I dreaming?" When you discover that you are, in fact, awake, allow yourself to feel the same sense of wonder and delight you would feel if you had discovered you were in a dream. Behave *as if* this were a wonderful revelation, filled with surprise and possibility. And why shouldn't it be just that?

• *Experiment* with your waking state. Explore its novelty. A lucid dreamer, after all, will experiment freely with the dream state, summoning up dream characters out of his or her subconscious, attempting to fly. *Be silly.* Solemnity and high-mindedness are incompatible with lucid waking. Try to levitate if you like. Try to materialize and dematerialize objects, or try to change the scene. If you don't succeed, attempt more modest things.

• Explore the possibilities, rules, and laws of waking reality—*as if* they were entirely new to you. Learn about gravity, air, liquids, solids, etc., as if they were novel concepts. Also, consider the presence of *other people* in your reality. How can you relate to these mysterious and puzzling creatures? Where do they come from? Are they like characters out of dreams, phantoms of your subconscious? Or are they tangible, flesh-and-blood entities with waking realities of their own? What are the rules that govern waking relationships?

• Keep a dual waking/dreaming journal. If you have succeeded in lucid dreaming, so much the better for your attempts at lucid waking. Compare revelations that come in either state. Do your sleeping/waking experiences complement or enhance each other?

RESOURCE

In *Memories and Visions of Paradise: Exploring the Universal Myths of a Lost Golden Age* (J. P. Tarcher, 1989), author Richard Heinberg further develops the thesis of his earlier book by the same title. Heinberg's premise is that the reason for the astonishing parallels in the mythology of many cultures is that the stories reflect racial memory rather than mere symbolism. He weaves his argument adroitly, citing hundreds of sources from dozens of cultures.

Virtually every people has told the story of a golden time when humanity was the steward of the Earth and aligned with divine will. Even the descriptions of the garden are surprisingly specific and consistent. Then came the fall from grace, a steady degeneration triggered by the eating of a forbidden fruit. Humanity was left with profound amnesia, diminished perceptual powers, and abbreviated life span.

The dream of return to the original state is not merely religious, Heinberg says. It is also evident in philosophy, literature, and even economic theory.

He also compares similarities among other cultural mythologies. For example, stories of a deluge, similar to that of the biblical Noah and his ark, are found in Babylonia, Greece, among the Transylvanian Gypsies; the Lolos, an aboriginal mountain tribe in China; the Navajos, the Algonquins, and the Papagos (North American tribes), and the Hawaiians.

In conclusion Heinberg shows the relevance of the paradise vision to the present crises of civilization. The hero's journey is a legitimate means to recapture within oneself the knowing of the "First People." We have dragons to tame, Heinberg is saying, and a quest at hand—the restoration of the world.

solved, meaningful transformation is impossible. It may well be time to go shopping for some new myths.

The transformational journey is an adventure in every sense—fraught with dangers, uncertainties, and disappointments. Its rewards are rich but unpredictable. And transformation is not just an individual affair. It can take place in any living system—from a single cell to a civilization.

You can anticipate some of the hazards and pitfalls of transformation, but no tactic can take the place of simple alertness, of staying in tune with yourself and your world.

Finding a New Myth

"The times call urgently for *a theory of the Earth* that will guide our destiny and secure our survival," James Huchingson, professor of philosophy and religion at Florida International University wrote in *Zygon* (16); *Leading Edge Bulletin* reported on his ideas in 1982.

"The goal of science is understanding; the goal of religion is transformation." These are not separate realms, he believes, since it is "one and the same person who seeks both understanding and transformation."

But we need more than spiritual impulse and scientific knowledge. We need a unifying symbol. Huchingson nominates the planet. The theory of evolution became a powerful human myth. Similarly, he said, we need a new shared story. "We are of the Earth, in the Earth—under its skin, so to speak." We are embedded in its dynamic systems, not just *on* it. And we also need to see the planet within its larger systems. He calls this emerging perspective "cosmic naturalism."

With the use of reason, imagination, and "deep sources of motivation," says Huchingson, we can generate vision and take action in ways that will reverse damaging global trends.

Myths and symbols serve to create social order. Concrete historical events, such as the Exodus, may be universalized by means of myth and applied across space and time. Martin Luther King, Jr., adopted this image during the civil rights movement, for example.

"Thus a myth may be acclaimed true when it faithfully expresses the meaning of human existence and when it recommends authentic action, sustaining and even furthering that meaning."

INVENTORY: TRANSFORMATIONAL WORLD VIEW

Jack Drach, member-at-large of the Association for Humanistic Psychology, contrasted two distinct images of man in relation to the universe in the *Association for Humanistic Psychology Newsletter* (July 19, 1982), now called the *AHP Perspective*. "Assumptions about the nature of the universe—whether it is friendly, unfriendly or neutral—lead to very different values and behaviors," he said. "The prevailing worldview assumes an unfriendly universe, and Western civilization has been evolving accordingly. The emerging transformational worldview, however, assumes a friendly universe."

Prevailing Worldview	*Transformational Worldview*
The universe is unfriendly. Therefore, it must be confronted, outwitted, controlled.	The universe is friendly. Therefore, it must be accepted, experienced, celebrated.
Space and time are components of a controllable universe. Therefore, they are measurable and predictable.	Space and time are relative. Therefore, there will always be infinitely large, infinitesimally small, and varying units of space and time.
Nature is a hostile environment, separate from human beings. Therefore, nature is ours to use, to control, and if necessary, to exploit.	Nature is an evolving ecosystem of which we, the human species, are a part. Therefore, by enhancing nature we enhance ourselves.
Life is a matter of survival in a hostile environment. Therefore, I must produce food, property, and children to enhance my security.	Life is a matter of contributing, through myself and others, to the universe. Therefore, in that service, I must realize my fullest potential of body, mind, and spirit.
Other human beings are separate from me. Therefore, I must compete with them for the power that assures my security. I'm most secure when I know my "role" and my "place" within my community and my culture.	I am unique, but I am also one with the human species. Therefore, the degree to which I can successfully connect my full potential to the potentials of other human beings in the service of the universe is the measure of my success.
The purpose of a human society is to provide orderliness, protection, and predictability for its members. To do this requires structure, property rights, laws, enforcement agencies, and a central hierarchy of authority.	The purpose of human society is to increase the service of its members to other human beings and to themselves. To do this requires an environment that supports and encourages self-actualization and self-responsibility.

RESOURCE

The Chalice and the Blade: Our History, Our Future (Harper & Row, 1987) is an extraordinary piece of revisionist history.  According to feminist, futurist, lecturer, and attorney Riane Eisler, human prehistory was marked by 20,000 years of partnership and cooperation, not dominance and aggression. Goddesses were worshiped, and sexual egalitarianism was the norm. In short, the mythical Eden may well have been a reality.

This idyllic world ended about 5,000 years ago in wars and barbaric invasions. Goddesses of fertility and bounty were replaced by male gods of vengeance and destruction. Societies based on partnership were replaced by those based on dominance. Sexual egalitarianism came to an end. Henceforth, history was made by men.

Since then, history has not been without its fluctuations. The times of Jesus and the Renaissance provoked a reemergence of partnering. But as any student knows, history is usually taught as a chronicle of the deeds and triumphs of "great men." And their accomplishments are frequently measured in terms of dominance—and not of liberation.

This historical paradigm has long left us with a sad sense of determinism. We have long been led to believe that conflict and dominance are, somehow, part of the natural order of things. We have become convinced that war and territoriality are facts of human experience, and that things have always been so.

But, as Eisler benignly points out, this man-made paradigm too conveniently skips 20,000 years of human experience. Our heritage is actually as much one of co-operation and partnership as it is one of territoriality and struggle. Might this give us hope for the future? Eisler suggests that it does.

Myths Affect Social Change

Myths may either quicken or inhibit cultural change. "Certain images encourage change by directing energy to the point of crisis," Huchingson said. They accelerate transitions at times of disturbance. The peace symbol, for example, heightened the awareness of contradictions during the Vietnam War.

On the other hand, myths may stabilize the status quo by legitimizing certain modes of behavior. The myth of rugged individualism, for instance, tends to support behavior inappropriate for a time of global interdependence.

The more urgent the cultural crisis, Huchingson said, the more quickly scientific knowledge gains meaningful images, becoming a source of wisdom. The view of the planet as a system offers such wisdom.

Huchingson urges people to stay aware of their connections with the whole. "We must practice a superior *oikonomia,* or caring for the planetary household," he said. "There is no such location as the last place on earth."

Planetary Transformation

In 1983, British science writer Peter Russell told *Brain/Mind Bulletin* that the planet may achieve its own equivalent of consciousness—a global brain. The majority of human beings now alive, he said, may experience an evolutionary shift from ego-centered awareness to a unified field of shared awareness.

Russell's hypothesis about the emergence of a "planetary brain" asserts that humankind may be on the threshold of "a completely new level of evolution, as different from consciousness as consciousness is from life, and as life is from matter." His analysis of social, technological, and psychological trends appeared in his book, *The Global Brain: Speculations on the Evolutionary Leap to Planetary Consciousness* (J. P. Tarcher, 1983).

Factors in the shift to planetary consciousness, Russell said, include environmental crises, technological breakthroughs, growth of data processing capabilities, and the rapid spread of consciousness-expanding techniques. All of these serve as catalysts whose combined effects are shifting the evolutionary process into overdrive.

Russell also speculated on the role of human population growth as an evolutionary catalyst. He observed that human population is now within a numerical range associated with two previous evolutionary thresholds: the one between inanimate matter and life and the one between living matter and self-reflective consciousness.

Just as personal consciousness is more than the bio-chemical interactions of individual brain cells, planetary consciousness will be other than the sum of interacting individual brains, Russell said. "The global brain is likely to possess entirely new characteristics that are unimaginable by our present consciousness."

INVENTORY: TECHNOLOGY AS A KIND OF EVOLUTION

Numerous technological breakthroughs are also precipitating the shift to planetary consciousness, Russell said. Each is comparable to previous evolutionary breakthroughs:

• *Genetic engineering.* "The only innovation that similarly expanded biological diversity was the development of sexual reproduction by simple cells two billion years ago. While this capacity took the previous billion years to evolve, human science has achieved a comparable step in just a few hundred years."

• *Manipulating the atom.* "New elements were last synthesized in this area of our galaxy in a supernova explosion prior to Earth's formation. Humanity is thus initiating a process that has not occurred locally for more than four billion years."

• *The solar cell.* Direct conversion of solar energy represents an evolutionary development "as significant as that of photosynthesis three and a half billion years ago."

• *Mobility.* Our increasing capability for colonization of space "is a development as significant as the colonization of land by the first amphibians 400 million years ago."

• *Communications.* Russell compared global telecommunication networking to the emergence of multicellular organisms one billion years ago. "As communication links within humanity increase, we will eventually reach a point when the billions of information exchanges shuttling through the networks at any one time can create patterns of coherence in the global brain similar to those found in the human brain."

Advances in each of these technologies accelerate progress in all of the others, Russell said. Their combined effects are raising to a new level of complexity the three major factors that govern evolutionary shifts: diversification, organization, and interconnection. "The cross-catalytic effects of these technologies suggest that we are in the midst of a phase that has no evolutionary precedent."

RESOURCE

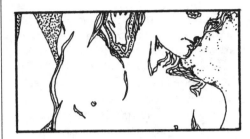

Gods in Everyman: A New Psychology of Men's Lives and Loves (Harper & Row, 1989) by Jean Shinoda Bolen is a sequel to her bestselling *Goddesses in Everywoman: A New Psychology of Women* (Harper & Row, 1985). ß "Men who have heard me lecture on the goddesses have repeatedly asked, 'What about us?'"

Bolen, a psychiatrist and Jungian analyst, used the Greek pantheon to lay out a system of archetypes that "shape men from within. These 'gods' are powerful, invisible predispositions that affect personality, work, and relationship."

These archetypal visions that men admire and try to imitate eventually affect every aspect of their lives.

Male readers can recognize their own antipathy or sympathy for Zeus, Hades, Ares, Dionysus, and others. Bolen shows how relationships between fathers and sons can parallel those depicted in the Greek myths. Finally, she suggests a new archetype, the son of Metis, the emerging archetype of the wise mother.

Optimal Experience: Psychological Studies of Flow in Consciousness, edited by Mihaly and Isabella Csikszentmihalyi (Cambridge University Press, 1988). In his contributions to this superbly edited volume, Mihaly Csikszentmihalyi of the University of Chicago traces contemporary interest in the flow state to various sources, including Abraham Maslow's fascination with intrinsic motivation.

The concept of flow, now a technical term in psychology, originated in the last two decades. Csikszentmihalyi first identified the "flow experience" while studying creative artists in the 1960s. He first used the term in the mid-1970s. Flow was apparently a state whose time had come.

Why do people pursue certain activities for their own sake? What is the feeling they achieve, and what contributes to it? Psychologists may have come late to an interest in the flow state because, as Csikszentmihalyi puts it, in their efforts to be scientific they ignored or discounted "the most obvious aspect of the human phenomenon, namely the existence of a conscious self."

The attributes of flow:
• Challenge level and skill are closely matched and high.
• Feedback is clear. There is a way to evaluate progress.
• Action follows close upon inspiration.
• You can focus on relevant stimuli.
• There is a sense of control.
• You are unself-conscious.
• You are relatively unaware of the passage of time.
• Motivation is intrinsic. The action itself is rewarding.

The book includes contributions from flow researchers in Japan, Italy, and Korea. Topics include the experience of flow in Japanese motorcycle gangs, in women at work, in solitary ordeals, in high school students, and in daily experience.

Noogenesis

None of the preceding evolutionary orders was predictable from previous ones, Russell maintained. "The dynamics of subatomic particles do not foretell the behavior of individual atoms any more than physics fully accounts for chemical phenomena. Chemistry in turn does not predict the principles that govern living organisms, nor can biology account for consciousness. Each level is a newly emergent order of existence."

The fifth evolutionary order, planetary *noogenesis* (from the Greek "knowing"), will be describable only after its emergence, he says.

Russell sees possible evidence of a noogenetic threshold in the vast acceleration of information and consciousness processing. The information-processing industry currently doubles every six years in the number of people it employs, while computer data-processing capacity doubles almost annually.

Even more dramatic is Russell's estimate that consciousness-raising—concern for self-growth and spiritual enlightenment—follows a three-year doubling trend. His estimate is based on a survey of numbers of people involved, organizations formed, and publications issued. The growth curve for information processing overtook the industrial growth curve in 1975. Russell predicts that the consciousness-raising curve will in turn overtake the information curve.

In Russell's view, popular attainment of "higher" consciousness is a prerequisite to noogenesis. Human conflict will cease only as millions of individuals develop deeper inner awareness. "The global brain will emerge from a blending of inner and outer evolution," he said. This blend requires a widespread shift in personal identity, the experience of underlying interpersonal unity that transcends the "skin-encapsulated ego."

Pitfalls to Transformation

Have you ever gone through a meaningful change, only to backslide at some point? Have you ever found yourself doing something you *know* to be beneficial for yourself and everyone around you, only to experience a backlash that stops you from doing it? The experience of transformation seems rife with such moments—and we greet them with disappointment and self-punishment.

At the previously mentioned "New Visions" conference in Lincoln, Nebraska, George Leonard, author of *The Transformation* (J. P. Tarcher, 1972, 1987) and *Walking on the Edge of the World* (Houghton Mifflin, 1988), discussed some of the pitfalls of transformation, and how we can deal with them. Leonard posed the question, "Is there something in the very structure of life to resist change?"

The answer is yes, he says. That something is called *homeostasis*.

Leonard pointed out that *change,* according to the dictionary, means to render something essentially different from what it was. In a sense, we undergo changes all the time. "Every seven years," he said, "every cell in our body is replaced. Every few months, all protein cells are replaced. Every day the epidermal level of the skin is replaced. Two and a half million red blood cells are destroyed every second—and replaced at approximately the same rate."

With all this change, there is an imperative to keep some things the same. We want cells to grow back in more or less the same way. When they don't, the results are disastrous. Cancer is an example.

"This process of self-regulation," explained Leonard, "is called homeostasis. So before we talk about change, let's sing the praises of staying the same."

Homeostasis is, literally, "the tendency of any self-regulating system to remain in a viable state—to remain within certain limits *as it is.*" And homeostasis applies to *all* such self-regulating systems—including single cells, human beings, families, organizations, and cultures.

The thermostat is a classic example of homeostasis. And homeostasis resists all change, whether *we* consider it beneficial or not.

In *Finite and Infinite Games* by James Carse (Macmillan, 1986), a popular professor of religion at New York University has captured in metaphor the essential confusion of form for substance. He lays out the options—life as a scary contest or never-ending adventure. "A finite game is played for the purpose of winning, an infinite game for the purpose of continuing the play."

Finite games have definite beginnings, endings, roles, boundaries, and rules that can't be changed during the course of play.

The rules of an infinite game "are like the grammar of a living language, where those of a finite game are like the rules of debate." Infinite play evolves, it doesn't conclude.

Societies serve to convey and maintain titles (chairman of the board, baton twirling champion of Indiana), which serve as acknowledgments that one has won. Although we seem to assume our roles freely, we soon experience them as necessary. We veil our free choices from ourselves.

Surprises, which can end a finite game, are the reason for infinite play to continue. "The finite play for life is serious; the infinite play of life takes joy. . . in learning to start something we cannot finish."

Carse distinguishes between playing and "playing at" drama. A society is a collection of finite games; culture is infinite. "To the extent that the Renaissance was true culture it has not ended. Anyone may enter into its mode of renewing vision."

INVENTORY: NEGOTIATING WITH HOMEOSTASIS

Homeostasis is a beneficial attribute of all self-regulating systems that resists change. But what can we do about homeostasis when it interferes with desired change? George Leonard lists the following points of advice:

- *Be aware of the machinery of homeostasis.* Said Leonard, "When you go through a wonderful change and then you get depressed six weeks later—expect that! It's almost inevitable if the change is really important."
- *Be willing to negotiate with homeostasis.* Don't be rigid. And beware of *hoping* for things. "Hope puts you in the future," said Leonard. "Try to focus on the present. Be there to negotiate."
- *Have a practice.* Leonard considers this point to be one of the most important. Leonard's own longtime practice is the martial art *aikido*. In aikido, the word for such a practice is *do*. In Chinese culture, it is called *tao*. These words literally mean *road* or *path*.

"A practice," said Leonard, "is something you do not because you can get something out of it—although you will—but because you're *doing* it. It's part of you. A practice offers you grounding, a basis for life. It is the path on which you walk. So many of us don't have paths on which to walk."

You can choose almost anything for your practice. But it is important to carry it out regularly, regardless of circumstance or disposition—no matter how depressed or tired you get. Franklin Roosevelt, during the worst days of World War II, took time out regularly to work on his stamp collection.

Groups of people and institutions require practices, too. For example, Leonard recommends that a family sit down to dinner every evening. "If you have candles with dinner, light them every night."

- *Involve your body in your personal change.* During the sixties people tended to say, "Just change your head!" This is simplistic advice. Rather, he says, "Get some physical discipline, get centered, get balanced. Get in touch with your body and find out what's going on in there."
- *Get a support group.* If you're going through personal change, don't try to do it alone. Keep each other in touch about your progress. Leonard suggested "negativity sessions," in which everyone can talk freely about everything that's going wrong, and nobody says anything in reply except, "I hear you."
- *Be a lifelong learner.* True learning is rare in our culture. Many of our educational institutions are actually set up to *prevent* learning, Leonard commented. But what does it mean to be a learner? Citing his book *Education and Ecstasy,* he said, "Education is a process that changes the learner; to learn is to change."

Some Closing Thoughts

PragMagic has been a collection of scientific discoveries and theories. It has also been an exhortation to live like a scientist—to experience everyday existence as a process of discovery.

Like all news, the information presented in *PragMagic* is a perishable commodity. Many of the facts, theories, and ideas are being amended, revised, and expanded even as you read about them.

Others will be disproven.

This does not make them bad science. To the contrary; a theory's validity depends on its ability to be disproven. And so, in order to live like scientists, we must prepare to have our day-to-day observations and assumptions contradicted. We should even exult in it. As epistemologist John Brockman puts it, "Success is when you prove I'm wrong."

In "Changing Magic," we've gotten a taste of how much science itself has changed during this extraordinary century. There was a time when *certainty* seemed possible, when our universe could be understood as something separate from consciousness.

Thomas Jefferson, a contemporary of that departed age, once wrote: "On the basis of sensation, of matter and motion, we may erect the fabric of all the certainties we can have or need . . . A single sense may indeed be sometimes deceived, but rarely; and never all our senses together, with their faculty of reasoning."

To say that Jefferson was mistaken is inaccurate. That's what his universe was like. As we have seen, our universe is different. Quantum physics tells us that our observations actually change reality—something that Jefferson could never have reckoned on.

The millions are awake enough for physical labor; but only one in a million is awake enough for effective intellectual exertion, only one in a hundred million to a poetic or divine life.
To be awake is to be alive.
I have never yet met a man who was quite awake.
How could I have looked him in the face?

—Henry David Thoreau, *Walden*

The world of science lives fairly comfortably with paradox. We know that light is a wave, and also that light is a particle. The discoveries made in the infinitely small world of particle physics indicate randomness and chance, and I do not find it any more difficult to live with the paradox of a universe of randomness and chance and a universe of pattern and purpose than I do with light as a wave and light as a particle. Living with contradiction is nothing new to the human being.

—Madeleine L'Engle
From *Two-Part Invention*
(Farrar, Straus & Giroux, 1988)

"Creative science is always a mixture of facts and ideas," wrote biologist Stephen Jay Gould in *An Urchin in the Storm* (W. W. Norton, 1987). "Great thinkers are not those who can free their minds from cultural baggage and think or observe objectively (for such a thing is impossible), but people who use their milieu creatively rather than as a constraint . . ."

It is useless nowadays to think of "knowledge" as a thing that exists *apart from* our personal and cultural biases and preconceptions. To try to do so is to become trapped by those very biases and preconceptions.

What About Answers?

All this is wonderful—and scary. It raises the haunting question: *What can I know?*

You won't find an answer here.

Our parting advice is simple. And it is the same advice that has been repeatedly offered throughout this book: *Pay attention.*

Pay attention to the world around you, and the people who inhabit it. They are your raw data.

Pay attention to your biases and preconceptions. Don't pretend they don't exist. That's bad science. Try to think *beyond* biases and preconceptions, not merely *past* them.

Pay attention to the ongoing, ever-changing flux of ideas and information in the world.

Pay attention to how certain important concepts—such as the Golden Rule—seem to emerge again and again, although they may appear in new forms.

In her book *The Aquarian Conspiracy* (J. P. Tarcher, 1987), Marilyn Ferguson quotes Pierre Teilhard de Chardin as saying that the aim of evolution is "ever more perfect eyes in a world in which there is always more to see."

In "a world in which there is always more to see," we lose the privilege of certainty. It is a commodity that we can no longer afford. But uncertainty, too, has its rewards. Not the least of these is unending adventure.

EXERCISE: THE HAPPINESS PARADOX

Perhaps—just perhaps—there is nothing new whatsoever in this book. Not a few of the researchers cited here acknowledge that their ideas merely confirm ancient wisdom. Can it really be true that "there is nothing new under the sun"?

Try the following simple experiment and see what you think.

- List ten people you know best.

_____   _____ _____
_____   _____ _____
_____   _____ _____
_____   _____ _____
_____   _____ _____
_____   _____ _____
_____   _____ _____
_____   _____ _____
_____   _____ _____
_____   _____ _____

- After each name, write an H if the person is happy, or an N if the person is not happy.

- Then write an S if the person is selfish or a U for unselfish.

This experiment is based on a study conducted by Bernard Rimland, a San Diego psychologist who produced what he calls "striking empirical support" for a very old and familiar (if too rarely followed) standard of conduct. Rimland's study appeared in *Psychological Reports* (51); *Brain/Mind Bulletin* reported on his research in 1983.

Rimland defines *selfish* as "a stable tendency to devote one's time and resources to one's own interests and welfare—an unwillingness to inconvenience oneself for others." Of 1,988 individuals who have performed this experiment, very few have listed anyone who was both happy and selfish.

"The findings represent an interesting paradox," Rimland noted. "Selfish people are, by definition, those whose activities are devoted to bringing themselves happiness. Yet, at least as judged by others, these selfish people are far less likely to be happy than those whose efforts are devoted to making others happy."

Rimland's conclusion: *"Do unto others as you would have them do unto you."*

EXERCISE: PRACTICING EMPATHY

It is not news that the Golden Rule is not news. It was not even news at the beginning of the Christian era. In a conversation with Bill Moyers in *The World of Ideas* (Doubleday, 1989), ethicist Michael Josephson remarked, "The Golden Rule occurred in Greek culture and in the Chinese culture thousands of years before Christ articulated His version."

Through the ages, the Golden Rule has had very few dissenters. Perhaps the only one to go on record was the ever-iconoclastic George Bernard Shaw. He wrote, "Do not do unto others as you would that they should do unto you. Their tastes may not be the same."

But when one thinks about it, this isn't so much a refutation as a corollary. As with any maxim, the *letter* of the Golden Rule is not enough. We should strive to live its *spirit*. And the spirit of the Golden Rule is one of generosity and altruism. But that spirit is negated when the Golden Rule is used as an excuse to self-centeredly project one's needs and desires onto others.

So how does one live the *spirit* of the Golden Rule? Shaw's riposte suggests that *empathy* is the answer.

Empathy is a troublesome word. It seems an almost mystical commodity. We think of it as a special, almost telepathic skill: an uncanny ability to experience the thoughts and feelings of someone else. It almost seems the province of saints and psychics, not ordinary people.

This mystique is easily defused.

The next time you are sitting in a room conversing with three or more people, try this very simple activity:

Temporarily remove yourself from the conversation. Be quiet for a few moments. Pay particular attention to the person doing the most talking. *Imagine* the following things:
• Imagine the *physical sensations* the speaker is experiencing. Mentally place yourself in that person's body, sitting or standing in a particular position, drinking the same drink, eating the same food. Mentally *become* the person. Do you feel tired? Energized? Irritated?
• Use whatever knowledge you may have of the speaker's life to imagine *what kind of day* he or she has had. If you know little about the person, guess. Continue to *imagine yourself* that person. How does your day color and affect what you are saying?
• Carefully consider the *person's relationships* to everyone in the room—including yourself. Continue to *mentally be* that person. What kind of feelings are generated by the people around you? How do they affect the things you say?
• Now, step back into yourself and rejoin the scene. Does your own role in the conversation feel different?

Keep in mind your fallibility. Every hypothesis you form about the other person's thoughts and feelings could well be wrong. This is not mind reading or telepathy. It is, quite simply, *applied imagination*. Empathy, like memory, is a creative act, not a mystical property, and it requires imagination. It also requires a little exertion and discipline. But it lies within the grasp of all of us.

NOTES:

APPENDIX A

SOURCES & RESOURCES

Most books mentioned in these pages can be ordered through your local bookstore or obtained from public libraries. You can check availability through *Books in Print,* and you can also find out-of-print books through book-search services.

Because availability and prices change from time to time, we have not included such perishable information. However, we will be happy to pass along our best current data on harder-to-locate resources. Send your inquiry in a stamped, self-addressed business-size envelope to *Brain/Mind Bulletin,* P.O. Box 42211, Los Angeles, California, 90042. For inquiries from outside the U.S. please include an international postal coupon.

Those who require specific volume and page references to journals cited in *PragMagic* should request "Journal References."

Subscriptions to the *Bulletin* are $35 a year ($40, first-class mail) for the U.S., Canada, and Mexico. All other countries, $45 (airmail). Two-year and institutional rates are available. For telephone credit-card orders: (800) 553-6463 or (213) 223-2500 in California.

Special "state-of-the-art" reports are now available on specific topics—for example, "Challenge and the Brain," "Imagery," "Reading Disabilities"—as well as Theme Packs on broader subjects (learning, psychiatry, consciousness). These incorporate everything *Brain/Mind Bulletin* has published under a specific category since 1975. Send SASE for Theme Pack catalog listing available titles.

PragMagic was designed in part to complement Marilyn Ferguson's *The New Common Sense: Secrets of the Visionary Life* (New Stream Books).

EXERCISES

Throughout *PragMagic* we suggest exercises and inventories of many different kinds for your use, or to stimulate your own ideas for experiments. We have placed a few additional examples that are long, complex, or that require a certain kind of concentration in this Appendix. Each of these is related to a specific section of the main text.

Some of these Appendix materials will be most useful either taped or read aloud—so that you can follow them without having to interrupt yourself to see what comes next. In those cases, be sure to allow enough time between each set of ideas for the images or experiences to develop.

2. BEING MAGIC

Cycles:

Chronopsychology
On the following two pages is an inventory designed to help you determine whether you are basically a morning or evening person.

INVENTORY: MORNINGNESS-EVENINGNESS

This self-assessment questionnaire is designed to determine morningness-eveningness in human circadian rhythms. This English-language version was designed by J. A. Horne (Department of Human Sciences, University of Technology in Loughborough, Leicestershire, England) and O. Östberg (Department of Occupational Health, National Board of Occupational Safety and Health, Stockholm, Sweden) and was based on an earlier Östberg Swedish-language test.

INSTRUCTIONS:

1. Please read each question very carefully before answering.
2. Answer all questions.
3. Answer questions in numerical order.
4. Each question should be answered independently of others. Do NOT go back and check your answers.
5. All questions have a selection of answers. For each question check one answer only. Some questions have a scale instead of a selection of answers. Mark the appropriate point along the scale.
6. Answer each question as honestly as possible.

THE QUESTIONNAIRE, WITH SCORES FOR EACH CHOICE:

1. Considering only your own "feeling best" rhythm, at what time would you get up if you were entirely free to plan your day?

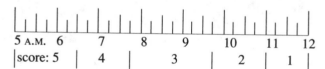

2. Considering only your own "feeling best" rhythm, at what time would you go to bed if you were entirely free to plan your day?

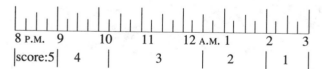

3. If there is a specific time at which you have to get up in the morning, to what extent are you dependent on being woken up by an alarm clock?

Not at all
   dependent   ❑ 4   Fairly dependent ❑ 2
Slightly
   dependent   ❑ 3   Very dependent   ❑ 1

4. Assuming adequate environmental conditions, how easy do you find getting up in the morning?

Not at all easy   ❑ 1   Fairly easy   ❑ 3
Not very easy   ❑ 2   Very easy   ❑ 4

5. How alert do you feel during the first half hour after having woken in the morning?

Not at all alert   ❑ 1   Fairly alert   ❑ 3
Slightly alert   ❑ 2   Very alert   ❑ 4

6. How is your appetite during the first half hour after having woken in the morning?

Very poor   ❑ 1   Fairly good   ❑ 3
Fairly poor   ❑ 2   Very good   ❑ 4

7. During the first half hour after having woken in the morning, how tired do you feel?

Very tired   ❑ 1   Fairly refreshed ❑ 3
Fairly tired   ❑ 2   Very refreshed   ❑ 4

8. When you have no commitments the next day, at what time do you go to bed compared to your usual bedtime?

Seldom or
   never later   ❑ 4   1–2 hours later   ❑ 2
Less than
   1 hour later   ❑ 3   More than
                       2 hours later   ❑ 1

9. You have decided to engage in some physical exercise. A friend suggests that you do this one hour twice a week and the best time for him is between 7 and 8 A.M. Bearing in mind nothing but your own "feeling best" rhythm, how do you think you would perform? Would you:

Be in good form   ❑ 4   Find it difficult   ❑ 2
Be in reasonable
   form   ❑ 3   Find it very
                   difficult   ❑ 1

10. At what time in the evening do you feel tired and as a result in need of sleep?

INVENTORY: MORNINGNESS-EVENINGNESS, continued

11. You wish to be at your peak performance for a test that you know is going to be mentally exhausting and lasting for two hours. You are entirely free to plan your day, and considering only your own "feeling best" rhythm, which ONE of the four testing times would you choose?

8:00–10:00 A.M. ❏ 6   3:00–5:00 P.M. ❏ 2
11:00 A.M.–1 P.M. ❏ 4   7:00–9:00 P.M. ❏ 0

12. If you went to bed at 11 P.M., at what level of tiredness would you be?

Not at all tired ❏ 0   Fairly tired ❏ 3
A little tired ❏ 2   Very tired ❏ 5

13. For some reason you have gone to bed several hours later than usual, but there is no need to get up at any particular time the next morning. Which ONE of the following events are you most likely to experience?

Will wake up at usual time
  and will NOT fall asleep ❏ 4
Will wake up at usual time
  and will doze thereafter ❏ 3
Will wake up at usual time
  but will fall asleep again ❏ 2
Will NOT wake up until
  later than usual ❏ 1

14. One night you have to remain awake between 4:00 and 6:00 A.M. in order to carry out a night watch. You have no commitments the next day. Which ONE of the following alternatives will suit you best?

Would NOT go to bed
  until watch was over ❏ 1
Would take a nap before
  and sleep after ❏ 2
Would take a good sleep
  before and nap after ❏ 3
Would take ALL sleep
  before watch ❏ 4

15. You have to do two hours of hard physical work. You are entirely free to plan your day. Considering only your own "feeling best" rhythm, which ONE of the following would you choose?

8:00–10:00 A.M. ❏ 4   3:00–5:00 P.M. ❏ 2
11:00 A.M.–1 P.M. ❏ 3   7:00–9:00 P.M. ❏ 1

16. You have decided to engage in hard physical exercise. A friend suggests that you do this for one hour twice a week and the best time for him is between 10:00 and 11:00 P.M. Bearing in mind nothing else but your own "feeling best" rhythm, how well do you think you would perform? Would you:

Be in good form ❏ 1   Find it difficult ❏ 3
Be in reasonable
  form ❏ 2   Find it very
  difficult ❏ 4

17. Suppose that you can choose your own work hours. Assume that you worked a FIVE-hour day (including breaks) and that your job was interesting and paid by results. Which FIVE CONSECUTIVE HOURS would you select? (Circle the time, check score below.)

Midnight   NOON   Midnight
12 1 2 3 4 5 6 7 8 9 10 11 12 1 2 3 4 5 6 7 8 9 10 11 12

|score:1| 5 |4| 3 | 2 | 1 | |

18. At what time of day do you think that you reach your "feeling best" peak? (Circle the time, check score below.)

Midnight   NOON   Midnight
12 1 2 3 4 5 6 7 8 9 10 11 12 1 2 3 4 5 6 7 8 9 10 11 12

| score: 1 | 5 | 4| 3 | 2 | 1 |

19. One hears about "morning" and "evening" types of people. Which ONE of these types do you consider yourself to be?

Definitely a "morning" type ❏ 6
Rather more a "morning"
  than an "evening" type ❏ 4
Rather more an "evening"
  than a "morning" type ❏ 2
Definitely an "evening" type ❏ 0

HOW TO SCORE YOURSELF:
Numerical values are listed to the right of each box and beneath each horizontal scale. When you have finished the questionnaire, record the numbers nearest your answers and add them together.

Score:
70–86   Definitely Morning Type
59–69   Moderately Morning Type
42–58   Neither Type
31–41   Moderately Evening Type
16–30   Definitely Evening Type

2. BEING MAGIC

Consciousness:
Open Focus

**EXERCISE: OPEN FOCUS®—
GENERAL TRAINING**
by Les Fehmi

Can you imagine what it would feel like to experience your thumbs, the sense of presence of your thumbs, the three-dimensional presence of your thumbs intimately and subtly?

Can you imagine what it would feel like to experience your thumbs, the volume of your thumbs, even more sensitively?

Can you imagine experiencing your index fingers, the fingers closest to your thumbs, just as sensitively as you experience your thumbs?

Can you imagine experiencing your thumbs and index fingers simultaneously as a three-dimensional presence?

Can you imagine what it would feel like to experience the space, the sense of absence, between your thumbs and index fingers as sensitively and as intimately as you experience the presence of your thumbs and index fingers?

As you already know, an atom of matter is more space than matter. The nucleus of the atom is 200 thousand times smaller than the diameter of the atom. The electrons are much smaller than the nucleus and revolve around the nucleus in space. By volume, the particles of the atom are just specks compared to the magnitude of the vast space of an atom.

Can you image that you can experience your thumbs and forefingers as clouds of atoms, clouds of particles floating in space right where your thumbs and forefingers are experienced to exist? Floating in space, permeated by space, surrounded by space.

Can you imagine that all your fingers—middle fingers, ring fingers, little fingers—are also clouds, clouds of particles floating in space, permeated by space?

Can you imagine experiencing this space between and continuously through all of your fingers as intimately and as subtly as you experience a sense of presence of the clouds of particles which are your fingers?

Can you imagine what it would feel like to experience your fingers as mist, as fog, permeated by space?

Can you imagine the feeling of basking in the space in which the fog, the mist, the cloud of particles floats?

Can you imagine experiencing the silence out of which the phone's ringing emerges, just as intimately as you experience the space in which the cloud of particles which is your fingers floats?

Can you imagine what it would feel like to use your fingers and the space around the flowing through your fingers as models of how you might experience the rest of your body?

Can you imagine experiencing your feet and toes as clouds of particles floating in space, permeated by space, just like your fingers and at the same time as your fingers?

Can you experience your whole hand, wrist, and forearm just as intimately as you experience your fingers filled with space, permeated by space, surrounded by space?

Can you imagine experiencing your ankles, your lower legs as filled with space, floating in space, permeated by space just like your feet and toes, hands and fingers, wrists and forearms?

Can you imagine what it would feel like to experience your elbows, upper arms, your shoulders, and the region between your shoulders as permeated by space, as well as your knees, upper legs, your hips, and the region between your hips just as intimately as you experience your hands, fingers, feet, and toes?

Can you imagine experiencing your shoulders, arms, hands, and fingers, and your hips, legs, feet, and toes simultaneously and equally, as clouds of particles floating in space right where they are, permeated by space?

Can you imagine feeling that your lips are clouds of particles floating in space just like your fingers and toes, your hands and feet?

Can you imagine now also experiencing your tongue as a cloud of particles permeated by space . . . the feeling of your teeth and gums intimately as clouds of particles, clouds of feeling permeated by space . . . and your jaw and your chin floating in space just like your lips, teeth, gums, shoulders and arms, hands and fingers, hips, legs, feet and toes?

Can you imagine feeling that your cheeks and your cheekbones and the region between them, and your ears and the region between your ears, are filled with space, permeated by space, just like your face, your hands and fingers, and feet and toes?

Can you imagine what it would feel like to experience your nose and your sinuses, the region between your upper lip and the base of your nose, the bridge of your nose and the region between the bridge of your nose and your eyes, and the region between your eyes permeated by space?

Can you imagine what it would feel like to experience your eyes more intimately, more subtly as clouds of experience floating in space . . . not trying to see, letting sight and visual imagery be permeated by the space around your eyes, the space behind your eyes, the space in front of your eyes . . . feeling the touch of space upon and through the cloud of feeling which is your eyes?

Can you imagine that your temples and the region between your temples and your eyebrows, and the sides of your head and the region between the back of your head and the front of your head, and the top of your head, are all clouds of feeling floating in space just like your lips, your jaw, eyes, tongue, shoulders, arms, hands, fingers, hips, legs, feet, and toes?

Can you imagine that any feeling that is present in you right now—emptiness, anxiety, impatience, boredom, fidgetiness, whatever—is a cloud of that particular feeling floating in space surrounded by space, permeated by space, just like your head, and hands, and feet?

Can you imagine feeling your neck surrounded and permeated by space?

Can you imagine feeling your throat and the space inside your throat, equally intimate with that sense of emptiness inside your throat as you are with the cloud of presence which is your neck?

Can you imagine experiencing the region between your breastbone and your backbone, the region between all of your ribs permeated by space . . . space flowing right through your chest from side to side, front to back, back to front, from shoulders down and diaphragm up, right through your back, and the muscles of your back and chest?

Can you imagine experiencing all the organs in your chest—your heart, your lungs, esophagus, bronchial tubes, trachea, liver—intimately as clouds of feeling floating in space?

Can you imagine feeling your mid-section . . . your kidneys, stomach, the whole region around your waist, your navel, the region between your navel and your backbone, just like your hands and feet and your head all floating in space, permeated by space?

Can you imagine what it would be like to experience now your lower back, your abdomen, the sides of your lower trunk, the region between, as clouds of feeling floating in space?

Can you imagine your buttocks filled with space, the sense of pressure on your buttocks as a cloud of pressure floating in space, permeated by space?

Can you imagine that even compressed tissue is mostly space?

Can you imagine what it would feel like to experience your whole body as a cloud of feeling floating in space right where it is, space flowing right through the soles of your feet, palms of your hands, your whole body in every direction, experiencing the space,

basking in the space as intimately as you bask in the sense of presence?

Can you imagine that your awareness of the sense of absence and sense of presence is also a cloud, a cloud of particles floating in space, surrounded by space, permeated by space?

Can you imagine that this cloud of awareness is attending to the cloud of experience of your whole body, the space which permeates your body, the space between your awareness and your body sensations, and the common space permeating both your awareness and your body sensations?

Can you imagine that now you can witness how you are aware of your feelings of space and presence?

Can you imagine witnessing how you are attending to your somatic sensation?

Can you imagine intimately witnessing, basking in your awareness of how you feel, of how you are attending to feeling your whole body and all the space around you and the space permeating you and all the other people and objects in the whole room?

At the same time you are witnessing how you are attending to what you feel of space as intimately as you can, can you imagine experiencing the silence in that space in this room, the silence behind you, above, in front of you, below you, to the sides of you, the silence that is pierced by sound, a three-dimensional silence from which sound emerges and exists and again dissolves . . . the silence and the feeling of space, simultaneously?

Can you imagine being aware of the direction out of which sound comes through you?

Can you imagine that sound comes from a specific direction, and that there is silence in the other directions, silence above you, and in between the directions from which sounds come?

Can you imagine also visualizing the space in this room, the space above you, below you, and to the sides of you, as you feel the space, and as you hear the silence in that space? And imagine what it would feel like and what it

would look like to feel and see right through the walls, the ceiling, the floor, the people, and the objects . . . feeling and looking to infinity in every direction at once.

Can you imagine experiencing the space in which smells would arise if they were present . . . and the sensory emptiness out of which tastes would arise if they were present?

Can you imagine feeling space, hearing space, visualizing space, tasting and smelling space, all as the same space, one space? Can you imagine experiencing all your sensations simultaneously in that same space?

Can you imagine experiencing that space in your mind in which thoughts and images and dialogue occur as the same space that you visualize, hear, taste, smell, and feel?

Can you imagine that all experiences exist in the same space, a space witnessed by a cloud of awareness floating in space, permeated by space, that opens to integrate all of these experiences of space, an awareness that merges with and basks in that infinite space?

Can you imagine what it would feel like to float, to bask in the experience of space, the universal solvent, more intimately, and all the sensations that arise in it . . . witnessing these sensations and becoming one with all simultaneously and equally?

Can you imagine attending to how you are attending to all of this experience?

Can you imagine attending to who is attending, experiencing this attender as a cloud of experience floating in space, permeated by space?

Is it possible for you to experience yourself in space and in time, in timelessness? Who is experiencing how you are attending to what you are attending to more intimately, more subtly now? Who is this witness? Who is this you? How do you experience this you?

Can you include now any experiences which you have excluded thus far? Any feelings, emotions, pains, aches, discomforts, boredom, apprehensions, fears, voids, as part of a more intimate experience of attending to what and how you are attending?

® OPEN FOCUS is a registered trademark of Biofeedback Computers, Inc. General Training © was copyrighted 1984 by Biofeedback Computers, Inc.

2. BEING MAGIC

Consciousness:
Altered States of Consciousness

EXERCISE: LEFT BRAIN/RIGHT BRAIN
by Jean Houston
and Robert Masters

In *The Possible Human,* Jean Houston begins her chapter on "Awakening the Brain" with an adaptation of an exercise created by her husband, Robert Masters.

Houston says: "Of all the exercises we have developed of this type, it seems to have the most profound effect. Although we have called this exercise 'Left Brain/Right Brain' and work with the metaphor of right and left sides of the brain, we cannot claim that this exercises the function of two distinctly separated hemispheres of the cerebral cortex. Instead, this exercise would seem to integrate many functions of the brain, bringing together words and images, senses and emotions, the abstraction of numerical symbols, and the unity of the mind field."

Allow sixty minutes for this exercise.

PREPARATION
Seat yourself comfortably with your spine straight and your body in a supported and relaxed position that you can maintain comfortably for about forty-five minutes.

Consider now what you would say to your brain if you could speak to it directly. Apart from "Hello there," "Wake up, stupid!" or "Where have you been all my life?" what would you really say if you had the opportunity to begin a friendship and ongoing communication with your own brain? Remember what this is, because toward the end of this exercise you will have the opportunity to say these things directly to your own brain.

THE EXERCISE
Close your eyes and direct your attention to your breathing. Allow the rhythm of your breath to become regular. As you do this, allow your consciousness to rest in your solar plexus and gradually move up through your body, passing through your lungs and then your heart, moving up the left carotid artery to the left side of your brain. Move your awareness forward now to your left eye.

Keeping your eyes closed, look down with your left eye. Now up. Look to the left . . . and to the right. Keeping your awareness in your left eye, allow that eye to circle clockwise . . . and counterclockwise. Which direction is easier? You may find it easier if you imagine you are looking at a clock and follow the numbers of the clock as you move your eye.

Now shift your attention to your right eye. Keeping your eyes closed, look down and then up. Repeat this several times. Now move your eye from right to left. Allow your right eye to circle to the right and then to the left, clockwise and counterclockwise. Is this easier with the right eye than the left?

Relax your eyes, feeling them get soft and releasing the muscles around the socket. Rest for a minute.

* * *

Keeping your eyes closed, direct your attention to the right side of the brain . . . and now to the left. Shift back and forth easily a few times, noting any differences between the

two sides of your brain. Does one seem more accessible than the other?

Keeping your eyes closed and relaxed, imagine the images that will be suggested as vividly as possible. Don't strain as you do this.

On the left side of your brain, imagine the number 1 . . .

And on the right side the letter A . . .

On the left side the number 2 . . .

And on the right side the letter B . . .

On the left the number 3 . . .

And on the right the letter C . . .

On the left the number 4 . . .

And on the right the letter D . . .

On the left the number 5 . . .

And on the right the letter E . . .

Continue with the numbers on the left and the letters on the right, going toward the number 26 and the letter Z. You don't have to actually reach 26 and Z. Just continue for a minute or so. If you get confused or lost, go back to the place where the letters and numbers were clearly together and begin again.

Rest for a minute, relaxing your attention as you do so.

Now reverse the process you have just done, putting the letters on the left and the numbers on the right.

On the left image the letter A . . .

And on the right the number 1 . . .

On the left the letter B . . .

And on the right the number 2 . . .

Keep going toward the letter Z and the number 26.

Stop and rest for a minute. Note whether it was easier on one side than the other, whether numbers or letters were more clearly imagined.

* * *

Continuing with your eyes closed, on the left side of your brain imagine a festive outdoor scene with a big picnic and fireworks.

On the right image a couple getting married.

Let that image go, and on the left, imagine a procession of nuns walking two by two through a lovely medieval cloister.

On the right there is a hurricane

sweeping through a coastal town.

On the left is an atom.

On the right is a galaxy.

On the left are fruit trees bearing new blossoms.

On the right the trees are weighted down with frost and snow.

On the left is the sunrise.

On the right is the sunset.

On the left is a green jungle forest.

On the right is a snow-covered mountain in the Alps.

On the left is a three-ring circus.

On the right is a thick fog.

On the left is the sensation of climbing rocks. Try to capture the feeling and sensation of the rocks and breathe easily as you experience it.

On the right, imagine how your hand feels caressing a baby's skin.

On the left, the feeling of plunging your hands into warm, soppy mud.

On the right, that of making snowballs with your bare hands.

On the left you are pulling taffy.

On the right you are punching a punching bag.

Now, on the left hear the sound of a fire engine.

On the right the sound of crickets chirping.

On the left the sound of a car starting up.

On the right somebody is singing in a very high voice.

On the left the sound of ocean waves on a beach.

On the right the sound of your stomach growling.

Now on the left the smell of a pine forest.

On the right imagine smelling freshly brewed coffee.

On the left the smell of gasoline.

On the right the smell of bread baking.

Now on the left brain, the taste of a crisp, juicy apple.

On the right the taste of hot buttered toast.

On the left the taste of a lemon. On the right the taste of nuts.

Now on the left side of the brain, experience as fully as you can the following scene: You are riding a horse through the snow and sleet carrying three little kittens under your coat, and you are sucking on a peppermint.

On the right side of the brain you are standing under a waterfall singing "You Are My Sunshine" and watching a nearby volcano erupt.

* * *

Now, eyes still closed, with your left eye look up toward your left brain. Move the eye so that it circles and explores this space. Roam around for a while.

Now do the same thing for a while with your closed right eye on the right side of the brain.

Now with the left eye trace some triangles on the left side of the brain. Now make some rectangles. Now make some stars.

With the right eye trace some triangles on the right side of the brain. Now make some rectangles. Now draw some stars.

Now make many overlapping circles on the left side, leaving spirals of light streaming from these circles into the left side of the brain. Imagine the brain as charged with energy by this light.

Make many overlapping circles on the right side with the right eye, leaving energizing light streaming from these circles.

Now, with both eyes, circle vertically just in the middle of the head. You should circle along the corpus callosum, the ridge where the hemispheres of the brain come together. With both eyes together, circle as widely as you can inside your head.

With both eyes, create spiraling galaxies throughout your brain. Fill the whole of your brain space and the inside of your head with them.

Stop and let your eyes come completely to rest.

* * *

Try to make horizontal circles with both eyes just at the level of your eyes, and circling as widely as possible inside your head. Now try making smaller circles horizontally at the level of your eyes. Make them smaller . . . and smaller . . . and smaller . . . until you get down to a space that is too small for circling and then you will want to fix on that point and try to hold it. Continue to breathe freely with your muscles relaxed as you do this. If you lose the point, make more large circles, letting them become smaller and smaller until you get back down to a point, staying fixed on that point for as long as you can easily.

(Circling inward and holding on the point in the center is an excellent meditation exercise when done by itself.)

Rest for a moment. Then, in the middle of your forehead, imagine a huge sunflower. Then erase the sunflower.

Simultaneously, imagine a sunflower on the left and some green, damp moss on the right. Let them go.

Imagine that there is a big tree growing right in the middle of your forehead.

Let go of that, and imagine that there is a golden harp on the left, and just a little to the right of the harp is a drum. Try to hear them as they play together.

Let them go and imagine on the left an eagle, and on the right a canary, both of them there together at once. Let them go now, and imagine the canary now on the left and the eagle on the right.

Let them go, and imagine two eagles on the left and two canaries on the right. Let them fade away.

Breathe easily, and if you need to adjust your position to be more comfortable, do so.

Now in the middle of your forehead, imagine a small sun. Then imagine the sun just inside the top of your head. Try to roll it down the inside of your skull to the inside of the back of your head, so that if your eyes could turn completely around in your head, they would be looking at it.

Now raise the sun along the back of your head to the top and then down to the forehead. Now raise it along the inside of the head from the forehead back to the top and then to the back of the head, and then to the top of the head and back to the forehead. The sun should be making vertical semicircles on the inside of your skull.

Now let that sun move out in front of you and see it setting over the sea. From somewhere in the direction of the sunset comes a sailboat. From what direction is the sailboat coming? From the left, from the right, or from some other direction?

Let that image fade away and imagine an elephant walking. Try to become more and more aware of him as he walks. He stops and eats something, pushing his long trunk into his mouth, then he walks some more, then he sees you and breaks into a run. He slows down and then he stops and eats some more.

Let the elephant go, and imagine seeing Santa Claus in a sleigh pulled by reindeer. Observe the sleigh and watch it accelerate, then slow down and stop, then start up again, going faster and faster as it circles around and down a spiral track that is inside of your head.

Starting from your chin, the sleigh spirals up and around and around and around until it reaches to the top of your head. Then it spirals down and around and around and around to your chin. Then it rushes up and around and around to the top of your head. Then it circles down and around and around to your chin. Circling now up and around and around and around to the top of your head. Let it stop there poised on the edge of the front of the top of your head.

Now yawn and let Santa and his sleigh and reindeer drive down over your nose and into your mouth, swallow the sleigh, and forget all about it!

* * *

Now focus attention on the left side of your brain for a while. Concentrate on it and try to see or imagine what your brain looks like on the left side. Be aware of the gray matter and the convolutions of the brain. Concentrate in the same way on the right side of the brain. Pay attention to the thick bands of fibers that connect the two hemispheres of the brain.

Now try to sense both sides at once, the whole brain. Sense its infinite complexity, its billions of cells intercommunicating at the speed of light. Meditate on it as a universe in itself, whose dimensions and capacities you have only begun to dream of.

Now, breathing very deeply, imagine that by inhaling and exhaling you can expand and contract your brain. And do this for a while, expanding your brain when you inhale slowly and deeply, and contracting your brain when you exhale slowly and completely.

* * *

Let your brain rest now, and holding its image, speak directly to your own brain, suggesting, if you wish, that its functioning will get better and better.

Suggest that you will have more brain cells accessible to you and that the interaction of the cells and all the processes of the brain will continuously improve as time goes by.

Tell it that the right and left hemispheres will be better integrated, as will older and newer parts of the brain.

Advise your brain that many of its latent potentials can now become manifest and that you will try to work together with the brain in partnership to allow these potentials to develop in your life.

Listen now and see if your brain has any messages for you. These messages may come as words or images or feelings. Give the brain time to respond, withholding judgment. Does your brain want something from you? What does your brain want to give you?

Again being aware of the whole of the brain, begin to feel a real sense of both communication and communion with your brain.

Think of it as a new friend and of this friendship as a profound and beautiful new fact in your life. In the weeks to come, spend time nurturing and deepening this friendship so that the two of you (your brain and your consciousness) can work together in useful ways. But now, spend some minutes communing with your brain. Images may come to you, or feelings, or words, as together you move into a more complete partnership and friendship.

If you wish, while you do this, place your hands about half an inch above your head and have the sense that you are caressing the "field" around your brain, in the same way that you might pat or stroke the hand of a dear friend. (Allow about three or four minutes for this to happen.)

* * *

If you have some special intention for your brain, offer it now.

Continuing to feel a communion with your brain, open your eyes and look around. Observe whether there are any changes in your sensory perceptions. How do you feel in your body? What is your mood and your sense of reality? Do you feel that your possibilities have changed? Observe these things.

As you do this, stretch and move around the room. When you wish to, suggest to yourself that you are becoming more and more wide-awake.

DISCUSSION

What seems to be happening here? Certainly, many things on many levels. Teachers who have used this exercise with their classes report that their students enjoy the experience and then are more relaxed and alert as they address the other areas of their schoolwork. They begin to regard their brains as allies rather than poorly programmed robots, and they are delighted to find that their brains have a sense of whimsy and play. Some who have felt sluggish and sleepy experience renewed energy. One Texas rancher found his brain saying to *him*, "Where have *you* been all my life?"

Many experience an unexpected sense of reverence for their brain; the brain has truly become Thou, an active partner in the process of co-creation.

As attention of this kind and duration is directed toward the brain, more blood goes to the brain, bringing nourishing oxygen. As this attention is directed toward different areas of the brain in different ways, more of the brain seems to be nourished and available. The principle is the same as that used in autogenic training for the relief of migraine headaches. As you image the hand becoming warm and heavy and the forehead cool, the congested blood in the head is relieved and more blood is directed toward the hand. Patterns of blood circulation are thus directed by conscious imaging. For this same reason, some people experience a temporary feeling of constriction in the skull after doing this exercise. This is often followed by increased mental acuity and cognitive clarity.

If you feel fatigued after this exercise, you may have been trying too hard. As in all psychological exercises, it is important to work without strain, letting images happen rather than making them happen. Your brain will cooperate with you if you let it, but if you bully it, the level of cooperation drops drastically. Scolding yourself or feeling inadequate if Z and 26 do not come out together at the end won't help Z or 26. With practice, you will find this exercise increasingly easy, indeed child's play. Then you may want to vary it in your own way or follow any of the suggestions in the Extensions section [in *The Possible Human*].

From Jean Houston, *The Possible Human: A Course in Extending Your Physical, Mental, and Creative Abilities* (J. P. Tarcher, 1982)

7. CHANGING MAGIC

The Paranormal:
Out-of-Body Experiences

**EXERCISE:
FREE FLIGHTS TO NOWHERE:
LET YOUR PSYCHE
DO THE WALKING**
by Keith Harary

It could happen spontaneously while you're relaxing in your favorite chair, listening to music, or falling asleep. It could also occur while you're lying on an operating room table, with your heart stopped, or as you're bleeding to death in an overturned car. Centuries ago the Chinese called the experience magical flight. Since then it has been called astral projection, traveling clairvoyance, and ecstasy. Modern psychologists prefer the term *out-of-body experience,* or OBE, when referring to the sensation that your awareness is separated from your body. Whatever you choose to call it, the experience may be as familiar as the feeling that you're falling out of bed or as startling as waking up and floating near the ceiling in the middle of the night.

People who have had OBEs insist the experience is different from dreams or waking fantasies. Preliminary research suggests that there may be some objective basis for these claims. Those who have OBEs, some experts say, can report on distant events and influence the behavior of distant people and animals. Occultists and mystics take these claims further, suggesting that OBEs prove the existence of a soul that survives bodily death. Skeptics, on the other hand, say that OBEs are just particularly vivid dreams or hallucinations brought on by fatigue and intense or psychological stress.

While scientists and mystics debate the ultimate meaning of OBEs, chances are that you or someone you know has spontaneously had such an experience at least once, if not many

times. OBEs are so commonplace, in fact, that it strains credibility to consider the popular notion that having an OBE is a sign of unusual spiritual development. More likely, the OBE represents a fascinating experience and state of mind that may be available to most, if not all, of us.

Perhaps the best way to understand the OBE is to explore the experience firsthand. These exercises can help you deliberately induce your own OBEs *without* following an occult belief system or approaching death.

Since OBEs tend to reflect your state of mind when you enter them, you may find that they're most enjoyable when induced under positive psychological conditions. We therefore recommend that you practice these exercises only when you're feeling emotionally comfortable and relaxed. If you have a history of sleepwalking or any other sleep or psychiatric disorders, we recommend that you check with your doctor before you begin.

As you practice these exercises, don't try to force the experience. Rather, allow it to evolve as part of an ongoing process. The more relaxed you are, the more likely it is that an OBE will spontaneously emerge. For each of these exercises, choose a practice location where you feel safe and won't be interrupted. We recommend sitting in a stuffed or reclining chair, where you can relax without getting so cozy that you'll just fall asleep. Loosen any clothing or jewelry that makes you feel constricted.

Before each practice session take a deep breath and close your eyes. Allow yourself a few moments to get grounded. And be sure to quietly affirm that you'll allow yourself only to have experiences you can easily handle. If you should feel uncomfortable during any of these exercises, you can return to the waking state instantly by remembering how it feels to be completely alert and aware of your body.

Remember, you may or may not have an OBE as you practice each of the individual exercises. But practicing a few of these exercises on a regular basis can help you stimulate more OBEs than you might otherwise have.

EXERCISE 1: GETTING GROUNDED

Exercise 1 teaches you the basic technique of progressive relaxation. To begin, imagine that warm currents of mental energy are slowly moving up through the soles of your feet toward the top of your head, warming and relaxing each muscle in turn. Imagine the currents turning around to move downward through your arms, toward your fingertips, then moving upward once more through your arms and neck to the top of your head.

The key to success here is learning to enter a state of deep physical relaxation while remaining mentally alert. In order to maintain this desired state, you may find it helpful to imagine the currents passing through your body in a variety of interesting patterns or colors. You may also find it helpful to practice Exercise 1 only when physically and emotionally rested and easily able to remain awake for the entire exercise.

As you practice Exercise 1, you may find that remaining alert while entering a state of deep relaxation can create the sensation that your mind is somehow separated from your body. This sensation is the most basic form of the OBE. To pursue the OBE further, however, you may decide to practice Exercise 1 in conjunction with some of the exercises that follow.

EXERCISE 2: GEARING UP

In Exercise 2 you'll create a mental image that simulates one aspect of an actual out-of-body experience: the sensation of existing apart from your body. This sensation may not only prepare you for the OBE, it may also help to induce the experience.

Begin Exercise 2 by noticing how it feels to be "inside" your body. Notice, for example, how it feels to "look" through your closed eyelids or how you focus your attention on the world around you from "inside" your physical form. Quietly note the sensations associated with breathing.

Now stay perfectly still, and as you exhale, imagine how it would feel to experience these sensations from a position a few inches above your body. Imagine that you can simultaneously feel yourself floating above your body and see yourself floating there from your familiar perspective within your body. Allow yourself time to fully create this experience in your mind; then gradually move your attention back and forth between the inside of your body and the point you have imagined a few inches above.

Continue to practice until you're able to maintain the imagined experience of floating above yourself for several minutes without straining. Once you've accomplished this, imagine you're floating a few inches above yourself, your disembodied face looking directly back at the physical face below.

As a way of easing into the next stage of this exercise, combine Exercise 2 with the progressive relaxation techniques learned in Exercise 1. Imagine yourself floating a few inches above your body, face-to-face with yourself, while entering an alert state of deep physical relaxation.

Then imagine your mind moving away from your body to another part of your environment. Look back on your physical position from the new perspective. Practice focusing as little attention as possible on your body and as much as possible on the mental part of you floating some distance away. Create as complete a mental image as possible until, perhaps for only an instant, detailed visual, tactile, and auditory impressions seem to become vivid enough to be real.

The experience of looking back on the physical body from an independent location is one of the most commonly reported forms of the OBE.

EXERCISE 3: TAKING OFF

Exercise 3 may be practiced either as an extension of Exercise 2 or as a separate exercise. Begin by entering a state of deep but alert relaxation. This time, instead of imagining that you're floating directly above your body, focus your attention on a location far removed from where you are now. Imagine that you're a point of consciousness in space, floating above the location in question. Take time to allow this perception to form in your mind. Then focus your attention on a different location, allowing the sensations associated with this new place to form as those associated with the old place dissolve.

Exercise 3 can help you overcome the common misconception that OBEs involve a second body that somehow separates from the first, then flies around from one locale to the next. In fact, many people report OBEs in which they feel like an independent point of consciousness traveling from place to place purely through the power of thought.

As you did in the previous exercise, focus on making your mental exploration of the distant location as vivid as possible. Don't try to just picture or sense the area in your mind. Instead concentrate on creating a vivid sensation of actually being present in the place you've chosen. The more detailed your images, the more likely you will be to have an OBE while practicing the exercise or sometime soon after.

EXERCISE 4: TOURING THE LOUVRE

The Louvre method was named after the experience of writer Darlene Moore, who first practiced this exercise one afternoon in the courtyard of the Louvre museum in Paris. That night in her hotel room on the Left Bank, she had her first spontaneous out-of-body experience. The exercise put Moore in touch with her sensory experiences, evoking the varying levels of perception that entered into her everyday waking consciousness. By becoming more aware of the sensations associated with her body, she was able, paradoxically, to open up her unconscious mind to the possibility of having an OBE.

To practice the Louvre method you'll need a companion to help guide you through the exercise. Choose an unfamiliar location rich in a variety of forms, textures, and sounds. A plaza, park, or beach would be perfectly suitable for this exercise.

Your eyes should remain closed for the duration of the session, which should take at least two hours to complete. You and your companion are not to talk with each other or anyone else for the duration of the exercise. Instead you should communicate with each other through gentle, direct physical contact intended to guide you safely around the area and offer you a selection of stimulating nonvisual sensory experiences.

Begin by standing with your companion at one end of the site you've selected. Then take a deep breath and close your eyes. Pay deliberate attention to the sound of your own breathing as well as to the sounds around you. Notice how you perceive the sounds in multiple layers that overlap and blend with one another. Take a few moments to absorb these layers, then signal your companion that you're ready to proceed by tapping his or her shoulder.

Your companion should provide you with a variety of contrasting and surprising sensory experiences, taking special care to guide you safely around your environment. He or she may, for example, introduce you to a running fountain by placing your hand under it. Listen to the sound of the fountain, slowly run your hands along the edge, then feel the surface of the water. Your companion may then surprise you with a contrasting experience by, for example, offering you a handful of fragrant dried leaves to smell and crumble in your hands. Listen to the leaves as you crumble them, and continue to notice the sounds of your breathing and the fountain in the background as well. Notice how the leaves may smell subtly different before and after you crumble them in your hands.

Be curious. Throughout the exercise your companion should provide you with opportunities for stimulating all your nonvisual senses. You, on the other hand, must pretend this is your first experience having a body, taking the opportunity to explore your physical senses as though you had never done so before.

After a predetermined period of time has passed, have your companion instruct you to open your eyes. Take a deep breath, open your eyes, and notice the ways in which your awareness of yourself and your environment subtly shifts. Take a few minutes to adjust to your overall experience and to visually observe the location in which you've chosen to practice your out-of-body experience.

To follow through to the next stage of Exercise 4, find a safe and quiet spot at the location you've chosen, relax in a comfortable position, and once again close your eyes. Take a deep breath, and imagine that you're mentally exploring your surrounding environment, this time without bringing your body along.

You may find that there are moments when the sensation of floating apart from your body feels more real than imaginary. Instead of trying to figure out whether you're having an OBE, or comparing this experience with your expectation of what an OBE should be like, you may find it more helpful to just allow the experience to form and express itself.

You may be surprised to discover yourself feeling as though you're momentarily back at some especially interesting spot, having sensations very much like those you had when you were practicing the first phase of the exercise.

EXERCISE 5: NOCTURNAL FLIGHTS

Exercise 5 can be practiced just as you're falling asleep. As you're nodding off, clear your mind and casually give yourself permission to have an OBE sometime during the night. You may, for example, repeat the following sentence: "I'll allow myself to have an out-of-body experience."

One caveat: Don't tell yourself you're going to try to have an OBE, since we only *try* to do things we believe we might not be able to accomplish. Simply allow your conscious mind to express your openness to the idea.

The key to success in Exercise 5 is clearing your mind of all other thoughts the moment that you give yourself permission. Then let go of the thought of having an OBE the moment you acknowledge that permission. Keep things simple and positive. Focus on having an OBE sometime in the future, when your unconscious mind decides it is appropriate to do so.

Depending on your personal predisposition, Exercise 5 may lead to many different types of OBEs. For example, you may find yourself feeling as though you were waking up and getting out of bed sometime during the night, only to look back and notice your body still lying in bed.

Conversely, you may find yourself having a vivid dream that gradually or suddenly transforms itself into an OBE.

If you're prone to lucid dreaming, in which you're aware of having a dream *while* the dream is in progress, you may try a variation on Exercise 5 by giving yourself permission to have an OBE sometime during the course of one of these dreams.

EXERCISE 6: FLYING HOME

Exercise 6 is a simple technique for inducing an OBE and may be practiced anytime you find yourself on the verge of falling asleep or waking up in a strange environment. Close your eyes and imagine that you're lying in your own bed, experiencing all the sensations that you usually associate with sleeping in your own home.

You may also practice Exercise 6 without leaving home. Just lie down in a place where you wouldn't normally sleep, such as the sofa or even the kitchen floor. Then just as you're falling asleep or waking up, imagine that you're lying in your own bed, experiencing all the familiar sensations you associate with being there. Exercise 6 may be particularly effective when combined with Exercise 5, in which you give yourself permission to have an OBE as you're falling asleep. By imagining you're in a familiar place other than where you are physically, you may induce a powerful OBE.

EXERCISE 7: NIGHT MISSIONS

The next time you notice some out-of-place object in your everyday surroundings, don't set it straight. The object may be a crooked picture, a book positioned oddly on a shelf, or a glass that you forgot to put away.

Later, when you're about to fall asleep, remember the feeling you had when you first noticed the displaced object, and allow yourself to experience the annoyance of not having the object right. Don't exaggerate these feelings, but allow them to surface naturally. Then give yourself permission to have an OBE and imagine yourself getting up in the middle of the night and setting the object straight.

For the best results, don't deliberately "misplace" objects to provide artificial reasons for practicing this exercise. Practice only when the opportunity presents itself.

EXERCISE 8: PILOT TO COPILOT

Exercise 8 is practiced when two adults, accustomed to sleeping together, find themselves sleeping apart. The couple must agree to synchronize practice sessions from two different locations. The exercise may be practiced while both parties are falling asleep or while they are in the relaxed but alert state described earlier. It may even be practiced while both people are asleep.

Begin by entering a deeply relaxed state, and start to remember the physical sensations you associate with your partner. If your loved one is in a familiar environment, such as your bedroom, you may help this exercsie along by remembering the room and all the attendant sensations in as much detail as you can. If your loved one is away, imagine him or her in a familiar position beside you. You and your partner may follow this exercise as far as your imagination comfortably allows you to go, mentally incorporating as much of your physical experience as you can. The result may be a mutual OBE that adds a new dimension to your relationship. You may find it useful to prepare independent descriptions of your experiences so you can compare notes.

If your partner agrees, you may also conduct this exercise without synchronizing your practice sessions. In this case, you may give yourself permission to have an OBE and visit your partner in the middle of the night; you may induce the experience of being with your partner just as you're waking up; or you may simply enter a relaxed state and induce an OBE whenever it's comfortable for you to do so.

Once you've begun to induce OBEs in the course of your practice sessions, you may decide to expand the focus of the exercises to include a wider variety of references in space and time. In other words, you may focus your subjective attention on mentally "visiting" places at increasingly greater distances from your body, as well as focusing your awareness on events in either the distant past or future.

If you feel comfortable doing so, you might consider using the exercises above to induce OBEs in which you don't predetermine the particular locations or events upon which you focus your awareness. Instead you can allow the experience to emerge from the unconscious. In this case you may discover your unconscious mind leading you to experiences that reflect concerns and interests of which you are not even consciously aware. For this reason we strongly suggest that you consider pursuing such unconsciously directed experiences only under the guidance of a sympathetic psychotherapist.

You may discover that OBEs are different in many ways from what you expected and can be as varied and interesting in their content as your activities in everyday life. Remember to maintain a balanced perspective as you explore the deeper potential of this experience. OBEs can teach you some important things about your inner world and your relationship to the world around you as well.

From *The Whole Universe Catalog* insert in *Omni,* April 1988